Joe Ledger: Special Ops

By
Jonathan Maberry

JournalStone
San Francisco

JOURNALSTONE
YOUR LINK TO ARTISTIC TALENT

JournalStone books may be ordered through booksellers or by contacting:

JournalStone

www.journalstone.com

ISBN: 978-1-940161-39-6   (sc)
ISBN: 978-1-940161-40-2   (ebook)
ISBN: 978-1-940161-41-9   (hc)
ISBN: 978-1-940161-42-6   (hc—limited edition—leather binding)

JournalStone rev. date: April 25, 2014

Library of Congress Control Number: 2014930041

Printed in the United States of America

Cover Design: Rob Grom
Cover Photograph © Shutterstock.com

Edited by: Dr. Michael R. Collings

This book is dedicated to Michael Homler, editor and friend.
Thanks for always being there.

And, as always, for Sara Jo.

Endorsements

"Brilliant, shocking, horrifying, it puts the terror back in terrorist." —**James Rollins**, *New York Times* Bestselling author of *The Last Oracle*

"Jonathan Maberry is the king of the fictional occult and his Joe Ledger is a one-man wrecking crew for zombies and bioterrorists. These action-packed tales read fast and hard. Pick up this book and you won't put it down." —**Gregg Hurwitz**, *New York Times* Bestselling author of *Tell No Lies*

"The hard-shelled hero, Baltimore shamus Joe Ledger, deserves to stand alongside F. Paul Wilson's Repairman Jack in the pantheon of genre icons. Highest recommendation!" —**Jay Bonansinga**, *New York Times* Bestselling author of *The Walking Dead: Fall of the Governor*

"Wow! Maberry's *Patient Zero* made me pleasantly nervous for one long afternoon, when I consumed it. It's a fast-paced, creepy thriller that's as prickly as a hospital needle and sounds a little too convincing. This guy is good." —**Joe R. Lansdale**

"Jonathan Maberry has found a delightful voice for this adventure of Joe Ledger and his crew: while the action is heated, violent, and furious, the writing remains cool, steady, and low-key, framing all the wildness and exuberance in a calm rationality." —**Peter Straub**, *New York Times* Bestselling author and horror master

"Joe Ledger and the DMS have my vote as the team to beat when combating terrorist threats on a grand scale. Jonathan Maberry has struck upon gold, a perfect blend of military thriller and science-based horror." — **David Morrell**, *New York Times* Bestselling author of *First Blood* and *Creepers*

"Maberry's prose sears, his dialog cuts like a knife, and his characters crackle with life. Joe Ledger rules." — **Douglas Preston**, co-author of *The Wheel of Darkness* and *The Book of the Dead*

"Hooray for Jonathan Maberry. Please give us more Joe Ledger right now!" — **Victor Gischler**, author of *Shotgun Opera* and *Go-Go Girls of the Apocalypse*

"Jonathan Maberry has created a new genre. Mixing technology, thrills, chills, and procedural noir, Maberry shows why he is one of the freshest voices in fiction. Every reader will want to ride shotgun on Joe Ledger's adventures." — **Scott Nicholson**, author of *The Skull Ring*

"[Maberry] weaves science, police procedure, and modern anti-terror techniques into a unique blend, and tops it off with a larger than life character who is utterly believable. I couldn't put it down." — **Jerry Pournelle**, *New York Times* Bestselling co-author of *Footfall* and *Lucifer's Hammer*

"Smart, scary, and relentless!" — **Jon McGoran**, author of *Drift*

Table of Contents

Countdown

NOTE: This story was written as a teaser for the impending release of *Patient Zero*.
The storyline here picks up in that novel.

Chap. 1

I didn't plan to kill anyone.

I wasn't totally against the idea, either.

Sometimes things just fall that way, and either you roll with it or it rolls over you. Letting the bad guys win isn't how I roll.

Chap. 2

When I woke up this morning it was going to be another day on the job. I've been Baltimore PD for eight years now. I did four in the Army before rotating back to my life with a Rangers patch but no ribbons for doing anything of note because nothing of note was happening at the time. I got out right before 9/11.

It was different on the cops. Baltimore's been a war zone ever since crack hit the streets during the 80s. Families fell apart, kids took to the street in packs, and every corner belonged to one of the drug gangs. Down there, "murder" is so common a word it doesn't even give people pause. I wore the blue and knocked a few heads, made some busts, climbed the ladder. Couple of times it got Old West on me and there was gunplay. They taught me well in the Rangers, and the other older beat cops taught me even better. It's never been about who draws fast or draws first—it's only ever been about who hits what he aims at. I'm good at that. And if the scuffle is hands or knives or broken broom handles, well, I'm okay there, too. Baltimore isn't the richest city in the world, and it definitely has its issues, but it doesn't breed weaklings. The streets taught me a lot I didn't learn from the Army or in a dojo.

In the years since the planes hit the towers, every police department in the country grew an umbilical cord attached to the bureaucratic monster that is Homeland Security. Shortly after I got my shield I got "volunteered" to be part of a joint task force that was cobbled together by lend-lease cops from Baltimore, Philly, and D.C., all of us on Homeland's leash. We profiled suspects, invaded a lot of personal privacy, listened to thousands of hours of wiretaps, and tried to build cases—mostly against people whose closest ties to Middle Eastern terrorists was a collection of Sinbad movies at home. Every once in a while we'd get a minnow, but we never even caught a whiff of a shark.

Until we did.

I was sitting wiretap on a warehouse down by the docks. Our big break started as a fragment of info here and another fragment there—sketchy stuff, but we started seeing some movement patterns that looked covert. Conversations over the tapped phones started sounding like code, people talking about importing agricultural products when the warehouse was licensed to a shoe business. Stuff like that. Then somewhere in the middle of the night I caught a brief conversation on a cell phone line that was hardly ever used. Just a little bit of back-and-forth in which one of the players dropped the name "El Mujahid." The immediate response from the other party was to hang the hell up.

El Mujahid.

The name was so frigging big that I had about three seconds of thinking it was a joke, like everyday Schmoes might drop the name Bin Laden into the middle of a conversation or as the punch line to a joke. We all do it. But this didn't have that feel.

The transcript of the line I'd heard was this: ". . . that will all change when El Mujahid—"

At which point the other guy curses in Farsi and hangs up. Farsi's one of the languages I know. Actually, I know a lot of languages—that stuff's always been easy for me.

I called my lieutenant and he called the major who woke up the colonel who woke up the Homeland supervisor. Suddenly I was the golden boy, and when a full-team hit was planned on the warehouse, I got to play. Perks of ringing the bell.

El Mujahid was the right name to hear on the wire. It means "the fighter of the way of Allah." That son of a bitch was only a short step down from Bin Laden. If U.S. soldiers roll their Bradley over a landmine, chances are this asshole is responsible. If there was even the slightest chance to get a lead to him we had to move and move fast.

Chap. 3

There were thirty of us the next morning, everyone in black BDUs, helmet-cams and full SWAT gear. Each unit was split into four-man teams: two guys with MP-5s, a point man with a Glock .40 and a ballistic shield, and one guy with a Remington 870 pump. I was the shotgunner on our team. The task force hit the warehouse hard and fast, coming in every door and window in the place. Flashbangs, snipers on the surrounding buildings, multiple entry points, and a whole lot of yelling. Domestic shock and awe, the idea being to startle and overpower so that everyone inside is too dazed and confused to offer violent resistance. Last thing anyone wanted was an O.K. Corral.

My team had the back door, the one that led out to a small boat dock. There was a tidy little Cigarette boat there, and while we waited for the go/no-go, the guy next to me—my buddy Jerry Spencer from DCPD—kept looking at the boat with the calculating lust of a cop nearing early retirement. I bent close and hummed the *Miami Vice* theme, and he grinned. He had a few weeks before getting out, and that boat must have looked like a ticket to paradise for him.

The "go" came down and everything suddenly got loud and fast.

I had a Shok-Lok round chambered in the shotgun, and I blew the steel deadbolt to powder. We went in yelling for everyone to freeze, to lay down their weapons. Even if the bad guys don't speak English there's no one alive who doesn't get the gist when SWAT waves guns, yells, and points at the floor. I've been on maybe fifteen, eighteen of these things in my time with Baltimore PD, and only twice was anyone stupid enough to draw a gun on us. Cops don't hotdog it and generally neither do the bad guys, 'cause it's not about who has the biggest balls— it's about overwhelming force so that no shots are ever fired. I remember when I went through the tac team training, the commander had a quote from the movie *Silverado* made into a plaque and hung up in the training hall: "I don't want to kill you and you don't want to be dead." That's pretty much the motto.

So, the bad guys usually stand around looking freaked out and everyone bleats about how innocent they are, yada yada.

This wasn't one of those times.

Jerry, who was the oldest man on the task force, was point man for our team, and I was right behind him with two guys at my back. We hustled down a short corridor and then broke left into a big conference room. Eight Middle Eastern guys around a big oak table. Just inside the door was a big blue phone booth-sized container standing against the wall. "Freeze!" I yelled in three different languages. "Put your hands above your heads and—"

That was as far as I got because the eight guys threw themselves out of their chairs and pulled guns. O.K. Corral, no doubt about it.

When IAD asked me later to recollect how many shots I fired and who exactly I fired them at, I laughed. Twelve guys in a room and everyone's shooting. If they're not dressed like your buddies—and you can, to a reasonable degree of certainty, determine that they're not civilian bystanders—you shoot and duck for cover.

I shot the first guy to draw on us, taking him with two to the body. It spun him against the wall even as he opened up with a Tech-9, and as he spun he poured half a mag into one of his buddies. A ricochet burned the air three inches from my face. The only lucky part of a free-for-all shootout is that everyone is so caught up in not getting shot that they don't have time to aim. That's a little less true for SWAT, and the ratio of aim-to-hit improves once the shock of the moment wears off.

The unlucky part—and this is a real bitch—is that no matter how much you prepare for a shootout, you never really expect one. Most people have this moment—it feels like an hour but it's really a splintered part of a second—where they don't think or move or do anything the way that they should. It's not called fatal hesitation for nothing, and in that fragment of a second I saw two of our guys take hits. One was aimed and well placed and the other was a wild shot from the melee, and it could have as easily been friendly fire as a bullet from a bad guy.

I wasn't caught in that moment. For whatever reason—martial arts, Ranger training, years or the street, or maybe I'm wired different—I don't hesitate. As soon as the game started I was in my groove. I pivoted toward the guy who'd just shot one of mine and I took him off at the knees with two rounds from the shotgun. Take this message home: don't shoot at cops.

I spun out of the way of some return fire and ducked behind the big blue case. I fired the Remington dry and then dropped it so I could pull my Glock. I know the .40 is standard but I've always found the .45 to be more persuasive.

A bad guy rose up behind a stack of file boxes and pointed a SIG Sauer at me in a very professional two-handed grip. I gave him a double-tap—one to the sternum to make him stand at attention and the next through the brain pan.

After that it was duck, scream, shoot, reload. Everyone doing the same damn dance. Jerry Spencer was near me, and we covered each other during reloads. The report says I dropped four hostiles in that initial firefight. One of them was the *thirteenth* man.

Yeah, I know I said that there were eight of them and four of us, but during the firefight I caught movement to my immediate right and saw the door to the big blue case hanging loose, its lock ripped up by gunfire. The door swung open and a man staggered out. He wasn't armed so I didn't fire on him; instead I concentrated on the guy behind him who was tearing up the room with a QBZ-95 Chinese assault rifle, something I'd only ever seen in magazines. Why he had it and where the hell he found ammunition for it I never did find out, but those rounds punched a line of holes right through Jerry's shield, and he went down.

"Son of a bitch!" I yelled and put two in the shooter's chest.

Then this other guy, the thirteenth guy, comes crashing right into me. He was pale and sweaty, stank like raw sewage, and had a glazed bug-eyed stare. I thought, *drug addict*. He wasn't armed, so I gave him a flat kick in the upper leg to drive him off. That usually takes a man down with a knot of screaming cramps in the dense meat of the thigh, but all it did to him was knock him against the edge of the conference table. He rebounded and lunged at one of my guys—a tough little monkey named McGoran—and I swear to God the dope fiend tried to bite him. McGoran butt-stroked him with his rifle stock and the pale guy went down.

I turned to offer cover fire while McGoran dragged Jerry to cover, but I caught movement to my left and there he was again: the fruitcake with the bug eyes. He snarled at me, his lips peeling back from green and grimy teeth. I don't know what kind of drugs this guy was taking, but he was having a really freaky high. I stepped back to avoid his lunge, but my back slammed hard into a file cabinet and the sweaty guy clamped his teeth on the forearm I put up to ward him off. He tried to tear a chunk out, but he had a mouthful of sleeve and Kevlar. All I could feel was a bad pinch, and in the madness of the moment part of my mind lingered to marvel at how determined he was to chow down on my arm.

"Get off!" I screamed and gave him an overhand left that should have dropped him, but only shook him loose. He dropped to a crouch and scuttled away like a cockroach, pushing past me to make for the back door. The firefight was still hot so I couldn't give chase even though I figured he was making for that sweet Cigarette outside—Jerry's boat— so I leaned out into the hall and parked two in his back, quick and easy.

He hit the deck and skidded five feet before he stopped, then he simply sagged against the floor and stopped moving. I spun back into the room and now McGoran provided cover fire so I could pull Jerry behind the table.

A second team crowded into the room and now we had the numbers to turn the place into a shooting gallery.

I heard gunfire coming from a different part of the warehouse so I peeled off from the pack to see what was happening and immediately spotted a trio of hostiles in a nice shooting-blind laying down a lot of fire at one of the other teams. The team under fire had a wooden crate for cover, and the automatic fire was chopping it to kindling. The hostiles knew their business, too: they fired in sequence so that there was always a continuous barrage while the others reloaded.

Screw this, I thought as I raced forward. I ran as fast as silence would allow, well out of their line of sight. I had my pistol out, but to open fire from that distance would have been suicide. I might get one or two but the other would turn and chop me up. There was no cover at all between me and the hostiles, but I hugged the wall, running on cat feet, making no noise that could have been heard above the din of the gunfire.

When I was ten feet out I opened fire. My first shot caught one of the hostiles in the back of the neck, and the impact slammed him into the crates. As the other two turned I closed to zero distance and fired one more shot, which hurled the second hostile backward, but then the slide on my gun locked open. There was no time to change magazines. The third shooter instantly lunged at me, swinging his rifle barrel to bear. I parried it one-handed with my gun arm, and while I was still in full stride I used the empty pistol to check the swing of his rifle while simultaneously jabbing forward with my left hand, fingers folded in half and stiffened so that the secondary line of knuckles drove into the attacker's windpipe. A Leopard Paw punch, nasty but useful. As this was happening I made a quick change midstep so that my left foot went from a regular running step into a longer lunge and the tip of my combat boot crunched into the cartilage under the hostile's kneecap. I brought my gun hand up and jabbed the exposed barrel of the pistol into the hostile's left eye socket.

The attacker flew backward as if he'd been hit by a shotgun blast.

As I completed my step I reached to my belt for a fresh magazine.

But this alley fight was over and all the dogs were down. The main warehouse doors blew open and a second wave of SWAT came in like a swarm of pissed-off scorpions and anyone dumb enough to be still holding a gun went to meet Jesus—or whoever—in nothing flat.

Chap. 4

In the end, eleven alleged terrorists were shot, six fatally, including the cowboy with the Chinese assault rifle and the biter I nailed in the back—who according to his false ID was named Javad Mustapha. A terrorist with ties to El Mujahid. Turned out that none of our team was killed, though eight of them needed treatment, mostly for broken ribs. We were all rattled, but in the end it was a damn good day's work.

I checked on Jerry. Kevlar stops bullets but it can't stop foot-pounds of impact. Jerry had a cracked sternum and was one hurting pup.

"How you feeling, ya old fart?" I asked, squatting next to the gurney to which the EMTs had strapped him.

"Steal me that Cigarette boat and I'll feel right as rain." He ticked his chin toward my arm. "Hey, how's your arm? EMT said you got bit."

"Didn't even break the skin. Weird sumbitch though, wasn't he?"

"Looked to me like he came out of that blue box. The lock blew off and he stepped out, batshit crazy and looking at us like we're Sunday dinner. McGoran said you popped him."

"Seemed like the thing to do at the time."

Jerry nodded, then gave me a faint smile. "Everybody's talking about you, Joe. You saved some fellow officers today. I been hearing the 'H' word floating around." When I looked puzzled he explained, "'Hero,' son. That's what they're calling you."

"Oh, please. I'm just one of the crowd, doing my job."

He gave me a funny look, but it might have been the painkillers.

The EMTs took him away, and I watched as a bunch of federal agents in unmarked black BDUs came in to take over the crime scene.

Far as I was concerned it was all over.

Funny how wrong you can be about some things.

Chap. 5

Nobody who worked for him or with him knew his real name. The President called him Mr. Church, and that would do for now. He sat in a temporary office in a disused records storage warehouse in Easton, Maryland. He had a laptop on his desk, a glass of water, and a plate of cookies. Nothing else.

Mr. Church selected a vanilla wafer and munched it thoughtfully as he watched the replay of the video feeds from the raid in Baltimore. He punched the pause button and turned the laptop around toward the three big federal agents who sat across from him. A man's face filled the screen.

"His name is Detective Joe Ledger," said Mr. Church. His eyes were almost invisible behind the tinted lenses of his glasses, and his face wore no expression. "Baltimore PD, attached to a Homeland task force. This footage was taken two days ago. This is the one I want. Bring him in."

The agents exchanged looks, but they left without comment. Questioning Mr. Church was never fruitful.

When they were gone, Mr. Church restarted the video and watched it again.

And again.

~The End~

Zero Tolerance

NOTE: This story takes place a few weeks after the events of *Patient Zero*.

Chap. 1

Battalion Aide Station
Near Helmand River Valley, Afghanistan
One Hour Ago

"I never thought that anyone that beautiful could scare the shit out of me."

"Tell me about her, Sergeant," I said.

He looked away so quickly that I knew he'd been waiting for that request. He tried to keep a poker face, but he was a couple of tics off his game. Sleep deprivation, pain, and the certain knowledge that his ass was in a sling can do that. Even to a tough son of a bitch like Sergeant Harper. As he turned I saw the way guilt and shame twisted his mouth, but his eyes had a different expression. One I couldn't quite nail down.

"Tell you what? That I can't bear to close my eyes 'cause when I do I see her! That I've had the shivering shits ever since we found her out there in the sand! I don't mind admitting it," said the sergeant. He started to say more, then closed his mouth and shook his head.

The sergeant's uninjured hand was freckled with powder burns and skin was missing from two knuckles. He ran his trembling fingers through his sandy hair as he spoke. He did it two or three times each minute. His other hand lay in his lap, cocooned in gauze wrappings.

I waited. I had more time.

After a full minute, though, I said, "Where did she come from?"

Harper sighed. "She was a refugee. We found her staggering in the foothills."

"A refugee from what?"

"From the big meltdown out in the desert."

"In the Helmand River Valley?"

"Yes." He didn't tack on "sir." He was fucking with me, and I was okay with that for now. He didn't know me, didn't really know how much shit he was in, or how deep a hole he'd dug for himself. All he knew was that his career in the Marines had hit a guard rail at seventy miles an hour, and now he was sitting across a small table from a guy wearing captain's bars and no other military insignia. No medals or unit patch. No name tag. Harper had to be measuring that against the deferential way the colonel treated me. Like I outranked him, which I don't. I'm not even in the military anymore. But in this particular matter I was able to throw more weight than the base commander. More weight than anyone else in or out of uniform on the continent. As far as Harper was concerned, when it came to throwing him a lifeline it was me and then God, and God was off the clock.

Harper couldn't really know any of that, but he was smart enough and sly enough to know that I had some juice. On one hand, he rightly figured that I could drop him into a hole deeper than the one he'd dug for himself. On the other hand, he had information that I wanted, and he was stalling to see how to play his only good card.

"How long are they going to keep me here?"

"To be determined, Sergeant. Do you feel you're being inconvenienced?"

He didn't rise to the bait.

"It's been three days."

"Not quite. Forty-seven hours and change."

"Seems longer." He didn't even know that we'd already met. Not sure when I was going to spring that on him. It wouldn't do anything to calm him down.

I opened my briefcase and took out a file folder.

"I'd like you to look at some photos," I said and took two color eight-by-tens from my briefcase and laid them on the table. If I'd tossed a scorpion on the table he couldn't have jerked back faster.

"Jesus Christ!"

I nodded at the print. "That's her?"

"Fuck me," muttered the sergeant. "Oh fuck me fuck me fuck me."

Take that as a yes.

I sat back and waited him out. Sweat popped all along his forehead and leaked out from his hairline. He smelled like urine, cigarette smoke, and testosterone; but I could smell fear, too. A whole lot of it. I used to think that was a myth, or something only dogs and horses could smell; but lately I've learned different. The kind of shit I deal with I smell it a lot, and on myself, too. Like now, but I wasn't going to let this asshole know it.

"Could...could you turn the pictures over? I don't mean to be a pussy, but I don't want her staring at me the whole time, y'know?"

"Sure," I said, and did so. But I left them on the table. "Try to relax. Smoke one if you got any."

He shook his head. "Never took it up. Jesus H. Christ. Wish I had."

I opened my briefcase and took out two bottles of spring water, unscrewed one, and handed it to him. He drank half of it down. Then I took some airline bottles of Jack Daniels and lined them up in front of him. One, two, three.

"If it helps," I said.

He snatched one off the edge of the table, twisted off the cap and chugged it, then coughed. More bravado than brains.

"Tell me about the woman," I said. "And what happened in the cave."

He gave that some thought, drank half of the second bottle of Jack.

"Do you know my outfit? Second Marine Expeditionary Brigade, Light Armored Reconnaissance Battalion. We were part of Operation Khanjar, working that corner of Helmand Province, doing some recon stuff up in the hills," he began. "Counterinsurgency work, and some fox hunts to flush the Taliban teams running opium through the area. That whole part of the province is nothing but dead rock riddled with a million caves. You could hide a hundred thousand people in there, camels and all, and it would take us fifty years to find half of them. That's why this war was fucked from the snap. The Russians couldn't do it twenty years ago, and we can't do it now. Besides, nine out of ten people you meet are friendlies who look and dress just like the hostiles, so how you going to know?"

"Skip the politics, Sergeant. Talk about the woman."

He shrugged. "It was weird out there because last week the whole place was lit up by some kind of underground explosion. We got word that some Taliban lab blew up, but the blast wasn't nuclear. Something to do with geo-thermal chambers or shifting plates or some bullshit like that. A whole section of desert just fell into itself, and there was this spike of fire that shot a couple hundred feet in the air."

"No radiation?"

"No. Most of us still had TLD badges and the badges stayed neutral. The area was hot, though…not with radiation, but actually hot. Like a furnace. When we reached the outer perimeter of the event zone we could see a weird shimmer, and I realized that big sections of the desert had been melted to glass. It looked like a lava flow, rippled and dark."

"And is that where you found the woman?"

He drank the rest of the second bottle of Jack Daniels and chased it with a long pull on the water bottle. He was pale, his eyes sunken and dark, his lips dry. He looked like shit and probably felt worse. Just mentioning the "woman" made his eyes jump.

"Yeah," he said. "Locals started calling in sightings of burned people, and then word came down to scramble a couple of recon teams. We went in…and after that everything went to shit." He turned away to hide wet eyes.

Chap. 2

The Warehouse
DMS Tactical Field Office / Baltimore
Ninety-two Hours Ago

I was on the mats with Echo Team's newest members—replacements for the guys we lost in Philadelphia. There were four of them, two Rangers, a jarhead, and a former SWAT guy from L.A. For the last couple of hours Bunny and I had taken turns beating on them, chasing them with paintball guns, trying to carve our initials in them with live blades, swinging at them with baseball bats. Everything we could think of. Actually, let me rephrase that. There were ten of them this morning. The four who were left were the ones who hadn't been taken to the infirmary or told to go the fuck back to where they came from.

We were just about to enter a practical discussion on pain tolerance when my boss, Mr. Church, came into the gym at a fast walk. He only ever hurries when the real shit is coming down the pike. I crossed to meet him.

"Good evening, Captain Ledger," said Church. He nodded toward the recruits. "Are these four men in or out?"

"Is something up?"

"Yes, and it's on a high boil."

"They're in."

Church turned to Bunny. "Sergeant Rabbit, get these men kitted out. Afghanistan. No ID, no patches. You're wheels up in fifteen."

Bunny flicked a glance at me, but he didn't question the order. Instead he turned and hustled them all toward the locker room. Bunny was a nice kid most of the time, but he was still a sergeant. And we'd been through some shit together, so he knew my views on hesitation. Don't.

"What's the op?"

Church handed me the file. "This came in as an email attachment. Two photos, two separate sources."

I flipped open the folder and looked at two photos of an incredibly beautiful woman. Iraqi, probably. Black hair, full lips, and the most arresting eyes I'd ever seen. Eyes so powerful that despite the low res of the photos and graininess of the printout, they radiated heat. Her face was streaked with dirt and there was some blood crusted around her nose and the corner of her mouth.

I looked at him.

"These were relayed to us by the people we have seeded into a Swiss seismology team studying an underground explosion in the

Helmand River Valley. We ran facial recognition on them and MindReader kicked out a ninety-seven percent confidence that this is Amirah."

My mouth went dry as dust.

Holy shit.

When I was brought into the DMS a month ago my first gig was to stop a team of terrorists who had a bioweapon that still gives me nightmares. I'm not kidding. Couple times a week I wake up with the shivers, cold sweat running down my skin, and clenched teeth that are the only things between a silent room and a gut-buster of a scream.

There were three people behind that scheme. A British pharmaceutical mogul named Gault, a religious fanatic from Yemen called El Mujahid, and his wife, Amirah. She was the molecular biologist who conceived and created the *Seif al Din* pathogen. The Sword of the Faithful. They test-drove the pathogen with limited release in remote Afghani villages, trying out different strains until they had one that couldn't be stopped. *Seif al Din.* An actual doomsday plague. El Mujahid brought it here, and Echo Team stopped him. But only just. If you factor in the dead Afghani villagers and the people killed here, the body count was north of twelve hundred. Even so, Mr. Church and his science geeks figured we caught a break. It could have been more. Could have been millions, even billions. It came down to that kind of a photo finish.

Most of the victims turned into mindless killers whose metabolism had been so drastically altered by the plague that they could not think, had no personalities, didn't react to pain, and were hard as balls to kill. The pathogen reduced most organ functions to such a minimal level that they appeared to be dead. Or…maybe they were dead. The scientists are still sorting it out. We called them "walkers." A bad pun, short for "dead men walking." The DMS science chief is a pop-culture geek. My guys in Echo Team called the infected by another name. Yeah. The "Z" word.

And you wonder why I get night terrors. Six weeks ago I was a Baltimore cop doing scut work for Homeland. Sitting wiretaps, that sort of thing. Now I was top dog for a crew of first-team shooters. Do not ask me how one thing led to another, but here I am.

I looked at the photos.

Amirah.

"The rumors of her demise have been greatly exaggerated," I said.

Church managed not to smile.

"If you're sending us then she hasn't been apprehended."

"No," he said. "Spotted only. I arranged for two Marine Recon squads to locate and detain."

"What if Amirah's infected?"

"I shared a limited amount of information with the appropriate officers in the chain of command, Captain. If anyone reports certain kinds of activity—from Amirah or anyone—then the whole area gets lit up."

"Lit up as in—"

"A nuclear option falls within the parameters of 'acceptable losses.'"

"Can you at least wait until me and my guys reach minimum safe distance?"

He didn't smile. Neither did I.

"You'll be operating with an Executive Order, so you'll have complete freedom of movement."

"You got the President to sign an order that fast?"

He just looked at me.

"What are my orders?"

"Our primary concern is to determine if anyone infected with the *Seif al Din* pathogen is loose in Afghanistan."

"Yeah, that'll be about as easy to establish as Bin Laden's zip code."

"Do your best. We'll be monitoring all news coming out of the area, military, civilian, and other. If there is even a peep, that intel will be routed to you and the clock will start."

"If I don't come back, make sure somebody feeds my cat."

"Noted."

"What about Amirah? You want her brought back here?"

"Amirah would be a prize catch, Captain. There's a laundry list of people who want her. The Vice President thinks she would be a great asset to our own bioweapons programs."

"And is that what you want?"

He told me what he wanted.

Chap. 3

The Helmand River Valley
Sixty-one Hours Ago

We hit the ground running. When Church wants to clear a path, he steamrolls it flat. Our cover was that of a Marine SKT—Small Kill Team—operating on special orders. Need to know. Everybody figured we were probably Delta, and you don't ask them for papers unless you want to get a ration of shit from everyone higher up the food chain. And when we did have to show papers, we had real ones. As real as the situation required.

Just as the helo was about to set us down near the blast site, Church radioed.

"Be advised, I ordered the two Marine squads to pull out of the area. One has confirmed and is heading to a pickup point now. The other has not responded. Make no assumptions in those hills."

He signed off without explanation, but I didn't need any.

The six of us went into the desert, split into two teams and heading into Indian country. We ran with combat names only. I was Cowboy.

Twilight draped the desert with purple shadows. As soon as the sun dropped behind the mountains, the furnace heat shut off and the wind turned cool. Not pleasantly cool. This breeze was clammy and it smelled wrong. There was a scent on the wind—sweet and sour. An ugly smell that triggered an atavistic repulsion. Bunny sniffed it and turned to me.

"Yeah," I said, "I smell it, too."

Bob Faraday—a big moose of a guy whose call sign was Slim—ran point. It was getting dark fast, and the moon wouldn't be up for nearly an hour. In ten minutes we'd have to switch to night vision. Slim vanished into the distance. Bunny and I followed, slower, watching as darkness seemed to melt from under rocks and rise from sand dunes as the sparse islands of daytime shadows spread to join the ocean of shadows that was night.

Slim broke squelch twice, the signal to close on him quick and quiet.

As we ran up behind him, I saw that he'd stopped by a series of gray finger rocks that rose from the troubled sands at the edge of the blast area. But as I drew closer I saw that the rocks weren't rocks at all.

I followed my gun barrel all the way to Slim's side.

The dark objects were people.

Eleven of them, sticking out of the sand like statues from some ancient ruins. Dead. Charred beyond recognition. Fourth-, fifth- and sixth-degree burns. You couldn't tell race and even sex with most of them. They were like mummies, and they were still too hot to touch.

"There was supposed to be some kind of underground lab?" murmured Slim. "Looks like the blast charbroiled these poor bastards and the force drove them up through the sand."

"Hope it was quick," said Bunny.

Slim glanced at him. "If they were in that lab then they were the bad guys."

"Even so," said Bunny.

We went into the foothills, onto some rocks that were cooler than the sands.

The other team called in. The Marine was on point. "Jukebox to Cowboy, be advised we have more bodies up here. Five DOA. Three men and two women. Third-degree burns, cuts and blunt force injuries. Looks like they might have walked out of the hot zone and died up here in the rocks." He paused. "They're a mess. Vultures and wild dogs been at them."

"Verify that what you are seeing are animal bites," I said.

There was a long pause.

And it got longer.

I keyed the radio. "Cowboy to Jukebox, copy?"

Two long damn seconds.

"Cowboy to Jukebox, do you copy?"

That's when we heard the distant rattle of automatic gunfire. And the screams.

We ran.

"Night vision!" I snapped, and we flipped the units into place as the black landscape suddenly transformed into a thousand shades of luminescent green. We were all carrying ALICE packs with about fifty pounds of gear—most of it stuff that'll blow up, M4 combat rifles, AMT .22 caliber auto mags on our hips, and combat S.I. assault boots. It's all heavy and it can slow you down...except when your own brothers-in-arms are under fire. Then it feels like wings that carry you over the ground at the speed of a racing tiger. That's the illusion, and that's how it felt as we tore up the slopes toward the path Second Squad had taken.

The gunfire was continuous.

As we hit the ridge, I signaled the others to get low and slow. Bunny came up beside me. "Those are M5s, Boss."

He was right. Our guns have their own distinctive sound, and it doesn't sound much like the Kalashnikovs the Taliban favored.

The gunfire stopped abruptly.

We froze, letting the night tell us its story.

The last of the gunfire echoes bounced back to us from the distant peaks. I could hear loose rocks clattering down the slope, probably debris knocked loose by stray bullets. In the distance the wind was beginning to howl through some of the mountain passes.

I keyed the radio.

"Cowboy to Jukebox. Respond."

Nothing.

We moved forward, moving as silently as trained men can when any misstep could draw fire. The tone of the wind changed as we edged toward the rock wall that would spill us into the pass where Second Squad had gone. A heavier breeze, perhaps. Moving through one of the deeper canyons?

A month ago I'd have believed that. Too much has happened since.

I tapped Bunny and then used the hand signal to listen.

He heard the sound, then, and I could feel him stiffen beside me. He pulled Slim close and used two fingers to mime walking.

Slim had been fully briefed on the trip. He understood. The low sigh wasn't the wind. It was the unendingly hungry moan of a walker.

I finger-counted down from three, and we rounded the bend.

Jukebox had said that they'd found five bodies. Second Squad made eight.

As we rounded the wall we saw that the count was wrong. There weren't eight people in the pass. There were fifteen. All of them were dead. Most of them moving.

Second Squad lay sprawled in the dust. The night vision made it look like they were covered in black oil. Jukebox still held his M4, finger curled through the trigger guard, barrel smoking. A man dressed in a white lab coat knelt over him, head bowed as if weeping for the fallen soldier, but as we stepped into the pass the kneeling man raised his head and turned toward us. His mouth and cheeks glistened with black wetness and his eyes were lightless windows that looked into a world in which there was no thought, no emotion, no anything except hunger.

Spider and Zorro—the L.A. SWAT kid and the other Ranger—were almost invisible beneath the seething mass of bodies that crouched over them, tearing at clothing with wax-white fingers and at skin with gray teeth.

"Holy mother of God," whispered Slim.

"God's not here," I said as I put the pinpoint of the laser sight on the kneeling zombie. It was a stupid thing to say. Glib and macho. But I think it was also the truth.

The creature bared his teeth and hissed like a jungle cat. Then he lunged, pale fingers reaching for me.

I put the first round in his breastbone and that froze him in place for a fragment of a second, and then put the next round through his forehead. The impact snapped his neck, the round blew out the back of his skull, and the force flung him against the rock wall.

The other walkers surged up with awful cries that I will never forget. Bunny, Slim, and I stood our ground in a shooting line, and we chopped them back and down and dead. Dead for good and all. Painting the walls with the same dripping black. The narrow confines of the pass roared with thunder, the waves of echoes striking us in the chest, the ejected brass tinkling with improbable delicacy.

Then silence.

I looked down at the three men. They'd been part of Echo Team for a day. Less. They'd been briefed on the nature of the enemy. They were highly trained men, the best of the best. But really, what kind of training prepares you for this? The first time the DMS encountered the walkers they'd lost two whole teams. Twenty-four seasoned agents.

Even so, the deaths of these good, brave men was like a spear in my heart. It was hard to take a breath. I forced myself to be in the moment, and I slung my M4 and drew my .22 and shot each of the corpses in the head. To be sure. We carried .22s because the low mass of the bullet will penetrate the skull but lacks the power to exit, so the bullet bounces around inside the skull and tears the brain apart.

Assassins use it, and so does anyone who has to deal with things like walkers.

"Bunny, drop a beacon and let's haul ass."

Bunny dug a small device from a thigh pocket, thumbed the switch and tucked it under the leg of one of the dead walkers, making sure not to touch blood or exposed skin. The beacon's signal would be picked up by satellite. Once we were clear of the area, an MQ-Reaper would be guided into the pass to deliver an air-to-surface Hellfire missile. Fuel-air bombs are handy for cleanup jobs like this. When you don't want a single fucking trace left.

We didn't take dog tags because the DMS doesn't wear them. We try to have a "leave no one behind policy," but that doesn't always play out.

We moved on.

The night was vast. Knowing that helicopters and armed drones and troops were a phone call away didn't make the shadows less threatening. It didn't make the nature of what we were doing easier to accept: hunting monsters in a region of the Afghan mountains dominated by the Taliban. Yeah, find a comfortable space in your head for that thought to curl up in.

This was pretty much the opium highway. The friendlies who lived in the nearby villages were little or no help, because even though they idealistically supported us and hated the Taliban, they also feared the terrorists more than they feared us; and without the trickle-down of drug money, they'd starve to death. It was a devil's bargain at best, but it was the reason that no one can win this war. The best we could hope for was to slow the opium shipments and keep the Taliban splinter cells underfunded and ill-prepared for a major, coordinated terror offensive of the kind they've always promised and we live in fear of.

Something flared ahead and I held up my fist. The others froze.

The pass we were following curled around the mountain like the grooves on a screw, turning and rising toward the peak on the far side. Sixty yards ahead, half-hidden by an outcropping of rock, light spilled from the mouth of a small cave. The overhang would have made the light invisible from aircraft, but not for us on the ground. A shadow seemed to detach itself from the wall and as I watched through narrowed eyes it resolved into the shape of a man. A Marine.

He walked to a spot outside the spill of light, looked up and down the pass, and then retreated into his nook. In the dark, he didn't see the three big men crouched behind boulders. The sentry went to the mouth of the cave and peered inside. The glow let me see his face. He was grinning.

Then we heard the scream.

A man's voice, pleading. A string of words in Pashto, ending in a screech of pain that was cut off by the sharp crack of a palm on flesh.

And the sound of a woman laughing.

It was not a pleasant laugh. It held no cheer, no goodwill. No warmth. It was deep and throaty, strangely wet, and it rose into a mocking screech that turned my guts to gutter water.

We did not hail the guard. The situation felt wrong in too many ways. I signaled Bunny to keep his eyes and gun barrel on the sentry as I circled on cat feet behind a tall slab of rock. That put me on the man's six o'clock, ten feet from his back. Even if this all proved to be a zero-threat situation I was going to fry this guy for his criminal lack of attention to duty. A sentry holds everyone's life in their hands; this guy was handing me everyone in that cave.

I screwed the .22's barrel into the soft spot under his left ear, grabbed him by the collar and slow-walked him back. Slim was there and he spun the guard and put him down. I didn't see the blow, but it sounded like a tree being felled. The guard went out without having said a word. Slim watched our backs as Bunny and I crept to the cave entrance…

…and looked into a scene from Hell.

The cave clearly saw regular use. There were chairs, a card table, ammunition cases, cots, and a stove with sterno burners. A Taliban soldier was tied to folding chairs, ankles and wrists bound with plastic cuffs. His clothes had been slashed and torn away to reveal his pale chest and shoulders. His turban hung askew, one end trailing down behind him where it puddled on the rocky ground between his heels. Several Kalashnikovs stood against the wall, magazines removed.

The other three men of the Marine squad stood in a loose semicircle around the man, laughing as he screamed and begged and prayed. All of them were sweating; a couple had red, puffy knuckles that spoke to the way this session had started. If this was just a group of frustrated Marines knocking the piss out of a Taliban grunt, partly to blow off steam and partly to try to get a handle on something that might result in some real good being done, then I might have just stepped in and calmed it down. Yelled a bit, given them the appropriate ration of shit, but basically dialed it all down with no charges being filed.

But that's not what we were seeing. These guys had taken it to a different level and in doing so had crossed the line between an attempt to gather useful intelligence and something else. Something darker that was not part of soldiering. Something that wasn't even part of torturing or "enhanced interrogation." Something that went beyond Abu Ghraib and into the darkest territory imaginable.

They had Amirah—scientist, designer of the *Seif al Din*, wife of one of the world's most hated terrorists. There were two ropes looped around her neck, each end pulled to an opposite side by a Marine so that she could not approach either of them. All she could do was lunge forward toward the prisoner. Her wrists were bound behind her. Her ankles were hobbled by a length of rope. She couldn't flee, couldn't run. The men had stripped her to the waist, revealing a body that was beautifully made but which now inspired only revulsion. Her once olive skin had faded to a dusty gray-green and there were four black bullet holes—one in her stomach, three in her back—that were crusted with dried blood and wriggling with maggots.

Amirah lunged forward to bite the man, but the Marines jerked on the ropes and stopped her when her gray teeth were an inch from the Afghani's face. Amirah snarled and then laughed. It was impossible to say whether she was enjoying this game or if she was completely mad.

As the men struggled to keep her in check they danced and shifted around, and I could see that there were two other Afghanis in the room. They lay sprawled like broken dolls. It looked like their faces had been eaten, and their throats were tangles of red junk.

"It's getting tough to hold this bitch," growled one of the men, though he was smiling when he said it.

"Please, in the name of God keep her away!" begged the bound man. He was already bleeding from half a dozen bites. Thin lines of dark red spider-webbed from each bite. The infection was slow for some, faster for others. Snot and spit ran from his nose and mouth as he pleaded in three different languages.

A big man with sergeant's stripes—the only one not holding a leash—bent behind the man and spoke with sharp impatience. "We'll fucking stop when you fucking tell us what we want to know."

"But I don't…. I don't…." He was filled with too much panic to complete a sentence.

The sergeant straightened and nodded, and the men slackened their holds on the rope leashes. Amirah instantly lunged forward and sank her teeth into the flesh of the man's shoulder. Blood spurted hot and red beside her cheeks, and even from where I crouched I could see her eyes roll high and white with an erotic pleasure. The man's piercing shrieks filled the whole cave.

"Okay, pull the bitch off him," snapped the sergeant, and she fought them, her teeth sunk deep into muscle. It took all three men to haul her back, two pulling and the sergeant pushing. He punched Amirah in the face and that finally broke the contact, but as they dragged her away a piece of sinew was clamped between her jaws and it snapped with a wet pop.

She licked her lips. "Delicious…," she said in English, drawing the word out, tasting the soft wetness of it, savoring the way the syllables rolled between teeth and tongue and lips.

Bunny made a soft gagging sound beside me.

This was what I was afraid of. What Church had been afraid of. During that fight against El Mujahid, we'd encountered several generations of the *Seif al Din* pathogen. Most of the early generations transformed the infected into mindless eating machines. The walkers. But at the end, when I'd squared off against El Mujahid himself, he'd been among the dead but he still retained his intelligence. It was the result of Generation 12 of the disease. He bragged about how his princess had saved him, had elevated him to immortality. The name *Amirah* meant "princess."

That had to be what we were seeing here. Amirah had become one of her own monsters. Was it an accident or part of some twisted plan? From the way El Mujahid bragged about it—right before I gave him a ticket to paradise—I had to believe that Amirah had chosen this path.

Chosen. God almighty.

"Fuck this," I murmured and stepped into the cave. Bunny was right beside me. I held my .22 in a two-hand shooters grip; he had his

M4. Our night vision was off, but we wore black balaclavas that showed only our eyes.

"United States Army," I bellowed. "Stand down, stand down!"

The sergeant whirled toward me, his right hand going for his sidearm. I put the laser sight on him.

"Stand down or I will kill you!"

He believed me, and he froze.

The other Marines froze.

The man in the chair froze.

Amirah, however, did not.

With a snarl of hunger, the mad witch twisted so suddenly and violently that she tore the ropes from the hands of the startled Marines. She tore her hands free from the plastic cuffs. She screamed like some desert demon from legend, leapt into the air and slammed into the sergeant, driving him against the torture victim. They crashed to the ground amid shrieks and blood and biting teeth.

The two Marines began to move toward the sergeant, but Bunny shifted to cover them with his M4. That left me.

I stepped in and kicked Amirah in the side of the head. The blow knocked her off of the sergeant, but she had his hand clamped between her jaws. And the bound man was screaming and beating his forehead against the side of the sergeant's head, mashing his ear.

"Holy shit, Boss—on your six!"

It was Bunny. I pivoted in place in time to catch the rush as something came out of the shadows and tackled me. It was one of the other Afghanis. One of the dead Afghanis.

His teeth were bared and spit flew from cracked lips as he lunged for my throat.

I braced my forearm under his chin as I fell backward and clenched my abs so that my flat back fall turned into a curled back roll. The Afghani went into the tumble with me and instead of him pinning me down we ended the roll with me straddling his chest. I jammed the barrel of the .22 into his left eye socket and fired. The bullet tore all his wiring loose, and he transformed from murderously vicious to sagging dead weight in a microsecond.

There were shouts all around, and I had to shove at the body to get free. As I came up, I saw that the second Afghani had clamped his teeth around the windpipe of one of the Marines. Bunny put six rounds into the Afghani: the first one knocked him loose from his victim, the second punched him in the chest to stall him, and the last four grouped like knuckles in a lead fist to strike him above the eyebrows. The man's head exploded and his body spun backward in a sloppy pirouette. The Marine dropped to his knees, trying to staunch an arterial spray with fingers that shook with the palsy of sudden understanding. His companion crouched over him, pressing the wound with his hands, but the Marine drowned in his own blood in seconds.

Slim was in the cave mouth, his weapon sweeping quickly back and forth from target to target, not knowing whether to take a shot or not.

I dove at Amirah, who had crawled back atop the sergeant. For his part, the Marine was putting up a good fight, but it was clear that terror of the woman he had been using as a tool of interrogation was off the scale, too much for him to handle. He shot me a single, despairing glance, and I saw the moment when he gave up. It must have been one of those instantaneous moments of clarity that can either save you or kill you. His interrogation had failed. His method of interrogation was indefensible, a fact that would never have mattered if we hadn't shown up. But we were here, and he was caught. His world had just crashed, and he knew it.

I locked my arm around Amirah's throat and squeezed, bulging my bicep on one side to cut off her left carotid and my forearm to cut off her right. In jujutsu that puts someone out.

It didn't do a fucking thing to her.

She bucked and writhed with more force than I would have thought possible for a woman of her size, alive or dead.

I shoved the hot barrel of the .22 against the back of her head, bent close, and whispered in her ear, speaking in Farsi.

"There is no shame to die in the service of Allah."

Her muscles locked into sudden rigidity. The cave was instantly still. Even the Afghani and the sergeant had stopped screaming. I held her tight against my chest, and my back was to the cold stone wall. She smelled of rotting meat and death, but in her dark hair there was the faintest scent of perfume. Jasmine.

"Amirah," I said. "Listen to me."

I whispered six more words.

"Your choice, Princess," I said. "*This*…or paradise?"

I leaned on the word *this*. From the absolute stillness, I knew that she understood what I meant. The cave, these men, all this destruction. She knew. And even though she had meant to sweep the world with her pathogen, the end goal—the transformation via Generation 12 of a select portion of Islam and the total annihilation of the enemies of her people—that was impossible. All that was left to her now was to be a monster. Alone and reviled.

The moment stretched. No one moved. Then Amirah leaned her head toward me. An oddly intimate movement.

She said, "Not…this."

I whispered, "*Yarhamukallâh.*"

May God have mercy on you.

And pulled the trigger.

Chap. 4

Battalion Aide Station
Now

I sat back and studied Harper for a long time.

He said, "What? You going to sit there and tell me that you wouldn't have done the same thing?"

I said nothing.

"Look," he said, "I know that was you in the cave. What are you? Delta? SEALs?"

I said nothing.

"You *know* what we're up against out there. They want us to stop the Taliban, stop the flow of opium, but our own government supports the brother of the Afghan president, and he runs half the opium in the frigging country! How the hell are we supposed to win that kind of war? This is Vietnam all over again. We're losing a war we shouldn't be fighting."

I said nothing.

Harper leaned forward, anger darkening his face. He pointed at me with the index finger of his uninjured hand. "You think Abu Ghraib's the only place where we had to do whatever it took to get some answers? It goes on all over, and it's *always* gone on."

"And look where it's gotten us," I said.

"Fuck you and fuck that zero tolerance bullshit. We were trying to *save* lives. We would have gotten something out of that man."

"You didn't get shit from the first two."

Now it was his turn to say nothing. After a minute he narrowed his eyes. "When you spoke to that...that...*thing*. That woman. At the end, you gave her a blessing. You a Muslim?"

"No."

"Then why?"

"Honestly, Sergeant, I don't think I could explain it to you. I mean...I could explain it, but I don't think you'd understand."

"You think I'm a monster, don't you?"

"Are you?"

"No, man," he said. "I'm just trying to...." And his voice broke. At first it was just a hitch, but when he tried to catch it and hide it, his resolve broke and he put his face in his unbandaged hand and sobbed. I sat back in my chair and watched.

I looked at him. The bandages on his other hand were stained with blood that was almost black. Red lines ran in a crooked tracery from beneath the bandage and up his arms. I could see the same dark lines beginning to creep up from his collar. It was forty-eight hours since he'd been brought to the aide station. Fifty-nine since Amirah had bitten him. Strong son of a bitch. Most people would have turned by now.

"What's going to happen to me?" he asked, raising a tear-streaked face.

"Nothing. It's already happened."

He licked his dry lips. "We...we didn't know."

"Yes you did. Your squad was briefed. Maybe it was all a little unreal to you, Sergeant. Horror movie stuff. But you *knew*. Just as you know how this ends."

I stood and drew my sidearm and racked the slide. The sound was enormous in that little room.

"They're going to want to study you," I said. "They can do that with you on a slab, or in a cage."

"They can't!" he said, anger flaring inside his pain. "I'm an American god damn it!"

"No," I said. "Sergeant Andy Harper died while on a mission in Afghanistan. The report will reflect that he died while serving his country and maintaining the best traditions of the U.S. Marine Corps."

Harper looked at me, the truth registering in his eyes.

"So I ask you," I said, raising the pistol. "This...or paradise?"

"I...I'm sorry," he said. Maybe at that moment he really was. Deathbed epiphanies aren't worth the breath that carries them. Not to me. Not anymore.

"I know," I lied.

"I did it for *us*, man. I did it to help!"

"Yeah," I said. "Me too."

And raised the gun

~The End~

Deep Dark

NOTE: This story takes place after the events of *Patient Zero*. It is an independent adventure.

Chap. 1

The Vault
Ultra High Security Biological Research Facility
The Poconos, Pennsylvania
Twenty Minutes Ago

It was the dirty end of a dirty job.

Three of us—Bunny, Top and I—were hunting horrors in the dark, seven thousand feet below Camelback Mountain. Even with night vision goggles, body armor, and weapons, we were lost in an infinity of shadows. If we blew this, if we couldn't wrap this before the clock ticked down, then the whole place would go into hard lockdown. Steel doors would drop, and explosive bolts would fire, triggering thermite charges that would seal the doors permanently in place. Federal and international biohazard protocols forbade anyone from digging us out if the failsafes went active.

The Vault would become our tomb.

The government would disown us; our own people would have to write us off.

But the things we hunted wouldn't care. When our lights and weapons and food ran out, they'd hunt us.

And, very likely, they would get us…and then get out.

Chap. 2

Camelback Mountain
Pocono Plateau, Elevation 2,133 Feet
Two Hours Ago

We touched down on a State Forestry helipad at the top of Camelback. Morning mist still clung to the off-season ski slopes. The sun was a weak promise behind a ceiling of white clouds that stretched into the dim forever. A bookish-looking man in a white anorak and thick glasses met us as we ducked out through the rotor wash. He was flanked by a State Cop, who looked confused, and a security officer from the Vault, who looked bug-eyed scared. Nobody shook hands.

We piled into an Expedition. The State Cop looked at the equipment bags we carried, and it was clear he wanted to ask, but he'd been told that questions were off-limits. All he knew was that we were 'specialists' on the Federal dime who came here to help solve a security problem. Which is another way of telling him to shut the hell up and just drive the car.

The geek with the glasses turned to me and started to speak, but I shook my head.

We drove in silence down the zigzag road that should have been packed with tourists here for the water park and other summer sports. We passed three police roadblocks and turned onto an access road before a fourth. A phalanx of Troopers were bellowing at the families and tour busses, waving them into U-turns and turning deaf ears to the abuse heaped on them by people who had driven since before dawn to get here. Top caught my eye and shook his head. I nodded. Inconvenience was a hell of a lot better than dying out here in the cold.

A smaller road split off from the access road and led into a big equipment barn, but the barn was just a cover for the entrance to The Vault. Four nervous-looking guards manned the entrance; their supervisor came over to us in an electric golf cart. He cut a look at the bookworm.

"These the pros from Dover?" He tried for the joke, but his voice cracked, spoiling it. I gave him a hard grin anyway. It was a nice try.

I turned to our driver as we climbed out. "Thanks, Troop…we're good from here."

He gave me a gruff nod, backed up, turned, and left, throwing suspicious looks at us through the side view mirror. The three of us unzipped the light windbreakers we'd worn on the flight and checked our weapons. We all wore Heckler & Koch Mark 23 .45 ACP pistols in nylon shoulder rigs. We each carried six magazines, and we had other toys in the equipment bags. Bookworm stared at the guns and flicked his tongue over his lips like a nervous gecko.

"Okay, run it down for us," I said to him.

"We'll talk on the way down," he said, and we piled into the golf cart. The security guy drove it into an elevator that began a descent of over a mile.

"I'm Dr. Goldman," said the guy with glasses. "I'm the deputy director of this facility. This is Lars Halverson, our head of security."

I shook hands with Halverson. His hand was firm but clammy, and his face and throat glistened with nervous sweat.

"You're Captain Ledger?" Goldman asked.

I nodded and jerked a thumb over my shoulder. "The old man behind me is Top Sims and the kid in diapers is Bunny." In my peripheral vision, I saw Top scratch his cheek with a middle finger.

First Sergeant Bradley Sims was hardly old—but at forty-one he was the oldest field operative in the DMS. He was nearly as tall as me, a little heavier in the shoulders, and though he was a calm man by nature, he could turn mean as a snake when it mattered.

The big kid next to him was Staff Sergeant Harvey Rabbit. Real name, so no surprise that everyone called him Bunny. He was just a smidge smaller than the Colossus of Rhodes, and somehow, despite everything we've been through together while running black ops for the Department of Military Sciences, Bunny still managed to keep his idealism bolted in place. My own was wearing pretty damn thin, and my optimism for rational behavior in people who should know better was taking one hell of a beating.

"What were you told?" asked Goldman.

"Not enough," I said. "You believe there's one or more infiltrators operating in your facility. You have one casualty, is that right?"

I caught the quick look that passed between Goldman and Halverson. It was furtive as all get-out, and at that moment I wouldn't have bought water from either of them if my ass was on fire.

"Actually," Goldman said slowly, "we have four casualties."

The engine of the elevator car was the only sound for a while. I heard Top clear his throat ever so slightly behind me.

"Who's dead?" I said sharply.

"Two of my people," said Halverson. "And another of the research staff."

"How and when?"

"We found the second guard half an hour ago," Goldman said. "The others were killed sometime last night. They didn't report for the breakfast meeting, and when the security teams did a search they found them dead in their rooms."

"How were they killed?"

Goldman chewed his lip. "The same as the first one."

"That's not an answer. I asked 'how?'"

He turned to Halverson, but I snapped my fingers. Loud as a firecracker in the confines of the elevator car. "Hey! Don't look at him. I asked you a question. Look at me and give me a straight answer."

He blinked in surprise, obviously unused to being ordered about. Probably thought his rank here at the facility put him above such things. Life's full of disappointments.

"They were...*bitten*."

"Bitten? By what? An animal? An insect?"

Halverson snorted and then hid it with a cough.

Goldman shook his head. "No...they were bitten to death by the...um...terrorists."

I stared at him, mouth open, unable to know how to respond. The elevator reached the bottom with a clang, and Halverson drove us out into the complex. We passed through a massive airlock that would have put a dent in NASA's budget. None of us said anything, because all around us klaxons screamed and red emergency lights pulsed.

Halverson stamped on the brakes.

"Christ!" Goldman yelled.

"OUT!" I growled, but Top and Bunny were already out of the cart, their guns appearing in their hands as if by magic. I was right with them.

The floor, the walls, even the ceiling of the steel tunnel were splashed with bright red blood. Five bodies lay sprawled in ragdoll heaps. Arms and legs twisted into grotesque shapes, eyes wide with profound shock and everlasting terror.

The corridor ran a hundred yards straight forward, angling deeper into the bowels of the mountain. Behind us, the hall ran twenty yards and jagged left into a side hall. Bunny put his laser sight on the far wall near the turn. Top had his pointed ahead. I swept in a full circle.

"Clear!" Bunny said.

"Clear," said Top.

"Jesus Christ!" said Goldman.

Halverson was saying something to himself. Maybe a prayer, but we couldn't hear it beneath the noise of the klaxons.

Then the alarms died. Just like that.

So did the lights.

The silence was immediate and dreadful.

The darkness was absolute.

But it was not an empty darkness. There were *sounds* in it, and I knew that we were far from alone down there.

"Night vision," I barked.

"On it," Bunny said. He was the closest to the golf cart, and I heard him rummaging in the bags. A moment later he said, "Green and go. Coming to you on your six."

He moved through the darkness behind me and touched my shoulder, then pressed a helmet into my hands. I put on the tin pot, flipped down the night vision, and flicked it on. The world went from absolute darkness to a surreal landscape of green, white, and black.

"Top," Bunny said, "coming to you."

I held my ground and studied the hall. Nothing moved. Goldman cowered beside me. He folded himself into the smallest possible package, tucked against the right front fender of the cart. Halverson was still behind the wheel. He had a Glock in his hand and the barrel was pointed at Top.

"Halverson," I said evenly, not wanting to startle him. "Raise your barrel. Do it now."

He did it, but there was a long moment of nervous indecision before he complied, so I swarmed up and took the gun away from him.

"Hey!" he complained. "Don't—I need that!"

"You can't see to shoot. Do you have night vision?"

"I have a flashlight." He began fumbling at his belt, but I batted his hand aside.

"No. Stay here and be still. I'm going to place your weapon on the seat next to you. Do not pick it up until the lights come on."

"But—"

"You're a danger to me and mine," I said, bending close. "Point a gun in the dark around me again, and I'll put a bullet in you. Do you believe me?"

"Y-yes."

I patted his shoulder—at which he flinched—and moved away.

"What are you seeing, Top?"

He knelt by the wall, his pistol aimed wherever he looked. "Nothing, seeing nothing, Cap'n."

"Bunny?"

He was guarding our backs. "Dead people and shadows, Boss. Look at the walls. Someone busted out the emergency lights."

"Captain Ledger," began Goldman, "what—"

"Be quiet and be still," I said.

We squatted in the dark and listened.

A sound.

Thin and scratchy, like fingernails on cardboard. Then a grunt of effort.

Top and I looked up at the same time, putting the red dots of our laser sights on the same part of the upper wall. There was a metal grille over an access port. The grille hung by a single screw, and one corner of it was twisted and bent out of shape, the spikes of two screws hanging from the edges. The grille hadn't been opened with a screwdriver; it had been torn out.

No. *Pushed.*

The scratching sound was coming from there, but as we listened, it faded and was gone.

"It's gone," whispered Goldman.

I noticed that he said *it*, not *him* or *them*. I could tell from the way he stiffened that Top caught it, too.

But Bunny asked, "What's gone? I mean…what the hell *was* that?"

The scientist turned toward Bunny's voice. His green-hued face was a study in inner conflict. His eyes were wide and blind, but they were windows into his soul. I doubt I've ever seen anyone as genuinely or deeply terrified.

"They…they're soldiers," he said.

"*Whose* soldiers? We were told this was a potential terrorist infiltration."

"God," he said hollowly. "There are a dozen of them."

I moved up to him and grabbed a fistful of his shirt.

"Stop screwing around, Doc, or so help me God—"

"Please," he begged. "Please…. We were trying to help. We were doing good work, *important* work. We were just trying to help the men in the field. But…but…."

And he began to cry.

We were screwed. Deeply, comprehensively, and perhaps terminally screwed.

Something moved in the green gloom down the hall. It was big and it kept to the shadows behind a stack of packing crates. It made a weird chittering sound.

"Is that a radio?" Bunny whispered.

I shook my head, but I really didn't know what it was.

"It's *them!*" Goldman said, and he loaded those two words with so much dread that I felt my flesh crawl.

"I got nothing down here," said Bunny, who was still guarding behind us. "What are you seeing, Boss?"

"Unknown. Top, watch the ceilings. I don't like this worth a damn."

The chittering sound came again, but this time it was behind us.

"What've you got, Bunny?" I called.

"I don't know, Boss, but it's weird and it's big. Staying out of range, just around the bend."

I turned.

"This is the U.S. Army. Lay down your weapons and step out into the hall with your hands raised."

My voice echoed back to me through the darkness, but whoever was around the bend did not step out.

The chittering sound was constant.

I repeated the challenge.

The sound changed, fading as the figure retreated. It was gone in seconds. I turned again, and the one ahead of us was gone as well.

"Cover me," I said, and Top shifted to keep his laser sight next to me as I crept over to the wall below the grille. I stood on tiptoes and strained to hear.

The chittering sound was there, but it was very faint, and as I listened, it faded to silence. Whatever was making that sound was too far away to be heard, but I knew that didn't mean it was gone.

I turned to the others. Doctor Goldman sat with his face in his hands, weeping.

"We're all going to Hell for this," he sobbed. "Oh, God...I'm going to Hell."

Chap. 3

The Vault
Forty-six Minutes Ago

When I finally got Goldman to stop blubbering and tell me what the hell was happening I was almost sorry he did.

Halverson was able to lead us to the breakers, and we got the main lights back on. The rest of the research team huddled in the staff lounge, a few of them with improvised weapons—a fire axe, hammers, that sort of thing. The lounge had a single door, and the filtration system vent in that room was the size of a baseball. We locked ourselves in and had a powwow.

Goldman said: "This facility was originally built as a secure bunker to house the Governor and other officials during a nuclear war. After the Cold War, it was repurposed for genetics and biological research."

"What kind of research?" I asked.

"That's classified."

I put my pistol barrel against his forehead. "Declassify it."

"Listen to the man," murmured Top in a fatherly voice—if your father was Hannibal Lecter.

Everyone gasped, and Halverson's hand almost strayed toward his sidearm. Goldman licked his lips. "We…we've been tasked with exploring the feasibility of using gene therapy for military asset enhancement."

"What kind of gene therapy?"

"Various."

I tapped him with the barrel. "You're stalling, and I'm disliking you more and more each second, Doc."

He winced. "Please…I can't think with that…." He gestured vaguely toward the gun. I moved it six inches away.

"Talk."

"We…I mean the government, the military, *see* the way things are going. The biosphere is critically wounded. Global warming is only the beginning. That's the pop-culture talking point, but it's a lot worse than that. Seas are dying because pollution has interrupted or eliminated key links in the food chain. Plankton and krill are dying while seaborne bacteria proliferate. Coral reefs are dying, the sea floor is a garbage pit, and even Third World countries are building centrifuges by the score to refine uranium."

"Yeah, I watch CNN. Life sucks. Get to the point."

"Some key people in government want to ensure that no matter what happens we'll still be able to maintain an effective military presence capable of response under all conditions."

"What kinds of conditions?"

"Extreme. Deep pollution, blight, even post-conflict radiation environments."

"Meaning?"

Goldman's face was bleak. "Meaning, that if you can't fix the world, then alter the inhabitants to adapt to the ambient circumstances."

I sat back and laid the pistol on my lap, my finger outside of the trigger guard.

"How?" asked Bunny. "How do you *make* people adapt?"

"Transgenics. Gene therapy. And some other methods. We explored some surgical options, but that's problematic. There's recovery time, tissue rejection issues, and other problems. Genetic modification is less traumatic."

"Let me see if I get this," I said. "You and your bunch of mad scientists down here alter the genes of test subjects to see if you can make them more adaptable to polluted and devastated environments."

"Yes."

"What kinds of genes?"

"Insect," he said. "Insects are among the most successful life-forms. Not as durable as viruses, or as hardy as some forms of bacteria, of course, but otherwise, they're remarkable. Many can live on very little food, they can endure great injury, and there are some who are highly resistant to radiation."

"You mean cockroaches?" Bunny asked.

Goldman shot him a quick look. "Yes and no. The idea that cockroaches would survive a nuclear war…that's a distortion based on urban myths. Cockroaches are only a little more resistant to radiation than humans. Four hundred to one thousand rads will usually kill a human. A thousand rads will cause infertility in cockroaches. Sixty-four hundred rads will kill over ninety percent of the *Blattella germanica* cockroaches. No…for increased resistance to radiation we explored genes from wood-boring insects and the fruit fly. Some species of woodborers can withstand forty-eight to sixty-eight thousand rads without measurable harm. It takes sixty-four thousand rads to kill a fruit fly; and if you're talking real endurance, the *Habrobracon*, a parasitoid wasp can withstand one hundred and eighty thousand rads."

"Hooray for garden pests," Top muttered.

"We experimented with various gene combinations and got mixed results. Many of those lines of research were terminated. We did come back to the cockroach, though," he said, and again he licked his lips with a nervous tongue. "Not for radiation resistance, but for other qualities."

"Like what?"

"They can run at incredible speeds. Even ordinary cockroaches can run at a speed of one meter per second. That's like an ordinary man running at one hundred and forty miles an hour. And they can change direction twenty-five times per second! Nothing else in nature can do that. Their elusiveness is one of the things that explains how they've survived in so many situations in which other animals were destroyed. They can also climb walls because the tiny *pili* on their feet allow them to adhere to surfaces as if they're covered in suction cups. It's like Velcro. They have light receptors in the ultraviolet range. And the list goes on and on." He took a breath, clearly caught up in the excitement of his life's work. "As we mapped the genome from the desired source animals, we began to see the potential emerge. A true super soldier. I...."

"Soldier?" Bunny interrupted.

Goldman turned to him, momentarily flummoxed. "Yes, of course....didn't I make that clear? All of our test subjects are soldiers."

"Whose soldiers?" asked Top.

"Why...ours, of course."

I leaned toward him. "Did they *know*?"

Goldman recoiled, but his voice was firm. "Of course! They all knew that they were volunteering for genetic experiments designed to make them better fighters. We had to tell them. There were letters of agreement, and every man signed." He looked at me accusingly, "You think we'd do this without telling them? God, what kind of monster do you think I am?"

I wanted to hit him. I wanted to drag him and his whole team into a quiet room and work them over.

"What went wrong?" I said, keeping my voice even.

He was a long time answering. He and the other scientists exchanged looks, and Halverson studied the floor between his shoes.

"They were all screened," Goldman said softly. "They knew the risks. But...gene therapy isn't yet an exact science. Mapping the genome isn't the same as truly indexing and annotating it."

"What are you talking about?" I asked. "What happened to them? Did they get sick?"

"Sick? No. No...they're very healthy. It's just that they...*changed*."

"Use the word, dammit," said Halverson in a fierce whisper. Apparently he wasn't as fully on board with all this as the science staff.

"Some of the insect genes coded differently than we expected. Most of the changes were mild and mostly irrelevant. Some skin changes. Thickening of the dermis, some color changes, follicular alterations. We tried to correct the problems with more gene therapy, but...we couldn't control the mutations." Goldman sighed, and said: "They *mutated*."

"Oh man," said Bunny. "My daddy wanted me to stay in Force Recon. Worst that could happen there is I get shot."

Top gave Goldman a hard look. "Why are they attacking your people? If they're volunteers...?"

Goldman shook his head, and nothing that I said could make him say it out loud. The rest of the science team looked ashamed and frightened. A few were openly weeping. None of them could look at us except Halverson. I saw the muscles at the corners of his jaw bunch and flex.

"Tell me," I said. We were past the point of threats now.

Halverson wiped sweat from his eyes. "These...*scientists*...had a protocol for incidents involving extreme aberrations. The entire project was to be terminated, along with any potentially dangerous aberrant forms."

"'Aberrant forms'?" I echoed. "God. You idiots were going to terminate a dozen U.S. soldiers? Citizens?"

"No," said Goldman. "They signed the papers! That officially made them property of the United States Army. And, besides...they were no longer soldiers."

"You mean that they were no longer *people*?"

He didn't answer, which was answer enough.

"You're a real piece of work, Doc."

"Look," he snapped, "we're at war! I did what I had to do to protect the best interests of the American people."

Suddenly there was a low rumble that shuddered its way heavily through the walls. The cement floor beneath our feet buckled and cracked. Dust puffed down from the ceiling, pictures fell from the walls. The scientists screamed and started from their chairs, but there was nowhere to run. Top and Bunny yelled at them to shut up, and they cowered back from the two big men with guns.

Halverson and I hurried to the door and peered out. There was a faint flickering red glow from down the hall. I could smell smoke. "Christ!" Halverson said. "I think that was the generator room."

There was a high whine from distressed engines, and then the lights dimmed again and went out. The staff room emergency lights kicked in after a few seconds, weak and yellow, giving each face a sallow, guilty cast.

"The generator *can't* be out," Goldman protested.

Halverson said nothing, but he looked stricken.

"What—?" Bunny asked.

The alarm took on a new tone as a prerecorded voice shouted from all the speakers. It told us why everyone in the room was looking even more terrified than they had been only a minute ago.

"This facility has been compromised. Level One containment is in effect."

The message looped and repeated. I turned to Goldman. "What does that mean?"

"It means that the generator is no longer feeding power to the airlocks or security systems. If the backup doesn't come on, then the system will move to Level Two."

"What happens then?"

"The whole place goes into lockdown," said Halverson. "This is a biological research facility, Captain. If containment is in danger of total failure, then the whole system shuts down. The doors will seal permanently."

"Did your test subjects know this?" I asked.

"I don't know," said Goldman. "Probably. I know the first subject, James Collins, knew it. He made a joke about it once. But...really, everyone knows, and it's posted on signs all over the facility."

I went to the door and opened it. Halverson joined me. "Looks like the backup generators are still on line. See—they are pulling the smoke out of the hall. The flames from the burning generator are dying down, too."

"I take it the backup generators aren't in the same room as the mains?"

"No, of course not. They're at the other end of the complex."

I pointed to the damaged access panel high on the wall. "That's the air duct system?"

"Yes."

"Does it go all the way into the chamber with the backup generators?"

He thought about it. "No. It terminates outside. The backups are on a totally separate system. Different venting, too. Smaller. No way *they* could use them to get into the chamber."

"How secure is it?"

"If you didn't have a key, then you'd need tools. Heavy pry bars and a lot of time. They were intended to protect against all forms of intrusion. The generator room is even hardened against an EMP."

"That's something."

I pulled Halverson out into the hall for a moment. "Tell me about James Collins."

Halverson paled. "He...he's a good kid. Young, in his twenties. No family, no one at home. No sweetheart or anything like that. It was one of the conditions. The men couldn't have families waiting at home. Better that way."

"Better for whom?" I asked, but he didn't answer.

"Collins was smart. He did a couple of tours with Force Recon. One in Iraq, one in Afghanistan. Took some shrapnel last time out. Lost a couple of fingers. It was while he was recovering at the evac hospital that he was approached about this project. He's been here almost seventeen months."

I stared at him. It was horrible. Some kid joins the Marines. Maybe he thinks he's helping to save the world from terrorists, or maybe he thinks he's saving his country. Or, maybe he's just lonely. Someone with no one at home and nowhere to be, so he makes the Marine Corps into his family, and it's a war so they're happy as hell to have him. They throw him into one meat grinder, and when he survives that they feed him into another. Then, when he's battle-shocked and mutilated, they make him an offer. Maybe money, maybe promotion. Or maybe they play off his sense of duty. God and country. That kind of pitch. They bring him to this place, hide him down in the dark, and when he's totally off the radar, they play God with him. If he lives, he's the prize hog at the fair. Someone to trot out to appropriations committees. If he dies, who's going to miss him?

But they never planned around a third option. What if they made him into a monster?

Hell, they wouldn't think that way. They're too limited, too conventional. They can *make* a monster, but to them it's just science. Pure science, divorced from conscience, separated from ethical concerns because no one is watching. People like Goldman and his masters in the military always think they have everything under control.

I know firsthand that, too often, they don't. I know because I'm the guy they send in to clean up their messes.

I don't know who I hated more in that moment: Goldman, because he made a monster; or me, because I knew that I had to kill it.

In the air vents I could hear a faint scuttling sound. Like fingernails on paper. I stepped closer to the vent, straining to hear it in the gaps between the bleats of the warning bells. It was there. Faint, and growing fainter.

They were moving away from us. Toward the other end of the complex.

Damn.

Chap. 4

The Vault
Twenty-two Minutes Ago

We left the others behind in a locked room. The emergency lights were smashed out along most of the hallway, so we flipped down our night vision. We had M4s from our equipment bags, and each of us wore light body armor. The stuff would stop most bullets, but I didn't think that was the kind of fight we were likely to have. Would it stop Collins?

Only one way to find out, and I didn't want to. Not one damn bit.

As he ran, Top whispered, "That door back at the staff room."

"Yeah."

"You saw the way those things tore at that vent grille. No way that chicken-ass door would keep them out."

"Yeah."

"You don't seem too broken up about the thought of those things getting in there."

"Are you?"

We ran for a dozen yards. Bunny said, "They're still civilians, Boss."

"Farm boy's right," agreed Top.

"Yep. So, if you want to go back and babysit them, you have my permission, First Sergeant."

Bunny cursed under his breath. We kept running down the hall.

We ran low and fast along the wall, guns out, moving heads and gun barrels in unison, the red eyes of the laser sights peering into every shadow. The Vault was enormous. It was one level, built into a series of interlocking limestone caves, but it spread out like an anemone, with side corridors and disused rooms and staff quarters and labs. There were three of us, and thirty wouldn't have been enough. Not without lights. Not with an enemy that could move as fast as these things could.

We looked for an ambush everywhere we went, and even then the monsters caught us off guard.

We were looking forward, we were looking side to side, we were covering our asses. Anything came at us in any normal direction, we'd have sent it home to Jesus in a heartbeat.

They tore open the damn ceiling and dropped on us.

There was a puff of dust, and then a screeching tear as the whole belly of the air duct tore open and they dropped out.

Like bugs.

The first one slammed down on Bunny. Two hundred pounds of it struck him between the shoulder blades, and the big man went down hard, knees cracking against the concrete, the air leaving his body in a surprised and terrified *whuf!*

Top screamed and spun, sweeping his gun up, firing as the second one fell, and the third. The rounds tore into them, punching through the dark, mottled skin, splattering the walls and ceiling with black blood. The creatures twisted in midair, trying to dodge the spray of lead, but instead soaking up the bullets.

The air was filled with a high-pitched keening and screeching as the things climbed through the torn duct and dropped into the hall.

Bunny was screaming as the creature on his back tore at him with fingers strangely thick and dark, the fingernails and the flesh beneath fused into chitinous hooks. Its back was to me, and I fired as I backpedaled, angling to shoot it and not Bunny. The creature threw back its head and screamed. Not like an insect, but like a man.

Bunny twisted under it, and slammed an elbow into the monster's side, and squirmed out from under. He was drenched with blood. I didn't know how much of it was his own.

"Cap!"

I turned at the yell and saw Top being driven backward against the wall. He had his M4 jammed sideways and pressed against the chest of a creature whose face was something out of nightmare. The eyes were human, but that was all. Its face was covered with thick scab-like plates, some of them overlaid like dragon scales, others standing alone on human skin. The nose was nearly gone, flattened against the armored face, and the mouth was a lipless slash surrounded by wriggling antennae. The creature was naked to the waist, the rags of fatigue pants hanging from its spindly legs.

Before I could close on him and offer help, Top pivoted and chopped out with a low, short side-thrust kick that shattered the creature's knee. As it reeled back, he came off the wall and swung the M4 in a tight upward arc, crushing its chin with the stock of the rifle. The blow was so powerful that the telescoping stock cracked and bent, but the thing that had once been a soldier flipped over backward and crashed down on the ground. Top stamped a foot onto its chest, and put two rounds into the misshapen skull.

I had my own troubles. Three of them swarmed at me in a three-point close. They tried to run me back against the wall, and if they had, I'd have been trapped and torn apart. They were so close that I only had enough room to bring my M4 up and hit the closest one with a burst to the chest. The impact flung him back, but the creature to his right lashed out and swatted the rifle out of my hands. It was a hugely powerful blow, way too strong for a man of his size. Whatever the doctors had done had amped up his strength. Or maybe he was mad with horror and rage and was pumping adrenaline. The rifle sling kept the weapon from flying away, but I lost my hold on it, and the creature reached for my throat with gnarled black fingers.

I parried and ducked and came up on the far side of his arms, then shoved him hard into the other attacker. They crashed into the wall, which gave me a short second of breathing space, so I grabbed at the rapid release folding knife clipped to the edge of my pocket. It was positioned to release into my hand, and I gave it a flick and felt the blade lock into place even while my hand was moving. There was a flash of green fire, and then the second of the monsters was spinning away, trying to staunch the flow of black blood from his throat.

The third one growled at me, his voice filled with clicks and hisses, and he slashed at my face. I ducked, and felt his ironhard nails tear through the fabric cover over my helmet. I didn't wait. I drove in low and hard and put my shoulder into his chest, driving him back against the wall. He hit with a crunch that tore a howl from his throat. I used a flat palm to knock his head against the wall, and then moved in to let the knife do its work.

He fell, and I pivoted, switching the knife to my left hand, drawing my pistol with my right.

And froze.

There was James Collins right in front of me. I knew immediately that it was him. Three fingers were missing from his left hand. He crouched ten feet away, legs wide to straddle the body on the ground.

Bunny.

Collins bent low so that he could touch Bunny's throat with the fingers of his right hand. The fingers were long, the nails thickened into talons, and from where each tip dented Bunny's throat, thin lines of blood leaked down the side of the big Marine's neck. Around us, the alarms rang and the lights flashed, but nothing and no one moved. Collins raised his horror-show face and I could tell, even with those dark and alien eyes, that he knew as well as I did that we were all sliding down a steep slope into hell.

I raised my pistol and put the laser sight on Collins, right over the heart. He looked down at it for a moment, and his fingers pressed more deeply into Bunny's flesh.

"Cap'n," murmured Top from a few yards away, but I ignored him.

Even though Goldman and Halverson had told us what to expect, I could feel a scream bubbling in my gut. This was wrong, and it was ugly, and it was scaring the living shit out of me. Sweat ran down inside my clothes and my mouth was as dry as mummy dust. If I could have run, I would have.

I said, "Collins."

The creature's head jerked up, and his slit of a mouth worked for a moment. All I could hear were clicks. His face was covered with the same platelike scabs as the others. It wasn't precisely an insect face, but it was too far away from human. There were tiny fibers or antennae around his mouth, and they twitched like stubby fingers. God only knows what sensory information those appendages fed that tortured mind.

"Listen to me," I said, and my voice cracked a little. I cleared my throat, and tried it again. "Collins…listen."

In the shadows, the other creatures clicked and hissed at the sound of my voice.

"I know you're in there. I know Corporal James Collins is still in there."

His mouth and throat muscles worked. Rasps and clicks, a stilted flow that was so alien and unnatural that it was painful to hear.

"J-J-J—"

I kept the red dot steady, my finger inside the trigger guard. I had my trigger adjusted to a five-and-a-half-pound pull, and I had about four pounds on it. Bunny was trying not to breathe, trying to sink into the floor, and he looked every bit as terrified as I felt.

"J-J-J-Jimm…J-J-Jimmy," said Collins.

My breath caught in my throat.

"Holy mother of God," Top whispered behind me.

"Jimmy?" I asked.

The misshapen head bobbed.

"You're Jimmy Collins, is that right? Jimmy, not James?"

Another nod. There was a light in his eyes. Fear. Anger. Maybe—relief?

"The docs," I said. "Jimmy—the docs said that you signed up for this."

His eyes hardened. The others hissed.

"They said that you knew the risks."

"Risks," he snarled and I knew that just framing the word had to hurt his throat. He used his maimed hand to touch his face. "Not…*this.*"

"No," I said emphatically. Almost a shout. "*Not* this. There's no way they told you that this would happen. But did they tell you what might happen?"

He tried to answer, but emotion—or whatever was left for him to feel—stole what little voice he had. Eventually he managed to get it out. Two words.

"They...lied."

"Yeah, brother, I pretty much figured that. That sucks more than I can describe, but listen to me, Jimmy....I can't let you hurt my man there. He's a good man. A friend."

"A—Army?" Collins said.

"No. He's Gyrene like you are. End of the day, though, he's another pair of boots on the ground in someone else's war." I eased off of the trigger and slipped my finger outside the guard. He watched me do it. I didn't lower the gun, though; and he saw that, too. "I know you never signed up for this, Jimmy. Who would? They think that because you enlisted and because you signed a piece of paper that they *own* you, that you're just a lab rat to them. If that's the case, if that's what we've all been fighting for, then God help the United States. Or maybe God help us all, because someone's missing the whole damn point. You with me on this, Jimmy?"

He paused, then nodded. It was impossible to read his face, hard to know if he was agreeing with me or giving me permission to keep talking.

"You want to know why I'm here? Why me and my team are here? The docs who did this to you called Homeland and said that this facility was being overrun by terrorists."

"T-T-T-T—" He couldn't even get the word out. The stubby antennae around his mouth twitched with wild agitation.

"Yes, sir, Jimmy. Terrorists. How's that for a thank-you from Uncle Sam? They rang the alarm, and we were sent in to drop the hammer on the bad guys. But...here's my problem, Jimmy, and maybe you can help me out with it."

His black eyes glittered like jewels.

"I'm not sure who the bad guys are. I mean...you're killing folks, and you know that I can't let that happen. I can't let it continue. But at the same time, I don't think you're doing these kills because you're a terrorist."

He said nothing. They all waited.

"I think you're doing it because you're scared. More scared than I am now, and that's saying something. But you know I can't let you go on killing these people. Even if I agree with why you're doing it, I got a job to do, and I know you understand that."

His antennae twitched.

"Now...*terror* is a funny word," I said. "We use it all the time, but we don't think about what it really means. Right now...I think my man on the floor there is feeling some genuine terror."

Collins looked down at Bunny and then up at me.

"And you've got to be feeling it. All of you."

The others clicked and hissed.

"And everyone else down here is feeling it because of you. There may not be any terrorists down here, Jimmy, but I have to stop the terror. That's my job. That's what I'm really here to do."

Jimmy Collins's eyes were wide, and dark, and wet.

"Can you help me with that, marine? Can you give me an out here?"

Collins looked at me, and raised his eyes slowly toward my helmet. Not at the night-vision unit, but at the small cylinder mounted on the left side of my tin pot. He nodded at me. At it.

"That's right, Jimmy," I said with a smile. "That's a video camera. We're on mission time here, everything's being recorded. Everything we've seen, and everything we've *heard* since we came down here is saved to memory in our helmet cams. Now how about that?"

Collins bent low until his deformed face was inches from Bunny's. He whispered something that I couldn't hear over the alarms.

And then he straightened and pulled his hand away from Bunny. The five little pinpricks still leaked blood, but there was no real damage. Collins took a step back, and another. Bunny scrabbled sideways and scuttled back toward me. He made a grab for his fallen M4.

"No," I said.

Bunny looked at me in surprise, then at Top, who nodded, and then at Collins.

The hulking figure stepped farther back. His companions clustered around him. They made chittering noises, and God only knows if it was some kind of speech or the screams of the damned. Behind them was the door to the secondary generator. Collins turned, looked at the door and then back at me. His eyes were intense, pleading.

I swallowed a lump the size of a fist.

"Boss," said Bunny, "if we get them out...maybe something can be done. Maybe there's some way of reversing this...."

His voice trailed off as the huddled monsters chittered and clicked. It wasn't words, but it was eloquent enough.

I shook my head.

"But...you know what they want to do," he pleaded.

Top put his hand on Bunny's shoulder. "If it was you, farm boy, what would you do?"

I raised my pistol. "Stand aside," I said to Collins.

After a moment, he and the others moved away.

It took six rounds to blow the lock open.

Smoke hung thick in the air. The klaxons continued to bleat.

"Give us ten minutes," I said.

Collins stared at me, his eyes unreadable in the green gloom of my night vision. Did he nod? Or was it simply the way his body trembled as he turned and slipped into the generator room? The others followed.

I holstered my gun and looked at Bunny and Top.

We ran like sons of bitches.

Chap. 5

The Vault
Now

The voice said: "Fail-safe is active. Hard lockdown commencing."

It was a female voice, very calm. She began counting down from one hundred.

"Top, Bunny...get everyone into the elevators."

"The generator—" Top said.

"...Eighty-nine, eighty-eight, eighty-seven...."

Halverson said, "The elevator has a separate power source. It's topside. As long as we get above the three thousand foot line we'll be fine. Below that charges in the wall will collapse the elevator into the shaft."

"...eighty, seventy-nine...."

"Get moving!" I ordered, and my men began herding the remaining scientists, support staff, and security personnel into the elevator.

"...sixty-three, sixty-two...."

I lingered in the staff room, watching as Doctor Goldman finished downloading his research files onto a one-terabyte portable drive.

"Is that everything?" I said as he pulled it out of the socket.

"...forty-four, forty-three...."

"Yes, thank God. Everything was in packets for quick hard-dump. We have everything we need to start over." He moved to the door, but I shifted to block his way.

"Give me the drive," I said.

"...thirty-six, thirty-five...."

"What the hell are you *doing*? This is no time for—"

I kicked him in the nuts and snatched the drive out of his hand. Yeah, it was a sneak shot, but who cares? He uttered a thin whistling shriek and grabbed his groin, sinking to his knees in shock and agony.

I set the drive on a counter top.

"...twenty-eight, twenty-seven...."

I drew my sidearm and used the butt to smash the drive to silicon junk. Goldman screamed louder than when I'd kicked him. He made a grab for it, but I batted his hand away.

"What are you doing?" he croaked.

I moved to the doorway. The elevator was a hundred yards down the hall. I could make it at a dead run.

I said, "I'm doing what I believe is in the best interests of the American people."

He stared at me and opened his mouth to say something, but a sound cut him off. Not the relentless female voice counting down. This was a thin, chittering noise that echoed out of the darkness at the far end of the corridor.

I holstered my gun, turned and ran like hell.

"...thirteen, twelve, eleven...."

"Where's the doc?" Halverson demanded as I skidded into the elevator car.

"They ambushed us," I lied. "Came out of nowhere. Now come on, get this damn thing moving!"

Halverson met my eyes for the briefest of moments, and I could see the realization in his eyes. He flicked a look out into the darkness. Maybe he could hear the skittering sounds. Probably not. The alarms were so loud that they even drowned out the sound of the screams.

He slammed the door shut and the car began to rise.

Three seconds later, we heard the *bang-bang-bang* as the steel doors dropped down and the thermite charges blew, fusing them shut. A moment later, the explosives in the elevator shaft blasted half a million tons of rock into the well of darkness below us. Dust clouds chased us all the way up into the light.

As the car slowed to a stop, I removed my helmet. The helmet cam was gone. I'd taken it off after we'd left Collins and the others outside of the generator room. The video file ended there.

Top, Bunny and I stepped out into the gloom of the building. State Troopers were everywhere, and soon there would be FBI, Marine Corps, and DMS choppers in the air. We didn't care. The three of us stood there in the darkness and said nothing. I reached into my pocket to touch the helmet cam, and closed my fist around it.

In silence, we left the shadows and walked out into the light.

~The End~

Material Witness

NOTE: This story takes place several weeks after the events in *Patient Zero*.

Chap. 1

Echo Team: Case File Report / DMS-ET 82fd1118
Events of August 16 / Prepared August 17; 11:30 a.m.
Team Leader: Captain Joseph Edwin Ledger

Preamble to the official statement of Dr. Rudy Sanchez:

I personally tested Captain Ledger and his men. Blood and urine, a full workup. There is no presence of alcohol or any controlled substance. Standard interview and psychological profiles demonstrate post-traumatic stress and nervous tension typical with recent combat, plus a degree of heightened nervousness that I believe should be ascribed to the unusual nature of the events as described by the members of Echo Team.

From the analysis of a voluntary polygraph test:

All three men were tested separately. I oversaw each test. Each man was given a number of unsequenced control questions as well as the set of questions prepared by Mr. Church. These questions were introduced randomly and without preamble. There is nothing in their responses or on the polygraph tape to suggest that any of them provided false or exaggerated answers. As disturbing and unlikely as it appears, these men believe that they saw and experienced everything exactly as described in Captain Ledger's after-action report and in the private interviews with Dr. Sanchez, Aunt Sallie, and Mr. Church.

Handwritten note included in Mr. Church's private copy of Dr. Sanchez's psychological evaluation of Captain Joseph Edwin Ledger, First Sergeant Bradley Sims and Staff Sergeant Harvey Rabbit. Note reads:

Per your question of earlier today...yes, I am certain that they believe that these events occurred. Please bear in mind the troubled history of that town. It has had far more than its share of troubles for many years. I respectfully but firmly decline your offer to go there and investigate matters for myself. No thank you! —RS

Chap. 2

The Warehouse
Department of Military Sciences Baltimore Field Office
August 16; 8:19 a.m.
One Day Ago

"God —*please!* They're killing me here. You got to get me out of this. Jesus Christ, you said this wouldn't happen."

I leaned forward to listen to the voice. Even with the distortion of a bad digital file I could hear the raw terror, the urgency.

"When did this come in?" I asked.

My boss, Mr. Church, sat on the other side of the conference table. He was neatly dressed, the knot of his tie perfect, his face impassive. But I wasn't fooled. This had to be hitting him every bit as hard as it was me.

"That's the problem," he said. "This message is three days old."

"*Three days?* How the hell...?"

Church held up a hand.

I paused, dialing it down a notch. "How did this get missed? Burke's handler should have called us right away."

"The handler didn't get this until this morning."

"Then how...?"

"This message was left on the home phone of the Special Agent in Charge."

He let that float in the air for a moment.

"Wait," I said, "*home* phone?"

"Yes," said Church, "and isn't that interesting. Simon Burke would have no way of knowing who the AIC was, let alone have access to his home number."

"Did the handler get a call?"

Church opened a folder and slid it across the table toward me. "These are the phone records for the handler, Dykstra. The top page is the direct line to Burke's safe house. The next pages are Dykstra's cell and home numbers. The previous call from Burke was the routine check-in last week. Nothing since then. Nothing from a pay phone or from any other line that Burke could have used."

"The handler's cell...."

"No," said Church. "There is no identifiable incoming call on any line associated with the AIC or the handler that could have resulted in that message."

I frowned. "I don't understand. If Burke left a message then there has to be a record."

Church said nothing. He selected a vanilla wafer from a plate of cookies which sat between us on the table. He nibbled off a piece and munched it thoughtfully, his eyes never leaving my face.

I said, "Then someone got to the records. Altered them."

"Mm. Difficult, but possible."

"Or...they have a way to erase their tracks, remove all traces of the call."

"Also possible, but...."

"...even *more* difficult," I finished.

He said nothing. He didn't have to. There were very few computer systems in the world capable of the kind of thorough hacking we were discussing; and even then there was only one computer that couldn't be fooled by any of the others and that was MindReader. That was *our* computer. It was a freak among computers, designed to be a ghost, to intrude into any other system and then rewrite its memory so that there was absolutely no footprint. All other computers left a bit of a scar on the hard drive. Not MindReader. And Church guarded that system like a dragon. Not even the President had access to it without Church personally signing him in.

"Okay," I said, "could someone have gotten to the answering machine directly and recorded a message onto it from the AIC's house?"

"No. Dykstra uses a service provided by AT&T, and the messages are stored on their server. If the call was made from Dykstra's home phone, there would be a record of that."

"And there isn't."

"No."

I reached over and took an Oreo from the plate. I can't come up with any good reason why a sane person would bother with vanilla wafers when the chocolaty goodness of Oreos was right there. It added to my growing suspicion that Church was a Vulcan.

"Who's looking for Burke?"

"The FBI has been looking for him since nine this morning. Except for us, no one else is in the loop."

"Local law?"

"They are definitely out of the loop. There have been some concerns about the police department, though admittedly that was under previous management. The current chief has no strikes against him, but otherwise he's an unknown quantity. This matter was deemed too sensitive to be shared with him."

"Even now?"

Church pursed his lips. "Only with direct supervision."

"Which doesn't mean the FBI."

"No." Church ate more of his cookie. "We've backtracked to a few hours before the call was left on Dykstra's voicemail, and nothing. Burke has not used a credit card or made transactions of any kind under his own name. His car is still parked in his garage."

I sighed. "I'm not liking the spin on this one, Boss. Burke's not a player. He might know in theory how to stay off the grid, but I can't see him managing it without making a mistake. Not for this long, not without help."

"Doubtful. And there's one more thing."

I waited, knowing that Church would save the kicker for last.

"Burke's clever. His whole life is built around creating plots that his readers won't see coming. Apparently he's used this same gift against his handler. We hacked the confidential reports between the handler and the AIC, and Burke's gone missing four times previously. Not for long, a matter of a few hours each time. The handler eventually realized that Burke was using a bicycle to get into town or out of town via one of the two bridges. I had Bug do computer pattern sweeps on commerce records of stores within bicycle distance of the safe house. We've been able to establish that on the dates in question, and inside the window of time, there were purchases of six disposable cell phones. Burke has been making calls."

"Who's he calling?"

"Add this to the equation," Church said. "Interest in Burke and his unstoppable novel plot has increased substantially in the weeks following those purchases."

"Well, that's interesting as hell."

"Isn't it, though?"

"You think he's trying to sell it?"

"We have to be open to that possibility."

What Church didn't say out loud was: *In which case Burke becomes a National Security liability.*

"We need to put this idiot in a bag," I said. "But we can't put out an APB. That would draw every shooter east of the Mississippi."

"Likely it would draw shooters from around the globe," said Church. "A dozen countries come to mind."

"What if he's already dead?"

He looked at me. Church wears tinted glasses that make it tough to read his expression. "Is that what you think?"

I thought about it, and shook my head. "No. Considering how important Burke is, a pro would either be under orders to get him out of the country or get him to one of *their* safe houses. Or they'd want him splashed all over the headlines. Either way, the odds on him seizing the opportunity to leave a message are pretty slim."

"Agreed." Church took another cookie. Another vanilla wafer. Weird.

I nodded to the recorder on the table. "Play it again."

"This is Simon Burke...look, you jokers said you'd protect me. They're going to tear me apart. Look...I don't have much time...this is really hard. You got to do something. God—please! They're killing me here. You got to get me out of this. Jesus Christ, you said this wouldn't happen."

He played it three times more. It sounded just as bad each time, and Burke sounded just as terrified. I rubbed my eyes and stood up.

"He sounds genuinely scared," I said. "And outraged. I can't see him making that call *after* he's contacted potential buyers. It would make more sense for him to do that as a result of getting no action on this kind of a cry for help."

"Agreed. Which means we are short on answers, and time is not our friend."

"Then I guess I'd better get my boys and get gone."

"Sergeant Dietrich is prepping a helo," said Church. He cocked his head at me. "Have you ever been to that town?"

"Pine Deep? Sure, but way back when I was a kid. My dad took me and my brother to the big Halloween Festival they used to have. That was before the trouble, of course."

The *trouble*.

Funny little word for something that stands as one of the worst disasters in U.S. history. More than eleven thousand dead in what has been officially referred to as an act of terrorism and insurrection by a domestic terrorist cell formed by members of a local white-supremacist organization. The terrorists dumped a lot of LSD into the town's drinking water. Had everyone convinced that half the town was turning into monsters.

"Terrible tragedy," said Church.

"I saw the movie they did on it," I said. "*Hellnight*, I think it was called. Hollywood turned it into a horror picture. Vampires and ghosts and werewolves, oh my."

Church chewed his cookie. "There was a lot of confusion surrounding the incidents. The *official* report labeled it domestic terrorism."

I caught the slight emphasis he put on the word *official*. "Why, was there something else going on?"

He very nearly smiled.

"Have a safe trip, Captain Ledger."

Chap. 3

Route A-32
Bucks County, Pennsylvania
August 16; 4:22 p.m.

The chopper put us down at a private airfield near Doylestown, Pennsylvania, and a couple of DMS techs had a car waiting for us. It looked like a two-year-old black Ford Explorer, but we had the full James Bond kit. Well, I guess it's more the Jack Bauer kit. No oil slicks or changeable license plates. Mostly we had guns. Lots and lots of guns. The back bay was a gun closet with everything from Glock nines to Colt M4 carbines fitted with Aimpoint red-dot sights. And enough ammunition to wage a moderately enthusiastic war.

Bunny whistled as he opened all the drawers and compartments. "And to think I asked for a puppy for Christmas."

"For when you care enough to send the very best," he said, hefting a Daewoo USAS-12 automatic shotgun. "I think I'll call her 'Missy.'"

"Freak," muttered Top Sims under his breath. First Sergeant Bradley Sims—Top to everyone—was a career noncom who had been in uniform nearly as long as Bunny had been alive, but for all that he'd never cultivated the testosterone-driven shtick of idolizing weapons. To him they were tools and nothing more. He respected them, and he handled them with superior professional skill, but he wasn't in love with them.

Bunny—Harvey Rabbit, according to his birth certificate—looked dreamy-eyed, like a man going courting.

They were the only two members of Echo Team left standing after our last couple of missions. We had more guys in training, but Top and Bunny were on deck and ready to roll when this Burke thing came at us. Like me, they were dressed in civilian clothes. Jeans, Hawaiian shirts. Top wore Nu-Balance cross-trainers that looked like they'd been spit-polished; Bunny had a well-worn pair of Timberlands.

I said, "Concealed small arms. We're here on a search and rescue. We're not declaring war on rural Pennsylvania."

Bunny looked hurt. "Damn, and here I thought it was redneck season."

Even Top grinned at that.

I looked at my watch. "Saddle up. We're burning daylight."

Even as I said it I heard a rumble of thunder and glanced up. The sky above was bright and blue and cloudless, but there were storm clouds gathering in the northeast. Probably ten miles from where we were, which put the clouds over or near Pine Deep. Swell. Nothing helps a manhunt better than fricking rain.

We climbed into the SUV, buckled up for safety, and headed out, taking Route 202 north and then cutting onto the snaking black ribbon that was State Alternate Route A-32. Top drove, Bunny crammed his six-and-a-half-foot bulk into the back, and I took the shotgun seat.

"So why's this Burke guy so important?" asked Bunny. "And since when do we screw around with Witness Protection?"

"Not exactly what this is," I said. "Simon Burke is a writer and—"

"I read his books," said Top. "Bit weird. Little paranoid."

I nodded. "He writes thrillers, and since the middle nineties he's built a rep for ultrabelievable terrorist plots."

"Yeah, yeah," said Bunny, nodding. "I saw the movie they made out of one of those books. The one about terrorists introducing irradiated fleas into the sheepdogs in cattle country. Jon Stewart had him on and kind of fried the guy because a couple of meatheads actually *tried* to do the flea thing. Burke kept saying, 'how is that *my* problem?'"

"That's the story in a nutshell," I said. "Burke's plots have always been way too practical, and he likes showing off by providing useful detail. There's a fine line between a detailed thriller and a primer for terrorists."

"Hooah," murmured Top. That was Army Ranger-speak for everything from "I agree" to "Get stuffed."

"Well, early last year Burke was doing the talk show circuit to promote his new book—"

"—*A Predator Species*," supplied Top. "Read it. Give it four stars out of five."

"—and Conan O'Brien asks him about his plots. Burke, who's a bit of a jackass at the best of times, according to what I've been told and the interview transcripts I've read, starts bragging about the fact that he has a plot that is so good, so perfect that his contacts with Homeland 'strongly requested' him not to publish it."

"We know who that was in Homeland?" Bunny snorted.

"It wasn't Homeland," I said, "it was Hugo Vox, the guy who does all the screening for people getting top secret and above clearance. He ran the plot out at that counterterrorism training center he has in Colorado. Terror Town. Teams ran it six times, and Vox said that the best-case scenario was a forty percent kill of the U.S. population. Low-tech, too. Anyone could make it work."

"Jeeeez-us," said Bunny.

"What was it?" asked Top, intrigued.

I told them. Top gave a long, low whistle. Bunny's grin diminished in wattage.

They considered it, shaking their heads as the logic of it unfolded in their imaginations. "Damn," Bunny said, "that's smart."

"It's damn stupid," countered Top. "Putting that in bookstores would be like handing out M16s at a terrorism convention."

"It was stupid for Burke to talk about it on Conan," I said. "Luckily he didn't actually describe the plot on TV. Just enough to give the impression he really had something. You can probably guess what happened," I said.

Top made a face. "Someone made a run at him?"

I nodded. "Within a day of doing the show he was nearly kidnapped twice. He must have realized his mistake and went straight to his lawyer, who in turned called the FBI, who called Homeland, who called us."

"And we did what?" asked Bunny. "Put a bag over him?"

"More or less. This is before we came on the DMS," I said, "so I'm getting this second hand from Church. I drew this gig because I know Burke. Or, used to. He did ridealongs with me and a couple other cops when I was with Baltimore PD. Bottom line is that Burke was set up in Pine Deep as a retired school teacher and widower. His handler's cover is that of 'nephew' who lives one town away. Place called Black Marsh, right over the river in New Jersey."

"So it's just protective custody?"

"No. Homeland is cooking up some kind of scam thing where they'll eventually use Burke as bait to lure the cockroaches out of the woodwork. Get them to make a run at him so we could scoop them up, take them off for some quiet conversation, say at Gitmo."

"Well…that's pretty much what just happened, isn't it?" asked Top.

"I guess…but it wasn't on a timetable. They wanted Burke completely off the radar for a year or so to let things cool down. Homeland wanted to scoop up high-profile hitters, not bozos with suicide vests. The plan was to start seeding the spy network with disinformation this fall that Burke was willing to sell his idea for the right kind of money. Let that cook on the international scene for a bit then set up a meet with as many buyers as we can line up. Then do a series of snatch-and-grabs. It's the kind of assembly-line arrests Homeland's been doing since 9-11. Doesn't put all their eggs in one basket, so even if they put four out of twenty potential buyers in the bag they celebrate it as a major win. And, I guess it is."

Top nodded. "So what went wrong, Cap'n?"

"He disappeared."

"Disappeared? Did he walk or was he taken?"

"I guess that's what we're here to find out." I told them the rest, about Burke going AWOL a few times; and about the cell phones and the buzz overseas.

"Are we trying to find him and keep him safe," asked Top, "or put a bullet in his brainpan. 'Cause I can build a case either way."

I didn't answer.

We'd caught up with the storm clouds, and the closer we got to Pine Deep the gloomier it got. I know it was coincidence, but I could live without subtle jokes like that from the universe. Luckily the rain seemed to be holding off.

We passed through the small town of Crestville, following the road so that we'd enter Pine Deep via a rickety bridge from the north. Both sides of the road were lined with cornfields. It was the middle of August and the corn was tall and green and impenetrable. Here and there we saw old signs, faded and crumbling, that once advertised a Haunted Hayride and a Halloween Festival.

As we crossed the bridge Top tapped my shoulder and nodded to a big wooden sign almost completely faded by hard summers and harder winters. It read:

Welcome to Pine Deep
America's Haunted Holidayland!
We'll Scare You to Death!

Somebody had used red spray paint to overlay the writing with a smiley face, complete with vampire fangs.

"Charming," I said.

We drove down another crooked road that broadened onto a feeder side street, then made the turn onto Main Street. The town of Pine Deep looked schizophrenic. Almost half of the buildings were brand-new, with glossy window displays and bright LED signs; and the other half looked at least fifty years old and in need of basic repair. Some of the buildings had been burned and painted over, and that squared with what I'd read about the place. Before the trouble, Pine Deep had been an upscale arts community built on the bones of a centuries-old blue-collar farming region. Even now, with its struggle to create a new identity, there were glimpses of those earlier eras. Like ghosts, glimpses out of the corner of the eye. But the overall impression was of a town that had failed. It wasn't dead, but it wasn't quite alive either. Maybe the economic downturn had come at the wrong time, derailing the reconstruction of the town and the rebuilding of its economy. Or, maybe the memory of all those dead people, all that pain from the trouble infected the atmosphere.

"Damn," murmured Bunny. "They could film a Stephen King flick here. Wouldn't need special effects."

"Town's trying to make a comeback," I said.

Top's face was set, his brows furrowed. Unlike Bunny and me, Top had read a couple of the books written about the town and its troubles. He shook his head. "Some things you don't come back from."

"That's cheery," said Bunny.

Top nodded to one of the buildings that still showed traces of the fire that had nearly destroyed Pine Deep. "That wasn't the first problem this place had. Even when I was a kid *Newsweek* was calling this place the 'most haunted town in America.' Had that reputation going back to Colonial times."

"Since when do you believe in ghosts?" I asked.

He didn't answer. Instead he said, "Places can be like people. Some are born good, some are born bad. This one's like that. Born bad, and bad to the bone."

Bunny opened his mouth to make a joke, but he left it unsaid.

We drove in silence for a while.

Finally Top seemed to shake off some of his gloom. "We going to check in with the local police? If so, what badge do we flash?"

"That's where we're heading now," I said, as I pulled into a slanted curbside parking slot. "The FBI has been the public face of this kind of witness protection, but Federal Marshals are also involved. We're both. I'm FBI, you guys are marshals."

They nodded and Top dug out the appropriate I.D.s from a locked compartment. We have fully authentic identification for most of the major investigative and enforcement branches of the U.S. government. The only I.D.s we don't have are DMS cards and badges, because the DMS doesn't issue any. We only exist as far as the President and one congressional subcommittee is concerned.

We got out and headed toward the small office marked PINE DEEP POLICE DEPARTMENT. There were potted plants on either side of the door, but both plants were withered and dead.

Chap. 4

Pine Deep Police Department
August 16; 4:59 p.m.

There were three people in the office. A small, pigeon-breasted woman with horn-rims and blue hair who sat at a combination desk and dispatch console. She didn't even look up as the doorbell tinkled.

The two men did.

They were completely unalike in every way. The younger man, a patrol officer with corporal's stripes, was at a desk. Early twenties, but he was a moose. Not as big as Bunny—and there are relatives of Godzilla who aren't as big as Bunny—but big enough. Six four, two-twenty and change. The kind of muscles you get from hard work and free weights. Callused hands, lots of facial scars. A fighter for sure. He had curly red hair and contact lenses that gave him weirdly luminous blue eyes.

Almost purple. Odd cosmetic choice for a cop. Little triangular plaque on his desk read: CORPORAL MICHAEL SWEENEY.

He remained seated, but the other man rose as we entered. He was about fifty, but he had a lean build that hadn't yielded to middle-age spread. Short, slender, with intensely black hair threaded with silver. He, too, had visible scars, and it was no stretch to guess that they'd gotten them during the Trouble. And, strangely, there was also something familiar about him. I felt like I'd met him somewhere...or heard something about him.... Whatever it was, the memory was way, way back on a dusty shelf where I couldn't reach it.

The older man wore Chief's bars and a smile that looked warm and cheerful and was entirely fabricated. He leaned on the intake desk. "What can I do for you fellows?"

I flashed the FBI badge. "Special Agent Morrison," I said. The name on the card was Marion Morrison. John Wayne's real name.

His smile didn't flicker. I also noticed that it didn't quite reach his eyes. "And your fishing buddies there?"

They held up ID cases, too, but I introduced them. "Federal Deputy Marshals Cassidy and Reid." Full names on the IDs were William Cassidy and John Reid. Hopalong Cassidy and the Lone Ranger. The guy at the DMS who does our IDs needs a long vacation.

"Malcolm Crow," said the smaller man. "Pine Deep Chief of Police."

He offered his hand, which was small and hard, and we shook.

"So...again, what can I do for you?" he asked.

"Missing persons case," I said. "Confidential and high-profile."

"Which means what? A special agent and two marshals? This a manhunt for a suspected terrorist or a missing witness?"

I shrugged, hoping he'd take that as a 'we're not supposed to talk about it' kind of thing. He ignored it.

"Can't help you if you won't share," he said.

I said nothing, giving him 'the look.' It usually makes people squirm. Chief Crow merely smiled his veneer of a smile and waited me out.

"Okay," I said, as if answering his question was the hardest thing I was ever going to be asked to do, "I can tell you this much. We had a protected witness living in Pine Deep. He's missing."

"Living here under what name?"

"Peter Wagner."

"Ah."

"Ah...what?"

"The writer."

I stepped closer to the intake bench. "And how would you know that?"

Behind Crow, Officer Sweeney stood up. He did it slowly, without threat, but there was still a lot of threat there. Unlike the chief, Sweeney's face was unsmiling. A good-looking kid, but one that you'd take note of, especially if he wasn't in uniform and you were both alone. Behind me I heard the soft scuff as Top and Bunny made subtle moves. Shifting weight, being ready.

Crow seemed amused by all of this. To me he said, "You take a guy as famous as Simon Burke, give him a bad dye job and color contacts, and you expect no one to recognize him? People in small towns *do* read, you know. And your boy is famous."

"Who else knows who he is?"

"Most people with two eyes and an IQ."

Crap.

"For what it's worth," said Crow, "people hereabouts know how to keep a secret." As if on cue the thunder rumbled. It made Crow smile more. "Can I ask why a bestselling novelist is in witness protection?"

"National security."

"Ri-i-ght," he said in exactly the way you'd say "bullshit."

"Do you know where he is?" I asked. "Has he come forward and—"

"No," Crow said, cutting me off. "I don't know where he is, but I suspect he's in some real trouble."

"Why do you suspect that, Chief Crow?"

He shrugged. "Because you're here. If he was out sowing some wild oats or getting hammered down at the Scarecrow Lounge, his handler would be on it. Or at most he'd get a couple of kids right out of Quantico to help with the scut work. Instead they send you three."

"We *are* the team sent to locate our witness."

"Ri-i-ght," he said again, stretching out the "I."

"Would you like to see our credentials again?" This guy was beginning to irritate the crap out of me.

"Look," said Crow, leaning a few inches forward on his forearms. I could see the network of scars on his face. "You're about as close to a standard paper-pushing FBI agent as I am to Megan Fox. You're a hunter, and so are your pals. I don't care what the IDs say, because you're probably NSA at the least, in which case the IDs are as real as you need them to be and I'm Joe Nobody from Nowhere, Pennsylvania. But here's a news flash. Just about nothing happens in a small town without everybody hearing something. Our gossip-train is faster than a speeding bullet. If you want to find your missing witness, then you can do it the easy way, which is with my help; or the hard way, which is without my help."

I had to fight to keep a smile off my face. Guy had balls, I'll give him that much. The big red-haired kid was hovering a few feet behind him, looking borderline spooky with his fake blue eyes and unsmiling face.

"What do you suggest, Chief?"

Crow nodded. "Cut me in on the hunt. Give me some details, and I'll see what I can find."

I considered it. Thunder rumbled again, and the sky outside was turning gray. My instincts were telling me one thing and DMS protocol was telling me something else. In the end, I said, "Thanks anyway, Chief. If it's all the same to you, we'll poke around on our own. I doubt the witness is in any real trouble. Not in a little town like this."

I meant it as a kick in the shins, but he merely shook his head. "You read up on Pine Deep before you came here, Agent Duke? I mean…agent Morrison."

Touché, you little jerk, I thought.

"Some," I said.

"About the troubles we had a few years back?"

"Everyone knows about them?"

"Well," he said, shifting a little. He glanced back at the redheaded kid and then at me. "Those problems were here long before we had our 'troubles.' I guess you could say that in one way or another we've always had troubles here in Pine Deep. Lots of people run into real problems here."

I smiled now, and it probably wasn't my nicest one. "Are…you trying to threaten me, Chief Crow?"

He laughed.

Behind him the redhead kid, Sweeney, spoke for the first time. "Just a fair warning, mister," he said. His voice was low and raspy. "It ain't the people you have to worry about around here. The *town* will help you or it won't."

Then he smiled and it was one of the coldest, least *human* smiles I think I've ever seen. It was like an animal, a wolf or something equally predatory, trying to imitate a human smile.

Then Officer Sweeney turned away and sat back down at his desk.

Chief Crow winked at us. "Happy trails, boys."

I stared at him for a few moments as thunder rattled the windows in the tiny office. Then I nodded and turned to go. Just as Bunny opened the door for me, Crow said, "Welcome to Pine Deep."

I turned and met his eyes for a few long seconds. He neither blinked nor looked away. For reasons I can't adequately explain, we nodded to one another, and then I followed Top and Bunny out of the office. As we walked to the car, I could feel eyes watching me.

Chap. 5

The Safe House
August 16; 6:28 p.m.

We got back in the car.

"Okay," said Bunny, "that was freaking weird."

No one argued.

"Want me to run him through MindReader?" asked Top.

"Yeah," I said. "I know him from somewhere."

"Cop thing?" asked Bunny. "You do a shared-jurisdiction gig with Pine Deep?"

"No."

"Something social? FOP weenie roast."

"Cute. But no. I don't think I've met him, but there's something banging around in the back of my brain about him. Crow. Could be a martial arts thing."

"He train?" asked Bunny.

"Yes," Top and I said together.

Top added, "Not karate, though. No calluses on his knuckles."

"Has them on his hands, though," I said, touching the webbing around my thumb and index finger. I had a ring of callus there, too. "Kenjutsu, or something similar."

"Kid uses his knuckles, though," Top said. "Hard-looking son of a bitch. Looks like he could go a round or two."

A few fat raindrops splatted on the windshield, and the glass was starting to fog. I hit defrost and waited while Bunny called the request in to Bug, our computer guru at the Warehouse. Bug did a search through MindReader and got back to us before we'd driven two blocks.

"Plenty of stuff here," he said. "Malcolm Crow grew up in Pine Deep. Medical records from when he was a kid show a lot of injuries. Broken arms, facial injuries…stuff consistent with physical abuse."

"Anyone charged for that?"

"No. His mother died when he was little. He and his brother were raised by his father, who has a loooong record of arrests for public drunkenness, DUI, couple of barroom brawls. Sounds like he was the hitter. Wow…get this. His brother was murdered by a serial killer thirty-five years ago. Your boy was the only witness. Couple dozen victims total before the killer went off the radar. Possibly lynched by the townies, and the local police may have been involved in that."

"Lovely little town," Top said under his breath.

"Chief Crow was a cop for a while," Bug continued. "Then was a drunk for a long time. He sobered up and opened up a craft and novelty store, and helped design a haunted hayride for a Halloween theme park. All of this was before that trouble they had there. Crow was deputized by the mayor about a month before the Trouble, and—here's another cool bit—the deputation was because *another* serial killer was in town killing people. Thirty years to the day from when Crow's brother was killed. Freaky."

"Damn," I said. "What else you got?"

"He's married. Wife is Val Guthrie-Crow. Hyphenates her last name. And they have two kids. One natural—Sara—and one adopted, Mike."

"Mike? What was his birth name?"

"Same as he's using now. Michael Sweeney. Never changed it."

"What else?"

"Crow, his wife, and Mike Sweeney were all hospitalized after the trouble. Various injuries. Their statements say that they don't remember what happened and they claimed everything was a blur," Bug said. "That more or less fits because the town water supply was supposed to be spiked with LSD and other party favors."

"Do we have *anything* linking Crow to the Trouble itself? Any involvement with white supremacist movements, anything at all?"

"No. Couple other guys on the Pine Deep police force might have been involved, though, including the chief at that time."

"But nothing that would connect Crow to it?"

"Nothing."

"What are his politics?"

"Moderate with a tilt to the left. Same for the missus."

"And Sweeney?"

"Registered independent but has never voted. Oh…hold on. Got a red flag here. Looks like Sweeney's adopted father—another asshole who liked to hit kids if I'm reading this right—was one of the men suspected of orchestrating the attack on the town."

"What about the kid?"

"I hacked the Pine Deep P.D. files and it looks like the stepfather filed a report for assault. The kid decked him and ran away."

I glanced at Top. "You read the kid as a bad guy?"

He shook his head, then nodded, then shrugged. "I really couldn't get a read on him, Cap'n."

I thanked Bug and told him to call us if he got anything else.

"So, what d'you think, Boss?" asked Bunny. "Crow one of the good guys or one of the bad guys?"

"No way to tell. We're not even sure we *have* any bad guys in this. Burke could be shacked up with some chick."

"And doing what?" asked Top. "Making crank calls to the AIC?"

"*And* terrorists?" added Bunny.

I grinned. "Yeah, yeah."

We drove through the town, which takes less time than it does to tell it. Couple of stoplights. Rows of craft shops. A surprising number of cafes and bars, though most of them looked run down. More for drinking than eating, I thought. The biggest intersection had the Terrance Wolfe Memorial Medical Center across the street from the Saul Weinstock Ball Field. The hospital looked new; the ball field was overgrown, and a hundred crows huddled in a row along the chain link fence. Ditto for the hospital.

I noted it away and kept driving. The place was starting to get to me, and that was weird because I worked a lot of shifts in West Baltimore, which is probably the most depressing place on earth. Poverty screamed at you from every street corner, and there was a tragic blend of desperation and hopelessness in the eyes of every child. And yet, this little town had a darker tone to it, and my overactive imagination wondered if the storm clouds ever let the sun shine down. Looking at these streets was like watching the sluggish flow of a polluted river. You know that there's life beneath the grime and the toxicity, but at the same time you feel that life could not exist there.

We left town and turned back onto Route A-32 as it plunged south toward the Delaware River. This was the large part of the township, occupied for the first mile by new suburban infill—with cookie-cutter development units, many still under construction, and overbuilt McMansions. More than three quarters of the houses had FOR SALE signs staked into the lawns. A few were unfinished skeletons draped in tarps that looked like body bags.

Then we were out into the farm country and the atmosphere changed subtly, from something dying to something still clinging to life. Big farms, too, like the kind you expect to see more in the Midwest. Thousands of acres of land, miles between houses. Endless rows of waving green corn, fields bright with pumpkins, and row upon row of vegetables. A paint-faded yellow tractor chugged along the side of the road, driven by an ancient man in blue coveralls. He smoked a cheap pipe that he took out of his mouth to salute us as we went by.

"We just drive into the nineteen forties?" asked Bunny.

"Pretty much."

Mist, as thick and white as tear gas, slowly boiled up from gullies and hollows as the cooler air under the storm mixed with the August heat.

The GPS told us that we were coming up on our turn.

The lane onto which I'd turned ran straight as a rifle barrel from the road, through a fence of rough-cute rails, to the front door of a Cape Cod that looked as out of place here in Pine Deep as a sequined thong looks on a nun. Heavy oaks lined the road, and the big front lawn was dark with thick, cool summer grass.

"Okay, gentlemen," I said softly. "Place should be empty, and except for a brief walk-through by the handler, no one else will have disturbed the crime scene."

"Wait," said Top, "you want Farmboy and me to play Sherlock Holmes?"

"We're just doing a cursory examination. If we find anything of substance we'll ship it off."

"To where? *CSI: Twilight Zone?*"

I rolled the car to a slow stop in a turnaround in front of the house. The garage was detached except for a pitched roof that connected it to the main house. A five-year-old Honda Civic was parked in that slot. The garage door was closed.

"Looks nice and quiet," Bunny said as he got out, the big shotgun in his hands.

We split up. Bunny and Top circled around to the back and side entrances. I took the front door. We had our earbuds in place, everyone tuned into the team channel.

"On two," I said. I counted down and then kicked the door.

The door whipped inward with a crack, and as I entered, gun up and out in a two-handed shooter's grip, I heard the back door bang open, and then the side door that connected to the garage breezeway. We were moving fast, yelling at the top of our voices—at whoever might be in the house and at each other as we cleared room after room.

Then it was quiet again as we drifted together in the living room, holstering our guns and exhaling slowly. No one felt the need to comment on the fact that the place was empty. It was now our job to determine how it came to *be* empty.

"You take the bedrooms," I said to Bunny. "Observe before you touch."

He was a professional soldier, not a cop. There were no smartass remarks when being given straight orders that could remind him how to do his job.

"Why don't I take the garage and around the outside?" asked Top, and off he went.

I stood alone in the living room and waited for the crime scene to tell me its story. If, indeed, it was a crime scene.

The doors and windows were properly closed and locked from inside. I'd had to kick the door, and a quick examination showed that the deadbolt had been engaged. Same went for the side and back doors. I went upstairs and checked those windows. Locked. Cellar door was locked and the windows were block glass.

Back in the living room I saw a laptop case by the couch, and one of those padded lap tables. The case was empty. The power cable and mouse were there, but the machine itself was gone.

Significant.

The question was…was Simon Burke crazy enough to actually *write* his novel about the unstoppable terrorist plot?

I hadn't met him, but I had read his psych evaluations. He had that dangerous blend of overblown ego and deep insecurity that creates a person who feels that any idea he has is of world-shaking importance and must therefore be shared with the whole world. They typically lack perspective, and everything I'd read in Burke's case file told me that he was one of those. Probably not a bad person, but not the kind you'd want to be caught in a stalled elevator with. Only one of you would walk out alive.

So…where was he?

My cell rang, and I flipped it open. The screen read UNKNOWN CALLER.

That's…pretty unsettling. Our phone system is run through MindReader, which is wired in everywhere. There are no callers unknown to MindReader.

It kept ringing. Before I answered it I pulled a little doohickey the size of a matchbox from a pocket, unspooled its wire, plugged the lead into the phone and pressed the CONNECT button. MindReader would race down the phone lines in a millisecond and begin reading the computer and sim card in the other phone. One of Mr. Sin's toys. He did not like surprises.

It rang a third time and I punched the button.

"Hello?"

"Joe?"

"Who's calling, please?"

"Joe? Is this Joe Ledger?"

"Sir, please identify yourself."

"It's me, Joe."

"Who?" Though I thought I already knew.

"Simon Burke." He paused and gave a nervous little laugh. "Guess you've been looking for me."

"Where are you, Mr. Burke?"

"C'mon, Joe, cut the 'Mister' stuff. Mr. Burke was my dad, and he was kind of a dick."

I looked through the window at the white fog swirling from the cornfields. It was so thick you couldn't see the dirt. Between the black storm clouds and the ground fog, visibility was dropping pretty fast. That wasn't good. I said, "You told me that same joke the first time I met you."

"Did I?"

"Can you verify *where* we first met?"

"Sure," he said. "Central District police station on East Baltimore Street."

"Okay," I said, "good to hear your voice, Simon. You want to tell me where the hell you are?"

He laughed. "Too far away for you to come get me. At least right now."

I turned away from the window just as tendrils of fog began caressing the glass. "We need to get you back into protective custody, Simon."

"Joe," he said, "listen…I'm sorry for doing this to you."

"Doing what?" When he didn't answer I said, "We know about the cell phones, Simon."

"Yeah…I guessed you'd figure it out. I just thought Church would send more people. I…I didn't know it would be just three of you."

My mouth went dry.

"Jesus Christ, Simon, what did you do?"

There was a sound. It might have been a sob, though it sounded strangely like bubbles escaping through mud. "Look...I was getting tired of waiting...and I knew that you'd be able to handle just about anything. So...I started reaching out to...."

"To *who*?"

"Potential buyers."

"Oh...Christ....*why*?"

"I wanted to draw them in, just like the FBI said they were going to do. Only the Feds were taking way too much time. I was wasting my life away in this crappy little town."

"Simon...."

"I offered to sell my plot. I...reached out to several buyers and told them that I had it all written down, and that they had to bring two million in unmarked bills. Don't worry, I'd have turned over the cash. I just needed it to look and feel real to them. And they bought it, too. They thought I was selling out."

"Who's bringing the money, Simon?"

"All of them."

"What do you mean? Damn it, Simon, how many buyers did you contact?"

"A lot."

"Simon...."

"Six," he said in a small and broken voice. "There are six teams of buyers. I told them to meet me at the house. I figured they'd get there and start shooting each other. It would be like a movie. I could sell that scenario. I could make a bestseller out of it...I could make a movie out of it..."

"Simon, when are the shooters expected here?"

"When? Joe...that's what I've been trying to tell you. That's why I was sorry it was just the three of you. They're already here. I...I didn't mean to kill you."

And the windows exploded in under a hail of high-caliber bullets.

Chap. 6

The Safe House
Pine Deep, Pennsylvania
August 16; 6:41 p.m.

I dove for cover behind the couch. It wasn't a good dive and it wasn't pretty, but it got me low and out of the line of fire. Then I tried to melt right into the carpet. High-caliber rounds were chewing the couch to splinters and threads. The air above me was filled with thunder. Plaster and chunks of wall lath rained down on me.

The shots seemed continuous, so there had to be multiple shooters. They were firing full auto, and even with a high-capacity magazine it only takes a couple of seconds to burn through the entire clip.

I shimmied sideways, trying to put the edge of the stone fireplace between me and the shooters. I had my Beretta out, but the barrage was so intense that I couldn't risk a shot.

Then the sound changed. There were new sounds. The hollow *pok-pok-pok* of small-arms fire and the rhythmic *boom* of a shotgun. Those sounds were farther away.

Top and Bunny returning fire.

The automatic gunfire swept away from me and split as the shooters focused on these two new targets. That gave me my moment, and I was up and running, pistol out. There was nothing left of the door except splintered wood and glass through which the fog rolled like a slow-motion tide. I went through it fast, feeling the splinters claw at my sleeves and thighs. I was firing before I set foot outside.

In combat you see more, process more, and all of it happens fast. That's a skill set you learn quick or you get killed. As I came out of the house I saw five men standing in a loose shooting line in the turnaround. The fog was thick enough to cover them to midthigh. They were dark-skinned. Middle Eastern for sure, though from that distance I couldn't tell from where. All four of them carried AK47s with banana-clips. Three were facing the garage, firing steadily at it; the other two were standing wide-legged as they leaned back to fire at the second floor.

I emptied my magazine into them. I saw blood puff out in little clouds of red mist as two of them staggered backward and fell, vanishing into the fog. Another one took a round through the cheek. Because he was shouting, the bullet went through both cheeks and left the teeth untouched. He was screaming louder as he wheeled around toward me.

I fired my last two rounds into his chest, and my slide locked back.

The remaining shooters opened up on me, and I dove behind the armored SUV. Their bullets pinged off of the heavy skin and smoked the window before ricocheting high into the sky.

The shooters wanted me so badly they forgot, in that one fatal instant, about Top and Bunny.

Bunny spun out a side door to the garage and fired three rounds with the shotgun, catching the left-hand shooter in the chest and face. Top leaned out of the second floor window and put half a magazine into the last shooter.

As the last one fell I swapped out the magazine in my Beretta and crept to the edge of the car. Simon Burke had said that there were six buyers. Five men lay sprawled on the bloody gravel.

Where was the sixth...?

I tapped my ear bud. "We have one more hostile," I began, but Top cut me off.

"Negative, Cowboy," he said, using my combat call sign, "we have multiple hostiles inbound."

I turned and saw the fog swirling around two cars barreling down the long dirt road. Then there was a roar to my right and I saw another pair of vehicles—ATVs with oversized tires—crashing our way through the cornfields.

"Where's this fog coming from?" demanded Top. "Can't see worth a damn?"

"I got a team coming in on foot," called Bunny. "Behind the house, running along a drainage ditch. Can't make out numbers with that mist out there. No, wait...there's a second team farther back in the corner. Damn! A third at nine o'clock to the front door. Four men in black. Geez...Boss...we're under siege here. We need backup."

We needed an army, but we weren't likely to get one. The closest help was the naval airbase in Willow Grove. Half an hour at least.

With a sinking heart I understood the enormity of what Simon Burke had done. Not six buyers. Six teams of buyers. Conservative estimate—twenty men. Depressing estimate—thirty.

Coming straight at us.

Chap. 7

The Safe House
Pine Deep, Pennsylvania
August 16; 6:46 p.m.

We needed five minutes. With five minutes we could have fitted out with Kevlar and ballistic helmets, strapped on vests heavy with fresh magazines, picked optimum shooting positions, and turned the whole farm into a killbox.

We needed five damn minutes.

We had thirty seconds.

"Talk to me, Cowboy," said Top.

"Sergeant Rock and Jolly Green," I barked. "Converge on me. Living room. Now."

I spun around, yanked open the door of the SUV, ground the key in the starter, spun the wheel and stamped down. The big machine took an awkward, ugly lurch, then found footing and rolled heavily away from the house. I went completely around the roundabout, then jerked the wheel over and put the pedal to the floor as I aimed for the front door. The SUV punched a truck-sized hole through the shattered doorway, ripped across the living room floor and slammed into the stairs with enough force to rock the house to its foundations. I hadn't had time to buckle up for safety, so I bashed forward and backward. I could taste blood in my mouth as I bailed out of the driver's seat and ran to the back.

"Sergeant Rock, coming in!" yelled Top as he pounded down the stairs. He vaulted the wreckage of the bottom steps, ran across the hood, onto the roof, and dropped with a grunt into a squat next to me. He yelped in pain as his forty-year-old knees took the impact, but he sucked it up and staggered to me as I raised the back hatch.

"Coming in!" yelled Bunny, and then he was there, coming at us from the kitchen.

I clumsied open the gun lockers, and immediately six pairs of hands reached for the toys. I grabbed a bag of loaded magazines and an M4 and peeled away.

"Yo!" Top barked and tossed another bag to me. "Party favors!"

I snatched it out of the air and flashed him a grin. He grinned back. This was a total nightmare scenario, and only an insane oddsmaker would give us one in fifty on getting out of this. So…might as well enjoy it.

"Where, Boss?" asked Bunny.

"Kitchen. The fog might work for us. It'll confuse everything out there. Go!"

"On it." He shoved five drum magazines for the shotgun into a bag and slung it over his shoulder. Then he was gone, running to the kitchen.

"Top," I said, "upstairs."

"Why you keep making the old guy run up and down stairs?"

We both laughed.

He grabbed his gear and climbed over the wreckage.

I glanced through the broken window. The lead car was almost to the roundabout. It had slowed, though, and I figured that the converging teams were suddenly aware of one another. Who knows, I thought, maybe Burke was right. Maybe they'd slaughter each other while Top, Bunny and I stayed in here and played cribbage.

And maybe tomorrow I'd wake up looking like Brad Pitt. About as much chance of that.

I heard voices shouting and car doors slamming.

Then gunshots.

The first rounds were fired away from us, off to my three o'clock, the direction of the team on ATVs.

Then three other guns opened up on the house.

So much for cribbage.

Chap. 8

The Safe House
Pine Deep, Pennsylvania
August 16; 6:51 p.m.

It became hell.

A swirling surreal white hell, with the red flashes of muzzle fire filtered by thick fog, and all sounds muted to strangeness. Overhead the storm grumbled and growled, but no rain fell.

Maybe one of these days I'll look back on that ten minutes under the August sun in backwoods Pennsylvania and laugh about it. Maybe it'll become one of those anecdotes soldiers tell when they want to story-top the last guy. Or, maybe when I think about it I'll get the shakes and go crawling off to find a bottle.

Everyone was shooting at everyone.

I've never seen anything like it. Don't ever want to see anything like it again.

One team was dead. That left five teams of shooters, sent by God only knows who. Three were Middle Eastern, I could tell that much, and that made sense. Then I heard someone yelling in Russian. Someone else yelling in Spanish.

I was yelling in every language I could curse in...and I am fluent in a long list of languages.

I crouched behind the open door of the SUV, reached around with the M4 and opened fire. I wasn't aiming. No-damn-body was aiming. But everybody was sure as hell capping off a lot of rounds. My hearing will never be the same. Ditto my nerves.

I think I even screamed for a little bit. I'll admit it, I'm not proud.

I fired the magazine dry, dropped it, slapped in another, fired, swapped it out, fired. The effort of holding the gun was rattling the bones in my arm to pieces, and I don't think I hit anything with the first four magazines. The mist was chest high now, and the men out there were crouching. It was like trying to fight in the middle of a blizzard.

So I set down the gun and dug into the bag for one of Top's 'party favors.' An M67 fragmentation grenade.

"Come to papa," I murmured.

The M67 looks like a dark-green apple, but instead of juicy sweetness the spherical body contains six-and-a-half ounces of composition B explosive. When it goes boom, the body bursts into steel fragments that will forever change the life anything within fifteen meters. I lobbed one out through the hole that had been the front wall of the house. I never heard it bounce, never heard it land.

Everyone heard it when it blew. A loud, muffled *whumph.*

And everyone heard the screams that followed.

Another thing I'm not too proud to admit. I enjoyed those screams. Part of me did. The Killer that shares my mind with the Civilized Man and the Cop. That's the part of me that's always waiting in the tall grass, face grease-painted green and brown, eyes staring and dead, mouth perpetually caught in a feral smile.

The Killer wanted more, so I popped the pin on two more party treats and threw them out. More bangs, more screams.

Then I was up, laying the M4 over the hinge of the open door. Hot shell casings pinged and whanged off of the SUV's frame and smoke burned my eyes. All I could taste was blood and gunpowder.

The smoke from the grenades wafted away on a breeze, and I could see one of the cars sitting on flat tires, its sides splashed with blood, windows blasted out. Two ragged red things lay sprawled on the gravel, and a trail of blood led toward the tall corn. The second vehicle was askew in the ditch that lined the driveway, its windshield and driver's side polka-dotted with hundreds of bullet and pellet holes.

"Hey, Cap'n!" yelled Top from upstairs. "I'm running out of wall to hide behind."

"I'm open to ideas," I yelled back.

I think I heard him laugh. Top's a strange guy. Like Bunny. Like me, too, I suppose. As much as the Civilized Man inside my head was cringing and whimpering, the Killer was totally jazzed. I'm kind of glad I didn't have Kevlar and a ballistic shield, or I might have done something stupid.

Luckily, someone *else* did something stupid.

No, correct that, a bunch of people did a bunch of stupid things, and that's why I'm still here to tell you about it.

It spun out this way....

The team that came in on the ATVs were yelling something in Farsi and trying to cut their way to the house. No way to tell if the guys who came in the cars were their enemies or simply business rivals. In either case, the ATV guys came rolling in, firing over the handlebars with their AKs, chopping the cars to pieces and ripping up the last three car guys. If this was a two-way fight, or even a three-way fight, they might have won. They were the biggest team. Eight men on four ATVs.

I leaned out and sighted on them and started to pick them off. I got both men in the lead vehicle with four shots, and the ATV twisted and fell over onto its side, slewing around with one of the men still in the saddle. The second ATV hit that one at about forty miles an hour and the driver and passenger tried to leap to safety. *Tried* wasn't good enough.

Suddenly a shooter stood up out of the mist and aimed a pump shotgun at me. He caught me flatfooted while I was watching the ATV wreck. He was twenty feet away, right outside the shattered wall, and I saw his face crease into a wicked smile as he raised the barrel.

Suddenly the fog around him changed from milky white to bright red. The shooter's fingers jerked the trigger, and the double-ought buckshot blew harmlessly into the gravel. The man canted sideways and fell, and as he dropped I saw another figure move like a dark shadow through the mist. It was small, and at first I had the irrational thought that it was Simon Burke, but this figure moved with oiled grace.

I aimed my M4 at him. Whoever he was, he belonged to one of the teams sent to take Burke. I mean, thanks for saving my life and all that, but this is one of those incidents where the enemy of my enemy wasn't necessarily my friend.

I unloaded half a magazine at him, but the bullets swirled the fog without hitting anything. The figure had faded out of sight.

There was a crash behind me and I spun to see Bunny running in from the kitchen. A fusillade of shotgun blasts tore the back of the house to kindling. Bunny overturned the oak dining room table and crashed a breakfront on top of that. It would give him a few seconds of cover, but these guys had enough firepower to chew through anything.

He threw me a wild grin. "America's Haunted Holidayland," he yelled. "We'll scare you to death."

I nodded to the SUV. "That's our last fallback. The armor should hold for a bit."

He made a face, but nodded. A "bit" wasn't much.

Bullets continued to hammer the house from all directions. But there were also occasional screams.

I cupped my hands and yelled, "You're my hero, Top!"

His face immediately appeared at the top of the stairs. "Not me, Cap'n. They're doing a good job on each other. Maybe we should try and wait this out."

Before I could answer, two men charged through the open doorway. Both were firing AKs, and I had to do a diving tackle to save Bunny from the spray of bullets. We hit the floor and rolled over behind the couch. There was an overlapping series of shots, definitely from a different caliber, and I peered around the edge of the couch to see the two shooters sagging to their knees, both of them already dead from headshots that had taken them in the backs of their skulls and blown their faces off. As they fell forward I caught another glimpse of the slim, dark figure vanishing into the fog.

Only this time I saw the shooter's face.

Just for a moment.

"Hey, Boss," said Bunny, "was that…?"

"I think so."

"He on our side or is he with one of the teams?"

I shook my head.

We crawled out, and I hurried over to the crumbling wall to recover my bag of grenades.

Only it wasn't there.

The killer in the mist had taken it.

"He took the frags!" I yelled, and suddenly Bunny and I were scrambling back, ducking behind the SUV. Bullets still hammered the back, and there was no cellar.

"Oh man," whispered Bunny, and now there was no trace of humor on his face. After a while even the black comedy of the battlefield burns away to leave the vulnerable human standing naked before the reality of ugly death. We were screwed. Totally screwed, and we knew it.

When the first grenade blew, Bunny closed his eyes and clutched his shotgun to his chest as if it was a talisman that would provide some measure of grace.

But the grenade didn't detonate inside the house.

The blast was close, but definitely outside.

There was a second. A third. A fourth and fifth, and between each blast there were spaced shots. Not automatic gunfire. Spaced, careful pistol shots.

Men screamed out in the mist.

Men died in the mist.

I saw another shape move through the gloom. Not small. This one was big, but he was only a shadow within the fog. He turned toward me and I expected to see blue eyes.

The blood froze in my veins.

The eyes that looked at me through the fog were as red as blood and rimmed with gold.

And then they were gone.

I blinked. My eyes stung from the gunpowder and plaster dust. Had I seen what I thought I saw or were my eyes playing tricks?

I didn't want to answer that, but...my eyes don't play tricks.

We crouched, weapons ready to make our last stand a damn bloody one.

But the battle raged around the house. Around us.

"Top!" I yelled. "Talk to me!"

"We got new players, Cap'n."

"What can you see?"

"Not a damn thing. No, wait...oh, holy—"

Three more blasts rocked the side of the house and suddenly all the gunfire in the front ceased.

There was a moment of silence from the back, too, but then shots started up again.

A voice called out of the mist. "In the house!"

I said nothing and waved Bunny to silence.

After a pause the voice yelled again. "Hey...John Wayne...you got some injuns on your six. You in this fight or are you waiting for Roy Rogers?"

I looked at Bunny.

"Well...son of a bitch."

And that fast we were on our feet and running back to the kitchen, firing as we went. The incoming assault was less fierce, and we made it to what was left of the brick wall. A bullet plucked my sleeve and chips of brick dust flew past.

We saw them. Three groups left, but only a few of each. Two burly Russians behind a stack of hay bales over to the left. Couple of Arabs across the back lawn, using a toolshed as a shooting blind. Three Latinos to the left, firing from behind a tractor.

The voice called out of the mist. "Game on?"

I grinned. "Dealer's choice!"

I thought I heard a laugh. "You guys take scarecrow and Tim Allen. I got John Deere."

Bunny frowned at me for a moment before he got it. Scarecrows are stuffed with hay. Tim Allen's comedy is all about tools. John Deere makes tractors.

Bunny said, "Yippie kiyay…."

I swapped out for a fresh magazine. "Say it like you mean it."

He took a breath and bellowed into the fog.

They had the numbers. We had the talent.

I saw muzzle flashes coming from two points in the mist, catching the tractor in a crossfire. Bunny and I turned the toolshed into splinters. Top emptied four magazines into the straw.

The white hell outside became a red desolation.

The thunder of the gunfire echoed in the air for long seconds, and kept beating in my ears for hours.

The mist held its red tinge for a while, and then with a powerful blast of thunder, the rain began to fall.

When we went outside to count the living and the dead, we only found dead. Six teams. Thirty-two men.

There was no one else in the yard. No one else anywhere.

"Cap'n," said Top as he came back from checking far into the cornfields, "that was Chief Crow and that Sweeney kid, wasn't it?"

I said nothing.

The shapes had matched. One small figure, one big. The voice had matched Crow's. Even the John Wayne reference.

But we never found footprints. Not a one. I blamed it on the rain.

The bullets dug out of the bodies of the shooters did not match any weapons found at the scene. When the service weapons of Chief of Police Malcolm Crow and Corporal Michael Sweeney were later subpoenaed for testing, the lands and grooves of their gun barrels did not match the retrieved rounds. Shell casings from a Glock similar to Sweeney's and a Beretta 92F like the one Crow carried did not match the test firings performed by FBI ballistics. Witnesses put Crow and Sweeney elsewhere at the time of the incident.

"I've never seen a cover up this good in a small town," I said to Church ten days later.

Instead of answering me, he stared at me for a long three count and ate another vanilla wafer.

Then he opened his briefcase and removed a manila folder marked with an FBI seal. He set it on the table between us, removed a folded sheet, placed it atop the folder, and rested his hand over them both.

"What's that?" I asked.

Still making no comment, he handed me the folded paper. It was a report by the National Weather Service for August 16. There was no report of a storm, no Doppler record of storm clouds or fog.

"So? Somebody missed it."

"When the forensics team took possession of the crime scene," he said, "their reports indicate that the ground was dry and hard. There had been no rainfall in Pine Deep for eleven days."

"Then we need new forensics guys."

Church said nothing. He handed me the FBI folder. I took it and opened it. Read it. Read it again. Read it a third time. Threw it down on the table.

"No," I said.

Mr. Church said nothing.

I picked up the folder and opened it. Inside were several documents. The first was a report from a forest ranger who found a body in the woods. The second was a medical examiner's report. It was very detailed and ran for several pages. The first two pages explained how a positive identification was made on the body. Fingerprints, dental records, retina patterns. A DNA scan was included. A perfect match.

Simon Burke.

He had been severely tortured. His wrists and ankles showed clear ligature marks, indicating that he had been tightly bound. There were also bite marks on his wrists consistent with his having chewed through the cords. His stomach contents revealed traces of fiber.

According to the autopsy, Burke had managed to free himself from bondage and escaped from a cabin where he was being held. He made his way into the forest and apparently became disoriented. He was seriously injured at the time and bleeding internally. Forensic analysis of the spot where he was found corroborated the coroner's presumption that Burke had collapsed and succumbed to his wounds. He died, alone and lost, deep in the state forest that bordered Pine Deep.

That wasn't the tough part.

I mean…I felt bad for the little guy. He'd become a character in one of his own books. The intrepid underdog who outwits the bad guys and manages to escape. Except that this wasn't a book. It was the real world, and the bad guys had already done him so much harm that it's doubtful he could have been saved even if Echo Team had found him.

But…that wasn't the reason Church sat there, staring at me with his dark eyes. It wasn't the reason that my heartbeat hammered in my ears. It wasn't the reason I threw the report down again.

The coroner was able to estimate the time of death based on the rate of decomposition. By the time he had been found on August 22, his body had passed through rigor mortis and was in active decay.

The estimated time of death was irrelevant.

It was the estimated date of death that was turning a knife in my head.

When the forest ranger had found him, Simon Burke had been dead for ten days.

Ten.

"No way," I said.

Church said nothing.

"Burke called the AIC on the thirteenth."

Church nodded.

"I spoke to him on the sixteenth."

Church nodded.

"It was him, damn it."

Church selected a vanilla wafer from the plate, looked at it, and set it down.

The date of death written on the report was August 11.

Mr. Church closed the folder, sighed, stood and left the room.

I sat there.

"God," I said.

My heartbeat was like summer thunder in my head.

~The End~

Changeling

NOTE: This story is set after the events in *The Dragon Factory*. You don't to have read that novel, but if you read this story first there are some spoilers.

Chap. 1

The world keeps trying to kill me.

It's taking some pretty serious shots and as the months and years pass, it hasn't lost any of its enthusiasm. Or it deviousness.

I keep sucking air, though. Each time I somehow manage to pick myself up and either slap off the dirt and stagger back to the fight, or someone medevacs me to an aide station or a trauma hospital and the doctors do their magic to ensure that I have another season to run.

You know that saying how a bone is stronger in the place where it broke? And the thing from Nietzsche everyone and his brother always quotes—about the things that don't kill you making you stronger? A lot of that is true.

I'm stronger than I used to be. Less physically vulnerable. Not that I have superpowers. Bullets don't bounce off my skin the way they do with Superman, and I don't have Iron Man's armor. I don't have spider sense or adamantium bones.

I'm stronger because each time I survive a fight, I learn from it. I become less trusting, less naïve.

Colder.

Harder.

It takes more to kill me because as time goes on it becomes easier for me to take the first shot and to make sure that shot is the last one fired.

This is part of the cost of war. A warrior may take up his sword and shield because his ideals drive him to do it, and his love of family and flag may put steel into his arms and an unbreakable determination into his heart. I was like that.

That love, that passion, makes you dangerous at first, but it also bares your breast to arrows other than those fired by your enemy. The glow of idealism makes it easier for the sniper in the bushes to take aim.

And so you get harder. You shove that idealism down into the dark, you dial the passion down because you don't want to draw the shooter's aim. It casts you into a kind of darkness. A predatory darkness. In those shadows you change from someone defending the weak—the prey—to someone who is as much a predator as the enemy.

Your motives and justifications may be better, cleaner, but your methods are not. But while fighting monsters you risk becoming one. Nietzsche warned about that, too.

And yet....

And yet.

There is a line in the psychological sand that any person fears to cross, yet which pulls us toward it.

Loss.

Grief.

Call it what you want.

On this side of the line, you feel the full horror of a love lost. A friend, a brother-in-arms, a son or daughter. A lover. Someone who means the world to you. You will burn down heaven to protect them. You believe—truly believe—that you would march into hell to keep them safe. No matter what happens to you.

You take those risks because you believe that after all of the gun smoke clears, if you're still alive, you and the person you love will have a life together. Both of you the same as you were before. You believe that, even while the world and the war try to make you a monster.

But when the person you love is taken and the war goes on....

Damn.

That's where the real monsters are made.

When you have nothing left to love and the enemy still stands before you, grinning at your pain, feeding on your loss. In those moments, the grief can kill you. It can drive you to a final act of passion in which you throw everything away. You attack without skill or art, merely with fury. And you die without balancing any cosmic scales, without inflicting punishment.

Maybe you spend the rest of eternity in your own private hell, feeling your loss and realizing your defeat.

Or....

Or you don't give into the passion of hate.

Instead you let that hate grow cold, and in the secret dark places of your soul you crouch over that unsavory meal and feed on it. You become a monster dining on the manna of the pit. On cold, cold hate. Knowing that with each bite you are less of the person who once loved. You are less of the person who, had you and your love survived, would have reclaimed joy and innocence and optimism.

That version of you wouldn't know this dark and rapacious thing.

But it is the monster that survives.

It's the monster that *can* survive.

I loved twice in my life. Really loved.

The first time was Helen. My first love, when I was fourteen and the world was filled with light and magic. Four older teenage boys trapped us in a deserted field and taught us about darkness and their own brand of sorcery. They beat me nearly to death, and while I lay there, bleeding and almost dead, I saw what they did to Helen.

Her heart continued to beat after that, after hospitals and surgeries and counseling. But she was dead. Years later when I found her at her place, the empty bottle of drain cleaner lying where it had fallen from her hand, I felt the darkness begin to take root in the soil of my soul. Flowers of hate have blossomed since.

Then last year I fell in love again. A woman named Grace Courtland. A fellow soldier, a fellow warrior against real darkness. A woman who saved the world. The actual world.

And died doing it.

I held her as she left me. I breathed in her last breath as all of the heat left her through a hole an assassin's bullet had punched into the world.

My friends and colleagues tell me that I've made a great recovery since then. That I'm my old self again. That I look happy.

Which is all the proof I'd ever need of that philosophic belief that we each exist in our own reality, each inside an envelope of a completely separate dream.

I will never be my *old* self again.

Can't be. That ship has sailed and it hit an iceberg.

And happy?

Sure, I can laugh. So do hyenas, and it means about as much.

My enemies don't think I'm a happy guy. When they look into my eyes, they see the truth that my friends can't see.

They see what I've really become.

I know this because I see the fear in their eyes when I kill them.

I used to be a nice man.

The world used to be a place of sunshine and magic.

Monsters, though, don't thrive in the light.

Chap. 2

My boss, Mr. Church, called me into his office on a May Tuesday. It was one of those days that seems tailor-made for baseball, hotdogs and cold beer, and I was taking a half day to see if the Orioles could earn their paychecks. I had on new jeans and an ancient team jersey, sneakers, and a pair of Wayfarers on my head.

As I entered the office he slid a file folder across the desk toward me. It was a blue folder with a red seal. It looked official.

I said, "No way. I have tickets for a doubleheader, and as far as all of our billions of dollars of intelligence surveillance equipment says, it's a slow day for the bad guys."

"Captain...."

"Get someone else."

He sat back and studied me through the lenses of his tinted glasses. Mr. Church is one of those guys who never has to say much to either piss you off or make you want to check that your fingernails are clean. Frequently both.

"This requires finesse," he said mildly.

"All the more reason to get someone else. I am finesse-deprived today."

"This requires your particular skill set."

I stood there and glared at him. I could almost hear the crack of good wood on a hard ball, the roar of the crowd, the howl of the announcer as the ball arced high toward the back wall.

Mr. Church said nothing.

He opened his briefcase and removed a packet of Nilla wafers, tore it open, selected one. Bit off a piece and chewed while he watched me.

The blue folder lay where he'd put it.

I said, "Fuck."

Mr. Church asked, "What do you know about the Koenig Group?"

"Yeah, a little." I shrugged. "It was a think tank based in Jersey. Cape May, right? Alternate technologies...am I right about that?"

"They called it alternative scientific options. ASO."

"Which means what?"

"A bit of everything," he said. "They were originally a division of DARPA, but they went private as part of a budget restructuring. Private investors propped them up during the economic downturn in '09."

"But they closed, right?"

He tapped crumbs off his cookie. "They were shut down."

"Why and by who?"

"They were under investigation by a number of agencies, including our own. Aunt Sallie had some people on it, and she lent a couple of agents to a joint federal task force that is a prime example of too many chiefs and not enough Indians. It's become a jurisdictional quagmire."

"Typical." American politics are fueled by red tape. Anyone who says differently isn't on the inside track.

"As to why this has happened," Church continued, "we'd gotten some word that the administration there was a little too willing to consider offers from foreign investors."

"Like...?"

"North Korea, China, Iran."

"Yikes. So we shut them down?"

"So we shut them down," he agreed. "The task force made arrests, cleared out the staff and sealed the building. Aunt Sallie has been assembling a team of special investigators, forensics experts, and scientific consultants to do a thorough analysis of the work done there and a full inventory of research and materials. Until then, no one is allowed inside, regardless of federal rank. Every agency in the alphabet wants in on it, and as a result the whole place has been sealed for months, pending the outcome of the jurisdictional knife fight that continues as we speak."

"But the bad guys are out of there?"

"Yes. And that was enforced with fines, termination of licenses, confiscation of some research materials and computer records, charges against two administrators and one senior researcher, and a pending court case that will likely result in prison for at least one of those persons, if not all three. There are also fourteen members of the senior scientific staff as yet unaccounted for."

"A second site?" I suggested. "Another lab elsewhere?"

"That's the thinking, but so far we haven't been able to get a line on where that lab is or even if it's on US soil—though none of the missing scientists has flown out of any domestic airport. In itself, that means little because there are too many ways to export people from this country without raising a flag."

"They could be in North Korea for all we know."

"Agreed. As far as the Koenig facility, the building has been under constant surveillance since the doors were shut. Two-man teams, alternating between foot patrols and in-car observation. That responsibility has been shared on a rotating basis. Every five days another agency takes the job. Currently it's ATF."

"Okay. Why am I warming up my helicopter?"

"Our agents were first in the door, so we're the organization of record that shut it down. By default, it's up to us to sweep up any debris."

"So, I'm what? A janitor?"

"Let's face it, Captain," Church said dryly, "it's not the worst thing either of us has been called in this job."

I sighed. Church shoved the cookies toward me, but I shook my head. There's no moral justification for a vanilla cookie when every store in the free world sells a variety of chocolate-themed cookies. Like Oreos. It's closer to an American icon than Mom's apple pie ever was. Church didn't have any Oreos, so I sat there cookieless.

"If this place has been sealed for a couple of months, what's the hurry?" I asked.

"Apparently, when we shut them down they didn't entirely take it to heart."

"Naughty, naughty," I said. "But this sounds like something the FBI should be doing. I know for a fact that they love this kind of bureaucracy. It gives them that tingly feeling in their nice gray wool trousers."

Church gave me a look that could best be described as pitying. "They haven't yet won the toss of the bureaucratic garter. If they go in, then someone in congress will be accused of favoritism."

"Jesus H. Christ."

He nodded. "There are times I envy drive-through window employees at McDonalds. Red tape isn't a factor when ordering fast food."

"No joke."

We gave each other small, bland smiles.

I folded my arms. "Again I ask—why now?"

"There was a police report of lights on inside the facility late last night. Officers on scene found the rear door broken open, but a quick search of the premises yielded no results. The intruders must have fled."

"Could the intruders have been some of the missing scientists?"

"Certainly a possibility."

"But why break in? What's left to steal?"

"Unknown. When the Koenig senior staff realized the hammer was about to fall they tried to clear things up in a hurry. A lot of material was destroyed to keep it from falling into our hands and, by association, a congressional committee. The task force recovered melted disks, destroyed hard drives, and that kind of thing. Bug put his team on it to see if there was enough left to determine whether they trashed the actual records or if what we recovered was pure junk. Computer records are small and easy enough to hide. The task force might have missed a flash drive or some disks. If someone was there last night, it's likely they removed whatever was hidden. However, we do need to check."

"Swell."

"What little we did recover," Church continued, "tied into something that's clanged a few warning bells for MindReader."

When the DMS was formed it was built around a real mother of a computer system that was entirely owned by Mr. Church. Aside from being enormously powerful and sophisticated, MindReader had two primary functions. First, it collated information from all major intelligence networks, including some who didn't know their data was being mined, and then looked for patterns. Often different agencies will have gotten whiffs of things or obtained pieces of information, but MindReader sorted through all of it and began assembling fragments into whole, actionable pictures. A lot of our effectiveness is built on being able to spot trouble before it literally blows up in our face.

MindReader's other function was actually its scariest aspect. It could intrude into virtually any other computer system, poke around, take what it wanted, and then rewrite the target's security software so there was absolutely no record of the intrusion. All other intelligence software leaves some kind of scar on the target system; MindReader is a ghost.

"What bells?" I asked, not really wanting to know.

"Sadly, it's vague. The North Koreans and Chinese were both providing funding for a project codenamed 'Changeling.' We don't know the nature of the program, but when nations who don't always have our best interests at heart are willing to transfer funds in excess of fifty million...."

He let the rest hang.

"Have you talked to Dr. Hu about this?"

Hu was the head of the DMS science division. He was both a super-genius in multiple disciplines and a world-class heartless asshole. We have failed to bond on an epic level.

"Dr. Hu is intensely interested in it because he feels it may be connected to a project we caught wind of last year that dealt with transformative genetics."

"I don't even like the sound of that."

"Neither do it. It's a radical branch of transgenics in which animals of various kinds are given gene therapy in order to provoke controlled mutations. We saw some of that in the Jakoby labs."

"Ah," I said, loading that syllable with as much scorn as I could. The Jakobys were a family of brilliant geneticists. Immeasurably dangerous. Their Dragon Factory laboratory was used to create animals that, at least, *looked* like mythical creatures. Big game hunters paid millions to hunt unicorns and centaurs. It didn't matter than the animals were genetic freaks whose DNA was now hopelessly corrupted. Nor did it matter that the resulting mutations were often painful for the animal and virtually guaranteed a short and agonizing life. None of that mattered. The novelty market allowed them to raise money for more destructive projects, including ethnic-specific pathogens intended to fuel a new genocide.

We shut them down. Hard.

It was at the Dragon Factory that Grace died.

"Do these Koenig assholes have the Jakoby research? 'Cause if they do, I'm going to find them and remove important parts."

"It's unlikely. MindReader would have flagged that. But it seems that their scientists were working along dangerously similar lines. To what end we don't know. Once the red tape is sorted out I intend to have our people be first through the door to do a thorough examination of any materials left intact."

"Must be pissing you off that we've had to wait so long."

He said nothing, and nothing showed on his face, but there was a palpable feeling of tension buzzing around him. Yeah, he was pissed.

When he finally spoke, it was a shift in topic. "Last night's police report opens a door of opportunity. We have a chance to put someone in the building. Not to remove anything, of course, but to have a quiet look around without eyes on him. I'd like that to be you."

"And I suppose if there was a file conveniently labeled 'Changeling' I shouldn't let it lay there and gather dust."

Church snorted. "If life were that simple, Captain, we would be out of jobs."

"I thought the ATF had feet on the ground there."

"They didn't see anything last night."

"And the cops did?"

He spread his hands. And I had a sneaking suspicion that he had something to do with that police drive-by and any subsequent report. Made me wonder if there was anything to see. ATF boys are usually pretty sharp.

"Besides," added Church, "the ATF team has declined to break the seal and enter the premises."

"Why?"

"Because if anything is disturbed or if there is any procedural error when someone does step inside, then that agency takes the political hit." He shook his head. "If you look too closely for logic you'll injure yourself."

"Okay, I get that the bullshit factor is high. But why me? Why send a shooter?"

"Because you were a cop before you were a shooter. If nothing else, you should be able to determine if the place has been broken into. Work it like a crime scene."

"And if I find someone poking around in there?"

His smile was small and cold. "Then you have my permission to shoot them."

Nice. You can never really tell when he's joking.

"One more thing," said Church as I stood, crossed the room, and reached for the doorknob. "Our friends in the U.K have expressed some interest in this matter. They red-flagged some of the negotiations between the Koenig Group and North Korean buyers, and they've been hunting for any possible information on Changeling. They're sending a special agent to liaise with you. Her name is Felicity Hope. Expect her call."

"She's with MI6?"

"No," he said, "Barrier."

Barrier was Great Britain's so-secret-we'll-bloody-well-shoot-you group that was the model for the DMS. Church had helped set it up, and once it proved to be invaluable against the new breed of 21st Century high-tech terrorist, he was able to sell Congress on the Department of Military Sciences. But just hearing that name was the equivalent of a swift kick in the nuts for me.

Grace Courtland had been a senior Barrier agent. She'd been seconded to the DMS at Church's request, and for a few years she was Church's top gun. Maybe the world's top gun. I worked alongside her, respected her, fell in love with her. And then buried her.

The pain was too recent and too real.

Church adjusted his tinted glasses. I knew that he was following my line of thought and gauging my reaction. I also knew that he wouldn't say anything. He wasn't the kind of guy who engaged in heart-to-hearts. What he gave me was a single, brief nod, just that much to acknowledge the memory. He loved Grace like a daughter. His pain had to be as intense as mine, but he would never show it.

It cost me a lot to keep it off my face.

Chap. 3

Twenty minutes later I was in a Black Hawk helicopter, heading away from Baltimore's sunny skies toward the coastline of southern New Jersey.

The rest of my team—all of the two-legged variety—were scattered around the country looking at potential recruits. We'd lost some players recently, and we had the budget and the presidential authority to hire, coax, or shanghai top shooters from law enforcement, FBI hostage rescue, and all branches of Special Ops. For guys like us it was like being turned loose in a candy store with a credit card.

We flew through sunlight beneath a flawless blue sky.

When the Koenig Group had gone private a few years ago, they moved out of a lab building on the grounds of the Joint Base McGuire-Dix-Lakehurst, an air force base sixteen miles southeast of Trenton, and purchased several connected buildings once occupied by a marine conservation group that had lost its funding. I pulled up the schematics of the place on my tactical computer. The place looked like it had been designed by whoever built the Addams Family mansion and the Bates Motel. The centerpiece was a faux Victorian pile that was all peaked roofs, balconies, widow's walks, gray shingles, and turrets. Almost attractive but overall too austere and grim-looking. To make it worse, the conversion people had added wings and side buildings to the main structure, all connected by covered walkways that gave the whole place a haphazard, sprawling appearance. Unlovely, unkempt, and supposedly unoccupied. Seen from above via satellite, it looked like several octopi had collided and somehow melded, then were covered with shingles and paint. Charming in about the same way a canker sore is appealing.

The files on the research being conducted at the Koenig Group were sketchy. On the books, the teams were collating and evaluating data from several thousand smaller biological and genetic projects from around the world. Dead-end projects that had been canceled either because they were too expensive when measured against predicted benefits or because they'd hit dead ends. The Koenig teams had scored some hits by combining data from multiple stalled projects in order to create a new and more workable protocol, largely influenced by recent advances in science. A transgenics experiment that was infeasible twenty-five years ago might now be doable. The original hypotheses were often well in advance of the scientific capabilities of the day. The Koenig people sometimes had to sort through mountains of old floppy disks—back when they were actually floppy—or crates filled with digital cassette tapes, and even tons of paper to put a lot of this together. It was painstaking work that was often frustrating and futile...but which now and then yielded fruit.

Shame that those bozos didn't share all of that fruit with the U.S. of A.

Dickheads.

The frustrating thing for us, though, was that we really didn't know all they'd discovered. When the task force kicked the door in, they found a lot of melted junk and very little else. And the management team at Koenig apparently kept their employees compartmentalized so that few of them knew anything of substance. Probably because most of them would have made a call to Uncle Sam if they were in on it. Or they'd want the Koenig people to pad their paychecks. Either way, from what I read in the file, there were only three genuine villains, and they were under indictment and under surveillance.

So who was messing around inside the building? And what were they looking for?

Church didn't think this was anything more than a look-see by someone who used to be a detective. He didn't offer backup except for a Barrier agent who would *liaise* with me. Whatever that meant, given the circumstances. Maybe whenever she landed Stateside we'd compare notes over diner coffee and that would be that.

But as I looked at the satellite photo of the sprawling, ugly building I began to get a small itch between my shoulder blades. Not quite a premonition, but in that neck of the woods. What my grandmother used to call a "sumthin'," as in "sumthin' doesn't feel right." My gran was a spooky old broad. In my family no one laughed off or ignored her sumthin's.

I gave myself a quick pat-down to make sure I'd brought the right toys to this playground. My Beretta 92F was snugged into its nylon shoulder rig; the rapid-release folding knife was clipped in place inside my right front pants pocket. There was a steel garrote threaded through my belt, and I had two extra magazines for the Beretta.

The sad part was that this was how I dressed all the time. I had this stuff on me when I went to Starbucks to read the Sunday papers. I would have had it on me at the ballpark watching the Orioles spoil the day for the Phillies. I would like to be normal. I'd like to have a normal life. But when I joined the DMS, I left normal somewhere behind in the dust.

The Black Hawk flew on through an untroubled sky.

Chap. 4

While I flew I read some reports from Dr. Hu. Even though he hadn't yet gotten concrete information on the Changeling Project, MindReader had compiled bits of information that added up to a pretty disturbing picture of what they *might* be doing at Koenig.

Transformational genetics is a branch of science that scares the bejesus out of me. It has some benign and even beneficial uses, but the DMS doesn't go after doctors trying to cure a genetic defect. No, the kind of scientist we tend to encounter is often best visited with a crowd of torch- and pitchfork-bearing villagers.

Here's an example, and this is why palms were sweating as I read those reports. Hu found clear evidence of several covertly funded studies to create an "elastic and malleable genetic code." One that was able to "withstand specific and repeatable mutagenic changes within desired target ranges consistent with military applications." These programs have an end goal of "at-will theriomorphy."

Yeah.

Short bus version of that—included courtesy of Dr. Hu, who has little faith in my ability to grasp basic concepts—is that the North Koreans and Chinese have been funneling money into research for practical science that would allow a soldier to change his physical structure at will and at need. To transform from human into something else.

Hu could only speculate on what that other shape might be. His speculations included an insectoid carapace, gills, resistance to radiation and pollutants, retractable feline claws, enhanced muscle and bone density, night vision. Stuff like that.

True super soldiers. But not entirely human super soldiers.

You see why I occasionally have to shoot people?

Before I joined the DMS this was science fiction stuff, comic book stuff. Now, it was nightmare stuff because the science was out there. All it required was enough funding, little or no oversight from either Congress or human rights organizations, and a flexible set of morals. Sad to say, all of that is possible.

We are living in a science fiction age. Or, maybe it's a horror story.

Mad scientists like Frankenstein? That's almost a joke. Frankenstein, at least, was trying to do some good for humanity. He was trying to conquer sickness and death.

Guys like the Koenig Group…well, what the hell do you even call men like that?

Chap. 5

I had the pilot do a slow circle of the Koenig place and then set me down in the parking lot. The building extended onto a wharf in the bay. There were slips for six small boats and one large one, but nothing was currently tied up. No cars in the parking lot, either. The left-hand neighbor was an industrial marina for craft that serviced the big dredging platform six miles off the coast which kept pumping sand back to shore to replace what Mother Nature and global warming were taking away. The right-hand side was protected marshland. A billboard proclaimed that an exotic animal park would be opening soon, but the paint was peeling and faded, and the board looked twenty years old. The only exotic animal I could see among the marsh grass was a Philadelphia pigeon looking confused and out of place.

There was a single car parked on the street, a dark blue Crown Victoria. It was unmarked but it was so obviously a Federal vehicle that it might have had FEDS stenciled on the doors. One of these days the government will grasp the concept that plainclothes and undercover should include a component of stealth. Just a tad would go a long way.

I jumped down from the open side door, bent low, and ran through the rotor wash as the Black Hawk lifted away. The pilot would take the bird to a helipad near the Cape May lighthouse and wait there. We have several Black Hawks at the Warehouse, and we used this one for jobs that required less of a shock-and-awe effect on the locals. It was painted a happy blue and had the logo of a news wire service on it. No visible guns or rockets. Not to say they weren't there, but this was not a time to show off. We already had some rubberneckers slowing their cars down to look at the big blue machine.

I let the helo vanish into the distance and silence return before I approached the building. The ATF agents were standing beside their car, both of them in off-the-rack suits and wearing identical expressions of disapproval. They both began shaking their heads as I approached.

"You can't be here," said the taller of the two.

I held up my identification. The DMS doesn't have badges or standard credentials. When we needed to flash something we picked whatever would get the job done. I had valid ID for CIA, ATF, DEA, FBI and every other letter combination. The one I showed them was NSA. It was as close to a trump card as you can get, and they were the only organization that didn't have boots on the ground during the raid on the place. Church was working with the director to use them as referees for the jurisdictional dispute.

The ATF boys glanced at the badge and at my civilian clothes— jeans and an Orioles home-game shirt—and gave me looks that said they didn't give a cold shit.

"Need to go inside," I said.

"Show me some paper," said the shorter of the two.

I dug into my back pocket and produced a letter Church had prepared for me. It was a presidential order allowing me access to assess the integrity of the scene. They read it carefully. Twice.

"You can't take anything out," said the tall one.

"Don't want to," I said.

"We'll have to search you when you come out, you know."

"Sure," I said.

"Don't fuck with anything in there."

"I won't."

"We don't want trouble," said the short one.

"I'm on your side, guys." I pasted on my most charming smile.

The short one gave me another up and down inspection. "NSA recruiting ball players now?"

"It was my day off," I said, leaning on "off" enough to convey irritation. Not at them, but at the system. "I had tickets for the doubleheader."

That did the trick; they relaxed and nodded.

"Sucks to be you," said the tall one and gave me half a mean grin.

"We have the game on the car radio," said the short one. He wore the other half of that same grin. "Phils are up by two in the second."

"I'm from Baltimore."

"Like I said, it sucks to be you," said the tall one. Laughing, they turned and walked back to their vehicle.

"And a hearty fuck you, too," I said under my breath as I headed to the building.

It was no less ugly from ground level and perhaps a little less appealing. It was bigger than I expected. Three stories in parts, with lots of shuttered windows and reinforced doors. A discreet sign on a pole read, THE KOENIG GROUP, with a phone number for information.

I removed a small earbud, put it on, and attached an adhesive mic that looked like a mole to the side of my mouth. Two taps of the earbud connected me to Bug, the computer *über*-geek who provided real-time intel for all fieldwork. Even though this was a low-profile job, DMS protocol required that I use my combat call sign.

"Cowboy's online."

"With you," said Bug.

"What've you got?"

"We did a thermal scan on the place, but it's cold. No one home."

"That's what I want to hear."

I walked around the building. It really was a large mess. The additions and walkways looked almost like they'd grown organically, expanding out of need like a cramped animal. The paint jobs didn't match section-to-section, and for a company with a lot of private funding the exterior of the joint was poorly maintained. Weeds, some graffiti, trash in the parking lot.

"Place is a dump," I said.

"Better inside, from what I hear," said Bug. "Some cool stuff."

A red DO NOT ENTER sticker was pasted with precision to the center of the front door. I ignored it and used a preconfigured keycard to gain entry.

"Going in," I said quietly.

"Copy that," said Bug. "Watch your ass, Cowboy."

"It's on the agenda."

The entrance lobby was small and unremarkable. A receptionist's desk, some potted plants, and the kind of framed pictures you can buy at Kmart. Bland landscapes that probably weren't even places in New Jersey. The lights were out, which was surprising since the key-reader was functional. The entrance hall was dark, and daylight didn't try too hard to reach inside. When I tried the light switches all I got was a click. No lights.

I tapped my earbud. "Bug, I thought the power was still on."

"It is."

"Not from where I'm standing."

"Let me check."

I removed a small flashlight from my pocket and squatted down to shine the light across the floor. The immediate entrance hallway had a thin coating of damp grime on the floor—a side effect of the building's position near a bay and a swamp. There were footprints in the grime, but from the size and pattern it was clear most of them had been left by responding police officers. Big shoes with gum-rubber soles. The prints went inside and then they came out again. If there were prints by an intruder, they were lost to the general mess left behind by the cops. Pretty typical with crime scenes, and pretty much unavoidable. Cops have to respond and they can't float.

I tapped my earbud again, channeling over to Church. "Cowboy to Deacon."

"Go for Deacon."

"Did anyone have eyes on the cops who came out of the building last night? Are we sure they weren't carrying anything? Or had something in their pockets?"

"The ATF agents on duty last night searched each officer," said Church. "It was not well-received."

"I can imagine."

And I could imagine it—responding blues getting a pat-down by a couple of Federal pricks.

"Why didn't the ATF agents accompany them inside?" I asked.

I could hear a small sigh. "The ATF agents had left the scene to pick up a pizza."

"Ouch."

"Those agents have been suspended pending further disciplinary action."

"Yeah, fair call."

"Which is why the ATF is rather prickly about your being there."

"Copy that."

I channeled over to Bug.

"Where are we with those lights?"

"Working on it."

The lights stayed off, though.

There was a closed door behind the reception desk, so I opened it and entered a hallway that was as black as the pit. There was no sound, not the slightest hint that I was anything but alone in here, but regardless of that I drew my pistol. It's hard to say if, at that moment, my caution was born out of a concern not to accidentally disturb any evidence left behind or because the place was beginning to give me the creeps.

The hallway hit a t-juncture. Each side looked as dark and uninformative as the other, but I took the right-hand side because that was my gun-hand side. I know. I'm a bit of a superstitious idiot. Sue me.

The side hallway wasn't straight but jagged and curved and turned for no logical design reasons that I could see. Maybe there was something about the foundation structure that required so unlikely a design plan, but I couldn't imagine what. The result was something that—as I walked through the shadows—triggered odd little thoughts that were entirely uncomfortable. The unlikely angles combined with the mildly curving walls and low gray-painted ceiling to give the whole place a strangely organic feel. Like a building that hadn't so much been designed as allowed to grow. Like roots of a tree. Or tentacles.

Yeah, I shouldn't be in here. I should be out in the bright sunlight watching a bunch of millionaires in white, black, and orange stretch pants hit a small white ball around a grassy field.

"You're a fruitcake," I told myself, and I had no counterargument.

I followed the flashlight beam down the crooked hallway until it ended at a set of double-doors made out of heavy-grade plastic. The kind meant to swing back when you pushed a cart through them, like they have in meat-packing plants.

A charming thought.

I pushed one flap open and peered into the gloom. The beam of the flashlight swept across a storage room stacked high with boxes of equipment and office supplies. There were bare patches on the floor where I assumed boxed files once stood, but they'd been confiscated by the task force. Motes of dust swirled in the glow, spinning like planets in some dwarf galaxy. They looked cold and sad.

As I began to let the flap fall back into place something caught my attention.

Nothing I saw or heard.

It was a smell.

A mingled combination of scents, pleasant and unpleasant.

A hint of perfume, the sulfur stink of a burned match, old sweat, and spoiled meat.

The movement of the swinging door somehow wafted that olio of scents to me, but it didn't last. It was there and gone.

It was such an odd combination of smells. They didn't seem to fit this place. And they were transient smells that should long ago have faded into the general background stink of dust and disuses. Except for the rotten-meat smell. That, I knew all too well, could linger. But this was a research facility not a meat-packing plant. There shouldn't be a smell like that in here.

My brain immediately started cooking up rationalizations for it.

An animal came in here and died.

The staff left food in the fridge when the place was raided.

And....

And.

And *what*?

I tapped the earbud.

"Bug, what's the status on those damn lights?"

There was a short burst of static, then Bug said, "—er company."

"You're breaking up. Repeat message."

"The power is on according to a representative of the power company."

I moved through the swinging doors and found a whole row of light switches. Threw them.

Stood in the dark.

"Negative on the power, Bug. Call someone who doesn't have his dick in his hand and get me some lights."

He paused, then said, "On it, Cowboy."

The storage room had two interior doors, one of which opened into a bathroom so sparkling clean it looked like it had never been used. The only mark was a smudged handprint on the wall above the toilet. The smell hadn't come from here.

The other door opened onto another jagged hallway that snaked through the building. The walls were lined on either side with closed doors. A lot of doors. This was going to take a while.

Dark and spooky as the place was, it seemed pretty clear that nobody was home but me. I snugged the Beretta into the padded holster but left my Orioles shirt open in case I needed to get to it in a hurry.

For the next half hour I poked into a variety of rooms, including storage closets of various signs, a copy center, a staff lunchroom, offices for executives of various wattage, and labs. Lots and lots of labs.

I entered one at random and stood in the doorway, doing what cops do, letting the room speak to me. There were rows of black file cabinets, sealed with yellow tape that had an ominous-looking federal seal from the Department of Justice. A dozen tables were crowded with computers and a variety of scientific instrumentation so sophisticated and arcane that I had almost no idea what I was looking at. The floor was littered with papers, and here and there were fragments of footprints on the debris.

Watching the room told me nothing.

I backed into the hall and did a quick recount of the laboratories just in this wing of the building. Nine.

"Bug," I said, tapping the earbud.

"Cowboy, the power company insists that there is no interruption to the Koenig Group facility. They are showing active meters."

I grunted and filed that away. Maybe it was something simpler, like breakers. To Bug I said, "How many labs are there in this place?"

"Twenty-two separate rooms designated on the blueprints as laboratory workspaces."

"Jeez..."

"And one designated as a proving station."

"Proving what?"

"Unknown. None of the employees interviewed by the task force has ever been in there, and the three executives under indictment aren't talking."

"So we have no real idea what they were doing there?"

"Not really," he said, and he sounded wistful about it. "I wish we could have gotten those computer records. I'll bet there was some cool stuff there."

Cool.

Much as I like Bug, he shares a single characteristic with Dr. William Hu. The two of them have an absolutely unsavory delight for any kind of bizarre or extreme technology. For Hu, the head of our Special Sciences Division, it bordered on ghoulishness. Hu loves to get his hands on any kind of world-threatening designer plague or exotic weapon of mass destruction. A few months ago, when Blackjack Team out of Vegas took down a Chechnyan kill squad who had a hyper-contagious version of weaponized Spanish Flu and were planning on releasing it into the water supply of a large Russian community near Reno, Hu was delighted. A total of fifty-three people dead and an entire water supply totally polluted for God knows how many decades, and he was like a kid with a new stack of comics. He actually admires the kind of damaged or twisted minds that can create ethnic-specific diseases, build super dirty-bombs, and create weapons capable of annihilating whole populations. I've wondered for years how much of a push it would take to shove Hu over to the dark side of the Force.

Bug, though, didn't have a mean bone in his body. For him it was a by-product of a life so insulated from the real world that nothing was particularly real to him. Only his beloved computers and the endless data streams. Something like this lab was probably no more real to him than a level in the latest edition of *Gears of War* or *Resident Evil*.

For my part, I am not a fan of anyone who would put extreme weapons into the hands of people so corrupt or so driven by fanaticism that they would turn the world into a pestilential wasteland just to make an ideological point.

Fuck that. For two pennies I'd call the Black Hawk and see what twelve Hellfire missiles and a six-pack of Hydra-70 rockets could do to sponge this place clean.

"Where's that proving station?" I asked. He sent a step-by-step to my mobile phone.

As I made my way along corridors lit only by the narrow beam of my flashlight, I thought about the work that went on here. During the flight I'd had time to go over some of the background on the Koenig Group. They were originally a deeply integrated division of DARPA—the Defense Advanced Research Projects Agency, which is an agency of the Department of Defense responsible for developing new technologies for the military. Koenig Group people worked on every aspect of DARPA before they went private, and that meant that they had the opportunity to see not only what was currently in development for modern warfare and defense, but also what was being looked at for future exploration.

Of late I've come to realize that when it comes to keeping in front of the global arms race, there is virtually no line of exploration that's definitely off the table. So, without government oversight, where had the twisted minds here at Koenig gone?

I reached the end of one hallway and passed through a security door that lead to another corridor lined with doorways that looked exactly like the one I'd just come from. So much so that I actually went out the door and stood looking at the doors and then turned around and looked at the new set. The absolute similarity was unnerving and disorienting.

I called up the floor plan on my mobile and studied it.

"Bug," I said, "somehow I made a wrong turn."

Bug didn't answer.

I tapped the earbud.

"Cowboy to Bug, do you copy?"

Nothing. Not even static.

I tapped my way over to the command channel. "Cowboy to Deacon," I said, trying to reach Church.

Still nothing.

I turned around and looked down the hall. The beam cut a pale line that pushed the shadows back, but not much.

Suddenly I caught the smell again.

Sulfur, human waste, and spoiled meat. And the aroma of perfume.

I don't remember moving or pulling open my shirt, but suddenly my gun was in my hand. Even though the whole place was absolutely still and quiet, I yelled into the darkness.

"Freeze! Federal agent. I'm armed."

My words bounced off the darkened walls and melted into nothingness.

Then, from behind me, someone spoke my name.

A woman's voice.

Soft.

Familiar.

Achingly familiar.

An impossible voice.

"Joe...."

I whirled, gun in one hand, flash in the other, pointing into the darkness.

A woman stood ten feet behind me.

She was dressed in black. Shoes, trousers, jersey, gun belt, pistol. All black. Dark hair, dark eyes.

Those eyes.

Her eyes.

My mouth fell open. Someone drove a blade of pure ice through my heart. I could see my pistol begin to tremble in my hand.

I stared at her.

I spoke her name.

"Grace...."

Chap. 6

I don't know what time does in moments of madness. It stops or it warps. It becomes something else. Every heartbeat felt like a slow, deliberate punch to my breastbone, and yet I could feel my pulse fluttering.

She held a pistol in her hand, the barrel raised to point at my chest, and I had an insane, detached thought.

You don't need a bullet to kill me. Be her *and I'll die.*

Not be her, and I think I'll die, too.

She licked her lips and spoke.

"Who are you?"

The accent was British. Like Grace's.

But....

But the tone was wrong.

It didn't sound like her.

Not anymore. It had a moment ago when she'd spoken my name. But not now. Not anymore.

"Grace," I said again, but now I could hear the doubt in my own voice. "I...."

She peered at me over the barrel of the gun, her eyes dark with complex emotions, fierce with intelligence.

Slowly, carefully, she raised her gun until the barrel pointed to the ceiling and held her other hand palm-out in a clear no-threat gesture.

"You're Captain Ledger, aren't you?"

I kept my gun on her.

"Who are you?" I asked, but my voice broke in the middle, so I had to ask again.

"Felicity Hope," she said. "Barrier."

I stood there and held my gun on her for another five seconds.

Then....

I lowered the pistol.

"God almighty," I breathed.

She frowned at me, half a quizzical smile. "Who did you think I was?"

"It doesn't matter."

Felicity Hope holstered her piece and came toward me. "You called me Grace."

I said nothing.

"You thought I was Grace Courtland, didn't you?"

"Grace is dead."

"I know." She stood there staring at me.

Up close, I could tell that it wasn't her. This woman's hair was paler, her eyes darker, her skin had fewer scars. But the height was the same, and the body. The same mix of dangerous athleticism and luscious curves. The movement was the same, a dancer's grace. And the keen intelligence in the eyes.

Yeah, that was exactly the same.

Damn it.

When the universe wants to fuck with you it has no problem bending you over a barrel and giving it to you hard and ugly.

I cleared my throat. "Did you know her?"

She nodded.

"Was she...a friend?" I asked.

Felicity shrugged. "Actually, we weren't. Most of the time I knew her I thought she was a stuck-up bitch." She watched my face as she spoke, probably wondering what buttons she was pushing. Then she added, "But I don't think I really knew her. Not really. Not until right before she died."

"How?"

"What?"

"How could you know what she was like right before she died?"

"Oh...we spoke on the phone quite a lot. She was officially still with Barrier and had to make regular reports. I was the person she reported to."

"You were her superior officer?"

She looked far too young. Grace had been young, too, but Grace was an exception to most rules. She'd been the first woman to officially train with the SAS. She'd been a senior field team operative in some of the most grueling cases on both sides of the Atlantic. There was nobody quite like Grace and everyone knew it.

Felicity shook her head. "Hardly. I was a desk jockey taking field reports. I know I'm not in Major Courtland's league."

"No," I said ungraciously. "You're not. Tell me why you're here."

She said, "Changeling."

"Which means what exactly? The name keeps popping up in searches but no one seems to know exactly what it is."

"What do you know about transformational genetics and self-directed theriomorphy?"

"Some," I said, dodging it. "What do you know about it?"

"Too much."

"Give me more than that."

"They're making monsters," she said.

I shook my head. "Not in the mood for banter, honey, and I'm never in the mood for cryptic comments, especially not from total strangers I meet in dark places. This is American soil and a legally closed site. Spill everything right now or enjoy the flight home."

She took a breath. "Okay, but I'll have to condense it because there's a lot."

"So," I said, "condense."

"Can you take that flashlight out of my eyes?"

"No," I said, and I didn't. The light made her eyes look large and moist. If it was uncomfortable, then so what? I was deeply uncomfortable, so it was a running theme for the day.

She said, "Ever since the dawn of gene therapy and transgenic science it's become clear that DNA is not locked. Evolution itself proves that DNA advances. Look at any DNA strand and you'll see the genes for nonhuman elements like viruses hardwired into our genetic code."

"Part of junk DNA," I said. "What about it?"

"Transformational genetics is a relatively new branch of science that is searching for methods of changing specific DNA and essentially rebuilding it so that a new tailor-made code can be developed."

"That's not new," I pointed out. "The Nazis tried that, and the whole Eugenics movement before that."

"That's selective breeding. That's cumbersome and time-consuming because it requires eggs and host bodies and so forth. This is remodeling, and recent advances have opened developmental doors no one imagined would be possible in this century."

I didn't say anything. During the firefight at the Dragon Factory we'd encountered mercenaries who had undergone gene therapy with ape DNA. And there were other even more hideous monsters there.

"The word *theriomorphy* keeps showing up. What's that?"

"Shapeshifting."

"Shape...?"

"The ability to change at will from one form to another." She smiled through the blinding flashlight glow. "From human form into something else."

"At...will?"

"Oh yes."

"Like from what to what? You're making this sound like we're hunting werewolves or something."

Her smile flickered. "Who knows? Maybe we are."

"That's not funny."

"I know."

"Wait…hold on…are we really standing here having a conversation about werewolves? I mean…fucking *werewolves*?"

After a three count she said, "No."

"Jesus jumped-up Christ in a sidecar, then why—"

"Werewolves would be easy," she said, cutting right through my words. "Werewolves would be a silver bullet and we'd take the rest of the afternoon off for a drink. I wish it was only werewolves."

I gaped at her.

Seriously…what do you say to that?

Chap. 7

"Okay," I said, "before I pee my pants here, how do you know about this and what can we do about it? This facility is sealed."

She flashed her first real smile, and it looked so much like the battlefield grin Grace used to give me that I almost turned away.

"When your task force shut down this place," she said, "they made a thorough video inventory of everything. High-res footage from where every piece of paper was all the way down to the way pencils sat in a pot on each desk. Everything, with a second camera filming what the first camera was doing in order to firmly establish the integrity of the scene and contribute the first real link in the sacred chain of evidence. Am I right?"

Church had told me about that, but I hadn't seen it. I nodded anyway.

"So we can take or touch anything recorded on that video."

"That's the size of it," I agreed.

"The federal order sealing this place contains an authorized copy of that video."

"Yup."

"And the teams who were here agreed that absolutely everything has been documented—at least in terms of its existence and placement."

"Sure."

Her smile brightened. "Therefore, anything that *isn't* on the video technically doesn't exist in terms of that federal order."

"Sure," I said again, "but how does that put us back in a discussion about werewolves? 'Cause, quite frankly I'm having a hard timing shaking loose of that conversation."

The smile dimmed but did not go out. "Not werewolves," she said quietly.

"What?"

"They're not werewolves. That's not what they were doing here."

Felicity turned and walked a few paces away, going along the hall in the direction I'd come. She stopped, looked through the shadows. "You were in the storage room?"

"Maybe."

"You were in the storage room," she repeated, not making it a question this time. "Did you look inside the bathroom?"

"Sure. Nothing there."

She sighed audibly.

"I wish I could say you were right about that, Captain."

Without another word she began walking down the hallway toward the storeroom. She didn't have a flashlight, and my beam was currently pointed at the floor in front of me; however, she seemed quite at home in the dark.

I felt like I'd walked into the middle of a play for which I had no script and no stage direction.

She paused once in the very outside edge of the light and looked back at me. I had seen Grace turn that way, stand that way.

Look that way.

Then Felicity Hope turned and vanished into the black.

My eye tingled at the corners, and I knew that given half a chance I was going to break down and cry.

"Oh, Grace...," I said very, very quietly.

Chap. 8

I caught up with her at the entrance to the storage room and followed her over to the small bathroom. As she approached the door she drew a small gun from a shoulder rig.

"What are you doing?" I asked.

"Getting ready," she replied crisply, "and I suggest you do the same. I don't know exactly what's down in there, but things could get very bad very quickly."

I almost smiled. "In a toilet?"

"I trust you have enough faith in Barrier agents to know that we don't typically feel the need to arm ourselves to take a piss." She opened the door and we looked inside. Toilet, sink, white-tiled wall, plastic trash can. And the partial handprint on the back wall.

I said, "Secret door?"

"Secret door," she agreed. "And your federal task force missed it."

"Balls."

With her pistol in her right hand, she placed her left on the back wall, over the partial print. She moved her hand to one corner and pressed. The tile tilted inward with an audible *click.*

The whole rear wall swung inward on silent hinges, revealing a set of metal stairs that went down into blackness. A smell wafted up at us.

Rotting meat.

Human waste.

And… something else.

A fish stink. Not actually unpleasant, like the way an aquarium supply store smells, or the kitchens at a low-end fish-and-chips restaurant.

There were sounds, too.

Machines. Whirring motors. Rhythmic pumps. Other mechanical sounds, all soft, all muted.

"How do you know about this?" I asked quietly.

Felicity shrugged. "This information was hard won, believe me. Literally blood, sweat, and tears."

She moved to the top of the steel steps.

I drew my Beretta. "What's down there? I mean really, no bullshit about werewolves or boogeymen. What the fuck are we going to find down there?"

Felicity turned toward me. In the crowded confines of the bathroom she was very close to me. I could smell her perfume. It was the same brand Grace used. What the hell was it, standard issue by Barrier? Or maybe it was the top-selling scent in England, and I was out of the stylistic loop.

Her body was achingly familiar and devastatingly female. It was the kind of body that no matter how well-balanced and normally nonsexist a man is, he can't help but be profoundly aware of it. Of hips and breasts, of long legs and a slender, graceful throat, of animal heat that was purely, inarguably, powerfully female.

And yet....

Standing this close to her there was something wrong about her.

Maybe it was because she was so like Grace that knowing she wasn't Grace made her feel fundamentally wrong. It was meeting a deliberate fake, a double or stand-in for someone I loved. Everything similar suddenly felt like a cheat, like a fraud perpetrated on my broken heart by a cruel and vindictive universe.

And beyond that, there was one other quality. One other thing that was not anything my senses or my personal pain perceived. This woman, this Special Agent Felicity Hope, seemed strange. Sure, I was still rattled by her sudden appearance in the dark, and by her similarity to Grace, but there was something else. She had a quality that made her not....

Not what?

I really had no idea how to finish that thought.

And no time.

Felicity moved away from me and began descending the steps. She moved well in the darkness, and if her feet made any sound at all on the metal stairs it was beyond my senses. With great reluctance and confusion, I followed.

The stairs zigzagged down two levels, and I realized that we had to now be at least twenty feet below sea level. Cape May is pancake flat and houses in the center of town had basements. Certainly nothing built this close to the bay would normally have a cellar. But the stairs went down and down.

With each step the smell of rotting meat increased.

I almost said, "There's something dead down there." But it would have been inanely obvious. Something was not only dead, it had been dead for some time.

Felicity slowed her pace and took her gun in a two-handed grip.

Sweat was beginning to run down the sides of my face and pool inside my shirt at the base of my spine. It would be nice to lie and say it was because the stairway was oppressively humid, but that would have been bullshit. I was scared. Really damn scared.

Changeling, whatever it really might be, in whatever horrific form the madmen at Koenig had conceived with their perverted science, was down here somewhere. Hopefully it was dead or it was nothing more than samples of transgenic animals that had died without food and water. I really didn't want to have to euthanize some kind of mutant rhesus monkey or lab rat. I like animals far more than I like people, and I've seen what scientists do to chimps and dogs and pigs in labs. Dead animals would be easier to take. Sure, that's a cowardly view, but fuck it.

Changeling.

What was it? Where were these guys going with research to allow deliberate shapeshifting? Where *could* they go?

Since I signed onto the DMS, my optimism for common sense and bioethics has taken a real beating. That thing Michael Crichton said in *Jurassic Park* rang true every time. We spend so much time wondering *if* we can, we don't stop to think about whether we *should.* Or words to that effect. I've encountered monsters and mutations already. I wasn't sure how many more I could face before something inside my head snapped. How long did you have to fight monsters until you really became one?

And how long could I dance at the edge of the abyss?

Bad questions to ask yourself in the dark.

Bad questions.

As we descended, though, the darkness changed, becoming cloudy and finally yielding to the glow of a security light in a metal cage mounted on the wall beside a big metal door.

It was massive, as solid and ponderous as a bank vault. There were several high-tech scanners beside it, and even though I had plenty of gadgets for bypassing all kinds of security systems, I could see that I wasn't going to need any of them.

The door stood ajar.

It was held open by a corpse.

I think it had once been a man.

But it was impossible to tell.

The body was swollen and black, the tissues distended by expanding gasses as putrefaction ran rampant.

And…it had no face.

The flesh had all been torn away to reveal the striated remnants of muscle and the white of naked bone.

This hadn't been done by a knife or any kind of weapon. The flesh was torn in very distinctive ways.

By teeth.

Not small rat teeth, either. And it didn't look like dog or cat teeth. The flesh was savaged by very large and very sharp teeth. Not fangs, but rows of teeth. There was enough left of the throat to see that much.

"Christ," I said. "What did that?"

Her voice was very small.

"Dear God," she whispered. "They're out...."

Chap. 9

"What's out?" I demanded, but she shook her head.

"I...don't know exactly. We've only had rumors. But...." Felicity shook her head and set her jaw. Tiny jewels of sweat glistened on her forehead. "Cover me."

"Hey, wait, dammit...."

But she was already in motion, stepping over the corpse, squeezing through the opening, disappearing inside. With a growl I gripped the edge of the massive door and hauled on it, swinging it wider to give me room to follow.

There was light inside, and I ran forward, gun up and ready, into a lab that looked like it was born in the fevered mind of Dr. Moreau. The vast chamber must have stretched hundreds of yards under the streets of Cape May and outward under the waters of the bay. The ceiling was twenty feet high, supported by massive steel pillars. The floor was pale concrete, stained by dried seawater, rust-red old blood, and a dozen chemicals of various sickly hues. There were ranks of computers—the high-end supercomputers used for gene sequencing—tables of arcane scientific equipment, and a dozen stainless-steel dissecting tables. There were also bodies in the room.

Many bodies.

Most of them were human, and none of those were whole. Legs and arms, ragged torsos, bodiless heads lay scattered across the floor.

I knew without counting that the bodies down here and the corpse blocking the door upstairs would add up to an even dozen. The missing scientists.

Not working at a separate site or in another country.

All of them here.

Forever here.

Each missing scientist…but not all of any of them.

Felicity and I stood nearly shoulder to shoulder, gaping at the slaughter.

But then, even with all of that carnage around us, our eyes were drawn to the far wall. How could we not look? How could anyone not stare at what was there?

Row upon row upon row of glass cylinders, each ten feet high and as big around as elm trees. Each filled with murky water that smelled of brine and decay.

And in nearly all of the tanks a body floated.

They were all naked.

Men and women.

Tall. Powerfully built, with corded muscles under layers of gray-green skin.

They floated in the water, tethered by cables and wires attached to electrodes buried in their chests and skulls. Pale hair floated around their faces. Pale eyelids dusted their cheeks.

There were at least fifty tanks.

Three of them were empty, the glass shattered, the wires hanging limp and unattached. Every other tank was full.

Each of the bodies was naked.

None of them were human.

"Holy Mother of God," murmured Felicity.

I felt myself moving forward, taking numb steps like a sleepwalker. My eyes were wide, burning from not blinking. The sight before me was hideous, appalling in its implications, but I couldn't look away. I stopped in front of one of the tanks and reached to touch the glass. The body inside floated on the other side of the thick glass, inches away from me, but worlds apart in so many ways.

The people—the *things* inside the tank—did not have hands.

Not as such.

They had long flat panels of flesh with segmented bony structures that had once been fingers, each connected by rough webbing. The feet were the same. And all along the waterlogged limbs, the flesh glistened with scales.

In movies, in Disney pictures, creatures like this are beautiful.

In these tanks, here in the real world, they were hideous.

I looked into the face of the body floating inches from me. The mouth was little more than a slash with rubbery lips, between which I could see row upon row of serrated teeth.

The creature's eyes were half-open. There was a trace of white around large, black irises.

On the sides of the creature's face, below stunted and useless ears, were gills.

The sound of a footfall in water startled me, and I suddenly whirled, bringing my gun up, but it was Felicity.

She was standing ankle deep at the edge of what I'd first thought was a large puddle but I could now see was a pool. It ended at a wall, and when I shone my flashlight at the water, we could see that the wall ended a few feet below the surface. Tendrils of seaweed wafted back and forth, and there were small fish in the water, darting here and there.

"It must lead to the bay," said Felicity.

We looked from the pool to the three broken cylinders and then at the decaying bodies.

"Three of them must have escaped somehow," she said. "They killed the staff and escaped."

I nodded. And though I was almost too sick to speak, I asked, "Do you know what this is?"

She gave me a quizzical look. "I should think it's effing well obvious."

"No...I can see what they're doing. Transformative genetics...theriomorphy...they've turned test subjects—"

"—or volunteers," she cut in.

"—or volunteers...into monsters. Into water-breathing...." I fished in my mind for the word.

"Into mermen," said Felicity Hope. "And mermaids."

"I thought mermaids were supposed to be beautiful."

She gave a short, ugly laugh. "You don't read your folklore. The mermaids of legend were monsters who lured men to terrible deaths. They drowned them and fed on them."

"So these madmen created genetically engineered...what's the word? Mer-*people*?"

"Close enough."

"But...for Christ's sake *why*?"

She cocked her head appraisingly. "What is your nation's primary weapon of response to deliberate aggression from either China or North Korea?"

"Generally speaking, lots of missiles."

She shook her head. "Which are launched from...?"

"Ah," I said, "our fleet."

"Top marks. The U.S. fleet in the Taiwan Strait is the most powerful weapon of war in existence. Aircraft carriers ready to launch the world's most sophisticated and lethal fighters and helicopters, battleships and cruisers, and nuclear submarines capable of launching nuclear and non-nuclear missiles. China is working on building a blue water fleet, but beyond hype, they are many years away from anything comparable, and it's doubtful they ever will achieve it. That's why they've worked so hard on their missiles and on a submarine fleet capable of slipping past your surface ships. It's why North Korea is developing its nuclear capabilities and building long-range weapons of mass destruction."

"What's your point?"

"No nation on earth can face your fleet in any version of a surface battle. You have more ships and better military technology, and you can call in more far more resources. Everyone knows this. But consider how the Taliban has been able to wage so long and costly a war with your army in Afghanistan, and how they fought the Russians to a standstill at the height of Soviet power. They have no army, no technology. So what do they have?"

"Hit-and-run terrorists who hide among the civilian population and comes at us in small and very mobile groups."

"Bloody right. It's the exact kind of warfare that greatly helped you Yanks fight off our larger and better-trained armies during your Revolution." She spread her arms to indicate the massive tanks, and the bodies floating inside. "Now imagine the hit-and-run terrorists needed for a war against a fleet. A fleet that can detect any metal ships and that can sweep away any network of mines. Imagine teams of *merpeople* who could swim undetected into the heart of your fleet, carrying small satchel charges and nonmetallic limpet mines. Enough of them, with the right equipment, could destroy your fleet without North Korea or China launching a single missile. And what defense could you offer? You can't patrol beneath the surface for something this small and mobile. It's impractical to the point of impossibility."

I wanted to tell her that she was out of her mind. That she was delusional. That such a plan was far too wild to ever work.

But the faces of the dead scientists mocked my denials. The powerful bodies floating in the brine told me that my view of the world was relevant to yesterday. Today was a different and much more terrible day.

"I have to call this in," I said. "I need to get someplace where I can get a clean signal and get every-fucking-body out here."

She looked at me with her dark eyes.

"Captain," she said, then amended it. "Joe…you do understand that if this technology is acquired by our people—yours and mine—they'll do the same thing, continue the same research."

I said nothing.

"They'll make monsters, too," she said, "because the proof is right here that monsters are the next viable weapon of war."

"Monsters," I said, echoing the word. It tasted rancid in my mouth. "But what options do we have? The Koenig people are in custody, their research is either slag or it's in these computers, and we don't know if they've already shared their secrets with the Chinese or North Koreans. If our enemies have these weapons, won't we *have* to…."

I heard what I was saying and knew that it was absolutely true and absolutely wrong. It was the trap that has escalated warfare since the invention of the longbow. Since the gun. Since the first nuclear bomb.

It was keeping up with the Joneses in a very real and very ugly way, and unless everyone suddenly came to their senses, how could we avoid committing sins of conscience to defend our people?

What's the answer to that question?

Where's the path that leads us away from ever escalating the arms race?

"Joe," she said as she walked over to the bank of supercomputers, "the Koenig people haven't sold the information yet. The secrets are all here. The research that was burned was a decoy. All of it is here."

"You can't know that."

"Yes, I can. I *do* know it."

"How can you be so sure?"

Without turning she said, "I'm sure, Joe."

And she said it in Grace's voice.

Exactly Grace's voice.

My mouth went dry.

I took a small step toward her. "Grace…?"

"If we destroy these computers, it stops here."

I licked my lips. "The senior Koenig people are—"

"It stops here. This abomination goes no further."

I wanted her to turn around. I wanted to see her face. I needed to see the light of Grace's soul shining out of her eyes. If that was an impossible wish, who cares. We stood in an impossible place.

"Grace…," I whispered again.

And then a sudden violent sound of splashing water broke the moment. I spun around as three monstrous shapes rose from the pool.

Gray-green skin.

Black eyes.

Rows of teeth.

And webbed hands that ended in terrible claws.

Two of them rushed at me, and one launched itself at Felicity and slammed her against the computers. Felicity screamed. It sounded like the call of a wounded seagull.

I heard myself yelling. Screaming, really. But the sound was lost beneath the roar of the mermen who ran at me and the thunder of my gun as I fired and fired.

One of them abruptly spun sideways, his face torn away by a bullet that went on to strike a cylinder. The glass shattered in a spray of jagged pieces and gushing water. The occupant of the tube tore loose of the wires and fell heavily to the floor.

I saw this only peripherally as the second creature slammed into me.

He was enormously strong and drove me ten feet backward and nearly crushed me against a concrete wall. Even with the impact I managed to keep hold of my gun, but the monster twisted its head and clamped its jaws around my forearm. Blood spurted, and I heard my wristbones break. Pain exploded with inferno heat inside my arm, and I almost blacked out.

But part of me is as cold and inhuman as these monsters. It's the part of me that survived the trauma of my childhood by being too vicious to die. It's the part that somehow allowed me to complete the mission that Grace had died to accomplish, even though it meant facing impossible odds. It was the part of me that could kill despite idealism and compassion. It was the part of me that, on some level that I have never wanted to examine with total clarity, enjoys all of this. The pain, the violence.

The killing.

As my flesh ruptured and my bones broke, that part of me shoved the civilized aspect of my mind to one side. In that moment I stopped being a man and became the thing I needed to be in order to survive this encounter.

I became a monster.

With a snarl as inhuman as the thing that attacked me, I drove my knee up into its crotch, then head-butted the thing so hard I could hear cartilage and bone shatter. I drove my stiffened thumb into its eye, bursting the orb. Then I kicked its screaming, writhing body backward.

My right arm flopped bloody and limp, the fingers feeling like swollen bags of blood. My gun was gone, I had no idea where.

I ran at the monster that now lay twisting on the floor, hands pressed to its bloody eye socket. Its other eye stared at me with uncomprehending horror. It had killed the scientists in this room. It was a predator thing, designed for slaughter, and now it was hurt and helpless and being stalked by something that did not fear its power.

It raised one hand in defense and I kicked it away, then stamped down hard on its throat.

Without even pausing to watch it die, I whirled toward Felicity.

She was not there.

Instead I saw the third merman sprawled in a growing lake of blood, its body torn apart so savagely that its arms and legs were only attached by strings of meat.

Something bulky and gray shot past me, brushing close enough to strike my uninjured arm. It moved so fast I could barely see it.

It plunged into the water and was gone.

It was not a woman, that much was clear.

It looked like an animal.

Almost like an animal.

Its gray fur was crisscrossed by jagged cuts and streaked with blood. Within a moment all that was left was a stain of blood on the eddying waters.

I stood alone in the cavernous lab.

Twenty feet away, the merman who had fallen to the floor when my bullet smashed its tube was beginning to stir.

I bent and picked up the pistol dropped by Felicity Hope.

With blood falling from my shattered arm, I walked over to the creature as it struggled to get to its misshapen feet.

I raised the gun.

Fired.

For a long, long time I stood there. Arm cradled to my body. Pain and adrenaline washing back and forth through me like tidewaters.

There was no sign of Felicity Hope.

I knew there would not be.

Though…I did not understand why.

As the monster in my mind crept back into its cave and the civilized man staggered out again, the mysteries of this place—of this afternoon—rose up above me like a tsunami and threatened to smash me flat.

In my mind I heard the echoes of her voice.

"Joe…it stops here."

I looked around at the computers. And at the tables piled high with equipment.

And chemicals.

And reams of paper.

With my good hand, whimpering at the agony in my arm, I reached into my pocket for my lighter.

Chap. 10

The fire burned the building to black ash.

I leaned against the fender of the ATF agents' Crown Vic and watched it burn. They both yelled at me, demanding to know what happened, threatening to arrest me, trying to get me to react to them in any way. But all I did was watch the place burn.

When the firemen and cops asked me how it started, I spun a bunch of lies.

I was taken in an ambulance to the hospital where they had to do surgery to repair my arm. The doctors had a lot of questions about my arm. I told them that there had been a moray eel in a tank and that I was dumb enough to put my arm inside. They didn't believe me. Mostly because they weren't stupid enough to accept that story. And because the wound signature was wrong for an eel. Then Mr. Church showed up and people stopped asking me questions.

The only one who heard the real story was Church.

He listened the way he does—silent, without expression, cold. When I was done, he used his cell phone and, with me sitting right there in the E.R., ordered a full battery of physical and psychological tests for when I got back to Baltimore.

Even a lie detector test.

Our forensics people lifted blood samples from my clothes. Dark brick red blood from my shirt. The blood of the mermen.

And brighter red blood from my sleeve.

Her blood.

They also lifted a full handprint from the back wall of the bathroom. The techs promised DNA and other lab work back as soon as possible.

Dr. Hu spent days picking through the ashes of the Koenig building, his face alight with expectation, hoping to find something he could play with, but I'd built a very hot fire.

He finally gave it up, defeated and mad at me.

The doctors ran their tests.

I passed them all. No hallucinogens or alcohol in my system.

The shrinks ran and then re-ran their tests, and when they got the same answers they began looking at me funny. Then they stopped making eye contact altogether.

On a warm summer evening ten days after the fire, Mr. Church called me into a private meeting. There was a plate of cookies—Nilla wafers and Oreos—and a tall bottle of very good, very old Scotch. There was also a stack of color-coded folders. I didn't touch them, but I could see that some folders were from other agencies.

After we sat and ate cookies and drank whiskey and stared at each other for too long, Church said, "Is there anything you would like to add to your report?"

"No," I said.

"Is there anything about the report you would like to amend?"

"No."

He nodded.

We sat.

We each had another cookie.

Church picked up two FBI fingerprint cards and handed it to me. I looked at them and read the attached report. The conclusion was this: "Both sets of prints are clearly from the same source. They match on all points."

I sighed and set the report down.

"Fingerprints can be faked," said Church. "There are various polymers which can be worn over the fingertips, and even the whole hand, that can carry false prints."

"I know."

"The FBI report is therefore inconclusive as far as we're concerned."

"Okay," I said. He studied my face but I was giving him nothing to read. My face has been a stone since the fire. I didn't want to show nothing to nobody.

Church removed a report from a DNA lab that we often used. He studied it for a moment but didn't pass it to me.

"The lab says that the blood sample from your sleeve was contaminated. They pulled two blood types from it, one human and one animal."

"Which animal?" I asked, even though I knew the answer.

"*Halichoerus grypus*," he said. "Commonly known as the Atlantic gray seal."

I said nothing.

"The blood was thoroughly mixed."

"Yes."

"So thoroughly mixed that they were unable to entirely separate the DNA strands. In fact the only complete DNA they've recovered is an even mix of human and seal genes." He placed the report on the desk and laid his palm on it. "The scientists are floating various theories which could account for that level of genetic degradation. The leading theory is that the heat somehow fused the DNA."

"Is that even possible?" I asked quietly.

He smiled. "No."

We sat there.

The wall clock ticked away two full minutes before he spoke again.

Church said, "There's a legend in Ireland and elsewhere about a magical creature called a *selkie*. They're mysterious women who are actually seals." He selected a cookie but didn't eat it. Instead he rolled it back and forth on his desk top. "But that's myth and legend."

"Yes."

"This is the real world."

"Yes."

"And we don't—or can't—believe in the impossible," he said. "Can we, Captain?"

I said nothing. Three more minutes burned off the day. The office was absolutely quiet. Beyond the big picture window the brown waters of the Baltimore Harbor flowed and churned as boats passed by.

"She's dead," murmured Church after a while.

"I know."

"As much as both of us want her back, as much as each of us wants it to be untrue, Grace is dead."

"I know," I said.

Church finished his whiskey, got up and walked over to the window and stood there, hands clasped behind his back, staring out at the water.

I looked at the fingerprint card.

The partial palm print was matched against an official fingerprint ten-card used to record a full set of prints when anyone enters government service. The card they'd compared the partial to was old. Someone had affixed a small gold star sticker to one corner. They don't give gold stars when you do something great or if you score on a test. They add that to your record when you die.

The name on the card was a familiar one.

Looking at it twisted a knife in my heart.

The name was GRACE COURTLAND.

I poured myself another glass of whiskey.

~The End~

Mad Science

NOTE: This story takes place after the events of *Assassin's Code*. There are some spoilers if you haven't read that book.

Chap. 1

We came in with the whole *Mission: Impossible* thing.

Dropping through on wires, black clothes, whole bag of high-tech gizmos.

No cool theme music, though.

The ultraclean, ultrasecure lab was supposed to be making pills for old ladies with bad backs and men who wanted marathon erections.

But an undisclosed source whispered something very nasty into the right phone. She said that someone at Marquis Pharmaceuticals was cooking up something very, very nasty. The kind of thing that gives any sane person a case of the shakes. Something that no one inside U.S. borders was supposed to be working on, and something world governments had agreed to ban under all circumstances.

Two words.

Weaponized Ebola.

Yeah, sit with that for a moment. The black duds I wore were a modified Level A hazmat suit manufactured specifically for special operators. I didn't look like the Michelin Man. More like a high-tech ninja, but there was no one around to tell me how badass I looked. Besides, I wasn't wearing it for the cool-factor. Like I said…Ebola.

This is what the caller said: "They're working on QOBE—quick-onset *Bundibugyo ebolavirus*. They already have buyers lined up."

Quick-onset Ebola.

It's exactly what it sounds like. Ebola that works really freaking fast. Aerosolized for tactical deployment and married to nearly microscopic airborne parasites that act as aggressive vectors. This is not science fiction. This is science paid for by people who have had time to sit down, calm down, and think it over...and who still want to write a check for a bioweapon that, once introduced, will hit and present within hours. The idea was to use it in confined areas to remove hostile assets. Introduce it into a bunker or secure facility, and everyone in there would die. Without living hosts, an insertion team in combat hazmat suits can infiltrate and gain access to computers and other materials. Infection rate is ninety-eight point eight percent; mortality rate among infected is one hundred percent.

Our people worked on this until the DMS found out about it and shut the facility down.

Now someone else was screwing with it.

Which is why I was hanging from wires ninety yards down an airshaft, wrapped in a nonconductive and nonreflective Hammer suit, armed to the teeth, and scared out of my mind.

Oh yeah...and cranky.

This one was making me very, very cranky.

Chap. 2

I had a handheld BAMS unit that I used to check the viral load in the air around me. These units were portable bio-aerosol mass spectrometers that were used for real-time detection and identification of biological aerosols. They have a vacuum function that draws in ambient air and hits it with continuous wave lasers to fluoresce individual particles. Key particles like bacillus spores, dangerous viruses, and certain vegetative cells are identified and assigned color codes. As I passed it in a slow circle all the little lights stayed resolutely green. Nice.

I unfastened the airtight bioseal, peeled back the flexible hood of the modified Hammer suit I wore, and tapped my earbud to open the channel to Bug, our computer guy. He provides real time intel for gigs like this.

"Talk to me," I said quietly. "You crack their encryption yet, or am I hanging here just for shits and giggles?"

"Yeah, Cowboy," he said. "We're in. Downloading a set of revised building schematics to you now."

I wore a pair of what looked like Wayfarers with slightly heavier frames. The frames contained micro-hardware that allowed the lenses to flash images invisible to anyone else but which displayed in detailed 3D to me. Suddenly I had an entire office building around me, floating in virtual space. A tiny mouse was built into my right glove, and I used the tip of my index finger against the ball of my thumb to scroll through the schematics.

First thing was to orient myself. We'd pulled the building plans they'd filed with the proper agencies, but now that Bug used MindReader to hack the facility's computers, we had the actual plans. The aboveground building was the same, but down where I was, four stories below street level, nothing looked the same. The 'basement' in the original plans was on the first of twelve sub-floors built into the bedrock of Blue Bell, Pennsylvania.

"Tell me about the floor," I said.

"It's wired nine ways from Sunday," said Bug, "but that's not the bad news."

"It's not? Then have MindReader go in there and kick over some furniture."

MindReader was the supercomputer around which the Department of Military Sciences was built. It was a freak of a computer, the only one of its kind, and it had a super-intrusion software package that allowed it to do a couple of spiffy things. One was to look for patterns by drawing information from an enormous number of sources, many of which it was not officially allowed to access. Which was the second thing: MindReader could intrude into any known computer system, poke around as much as it wanted, and withdraw without a trace. Most systems leave some kind of scar on the target computer's memory, but MindReader rewrote the target's software to erase all traces of its presence.

"Can't—" began Bug, but I cut him off.

"Don't tell me 'can't.'"

"Cowboy, listen to me. Their security runs out of a dedicated server that isn't wired into their main computers. Not in, anyway—

no WIFI, no hard lines. Nothing. You're going to need to find it and plug a router cable into a USB port so MindReader can access it."

"Ah," I said.

There were no computers visible in the room.

Not one. I wore a high-definition lapel cam, so he could see that, too.

"I'm open to suggestions," I said.

That's when another voice said, "I got this."

It should have been Top's voice. He was suited up to follow me down. Or, if not him, then Bunny. We were the only three agents authorized to be here.

It wasn't them.

It was a woman who dropped down on a second set of wires. Slim, gorgeous, with dark hair pulled back into a tight ponytail. No hazmat suit. She used the hand brake on the drop wire and stopped exactly level with me.

She smiled.

It was a big smile, full of white teeth and mischief.

"Hello, Joseph," she said.

"Hello, Violin," I said. "What in the wide blue fuck are you doing here?"

Chap. 3

Her smile didn't waver.

"I'm on a case," she said.

"You're not supposed to be on *this* case," I fired back.

"You're intruding into *my* case."

"Sorry, babe, this is U.S. soil, and I'm the one with official sanction."

"Really?" She pretended to pout. "You're going to throw proper procedure at me? After all we've—"

I cut her off. "Uh-uh. Don't you dare give me the 'after all we've been through' speech. You've used that too many times."

"I have not."

"Excuse me? Paris? Cairo? Rio? Any of that ring a bell?"

She dismissed it all with a wave of her hand. "You sound like a shrewish old woman, Joseph. It's really unattractive."

"And you're wanted on four continents, including this one, darlin'. So how much do you want to push this?"

We had to keep our voices to whispers, so there was an unintentional hushed comedy to the exchange.

She started grinning right around the time I did.

We hung there for a moment, smiling.

I wanted to kiss her. She wasn't my girlfriend, and I'm not sure the term 'lover' fit, either. We'd been through some terrible stuff together, and we'd both nearly died. Friends of ours *did* die. And, no joke, we saved the world. The actual world. So, every now and then, when we found ourselves in the same part of the world at the same time, and providing neither of us had any serious emotional commitments elsewhere, Violin and I celebrated our survival, celebrated the fact of being alive. When you've taken the kind of fire we have, you definitely take time for that. Some soldiers go to the Wall in D.C. and trace names. Some visit Ground Zero or sit in a church—any church that's handy—and they thank their higher power for us being on the good side of the dirt.

Violin and I? We celebrated it in a very primal, very steamy way. Clothes were torn. Furniture was broken. Cops were called more than once.

There was never any attempt at a relationship. Not for us. We were still at war. When our time was over, we—by mutual consent—walked away and went back to the killing.

But, as much as it lifted my heart to see her alive and well and smoking hot, she was not supposed to be here. This was a covert op. It wasn't an invitational.

I tapped my earbud. "Cowboy to Sergeant Rock."

"Go for Rock," said the deep voice of my second-in-command, First Sergeant Top Sims.

"Why am I talking to you on the radio instead of face to face?" I demanded in a tone that could burn the paint off an oil drum. "Why, instead, am I down here with a *civilian*?"

I leaned on the word to piss off Violin.

"Bastard," she hissed. She stuck her tongue out at me, so I stuck my tongue out at her.

"Wasn't my call." Top's voice was very calm and controlled. "Word came down from the big man. Said to afford every courtesy."

The big man was my boss, Mr. Church, founder and head of the DMS.

Balls.

I knew that I was being unfair in my assessment that Violin was a civilian. She was hardly that. Violin was a fellow soldier, but not a fellow American. She was born in captivity to a mother who—along with many others—was forced breeding stock in the world's oldest and ugliest Eugenics program. A group called the Red Order had been using captive women for centuries to ensure that they had enough male members of a weird genetic subgroup called the *Upierczi*. These were as close to actual monsters as Mother Nature was likely to cook up. They were offshoots of human evolution, unusually strong and fast, and hideous in appearance. They were the reason the myth of the vampire came into our collective consciousness. No, these guys didn't turn into bats, sparkle, or sleep in coffins. They weren't supernatural in any way. But they weren't my idea of natural, either, even if they were technically human.

They were called the Red Knights.

The Red Order used them as assassins in a campaign of carefully orchestrated religious hate crimes going back to the Crusades.

Violin's mother, Lilith, had escaped from the breeding pits. I don't know that whole story, but whatever happened left a psychic scar on the Red Knights. They feared Lilith the way people used to fear vampires. She was their boogeyman. When Lilith escaped, she took other women with her—and their children. Violin among them. As soon as they were free, they formed a militant group called Arklight, and they began hunting down the members of the Red Order and their *Upierczi* assassins.

I met Violin while I was hunting down some rogue nukes in Iran. There was an interesting learning curve before we began trusting each other, but when we realized that we shared the same enemies and a similar agenda, we went into battle together. That one was a doozy. Lots of good people died, including some of my guys from Echo Team. Men who'd walked through fire with me time and again. Arklight lost some heroes—well, heroines, too. And when it was all over we'd formed a rather sketchy alliance. Nothing official, of course, because Arklight did not respect national borders in its relentless search for the surviving members of the Red Order and the

Red Knights. The official U.S. stance was that Arklight was a terrorist organization.

My boss, Mr. Church, was working to change that, and so far no one from Arklight had ever spent a night inside an American jail cell. After what they'd been through, Church and I were going to make sure no one put those women into any kind of cage ever again.

All of which explains her, but didn't explain why we were being Spider-Man and Spider-Woman in a bioweapons lab.

"Talk," I told her.

"Let me get to the computer first."

I gestured around. "We're in an empty chamber, honey. Unless I'm missing something...."

She produced a spray can from a Batman utility belt. Shook the can. Sprayed it.

The gas inside was white and almost opaque. There wasn't enough particulate matter in the discharge to trigger even the most sensitive motion sensor, but the opacity was usually great for revealing electric eyes and laser tripwires.

However, that wasn't Violin's purpose. She turned in a slow circle and emptied at least half the can into the chamber. The sluggish air from the shaft above us stirred the gas. All I could see were black stone walls. No hidden doors, no side tunnels, no electrical outlets.

Then I saw how wrong I was.

The gas expanded and diffused outward until it caressed the walls. Except that it didn't.

It rolled out to touch *most* of the walls. But to my left, the gas swirled differently. The tendrils of gas seemed to rebound from empty air and eddy, as if confused. Violin ran a laser pointer over that section of wall.

The red beam ran straight for a few inches and then bulged outward at the same point where the gas had rebounded. Violin moved the beam slowly, and I could see that there was something there. The gas knew it, the laser light knew it, but my eyes didn't.

"What the hell?" I murmured.

She grinned, enjoying my confusion. "Holograph," she said.

And then I understood. The security system computer access panel was indeed bolted to the wall, but it was masked by a high-density holograph that made it look like empty wall. Without the gas and the laser, I would never have found it.

"Guess that answers the question as to whether this place is crooked," I said. "Can't work up any reason a legit lab would have that kind of security."

"I never trust pharmaceutical companies," she said with asperity.

I tended to agree. Sure, a lot of them are probably on the up and up, but in my trade I kept running into mad scientists cooking up bioweapons. Some of the most dangerous terrorists I've tackled have been pharmaceutical moguls or pharmacologists of one stripe or another. I'd have to watch that tendency toward negative bias, though. Subjectivity is a dangerous thing.

Violin adjusted the wires so that she tilted in the direction of the invisible box. It was slow work, and it took her some time to find the cover plate lock, disable it with a little electronic doohickey—that looked a whole lot like the doohickeys that only the DMS is supposed to have—and finally locate the USB port.

"Router?" she said, holding out a hand.

I sighed and handed it over.

Violin plugged it in, making sure not to touch any part of the panel with her hands. It probably had passive security, like contact and trembler switches. The router's cable slid easily into the port and a tiny green light flashed on.

"Bug," I said, "we're—"

"Got it," he said. "Acquiring the security system now. Hm, nice stuff. Too bad MindReader is going to bitch-slap it." He actually sang that last part in a mocking falsetto.

I work with some pretty strange people.

We hung there and waited. The white gas swirled around us, obscuring the wires so that it looked like we were flying.

"So," I said, "want to tell me what you're doing here?"

Her mouth kept smiling but her eyes held no trace of humor. "Hunting vampires."

My mouth went dry and my nuts tried to crawl up inside of my body. "Red Knights? You're saying they're here?"

"No," she said. "But somebody who works here is helping them, and I—"

Bug cut in. "Okay, Cowboy…we own that place."

"Copy that."

I swung my feet down toward the floor and hit the cable release on the wires. A moment later Violin dropped silently beside me. The wires swayed around us like web threads from a giant spider.

The hologram projectors that hid the computer access panel clicked off, revealing a flat gray box the size of a hardback book. The router no longer looked like it was floating in midair. But when the holograms vanished, we discovered that there had been a second bit of misdirection. Right below us, set into the precise center of the concrete floor, was a steel hatch. It was very well made and was designed such that it was perfectly flush with the concrete. It had a touchscreen keypad that was currently displaying: "RESTRICTED ACCESS."

"So far the intel is good," I murmured. "We were told that this air vent was the way in. Looks like it is."

Violin and I knelt on either side of it. I removed a flat gadget about the size of a pack of playing cards and pressed it onto the hatch. It connected to MindReader and began cycling through the hundreds of millions of permutations of the locking combination.

While we waited, I turned to Violin. "Okay, spill."

She spilled.

Arklight spies had gotten wind of a hitherto unknown cell of Red Knights operating out of the Philly suburbs. It was unclear if the cell was preparing to strike Philly or if they were simply using the city as a base for recruiting and training. The Knights preferred cities that had elaborate subways and tunnel systems.

"Why Blue Bell?" I asked. "The subway doesn't come all the way out here."

She shook her head. "They have a contact here at Marquis Pharmaceuticals. A developmental chemist named Ryerson."

"And what's Ryerson doing for the Red Knights?"

"I don't know. But my mother did a thorough background check on him. Ken Ryerson is forty-one, unmarried, no family, no apparent politics, has not voted in any recent elections, no police record."

I waited. She wouldn't give me that much if there wasn't more. Violin liked a little drama.

"Mr. Ryerson gambles."

"Ah," I said.

That was it. She laid it out for me. Ryerson had been a three-times-a-year gambler when Atlantic City was the only place you could lay down a legal bet unless you flew to Nevada. Then the Native Americans opened casinos in the Poconos, and that made him a once-a-month man. A few years ago they turned the racetrack in Bensalem into a casino, twenty minutes away on the Turnpike. Ryerson started going once a week, then three times a week. He wasn't a card player. From the way Violin described him, it was doubtful the man knew a straight flush from a toilet flush. Ryerson needed a more constant and predictable fix. He played nickel slots. A lot of nickel slots. Started getting later and later on his utility bills and car payments. The third time he was late on the rent, he had to move to a smaller apartment in a less attractive suburb. He gave up the leased car and bought a hooptie. Ate a lot of cheap takeout food. Didn't stop plugging nickels into the one-armed bandit, though.

As she talked I thought about what it must be like to be Ryerson. What specific bit of damage makes a man tear off tiny chunks of his life and feed them into a machine that everyone knows is specifically designed to give a debit on any long-term investment? Old ladies play the slots out of boredom and because they socialize with the other pensioners. The uninformed play them because the casino hype yells about the million dollar jackpots. Guys like Ryerson have to know that there's no happy ending because even a jackpot on the nickel slots is small change, comparatively speaking. This man was either a loser or he was sick, and he almost certainly knew it.

The first digit pinged on the combination.

"So what changed?" I asked, knowing that there had to be a second act to this sad story.

"He bought a new car," she said. "He cleared all his credit card debt. And he booked a vacation in Las Vegas."

"I'm guessing that he didn't win big at the slots."

"His largest jackpot to date is forty-eight dollars and fifty cents. However over the last month, he's made five cash deposits between twenty-five hundred and forty-five hundred dollars."

"Ah," I said. Banks are required to report deposits over a certain dollar amount. "Why doesn't he just take out an ad in the paper saying he's been bought?"

"He might as well have," she agreed.

"Bug," I said, "take a look at this guy Ryerson. See if he looks good as our informant. Hit me with anything that comes up."

"Copy that."

The second number pinged. Four to go.

"Why were you looking at him in the first place?" I asked Violin.

She shook her head. "We were looking at this facility. At everyone here. It's been on our list for years because two of the shareholders have business ties to known members of the Red Order. Strong ties. One of those shareholders also owns points in BioDynamics out of South Africa."

I nodded. I knew that from our own intel. Without the BioDynamics connection, our people might not have taken the nameless informant very seriously. But you can't ignore that kind of red flag.

If you don't remember the story, it was four years ago. BioDynamics made a name for itself by developing technologies that allowed groups like Doctors Without Borders and the World Health Organization to collect and process biological samples while still in the field. That was a godsend because it allowed the doctors to identify diseases and classify disease mutations without the time lag of sending samples to labs in Europe or America. Lives were saved every day because of that technology.

Here's the kicker, though: the biosampling equipment was also collecting a great deal of information about virulent strains of exotic diseases and storing it in concealed clean compartments within the machine housing. When BioDynamics techs went into the field every few months to collect the machines and replace them with fresh units, all of those samples were taken back to the main lab in Modderfontein, in the Gauteng province of South Africa. There, the diseases samples were processed, studied, weaponized, mass-produced, and sold to groups who intended to distribute them in the poorest black towns throughout the country. The strains they tried to release were designed to resist all known antibiotics. The goal? Win back South Africa for a small ultraextremist group of whites by simply eradicating the majority of the blacks. Simple, direct, utterly ruthless, and very effective. Similar distribution plans were in the works for Somalia and other countries with a high percentage of black Muslims.

It would have been effective if not for a joint action taken by the DMS, Barrier—the UK counterpart of the DMS—and a hotshot Recces team from the South African Special Forces Brigade. The facility was seized, and the staff arrested and put on trial for a list of crimes that was so long that the world court judges asked the prosecution to summarize. The courts had to make an example of the perpetrators because to not do so would be to ignite the fuse on a global race war.

It didn't surprise me that Red Order members were involved. They pretty much invented the concept of hate crimes back in the thirteenth century. Freaks.

The third and fourth digits pinged at the same time.

I went through my habitual self pat-down, quickly and lightly touching the handle of the Beretta 92F snugged into a nylon shoulder rig, the rapid-release folding knife clipped to the inside of one pocket, the BAMS unit hanging from my belt.

The fifth light pinged.

I glanced at Violin as I pulled my hazmat hood into place.

"You're underdressed for this party."

"I hope not."

"Hey, I'm serious, Violin," I said. "Maybe you don't know what I'm hunting down here."

"Protocols for developing a weaponized viral hemorrhagic fever. Arklight has been aware for some time of plans to sell a developed protocol along with viable samples of a crude prototype to several terrorist groups, including the Knights."

I stared at her. "You think you're down here to steal some computer files?"

"Sure."

"You do realize that MindReader is currently hacked into that system and whatever they have, we now have."

"You have MindReader, Joseph," she said, "but Arklight doesn't. And the Oracle system Mr. Church gave us is a poor substitute."

"Horse shit. Oracle is the second-best hacking system in the world. Besides, if you'd have brought this to us, Church would have Bug on this."

Violin's eyes shifted away, and I suddenly knew why she hadn't reached out.

"Your mother didn't want to ask Church for a favor," I said.

"No," she said, and sighed.

There is apparently a very long and complicated history between Mr. Church and Lilith. It is, however, a tightly closed subject.

Also…given her history, I would imagine that it would gall Lilith to ask for help from any man. I did not blame her one bit.

On the other hand, that lack of communication came with its own problems.

"Listen to me," I said, taking her by the arms, "I didn't come down here to hack a file any more than I'm here to intercept a sample. We have an informant who said that this thing is already fully developed and that they are mass-producing it for an established client."

That news hit her pretty damn hard. The way you'd expect it to hit someone. Her eyes flared and she recoiled from the hatch as if it was a coiled rattlesnake.

"Are you *sure*?"

"Sure? No. We have an anonymous voice on the phone. The call was made from a disposable phone that was purchased at a strip mall near here."

She considered this, then shook her head. "All of our intel indicates that they are months away from a stable bioweapon. Besides, this is a development facility, Joseph. The viruses will be in sealed containers in secured vaults. It's not going to be floating around."

"Under ideal circumstances, sure, but what if they realize that they're being infiltrated? Accidents happen. Believe me, I know. I've seen a lot of monsters, big and small, get off the leash."

Violin chewed her lip. It was an unconscious action with no hint of flirtation in it, but I still found it incredibly sexy.

Yes, even crouching in an airshaft over a lab that made weaponized Ebola, I'm still a horn dog. Not a news flash.

The last number pinged.

"You can't go in," I said.

"There's no way I'm staying out here."

"I can bring Top and Bunny down here and you can stay topside and watch our backs."

"Not a chance, Joseph."

"It's fucking dangerous in there, Violin."

"Well," she said with a coquettish smile, "then I'll have to be very careful, won't I?"

I didn't answer that. But I pulled the hood on and made sure the seals were perfectly tight. I don't mind taking risks—that's kind of a professional responsibility, and I'll be the first to admit that I've taken some really dumb risks over the years in situations where I didn't have the time to think up a better plan. But give me a few minutes to plan and I'm the most cautious guy you'd ever want to meet. There are no second chances when it comes to accidents involving one of the world's deadliest pathogens.

Violin and I drew our guns. We shared a nod, then I lifted the hatch.

Chap. 4

Bug fed us the route.

Down a metal ladder, along one corridor, through a doorway, down some stairs, through more doorways and more corridors. At each point we encountered a security barrier—a retina scan, geometric hand scanner, keycard box. MindReader was deep inside the system now, though, and as we approached each doorway the scanner lights went from red to green. Nothing and no one stopped us. Not surprising, since the first three levels were administrative. Funny that even evil and corruption generate a lot of mundane paperwork.

I tried to imagine who would come to a place like this to fix the copier.

Did they have evil copier companies?

Then we reached the bottom level and stood inside the stairwell, stealing covert glances through a small wire-mesh window in the door. Twenty feet away was a heavy-gauge steel door, and outside stood a guard. Big, tough-looking, and alert. He had a Sig Sauer in a belt holster and a Heckler and Koch rifle slung from one muscular shoulder.

Bug said, "Okay, Cowboy, we have sixteen rooms at that level. Employee records indicate a security staff and lab personnel working on all shifts. You're too deep for thermal scans, but figure anywhere from nine to fourteen people."

"We see one guard," I said. "How many others?"

"Four on the schedule. You want me to send backup?"

I cut a look at Violin. She was a superbly trained assassin. A world-class sniper and one of the deadliest knife fighters I'd ever met. Faster than me, and I'm really fast.

"We got it," I said, "but don't let anyone upstairs fall asleep."

I nodded to the door. "You as good with a pistol as you are with a sniper rifle?"

Violin cocked an eyebrow. I told her why.

Chap. 5

As soon as I opened the door the guard whipped around in my direction and brought his rifle up. What he saw was a man in a black hazmat suit.

Specifically, he saw a man in a hazmat suit who took a single wobbly step before collapsing as if dying.

The soldier stared in horror for half a second, caught between needing to know who I was and yelling for help.

Violin leaned out the door and put two bullets in him. One in the heart, one in the head.

Perfect shots, nearly silent, the *pfft* sounds following each other so quickly they almost sounded like a single report. The guard went down. Without a sound, without a pause. One moment he was alive, and the next he was meat slumping to the ground.

There is a part of me that is constantly appalled at the fragility of life and the grim candor with which an invitation to die is spoken to total strangers. I did not know this man, and it was likely that I'd never know his name or anything about him. Somebody else in another enforcement agency would handle clean up on him. Another person I didn't know would sweep this man's life into the trash can.

As I got up I glanced at Violin. There was no flicker of mercy or regret or anything on her face. I had the tiniest flicker of distaste at that before I reminded myself of where she'd been born and under what circumstances she'd been raised. In light of that, it was amazing that she was not, herself, a monster.

I checked the BAMS unit. The lights were still green.

I tapped my earbud. "We're at the door, Bug. Let us in."

The security locks clicked.

I took the lead as I nudged the door open with my shoulder. Directly inside was a small room with rows of hazmat suits on hangars, a sign-in log, and a pressurized door. We had to let the hall door close and seal before the inner door would open. The air had that distinctive smell of ultrafiltered air, which never smelled quite right to me. I guess I've become habituated to pollutants.

Still had green lights on the BAMS.

We went through the pressurized door and found ourselves in a kind of central courtyard that had three short corridors leading to big doors marked—I kid you not—One, Two, and Three.

Violin turned to me. "Do you know which lab has the Ebola?"

"Nope. Want to see what's behind door number one?"

She nodded without a smile. I doubted she watched many game shows. I let it go.

We crept toward that corridor, flanked the entrance, and were just about to make the short run to the door when it opened.

A small man in a white lab coat stood there.

He should have been shocked. He should have shrieked and yelled and called for backup.

Instead he smiled.

A small, cold smile.

The four security guards behind him all had guns; all of them had laser sights on me.

"So," said the small man in the lab coat, "this is fun, isn't it?"

I recognized his voice.

It was my informant.

I said, "Ah, balls."

Chap. 6

"Drop your guns," said the little man.

"Not a chance," I said, pointing the barrel at his face. He was almost close enough to grab and use as a shield; definitely close enough to kill with my first shot.

The guy seemed to guess what I was thinking. "Shoot me and my guys will kill you."

"Yeah," I agreed, "maybe. But you'll be deader'n shit."

"True." He contrived not to look impressed. I wondered why. "So where's that leave us?"

"Having a chat."

"What would you like to chat about?"

"It starts with an 'e.'"

He chuckled. It made his eyes crinkle, and I realized that he looked exactly like Mr. Rogers. Swap the lab coat for a cardigan and it's him. It gave this whole thing an extra layer of surreal weirdness.

"Can we pause to appreciate the wonderfulness of my trap?" he asked.

"Yes, hooray, I'm sure you'll get your Mad Scientist merit badge."

He pursed his lips. "Sadly you won't get the Be Prepared badge. You came in here alone?"

"He's not alone," said Violin. "He brought a date."

We all laughed about that. The laser sights never budged, though. Not theirs, not ours.

"You want to cut to it, friend?" I said. "You set a trap and we walked into it. Now we have a standoff. What's the punch line here?"

"Oh, it's pretty simple," he said. "I'm in charge of quality control here. Our clients had some questions about our security. Despite all of our assurances that we have excellent security as well as redundant, fail-safe and alternative systems, they were still jittery. So I arranged a practical demonstration. We, um, *leaked* some information to several law enforcement agencies, domestic and foreign, over the last fourteen months. Different information to each agency, and leaked in ways that would encourage them to keep that information in-house. You know how you fellows in the alphabet agencies hate to share. Since then we've had the FBI, the CIA, Homeland, the DEA, and a few other groups come poking around. Not here, of course, and never the same company twice."

"You're not Marquis Pharmaceuticals?"

"Oh, hell no. And, by the way, Marquis doesn't actually know we're down here. At least, no one in authority does. We own key members of maintenance and security, as we do with fifty or so other companies, including the construction company that built this place, the zoning board, and the various federal offices that watchdog facilities of this kind. That's the real way to get things done, you know. Forget about corrupting the high-profile executives. They're always being watched and audited. No, the secret is to own the blue-collar grunts and the watchdogs because nobody of consequence is looking at them. It's the same way with some of the financial games we have running—we have our people in the IRS, the SEC, as well as

Wall Street. We own the people who are paid to look for the bad guys."

"That has a familiar ring to it," I said.

His smile turned into a grin.

"I'll bet it does."

"You're the Seven Kings," I said.

His grin kept getting bigger.

Oh fuck.

The Seven Kings were the world's most powerful and elusive organization. They pretended to be an ancient secret society and reinforced that by hijacking the history and urban legends of other secret societies, from the Illuminati to the Neo-Templars. They also pretended to be terrorists, but in truth they used terrorist groups as pawns, funding and supporting them and ultimately aiming them at specific targets. Terror, however, was only a byproduct of their game, and they weren't in it for God or to further a political agenda. They were in it for the money. If you knew exactly when a major terrorist attack was going to happen, you could make an incredible fortune during the flight-to-safety stock market panic that always follows. The Kings were behind 9/11 and the 2009 economic crash. Three of the Kings—Osama Bin Laden, Sebastian Gault, and Hugo Vox—were dead. That left four of them, and any replacements they might have recruited.

"I am a very small cog in the machine that is the Seven Kings," he admitted. "The organization, however, is always growing. And in case you're wondering, we've filled all outstanding vacancies. Killing me won't stop this project, and it won't prevent our clients from receiving the fruits of our research."

"Let's see if that's true after I blow your nutsack off."

He just grinned.

"Okay, Sparky," I said, "so you duped me here with an anonymous phone call. You also put out the stuff about Ryerson?"

"Sure," he agreed. "Mr. Ryerson is one of ours. Very low level, but like I said, that's where the action is." He turned his smile toward Violin. "We were hoping for Interpol or a Recces operative from South Africa. But I don't think that's who you are."

"She's a Jehovah's Witness," I said. "She wants to know if you heard the word of God today."

"Cute."

Violin thought so, too. She laughed. There was a bit of a threat in the laugh, too. And a bit of fear.

"I wasn't clear on something," said the guy, "so let me correct that. When I said that I didn't know who you were, miss, I meant personally. I know which organization you belong to. Arklight has become quite a troublesome little sewing circle. That's why I invited representatives of our newest client to join us."

"Joe...," murmured Violin, and even as she said it I heard a soft scuff behind us. I turned. Door number two stood open, and two Red Knights stood there.

They were also smiling.

Their mouths were filled with jagged teeth. You see teeth like that in monster movies, but in the movies they're fake. They're special effects. That's not the case with the Knights. Those teeth are way too real. Both of the Knights carried weapons that looked like ice axes. Dagger-tipped on one end, hatchet blade on the other.

The Knights looked at me with their rat-red eyes and dismissed me with sneers. The looks they gave Violin were different. Women in general were less than nothing to the Red Knights, which was a viciously patriarchal society. Women were slaves and breeding stock. But Arklight was different. Those women had killed many of the Knights and hunted them around the world with the same ferocity as Nazi hunters after World War II. It was kill on sight on both sides, and I knew that they would go after Violin with every intention of killing her while making the torment last.

The fact that they didn't attack her immediately suggested that they didn't know who she was. If they knew that she was Violin, daughter of Lilith, there would already be blood on the floor.

I jerked my head toward the Knights. "And them? The Seven Kings are recruiting monsters now?"

"Oh, hell," said the scientist, "we've always recruited monsters. I believe you've encountered some in the past."

"So, what's the play?" I asked. "We all know how this ends, so tell me why we're still chatting."

He nodded. "You're right, we do know how it ends. Ideally I live, you die, my clients are satisfied that we know who's looking at us and, more importantly, how they're looking and how they typically respond. So far there have been no surprises. The administrator in me appreciates that, because it allows the Kings to continue working the way we've always been working, knowing that the blunt predictability of the United States government's various law enforcement agencies actually contributes to our success. However, the sociopath in me—and, yes, I admit it; in the Kings that's both a job requirement and pathway to promotion—that part of me is disappointed in how clumsily you've walked into this trap. I thought that the DMS would send someone of greater skill."

I shrugged. "Life sucks sometimes."

He gave a sad nod of agreement. "So true. Anyway, to answer your question, the 'play' is that you get a choice. We want to know exactly how the information we leaked was disseminated internally by your organizations. Who received it, who processed it, who had eyes on it, how and to whom was it shared. That sort of thing. A complete rundown."

"Let me get right on that," I said. "We betray our people and then you kill us. I have to tell you, Sparky, that your sales pitch eats dog turds."

"No, wait, hear me out," said the guy. "That's not the choice I was talking about."

"This should be good," murmured Violin. Behind her the Knights growled like dogs.

"It is," insisted the guy. "There are three possible scenarios. In one scenario—the one I think we can all be happy with—we sit down over coffee and you talk, and that talk will be viewed as part of the application process for joining our organization. In that scenario we're all friends and nobody gets trigger-happy. Nobody dies."

"Very generous," said Violin.

"Isn't it?" the guy said, nodding. "And your safety would be guaranteed. You become part of our team, and believe me, the pay and benefits are spectacular. We take very good care of our people and we reward loyalty. Loyalty to us, I mean. Sure, there's a vetting process and a probation period, but once you prove yourself, you're really part of the family. No threats, none of that. It's how they recruited me. Now I'm on the administrative level. You can be, too."

"Why do I get the feeling that your nose should be growing a foot every time you open your mouth?" I asked.

"I'm dead serious."

"Unfortunate choice of words," said Violin.

"Oops. Yeah, sorry. We really do want you to join, and if you do then you have a real future and a great life. Look at me, look into my eyes. Do I look like I'm lying to you?"

I did, and I think he was genuinely serious. He held a lot of good cards, so there wasn't much reason to lie to us.

"But the alternatives aren't as much fun," he continued. "In scenario two you still tell us everything we want to know, but you make us work for it. Make no mistake, you *will* tell us everything, but the process of encouragement is extreme, and what they bury afterward won't even look like people."

"Not a fan of that one," I said.

"No, of course not," said the guy. "Though my friends from the Red Knights are particularly fond of it."

"We will rip the truth from you," said one of the Knights.

"Shove it up your ass, Count Chocula," I said.

Violin laughed so hard she snorted. Even the guy chortled.

"What's the third scenario?" I asked, even though we all knew what that one would be.

"Gunfight at the O.K. Corral," said the guy.

I took a long breath and let it out slowly. "There's a fourth scenario," I said.

"Oh? Does it involve me suddenly coming to my senses and letting you arrest me?"

"Not exactly. It involves you unburdening your soul to me. You tell us everything you know about the Seven Kings, including the identity of each King, the names of your customers, and the locations of any bases you have."

He goggled at me for a moment, then he burst out laughing. Even his guards looked amused, and until now they'd been stone-faced. I laughed, too. Violin turned to the Knights and gave them a saucy wink.

"That's really funny," said the guy.

"I know, right?" I said.

"It's also the stupidest thing I've ever heard," he said.

"Not entirely."

I cut a look at Violin, and she wore a small, confused frown. She had no idea where I was going with this. I put a bland smile on my face.

"I will go this far," I said. "I'll tell you our names. It might matter in the way this all plays out."

"Please do."

"I'm Captain Joseph Edwin Ledger."

His face went slack for a moment and he lost some color. But he recovered fast and cleared his throat.

"And the, um, young lady?"

The young lady straightened, her chin lifting imperiously. "You can call me Violin, daughter of Lilith, senior field operative of Arklight."

You really could have heard a pin drop. I think I heard the Red Knights grinding their fangs together. The Seven Kings guy's face kept vacillating between horrified shock and the delight of a kid on Christmas morning who thought he was getting socks and underwear and instead discovered a pony with a bow tied around its neck.

"Oh my God," he breathed.

"Yeah. Bit of a jackpot moment," I said.

"This slut is ours," growled one of the Red Knights. "We will use her until she screams for death and then send her eyes to the demon Lilith."

"You are welcome to try," said Violin. "I'll break your teeth out and add them to my collection."

They hissed at her. Actually hissed, like cougars. The sound made the hairs on the back of my neck stand straight out from gooseflesh skin.

Into the ensuing silence, I said, "I'm going to give you two choices, Sparky. In scenario one, you tell your guys to lay down their weapons and you come and have a confessional moment with my boss and me."

He just stared at me as if I'd suggested he pour live scorpions into his tighty-whities.

"Scenario two," I said, "a whole bunch of people die, and you're the first to hit the deck. If you're really, really lucky, you die before I turn you over to my boss."

"You do realize," said the guy, "that there are four laser sights on your chest. Four."

"Sure. And there are three of 'em on your chest."

His smile flickered. I had my gun on him and Violin had her pistol on the closest Knight. "Three? But...."

The guy's voice trailed off as he looked down. My laser sight was rock-steady on his sternum. But two other dots flanked it.

"I don't...," he began, then he raised his eyes and looked at the doorway. The snouts of two rifles protruded only an inch into the chamber. An inch was enough.

"Call it, Boss," said Bunny in my ear.

The Knights whirled and snarled.

"Nine, three, go," I snapped.

The other laser sights shifted and found new targets. There were two *pffts* of silenced rifles and the guards on either side of the guy flew backward as 5.56 × 45 mm NATO rounds exploded their heads.

There was perhaps a single fragment of time when no one moved, when the realities of this new version of the game were painted in the air for everyone to read. Then it all became very fast and messy.

I kicked the guy into the two guards behind him. It was a hard damn kick, and they all staggered backward, but both guards fired at the same time. Wild shots that pinged and whanged all over the place. I dodged and drove forward as bullets burned around me. I felt one round tug my sleeve and another ricochet off the floor and clip my heel.

Behind me, Violin emptied her gun at the Red Knights. One of them slammed into her in a diving tackle that should have crippled her. It would have broken the bones of any ordinary person. But Violin was born in the breeding pits. That meant she was half human and half *Upierczi*. She's stronger, faster, and a hell of a lot more durable than anyone I ever met. She could bench press me. She did it once in bed just to prove she could.

I heard a scream, but I don't think it was hers.

The other Red Knight whirled and tried to find cover from the gunfire that had erupted from the doorway. But Top and Bunny were on their feet, running into the room, taking lots of quick little steps so as not to interfere with their aim. Their aim was superb. Rounds punched into the Knight and tore blood and screams and life from him. The rounds made him judder and dance, and the wall behind him became a splash painting of bright crimson.

I elbowed the Kings guy out of the way, and he rolled into the corner, spitting teeth. The two remaining guards were good. Tough, highly trained. Instead of trying to bring their long-guns to bear in what was becoming the most violent episode of WrestleMania, they tried to hammer me with kicks, catching me on the forehead, the shoulder, and the elbow of the arm I raised to block the barrage. I rammed my pistol up as one kick came at my face and shot the guard through the sole of his foot. The boot and the foot inside of it didn't even slow the nine millimeter round down; it punched through and hit the man on the point of the chin, blowing out the back of his head.

As he slumped, the second guard kicked the pistol out of my hand. I let it go and hurled myself at him, punching my way up his body, hitting him in thigh, groin, stomach, floating ribs, and throat. He managed to smash me in the side of the face with a knee, but I rolled with it and then twisted and bit hard on the inside of his thigh.

His scream hit the ultrasonic, and he twisted so hard I nearly lost my teeth.

I let go, reached up, grabbed his tie, and yanked it as hard as I could, which peeled him off the floor so that he sat up. I threw my weight sideways, spun on my right hip, and kicked him in the face with my left foot. I held onto the tie as I kicked him four more times.

I think two were enough, though. There was no resistance at all after that. He slumped back, his head lolling way too loosely on his slack neck.

I cut a sharp look over my shoulder and saw Violin and the Knight in the last moment of their encounter. The Knight had his axe; Violin's gun was gone, lost in the heat of the fight, but she'd drawn two slender knives from inside her clothes. I'd seen her use those knives twice before. I don't think I've ever seen anything as fast, as horrible, or as combatively balletic. She moved with a kind of athletic grace that I knew I could never possess, dancing around the swings of the axe, flicking out with the blades, seeding the air with rubies that splatted against the floor and wall and ceiling. The Red Knight seemed to disintegrate within the whirlwind of her dance. Before Top and Bunny could cross the room to give her backup, there was no need for any assistance. The Knight crumpled into red madness on the floor. He hadn't looked human before, and now it was hard to tell that he had ever been a living thing.

I caught movement to my left and scrambled to my knees just in time to see the Kings guy make a dive for my pistol. He snatched it up but didn't try to shoot me. He tried to eat the barrel, but I made the long reach and swatted the gun out of his hand. He even tried to fight, but he wasn't a fighter. I only had to dent him a little to quiet him down.

And then it was over.

Gun smoke hung in the air, tinged by red. The air smelled of cordite, copper, and pain.

I got to my feet as Bunny came over to grab and cuff the Kings guy. He patted him down for weapons and to make sure there were no suicide devices planted anywhere. There weren't any, and that was going to seriously suck for him. Life was not going to be much fun from now on.

Top and Bunny were both dressed in full hazmat Hammer suits. Just like me.

"I feel overdressed for this party," said Violin as she cleaned her knives.

"More like we're overdressed. I don't think there's anything here." I waved the BAMS around. Everything was in the green.

The Kings guy said, "There's nothing here. No protocols, no samples. This facility has been thoroughly stripped of everything."

He said it with an attempt at a grin. Bloody teeth spoiled the effect. Top and Bunny each had a hand under an armpit, holding the man on his feet. He was dwarfed by them. I got up in his face.

"This is what's going to happen, Sparky," I said. "You are about to disappear off the face of the earth. We know how long a reach the Kings have, so you're not going to go into the system. No prison, no vacation at Gitmo. The Kings will never find you."

"So what? You think I don't know about 'enhanced interrogation'? I've been conditioned against it. I don't care what you try and do to me, I won't say a fucking word."

Violin said, "Let me have him. Let me take him to Arklight. I'll bet my mother could open him up."

The little guy tried to smile his way through that, tried to construct an expression that said that her threat meant nothing. We all knew different. The Red Knights feared Lilith, and they were fucking vampires.

I sucked my teeth.

"You're not seriously considering this?" demanded the guy.

I turned to Violin.

"On one condition," I said. "You share one hundred percent of what you learn. No holdbacks."

She nodded. "I'll film the interrogations if you want."

"Christ," murmured Bunny.

"No thanks," I said. "A transcript would be fine."

The guy looked from Bunny to Top to me. "You can't do this. I'm an American citizen. Goddamn it, Ledger, I have rights."

"Too bad."

"You *can't* do this."

"Sure I can."

"You're bluffing," he said as tears broke and ran down his face. All throughout history there are stories of what happened to enemy men when they fell into the hands of the women. Women, as a rule, don't start wars, but anyone who thinks they're the weaker and gentler sex is seriously misinformed. "You're just saying this to make me talk."

"We both know you're going to talk, Sparky," I said. "If I give you to Arklight, it shortcuts the process. And it means no blood on American hands. Nice solution."

"You're only saying that...you're playing a game with me."

"Look at me, look into my eyes," I said softly. "Do I look like I'm lying to you?"

Hearing his own words was the trick. I think that's what broke him. That, and the fact that he did take a look into my eyes. A good, deep look.

He began sobbing.

He swore on his life, his mother, his children that he would tell us—and only us—everything. Freely, without coercion. He'd crack the Kings apart for us. He'd tell us where we could find the real lab that was manufacturing the weaponized Ebola. He'd tell us where the Kings' training camps were. Anything we wanted to know, he'd tell us—if we wouldn't turn him over to Violin and the women of Arklight. Tears and snot ran down his face, and he pissed his pants.

I felt a wave of disgust—at him and at myself.

"Okay," I said to Bunny, "take him out of here."

Bunny looked relieved. He was almost gentle as he led the sobbing man away.

When they were gone, I turned to Violin. "You played that well."

She gave me an enigmatic little smile and walked off to begin searching the facility.

It left Top and me standing there surrounded by dead people.

"Nice play, Cap'n," he said. "He really thought you were going to hand him over."

"Yeah."

Top started to go, then paused, glancing back at me. "You...were joking, right? I mean, that was all bullshit. You'd never have let those women have him. You're not that crazy...right?"

I smiled at him.

"Of course not," I lied.

~The End~

Artifact

Chap. 1

I hung upside-down inside the laser network of a bioweapons lab. Tripping the laser would trigger a hard containment, which would effectively turn the small subterranean lab on the picturesque little island in the south Pacific into my tomb.

I wish I could say this was the first time I'd been in this kind of situation.

Wish I could say—with real honesty—that it would be my last.

I was, as we say in the super-spy business, resource light.

All I had was a bug in my ear, a Snellig Model A19 gas dart pistol in a nylon shoulder rig, and the few prayers I still remembered from Sunday school. Sweat ran in vertical lines from chin to hairline, and one fat drop hung pendulously from the tip of my nose. The watch on my wrist told me that there was nineteen minutes left on the mission clock. I needed fifteen of those to do this job.

I needed another twenty to get out.

It wasn't the heat that was making me sweat.

The earbud in my ear buzzed.

"The laser grid is off," said a voice. Male, slightly nasal, young.

I composed myself before I replied. Barking like a cross dog at my support team would probably not yield useful results. So, I said, very calmly, "Actually, Bug, the laser grid is *still* on."

"It's off, Cowboy. All of the systems mark it as in shutdown mode."

The network of red lasers suddenly throbbed. The crosshatch pattern, once comfortably large enough for my body to slip through, abruptly narrowed to a grid with only scant inches to spare on all sides.

"It's on and it's getting cranky."

"What did you do?"

"I didn't *do* anything, Bug. I'm still hanging here like a frigging bat. The floor is thirty feet below me and the laser net is getting smaller. So…really, anything you could do to shut it down would be super. Very much appreciated. Might be a bonus in it for you."

"Um. Okay. Maybe there's a redundancy system…."

"And, Bug…?"

"Yeah, Cowboy?"

"If you don't stop humming the fucking *Mission: Impossible* theme song while you're working…I *will* kill you."

"But…."

"My whole body is a weapon."

"I know…you could kill me more ways than I know how to die, blah, blah, blah."

The laser grid throbbed again.

I knew that the lasers couldn't hurt me. This wasn't a science fiction movie. Passing through them wouldn't result in an arm falling off or my body being neatly diced into bloody cubes. However, they would trigger the alarms; and for the last hour and sixteen minutes I'd been very, very careful not to let that happen.

Bad things would occur if that happened.

Our best intel gave a conservative estimate of sixty security personnel on site, not one of whom was bound by international treaties, human rights agreements, or basic human decency. This place recruited from groups like Blackwater and Blue Diamond Security. The kind of contractors who give mercenaries a bad name.

They would shoot me. A lot.

Bug knew there was no reset button on the mission. It was a matter of getting it right the first time, which made the learning curve more like a straight line.

"Oh, wait," said Bug. "Looks like they have a ghost program hiding the real operations menu. You need to input a set of false commands—which work as a faux password—in order to reach the...."

"Bug...."

"Long story short," he said, "*voila.*"

The laser grid switched off.

I exhaled a breath I think I'd been holding for an hour and dropped the rest of the way down the main venting shaft to the concrete floor sixty yards below.

No alarms went off. No bells, no whistles.

No army of guards storming through the hatch to do bad things to Mama Ledger's firstborn son.

"Down," I said. I unclipped from the drop harness and stood back as the cables whipped up out of sight.

"Lasers are going back on in three, two...."

The burning grid reappeared above me.

"Good job, Bug."

"Sorry for the delay," he said. "These guys are pretty tricky."

"Be trickier."

"Copy that. Sending the floor plan to Karnak."

Karnak was the nickname of the portable MindReader computer tablet strapped to my left forearm. It's a couple of generations snazzier than anything currently on the market, but my boss, Mr. Church, always makes sure his people have the best toys. It's dual hardwired and wireless connected to a whole series of geegaws and doodads built into my combat suit. I had everything in the James Bond catalog, from miniature explosives to a small EDS—explosive detection system—and even a miniature BAMS—bio-aerosol mass spectrometer which sniffed the air for dangerous particles like viruses and bacteria. Dr. Hu, the head of our science division, has told me several times that the collective value of those gadgets was worth ten of me. Considering that the rig I wore had a three million dollar price tag, it was tough to build a convincing counterargument.

One-man army is the idea. Or, in this case, one-man high-tech infiltration team.

The thing that really tickled Hu is that if I happened to be killed during the mission, the suit would continue to transmit useful information. So...the next guy would know what killed me and maybe not get killed himself. And then, when all useful info had been uploaded, small thermal charges built into the fabric would detonate and turn all of the electronics—and the body inside the suit—into so much carbon dust.

Hu thinks that's hilarious.

He and I have not worked up much of a sweat trying to be nice to one another. If he stepped in front of a bullet train and got smeared along half a mile of tracks, I would—believe me—find some way to struggle on with my life. Sadly he doesn't play on the train tracks as much as I'd like.

So, there I was a mile below the April sunshine, wearing my science fiction getup, all alone, looking for something that none of us understood.

This is not an unusual day for me.

Chap. 2

It might be an unusual day for the world, though.

Hence the reason for my being here.

Hence the reason why our best intel suggested that I might not be the only cockroach in the walls. A lot of teams were scrambling around looking for the same thing. Good guys, bad guys, some unaffiliated guys, and maybe some nutjobs guys. Last time there was this much of a scramble was when a set of four, man-portable mininukes went missing from the inventory of former Soviet play toys supposedly under guard in Kazakhstan. I'd been hunting for those, too, but they were scooped up by Colonel Samson Riggs. He's the most senior of the DMS field team leaders. Kind of an action figure demi-superhero. Even has a lantern jaw, crinkles around his piercing blue eyes, and an inflexible moral compass. We all geek out around Colonel Riggs. He's the closest this planet will probably ever get to a real-life Captain America.

Riggs was gone, now, though. Swept away by recent events the way so many other top operatives are who maybe spend one day too long in the path of the storm. Leaving guys like me to take the next job. And the next.

This was the next job.

So far there had been fourteen separate attempts to recover the package.

Those fourteen attempts resulted in sixty-three deaths and over a hundred severe injuries. That butcher's bill is shared pretty evenly by all the teams in this game. There are six DMS agents in the morgue. Five more who will never stand in the line of battle.

And all for something that nobody really understands.

We call it "the package" or "the football" when we're on an open mic.

Between ourselves, off the radio, we call it "that thing" or maybe "that fucking thing."

Its designation in all official documents is simpler.

The artifact.

Just that.

It's as precise a label as is possible to give, at least for now.

Why?

Simple.

No one—no fucking body—knows what it is.

Or what it does.

Or where it came from.

Or who made it.

Or why.

All we know is that twenty-nine days ago a team in Egypt ran the thing through an X-ray machine at what was the Egypt-Japan University of Science and Technology in Alexandria.

Yeah. You read about Alexandria.

The news services said that it was a terrorist device. Some new kind of nuke. The authorities and the U.N. aid teams keep adding more numbers to the count. So far it stands at seven thousand and four. Everyone at the University. Everyone who lived within a two-block radius. Not that the aid workers are counting bodies. There aren't any. All that's there is a big, round hole. Everything—every brick, every pane of glass, every mote of dust, and every person—is simply gone.

Yeah, gone.

And the ball buster is that there is no dust, no blast debris, and no radiation.

There's just a hole in the world where all those people worked, studied, and lived.

All that was left, sitting there at the bottom of the crater, was the artifact.

One meter long. Silver and green. Probably made of metal. Nearly weightless.

Unscratched and untouched.

We saw it on a satellite photo and in photos by helicopters doing flyovers.

The Egyptian government sent in a team.

The artifact was collected.

Then their team was hit by another team. Mercs this time. Multinational badasses. They hit the Egyptians like the wrath of God and wiped it out.

The artifact was taken.

And the games began. The multinational hunt. The accusations. The political pissing contests. The media shit-storm.

Seventeen days later everyone is still yelling. Everyone's pointing fingers. But nobody is really sure who was responsible for the blast. Not that it mattered. Something like that makes a great excuse for settling old debts, starting new fights, and generally proving to the world that you swing a big dick. Even if you don't. If there hadn't been such a price tag on it in terms of human life and suffering it would be funny.

We left funny behind a long way back.

About one millisecond after the team of mercs hit the Egyptians, every police agency and intelligence service in the world was looking for the package. Everyone wanted it. Even though nobody understood what it was, everyone wanted it.

The official stance—the one they gave to budget committees— was that the device was clearly some kind of renewable energy source. A super battery. Something like that. Analysis of the blast suggested that the X-ray machine triggered some kind of energetic discharge. What kind was unknown and, for the purposes of the budget discussions, irrelevant. The thing blew the Egypt-Japan University of Science and Technology off the world and didn't destroy itself in the process.

If there was even the slightest chance the process could be duplicated, then it *had* to be obtained. Had to. No question.

That was real power.

That was world-changing power.

For two really big reasons.

The first was obvious. Any energetic discharge, once studied, could be quantified and captured. You just need to build a battery capable of absorbing and storing the charge. Conservative estimates by guys like Dr. Hu tell me that such a storage battery would be, give or take a few square feet, the size of Detroit. There were already physicists and engineers working out how to relay that captured energy into a new power grid that could, if the explosion could be endlessly repeated under controlled circumstances, power... everything.

Everything that needed power.

People have killed each other over a gallon of gas.

What would they do to obtain perfect, endlessly renewable, and absolutely clean energy?

Yeah. They'd kill a lot of people. They'd wipe whole countries off the map. Don't believe it? Go read a book about the history of the Middle East oil wars.

Then there was the second reason teams were scrambled from six of the seven continents.

Something like that was the world's only perfect weapon.

Who would dare go to war with anyone who owned and could deploy such a weapon?

For seven and a half days no one knew where it was. Everyone held their breath. The U.S. military went to its highest state of alert and parked itself there. Everyone else did, too. We all expected something important to go *boom.* Like New York City. Or Washington D.C.

When that didn't happen no one breathed any sighs of relief.

It meant that someone was keeping it. Studying it. Getting to *know* it.

That is very, very scary.

Sure as hell scared me.

Scared my boss, Mr. Church, too, and he does not spook easily.

Halfway through the eighth day there was a mass slaughter at a research facility in Turkey. Less than a day later a Russian freighter was attacked with a total loss of life.

And on and on.

Now it was twenty-nine days later and a shaky network of spies, paid informants and traitors provided enough reliable intel to have me sliding down a wire into a deep, deep hole in North Korea.

If the artifact was here, then any action I took could be justified because even his allies know that Kim Jong-un is a fucking psycho.

Basically you don't let your idiot nephew play with hand grenades. Not when the rest of the family is in the potential blast radius.

On the other hand, if the North Koreans *didn't* have it, then I was committing an act of war and espionage. Being shot would be the very least—and probably best—I could expect.

Which is why I had no I.D. on me. Nothing I wore or carried could be traced to an American manufacturer. My fingerprints and DNA have been erased from all searchable databases. Ditto for my photos. I didn't exist. I was a ghost.

A ghost can't be used as a lever against the American government.

I even had a suicide pill in a molar in case the North Koreans captured me and proved how creative they were in their domestic version of enhanced interrogation. I tried not to think about how far I'd let things go before I decided that was a good option.

I ran down a featureless concrete tunnel that was badly lit with small bulbs in wire cages. All alone. Too much risk and too little mission confidence to send in the whole team.

Just me.

Alone.

Racing the clock.

Scared out of my mind.

Hurrying as fast as I could into the unknown.

My life kind of sucks.

Chap. 3

"I'm losing your signal," Bug said. "Some kind of interference from...."

That was all he said. After that all I had in my ear was a dead piece of plastic.

I looked at Karnak.

The small HD screen still showed a floor plan, which was good. But it wasn't updating, which was bad. The data it showed was what Bug had sent me when I'd detached from the spider cable. We had an eye-in-the-sky using ground-penetrating radar to build a map, but that was a slow process, and suddenly I was behind the curve. The corridor ran for forty more yards past blank walls and ended at a big red steel door. Shiny and imposing, with a single keycard device mounted on the wall beside it. Knowing what was on the other side of that steel door was the whole point of the satellite. Pretty much no chance it was a broom closet. Before I tried to bypass the security I'd like to know that it was my target. Intel suggested that it was, but a suggestion was all it was. That's a long, long way from certain knowledge or even high confidence.

"Balls," I said, though I said it quietly.

Our timetable was based on the fact that two things were about to happen at the same time. A motorcade of official cars and trucks was headed here. We'd tracked it all the way from the Strategic Rocket Forces divisional headquarters in Kusŏng. Infrared on the satellites counted eighty men.

The second problem was a two-truck miniconvoy coming in hot and fast from the east. Six men and a driver in each truck. We almost didn't spot them because their trucks were shielded with the latest in stealth tech—radar-repelling scales that contained thousands of tiny cameras and screens so that it took real-time images from its surroundings and painted them all over its shell. You could look at it and look right through it. Only a focused thermal scan can peek inside, but it has to be a tight beam. We were able to do that because of the one flaw in that kind of technology—human eyes. One of our spotters saw the thing roll past. Video camouflage works great at a distance. Up close, not so much, which is why it's mostly used on planes or ships. The science is cutting edge but it's not Harry Potter's cloak of invisibility. Not yet, anyway.

If I wasn't out of here real damn fast I was going to get caught between three hostile forces—the guards here, the incoming military convoy, and whoever was in those two trucks. I did not think this was going to be a matter of embarrassed smiles, handshakes, and a trip to the local bar for a couple of beers.

I'd wasted too much time with the laser grid, and now I could feel each wasted second being carved off of my skin.

I quickly knelt by the door and fished several devices from my pockets. The first was a signal counter, which is a nifty piece of intrusion technology that essentially hacked into the command programs of something like—say—a keycard scanner. It's proprietary MindReader tech, so it used the supercomputer's software to ninja its way in and rewrite the target software so that it believed the new programs were part of its normal operating system. In the right hands, it's saved millions, possibly billions, of lives by helping the Department of Military Sciences stop the world's most dangerous terrorists. If it ever fell into the wrong hands, MindReader and her children could become as devastating a weapon as the device I was here to steal.

Which is why each of the devices I carried had a self-destruct subroutine. If I died, they blew up. If they were too far away from me for too long, they blew up. If Bug, Dr. Hu or Mr. Church hit the right button, they blew up.

Such a comfort to know that all the devices hanging from my belt near all my own proprietary materials were poised to go boom.

I placed the device on the side of the keycard housing and pressed a button. A little red light flickered, flickered, and then turned green. I plugged a USB cable into it and attached the other end to a second device I had, which was flat gray and the size of a deck of playing cards. After too many seconds, a green light appeared on it as well, and a slim plastic card slid from one end.

I removed it, took a breath, and swiped it through the keycard slot.

And prayed.

Nothing happened.

My balls tried to climb up inside my body.

I swiped it again.

Nothing.

"Shit," I said.

And tried one more time.

Slower.

There was a faint *click*, and then the big red door shifted inward by almost an inch.

I let out the air that was going stale in my chest. My balls stayed where they were. They didn't trust happy endings.

When I bent my ear close to the doorframe, all I could hear was machine noise. A faint hum and something else that went *ka-chug, ka-chug*. Could have been anything from a centrifuge refining plutonium to a Kenmore dishwasher. I don't know and didn't much care. All I wanted was the package.

No voices, though. That was key.

I nudged the door so that it swung inward, slowly and only slightly. Light spilled out. Fluorescent. Bright. The machine sounds intensified.

No one shouted. No voice spoke at all.

I pushed the door open enough to let me take a look inside. Not one of those dart-in, dart-out looks you use in combat situations. When there's no action, the speed of that kind of movement was noticeable in an otherwise still room. I moved slowly and tried not to embrace any expectations of what I'd see. Expectations can slow you, and if this got weird, even losing a half step could get me killed.

The room was large and, as far as I could see, empty.

I held another breath as I stepped inside.

The ceiling soared upward into shadows at least fifty yards above me. Banks of fluorescent lights hung down on long cables. Bright light gleamed on the surfaces and screens and display panels of rank after rank of machines. Computers of some kind, though what they were being used for or why they were even here was unknown. I've seen a lot of industrial computer setups and there had to be eighty, ninety million dollars' worth of stuff here. Then I spotted a glass wall beyond which were rows upon rows of modern mainframe supercomputers, and I rounded my estimate up to a quarter billion dollars. The floor was polished to mirror brightness.

I tapped my earbud hoping to get Bug back on the line.

Nothing.

I faded to the closest wall and ghosted along it, taking a lot of small, quick steps. There was a second door at the far end of the big room. If any of my intel was reliable, the artifact had to be in there, or near there.

Fifty feet to go, and I was already reaching for another of the bypass doohickeys when a man stepped from between two rows of computers. A security guard. Young, maybe twenty-two. With a gun.

He stared at me.

I stared at him.

His eyes bugged, and he opened his mouth to let out a scream of warning.

Chap. 4

There are times in combat when you have options. You can take someone prisoner. You can use some hand-to-hand stuff and subdue him, leave him bound and gagged. Or you overpower him and juice him with some animal tranquilizers.

Those are options that let the moment become an anecdote for both of you, to allow it to be a story—however painful or embarrassing—to tell later on. Maybe over beers with your buddies, maybe at your court martial, maybe to your wife as she holds you to her breast in the dark of night.

Those are moments when mercy and a regard for human life are allowable elements in the equation. They're moments when even if blood is spilled, it's merely a price to be paid. A small price. No one dies. The price doesn't pay the ferryman's fee.

This wasn't one of those moments.

This was the kind of moment when there is no allowance for human life, for compassion, for choice.

The guard opened his mouth to scream and I killed him.

That's the only way the moment could end because there wasn't time for anything else. If he screamed, I'd die. If he screamed, the artifact would slip beyond the reach of people who wanted it stored and studied rather than used.

So he had to die. This young man. This peasant-soldier working for people who had no regard at all for his life.

Nor, in that terrible moment, did I.

As his mouth opened I moved into him, intruding inside his personal envelope of mental and physical safety. My left hand cupped the back of his neck, and I struck him under the Adam's apple with the open Y of the space between thumb and index finger. The blow slammed the side of the primary knuckle of the index finger against the eggshell-fragile hyoid bone. He stopped breathing. His face instantly turned a violent red and seemed to expand as he tried to drag air in through an impossible route. I swung him around, turning him so that his panicked face was pointed to the ceiling as I dropped to my right knee and broke his back over my left.

It all took one second.

One bad second that changed his world and broke a hole in the lives of everyone he knew and everyone who loved him, and slammed the door on every experience he would ever have. Bang. That fast.

And it chipped off a big piece of my soul.

I knew, with absolute certainty, that I would see his young face watching me from the shadows of my deathbed when it was finally my time to go. He would be waiting for me, along with too many others whose lives had ended because of the necessities of my job.

Yeah, I'm a good guy. Tell anyone.

Fuck.

Chap. 5

Tick-tock.

I laid him down on the floor and moved on.

Grief and regrets are for after the war.

I raced to the far end of the chamber, pulled the keycard scanner, reprogrammed my master key, and slid it through the slot.

It went green on the first try.

No, I wasn't going to suddenly start believing in good luck.

The door opened.

I stepped through.

The room was a lot smaller. Maybe twenty by twenty.

There was a big steel table in the exact middle of the room. A whole lot of weird-looking equipment was grouped around the table. Scanners and other stuff that looked like they came from a Star Trek movie were arranged to point at the thing under a glass dome on the table.

The artifact.

Right there. Closer than I could have hoped. Not hidden beyond an airlock, not wired up to fifty kinds of alarms.

I could have taken four paces and touched it.

Except.

The whole damn room was filled with people.

Three little guys in white lab coats. Not a problem.

Six bigger guys in uniforms.

Problem.

Chap. 6

We all went for our guns at the same time.

I was already totally wired, so I was maybe one heartbeat faster than the others.

The Snellig gas pistol fires tiny, thin-walled glass darts filled with a fast-acting nonlethal nerve agent. A new synthetic version of tetrodotoxin. Granted you fall down and shit your pants, but you do not die, so put it in the win column.

I was firing as I moved, rushing to put one of the lab coat guys between me and the guards, hoping they wouldn't want to risk shooting them. That bought me another heartbeat.

Two of the guards spun away, their eyes rolling high and white within a microsecond of the darts bursting on their skin. They went down hard. One of them collapsed against a third guard, dragging him down, too. The other three clawed at their side arms. I shoved my human shield against one, fired over the scientist's shoulder and took another guard in the cheek. He dropped and I closed on the one soldier left standing and pistol-whipped him across the chops. Teeth flew and he spun around so hard I thought he was going to screw himself into the floor.

Four guards down.

I pivoted toward the one who'd been accidentally dragged down and kicked him in the face. Twice. Real damn hard.

That left the one who was trying to push away the scientist I'd shoved at him. I shot the scientist in the back and when he crumpled I shot the sixth guard.

It was all over in the space of those salvaged heartbeats.

Bang, bang, bang.

That left me standing with the gun in my hand and them with their dicks in theirs. Metaphorically speaking.

They spent a couple of seconds being shocked, which is fine. I wanted them to fully appreciate the situation.

But all I could spare was a couple of seconds.

Then I said—in reasonably passable Korean, "Give me the device."

The two scientists looked blankly at me. Shock or training or good poker faces, it was all the same to me.

I pointed the gun at the closest guy's face.

"Now."

In this situation, you think they'd say, fuck it, we lost. All their security guys on the floor, snoring and shitting their pants. Them looking like book nerds. Me looking like the big hulking thug I am. Gun looking like a gun. You think this would be easy math. A no-win situation so clear that it was almost no-fault. They couldn't be expected to do anything here but acquiesce and hand it over.

That's what you'd think.

That was what logic and sanity dictated in no uncertain terms.

It didn't play out that way, and I knew it when one of them smiled at me.

This was not a smiling situation. Not even for me, and I had the gun.

The guy farthest from me—he was a half-step behind the other scientist—smiled. A small, ugly little smile.

Then he shoved his buddy right at me. It was so damn quick that it caught us both off guard. The closer man fell right against me, and I shot him more by reflex than intention. But his body was already falling, and it was a crowded room with bodies on the floor.

We both went down in a tangle.

Even little guys are a bastard when it comes to dead weight, and the dart made him totally slack.

I fell with him on top of me.

The other guy hit two buttons. One popped the glass dome over the artifact, which he scooped up and tucked under his arm, like a wide receiver.

The other was the central alarm button.

Fuck.

Klaxons began blaring with an ear-crushing loudness. Red lights slid out from slots in the walls and flashed with hysterical pulses. If I'd had epilepsy this would have triggered a fit.

I heard the hiss of a hydraulic door, and just as I shoved the unconscious scientist off of me I saw the other guy vanish through the doorway. The door began to slide shut.

I flung the guy off of me and shot to my feet, ran over several bodies—stepping on chests and faces and crotches as I fought to beat the close of that door. I leapt through a gap that didn't look anywhere near big enough, tucked to make sure I didn't lose a foot, hit the ground in a roll, felt the jolt as the concrete floor found every goddamn exposed piece of bone in my body, came up onto my feet, and pelted after the scientist. He was heading for another security door at the other end, faster than I ever saw Calvin Johnson run when there was nothing on the clock and the entire defensive squad on his ass.

He was already halfway down the hall when I capped off three rounds. Two hit the flaps of his lab coat and burst harmlessly. The third grazed him. He jerked sideways but didn't go down. Must have grazed him.

I fired again and got nothing. The magazine was out.

I dropped it, fished for a spare, slapped it in place, and emptied the whole thing as I tore up the hallway. The Snellig has a twelve-shot capacity. I think I hit him with number eleven, because he dropped and my last shot passed right over his head.

The artifact dropped, too.

It hit the ground and bounced.

I think my heart stopped.

It landed and rolled awkwardly against the wall while I skidded to a stop. Until now it had been a lumpy chunk of silver metal with no discernable seams or openings, no lights, no switches or dials. In every photo I've seen of it, the device looked like it had been molded rather than assembled.

Now it looked different.

Now it had lights.

When it hit the floor something happened to it.

As I bent over it a series of small green lights suddenly flicked on all along its sides.

The lights were intensely bright; the colors more striking than LED Christmas lights.

I hesitated before touching it.

I mean…of *course* I did. Who wouldn't?

After all, no one knows where this thing is from.

And right there I swear to God I heard a voice say, "Don't touch it."

I whirled, reaching for my last magazine, swapping out the old one with the speed borne of constant practice. But I brought the gun up and pointed it at nothing.

The hallway was empty except for the scientist who'd dropped the package. The room on the other side of the closed door was filled with his colleagues and their guards, and everyone was sleeping.

The alarms blared and the red lights flashed, but there was no one around to speak those words.

The voice repeated the warning.

"Don't touch it."

Here's the thing. The voice I heard sounded like my own.

Chap. 7

Granted, I make no claims about being sane. Or even in the same zip code as sane. On my best day I have three different people living inside my head. The Civilized Man—who is the innocent and optimistic part of me. The one who wasn't destroyed during the childhood trauma that otherwise turned me into a psychological basket of hamsters. Then there's the Killer, that rough, crude, dangerous part of my mind, always looking to take it to the bad guys in very ugly ways. And there was the Cop, the closest thing I have to a sane and sober central self.

Each of them spoke in a particular voice inside my thoughts.

This wasn't any of those voices.

The voice I heard was the one I use in normal conversation.

My regular voice.

Clear as day.

I spun around, bringing the gun up in a two-hand grip. There was an empty hall in front of me, and an empty hall behind me. Just the sleeping scientist on the floor. Red flashing lights on the walls. Nothing else.

No one else.

That voice, though…it had been real.

There's nothing in the playbook on how to react to that kind of situation. I didn't feel like I'd suddenly gone crazier than I already was. There was no way on earth the North Koreans had somehow sampled my voice and rigged a playback just to screw with me. It was too improbable and there was no point. So, that wasn't it.

The voice, though.

I *had* heard it.

I switched the gun to one hand and slowly knelt beside the artifact. The little green lights were pulsing now. Steady. Like a heartbeat.

I swallowed what felt like a throatful of dust.

"Fuck it," I said, and gently scooped up the object.

It weighed almost nothing. It felt like metal, but there was no heft to it at all. Lighter than aluminum or magnesium. Lighter than Styrofoam. I had to press my fingers against its planes and angles to assure myself that it was actually there.

That alone is strange. If this was some new alloy, then someone had broken through the ceiling of superlight design. If it was durable—and given the thing's history I had to believe it was—then that alone would be worth billions to the aeronautics industry. Durable superlight materials are the dream, the holy grail of metallurgy. If it could be studied and reproduced, it would totally revolutionize military aircraft. Maybe space travel as well.

And yet that was, as far as my team was concerned, a secondary benefit. An unknown benefit. It added another element of mystery to this thing. Science, as it's known by the teams working with the Department of Military Sciences—including the *über*-geeks at DARPA—couldn't do this. The energy discharge alone was freakish. Now this.

The artifact was warm to the touch.

Creepy warm.

Not warm like metal.

Touching it was like touching flesh. If I closed my eyes, that's what it would have been like. Skin, at normal body temperature.

Not metal.

"Jesus," I said, and I wished I could have dropped it right there and then. I wanted to. It was repulsive.

"Do it," said the voice. My voice. "Drop it and get out."

I whirled around again.

The hall was still empty.

"Fuck me," I told the emptiness.

The clock was ticking. I needed to be at the extraction point in ten minutes.

So I clutched the package to me, and I ran.

The corridors fed one into the other. I ran up flights of stairs. I ran down. I burned seconds I could spare bypassing locks on security doors.

Twice I encountered security personnel.

Twice I put them down before they could get off a shot.

After I dropped the last one, I passed through another door that took me out of the lab complex and into what was clearly an administrative wing. There were vault-style doors on that level, and the place was entirely deserted. Not sure if it was because of the hour—local time here was three in the morning—or because of the alarms. North Korean military protocols sent workers into secure bunkers during emergencies. I'd passed several locked chambers. Any staff working this late was probably squirrelled away in there. Good. Better for everyone concerned. Besides, I was down to three rounds in the Snellig. If I met any real resistance I'd have to switch to something lethal. I'd already killed one poor dumb son of a bitch; I didn't want to compound my crimes.

I hurried through the offices. At most of the desks, the chairs were neatly snugged into the footwells, computers were off or on screensaver, and the desk lamps were dark. A few were less tidy; those probably belonged to the workers hiding in the bunkers.

There were no security guards in this wing. That concerned me. Not that I wanted to meet any, but it seemed odd.

Everything, in fact, seemed odd.

Then I rounded a corner and found something even odder.

Three uniformed guards lay sprawled on the floor.

There was no blood. No marks of violence.

For all the world, they appeared to be…*sleeping*.

I think I actually said, "What the fuck?"

Beneath my arm the artifact throbbed.

Actually throbbed. It was a feeling of heat that pulsed so quickly and abated so immediately that the effect was like the device had expanded and contracted. Like something taking a breath.

I almost flung the thing away from me.

Instead I held it out at arm's length—despite its size I could easily hold it with one hand, it was that light—and looked at it.

Metal. Green lights.

Same as before.

But not exactly the same.

That pulse or throb or whatever it was….I didn't like it.

No, sir. Not one bit.

It felt wrong.

Like the surface temperature and texture of it was wrong. I was reacting to it as if it was not a machine at all. It felt to me like something….

The word is *alive*, but I can't really use it because that's stupid.

It's metal. It can't *be* alive.

The thing pulsed again.

The green lights went from a neutral intensity on a par with traffic "go" lights, to a glare that, for a split second, was eye-hurtingly intense. I winced and cried out and....

And, yes, I dropped the thing.

Or, maybe I flung it away.

Hard to say.

Hard to actually think about.

The artifact hit the ground and rolled bumpity-bumpity across the floor.

And stopped when someone placed the sole of his foot against it.

Someone who, I swear to God, was not there a moment ago.

Chap. 8

The man was dressed all in black.

All.

Head to toe. Black pants and pullover. Black socks and shoes. Black gloves. A black balaclava and black goggles. I couldn't see a single square inch of his skin. He could have been white, Asian or, yeah, black.

He was big, though. About my height. Not as bulky in the arms and chest, but close enough.

And he was just there.

Standing where he shouldn't have been standing, within arm's reach, and I hadn't seen or heard him approach.

So, fuck it, I shot him. Point-blank.

In the script in my head that I was writing for this scene, he should have folded up like a deck chair and that should have been that.

That wasn't how it played out.

I fired the dart gun, and he moved out of the line of fire.

It was weird. He was fast but not the Flash. It wasn't like he dodged a bullet, so to speak. He wasn't that fast. No, it was like he had such perfect timing that as I fired he was already moving—as if knowing exactly the timing and angle of my shot.

Then he pivoted and slapped the gun out of my hand.

There's a way to do that if you know what you're doing. You hit the gun at one angle and the back of the wrist at another. Do it fast and simultaneously, and the gun goes flying.

My gun went flying.

I have been disarmed exactly once in my adult life.

That time.

If anyone had wanted to wager on whether someone could do that to me, I'd have bet my whole pension on that answer being "no."

My gun went flying anyway.

I wasted no time goggling at it.

I kicked him in the knee.

Which he blocked with a raised-leg hoof kick.

I hooked a left at his short ribs, but he chop-blocked with his elbow and counterpunched me in the biceps, numbing my arm. Growling in pain and anger, I faked once, twice, and hit him with a jab in the nose.

Except that he turned his head two inches to the left so that my jab hit the point of his cheekbone.

Then he switched from defense to offense, throwing a series of punches and kicks at me that hammered me all the way across the hall and against the wall. He blocked every one of my counterpunches, parried every kick, even intruded into my attempted head-butt by head-butting me.

It was all very fast and very painful.

I won't lie and I won't sugarcoat it. He beat the shit out of me.

He humiliated me.

I didn't land a single solid punch on him, and he hit me as often as he wanted to, and it was pretty clear that he really wanted to.

Winded, bleeding, bruised and dazed, I sagged against the wall.

I tried to win that fight.

I've never really lost a fight. Not in years. Not any fight that's ever mattered to me. No matter how tough the other guy was, I was tougher. Or, if he was too tough then I won because I was crazier. I don't care if I get hurt, but I will win a fight. I'll burn down a house if that's what it takes to win a fight.

Except that I lost this fight.

Lost it fast, and lost it completely.

This man, whoever he was, outfought me.

I am a special operator. I'm a senior martial artist. I'm a warrior and I'm a killer, and he simply took me apart.

He even used some of my own favorite moves, some of the things I tried to use on him. He used them faster and he used them better and I went down.

On my knees, blood dripping from my mashed lips, I tried to change the game on him. I snagged the rapid-release folding knife from its little spring clip inside my trouser pocket. It came into my hand and with a flick I locked the three-point-seven-five-inch blade into place and I lunged in and up and tried to castrate the fucker.

He twisted away. I heard cloth rip. I saw droplets of blood seed the air, but he moved so fast that all I did was slash him. I could tell from the resistance that the blade hadn't gone deep enough to cut muscle or tendon. Only trousers and skin.

The blood was red.

The skin that showed through the torn fabric was white.

Not the light brown skin of an Asian. This guy was Caucasian.

He twisted and hit the side of my hand with a one-knuckle punch that turned my entire hand into a useless bag of pain. The knife clattered to the floor. He bent, scooped it up, and suddenly I was pressed back against the wall with the wicked edge pressed against the flesh of my throat. He held the knife the way an expert does when he wants you to know that you're not going to take that blade away from him. Not in this lifetime.

I was done.

I was cooked.

Beaten, bloodied, and disarmed.

With a knife to my throat and his fingers knotted in my hair to hold me still.

Then he bent close and spoke with quiet urgency into my ear.

"Believe me when I tell you that neither of us wants you dead," he said.

I froze. I didn't dare move a muscle.

"I need you to listen to me, and I need you to understand. You can't ask any questions. The best and *only* thing you can do is to listen and tell me you understand and agree."

He pressed the knife more firmly against my throat to emphasize his point. A drop of warm blood ran down alongside my Adam's apple.

"You listening, sport?"

"Y-yes...."

"Good, 'cause I'm only going to say this once." He was leaning so close that even through his mask I could feel the heat of his breath on my ear. "You don't know what this device is. None of you do. You can't know and, believe me, you shouldn't. You don't want to."

"Pretty fucking sure we *do*," I growled.

He made a sound. Might have been a laugh. "No, you really don't."

"Who are you?"

For a moment I thought he was going to move the knife away. Or cut my throat. His hand trembled.

"Let me ask you a question, chief," he said. "And you give me a straight answer. No bullshit. Can you do that?"

I said nothing. Wasn't really feeling all that chatty.

He took it as assent, regardless. "What do you think they're going to do with the device? I'm not talking about the North Koreans. What do you think *we're* going to do with it?"

I said nothing.

"Do you honestly and without reservation believe that once the U.S. government gets their hands on it that they'll hide it away and never use it? Do you think that if they *did* use it, they'd only concentrate on its potential for unlimited power? Do you think they can resist the temptation to study its potential as a weapon?"

I said nothing.

"You have good intentions, Joe," he said. I didn't ask him how he knew my name. I was pretty sure I didn't want to know that answer. "But sometimes you're naïve. You're too trusting. You think everyone has the same altruism as Mr. Church. You think that you can keep this thing from ever falling into the wrong hands. Tell me that's not true. Tell me I'm lying."

I still said nothing. My heart was hammering in my chest.

He sighed.

"I'm going to take the device out of play," he said. "Nobody gets it. Not our people, not theirs. Nobody."

"Bullshit," I said finally.

"No," he replied, "no bullshit. I know where it came from. I know what it is. And I know what will absolutely happen if anyone—*anyone*—fucks with it. And they will. You know it, sport.

They'll fuck with it and fuck around with it and then it'll all go to hell."

"You can't know that."

"No," he said, "*you* can't. I can. I do." He paused, and there was a strange quality in his voice. A kind of sadness that runs all the way down to the cellar of the soul. "I've seen it. That's why I can't let you take it."

He took the knife away, gave me a hip-check that knocked me sideways, and stepped backward out of reach before I could recover my balance. The device lay pulsing on the floor between us. Closer to him than to me.

Slowly, carefully, he knelt and scooped it up with the hand not holding the knife.

"Who are you?" I demanded. "Who are you working for?"

He hesitated, studying me, then dropped the knife on the floor and pulled the goggles off. He dropped them onto the floor next to the knife. The he pulled the balaclava over his head and dropped that as well.

I stared at him. The hinges of the world seemed to snap and crack off and for a moment the whole room seemed to tilt.

I know that face.

I knew those blue eyes and the scuffle of blond hair. I knew that crooked nose and the scars. Some of the scars. There were more of them than when I'd seen that face last.

More than there had been when I looked into the shaving mirror that morning.

I said, "I don't...."

It was all that would come out.

The face was older than mine. Harder, sadder, with deeper lines and more evidence of damage.

But it was my face.

He looked down at me with my own eyes.

There was such a look of deep hurt and enduring pain in those eyes.

"I'm taking it with me," he said. "Once I'm gone you'll have six minutes to get out. You'll need four and a half."

He smiled then.

There was no joy in it.

Not for him.

Not for me.

He turned and walked away. Within a few steps he was running. He rounded a corner and was gone.

I knew, with absolute certainty but with no understanding of why I knew it, that if I ran to that corner and looked around it, he wouldn't be there.

There was a brief squelch in my ear and then Bug's voice. "…To Cowboy, do you copy?"

I tapped my earbud but I had to suck some spit into my mouth and swallow it before I could trust myself to talk.

"Cowboy here."

"Thank god! We were having kittens and—"

"Shut up, Bug. How do I get out?"

"Do you have the package?"

I hesitated, trying to construct a reply that would make sense. "Mission accomplished," I said. Or something like that, I don't really remember.

He gave me the route.

I ran it.

I got out.

Chap. 9

They grilled me for days about it.

Days.

No sleep. No easing up.

My boss, Mr. Church. Dr. Rudy Sanchez. Aunt Sallie. Others.

They asked me hundreds of questions. Or, maybe it was the same few questions hundreds of times. It blurred together after a while.

They hooked me to a polygraph.

Someone—it might have been Dr. Hu—slipped me a Pentothal cocktail and grilled me through the haze.

They kept asking the same questions.

And I gave them the same story every single fucking time.

After a while they stopped asking.

They let me sleep.

Eventually they even let me go home.

Tomorrow the interviews or interrogations may start up again. I'm not sure. All I know for certain is that the artifact is gone. No one has seen it. I suspect no one ever will.

Where has it gone?

I have no idea.

I really don't.

What happened in the lab remains the biggest mystery of my life, and that is saying a whole lot.

I know what I saw. I know what I heard.

It's just that I am absolutely certain, without any margin for error, that I will never understand it.

Not, at least, until I'm older.

As *he* had been.

Older.

Sadder.

Stranger.

I don't believe in time travel, and I'm not sure I buy any bullshit about parallel dimensions. But, how else do I explain it? What else makes sense?

Nothing

Not a goddamn thing.

But...the device is gone.

Nobody has the weapon.

So...yeah...there's that.

~The End~

The Handyman Gets Out

Chap. 1

So, there I was.

Buck naked.

Duct-taped to a chair.

Couple of hard-cases with no-mercy eyes and a bag of tools. Big generator on a hand truck. Wires with clamps.

You get the picture.

There's shit creek, and there's me way the hell up it without a paddle.

I hate my job.

Chap. 2

Roll it back a few hours and I was fully clothed—an Orioles home-game shirt over jeans and flip-flops. Wayfarers up on my hair, cup of Starbucks cradled between my palms. Tickets for that evening's game against Philly. I had a Franklin on the game, and the oddsmakers were telling me I was going to see Philly go home in tears.

Life was a proverbial peach.

I'd come into the Warehouse to clean up a few things in my office. Some after-action reports I had to sign-off on. Equipment requisitions. Like that. Nothing important. For once the whole world seemed to be taking five, sitting one out. I'd taken Junie out dancing last night and, though I'm not exactly going to get my own reality show, *Dancing with Special Ops*, I didn't disgrace myself, break Junie's toes, or reinforce the stereotype that white boys from Baltimore cannot dance.

Even my dog, Ghost, was off the clock. Junie messaged me a selfie of herself in an electric blue string bikini with Ghost standing guard in case anyone who wasn't me got too friendly. They were at Ocean Beach with Circe O'Tree, Lydia Ruiz, and the new gal on Echo Team, Montana. Girls' day out. No testosterone allowed. Except of the canine variety.

At this point all I had to do was turn off my laptop and walk out of the building, ideally dropping my cell phone in a trash can in the parking lot. Sunny skies, baseball, way too much beer. Only a bloody fool who doesn't understand the way the universe works would even *think* about saying, "What could go wrong?"

I swear that thought didn't go through my head.

So, I turned off my laptop, got up, switched off the office lights, and reached for the doorknob.

Which is when my cell rang.

I don't have different ringtones for each person I know. I'm not thirteen. However I swear to God I can tell when a call is coming in from my boss, Mr. Church. Maybe I'm psychic. Maybe there's a tremor in the Force. Not sure. But I knew it was him before I even looked at the screen display.

Did I consider letting it ring through to voicemail?

Sure. Every time he calls.

Did I do that?

No.

I don't have that luxury. I can't.

Besides, Church isn't the kind to make social calls or to chat about last night's episode of *Game of Thrones.* Not much for the small talk.

And I knew for certain that he knew I was taking the afternoon off.

On the other hand, as I dug my phone out of my jeans I cursed him, his entire family to the seventh generation, his DNA, and his houseplants.

I punched the button and said, "Do I even want to know?"

"Probably not."

I sighed.

"Tell me anyway."

Chap. 3

He told me.

"Myron Bishop wants to come in."

I said, "Holy shit."

Chap. 4

Half an hour later I was pulling into a parking slot at Mercury Tower in Baltimore. Still in jeans and flip-flops. This was a pickup, not a combat mission. Had my piece, though, 'cause I'm not an idiot. Beretta 92f snugged into a clamshell shoulder holster under the Orioles shirt, and a rapid-release folding knife clipped to the inside of my right pants pocket.

The tower was forty-one stories, built during the let's-cover-everything-in-glass phase of the eighties and early nineties, so it was basically a featureless oblong that was a sun-glare hazard for miles. Lots of security. They had to buzz me into the lobby, then made me stand for five minutes at the desk. I can charm my way past most receptionists, but this one looked like they stuffed Clint Eastwood into a wool suit and wig. She was maybe six hundred years old. None of them good years.

She scowled at me like I was something the dog rolled in and demanded to see my I.D. I fished out a set that said I was "Jeffrey Book, Feng Shui Consultant." I batted my lashes at her and said that Mr. Bishop was thinking about redesigning his office and I was here to help him balance the energies to encourage a synergistic flow.

The receptionist—who had the improbable name of Mrs. Daisy—gave me a look that I was sure could cause some kind of liver damage. She called Mr. Bishop and looked pained when she found out I was expected. Her nails, as long and dark as a wicked witch's should be, tapped some keys, and a temporary I.D. came out of the printer. As I peeled off the back and pasted it to my shirt, two large security types came and flanked me.

I let Frick and Frack escort me to the elevator. They pushed all the buttons. They rode with me to the thirty-ninth floor. They didn't say a word.

Fine with me. Chris Tillman would be throwing the first pitch and the crowd at Oriole Park at Camden Yards would be yelling instead of me. I wasn't feeling chatty.

As we soared upward I thought about Myron Bishop.

He was, by everyone's estimation, a very bad man.

Brilliant, sure. Borderline supergenius, with more biotech patents on file than I've had hot dinners. His company, Accelerator Biologics, was at the absolutely bleeding edge of performance-enhancement science. And we're not talking about a new kind of Viagra. Bishop and his mad scientists were building better soldiers and better athletes. No human growth hormones or anabolic steroids. Nothing that crude. He was using transgenic science to rebuild the DNA so the right genes code for lean-mass builders, increase the natural $\beta2$-adrenergic receptor agonists, and new ways for the body to self-regulate testosterone so that the subjects were real manly men capable of greater feats of strength, speed and endurance but without having their nuts shrink to acorns or their brains turn to mush. In theory.

He started out doing this way off the radar for sports teams and got caught. That led to six years of litigation and rulebook burning to decide if genetic manipulation was covered under the standard doping rules. It wasn't. It is now.

By the time the court case was settled, Bishop had sold his interest in sports and was inking contracts with the military.

Not our military, though.

He was taking obscene amounts of money from Russia, from China, from North Korea, from Iran, and from a bunch of little countries who had more money than ethics.

The result? A new breed of super soldier.

Not exactly on a par with Captain America but pretty damn tough. On average, thirty percent more muscle density, fifteen percent greater potential for speed. Enhanced reaction time. Amped-up wound-repair system.

My guys in Echo Team had tussled with some of these jokers and very nearly had our asses handed to us. The whole "subdue and restrain" thing had to get tossed out the window. Instead we had to up the game on them in ugly ways that left a lot of hair on the walls.

Bishop and his company came under a lot of fire. We froze his accounts, had him audited, hacked his email, tapped his phone, and hauled him in front of subcommittees and judges.

We did that a lot, with enthusiasm.

He skated every goddamn time.

Apparently the thing he's smartest about is planning ahead. Before he went into the super-soldier business he hired enough lawyers to sink the *Titanic*. They were able to establish a lack of illegality because none of the customers in any of the named countries were in any way attached to the military nor were they associated with terrorist organizations. What Bishop had done, you see, was break the research into pieces and sell those pieces to medical researchers, hospitals, and pharmaceutical companies whose primary customers were kids and the elderly.

Fucker used a variation on the nuns-and-orphans gambit.

His lawyers put the burden on our State Department lawyers to prove that any single action Bishop took or sale he made could, in any way, be construed as a terrorist act. No, they could not. Could anything he did be construed as actions taken against the national security of the United States? No. Not really, because each single action was carefully tied to a humanitarian target market. The designer β2-adrenergic receptor agonists, for example, were only sold to hospitals and labs researching asthma and pulmonary disorders.

So, no one was able to prove within reasonable doubt that Bishop was anything more than a good businessman whose love of humanity transcended national borders and political agendas. Bishop's PR people tried the government in the court of public opinion, succeeding in painting us as the bad guys and him as a saint. There was even a picture on the cover of *Time* that showed him handing a puppy to sick kids in a rural Chinese hospital. The kids were smiling and cute, the puppy was adorable, and Bishop contrived to look like fucking Santa Claus.

Good place to pause and vomit.

Here's the truth that we knew but couldn't prove. Whereas the science was apparently innocent when viewed piecemeal, when combined those bits added up to biotech that could—and indeed did—create superior soldiers with significant physical enhancement.

That's who I was going to meet.

I'd met him before. Outside of a federal courthouse once. And again at one of his labs we raided. That raid, by the way, was based on bad intel. We busted the place up pretty good, and he handed us our collective asses in court to the tune of eleven million for repairs and a variety of nebulous damages.

When I saw him a third time at a sidewalk café in New Orleans where I knew he'd be, I had Top and Bunny with me, and they kept Bishop's bodyguards entertained while we had a chat. Over coffee and some very nice pastries I told him that we were, at that moment, in the process of dismantling the labs of several of his clients. It was a global, coordinated hit. Very illegal, very off the radar, and very well coordinated. Our boys plus some day-players from Mossad, Barrier in the U.K., the Belgian Pathfinders, an Austrian *Jagdkommando* team, and even Iceland's *Vikingasveitin*. Bunch of others. We didn't target the hospitals or civilian research labs, but we'd spent two years making a hit list of covert labs that were actually making super soldiers for sale to private contractors like Blackwater and Blue Diamond.

There was not one shred of actionable evidence to link Bishop to these labs, though everybody knew he was involved. He was just too good with burning any bridges that led to him. The best we could do was cut his client list by at least half—call it a thirty-billion-dollar annual loss—and maybe put the fear of god into the other half.

I had the job of making sure that Bishop didn't take any calls while this was happening. I wasn't in the field because I was healing from some injuries I'd taken on a gig. This was not long after I got shot during the Majestic Black Book affair.

So, it was a couple of guys sitting at a table drinking café-au-lait and eating beignets while half of Bishop's empire burned.

I made sure that we were photographed at that table. That photo was leaked to the right people.

Were we setting him up as the guy who sold out his own people to the Feds?

Fuck yeah, we were.

It was less than four hours before he started getting death threats.

Over the next few months there were sixteen separate attempts to assassinate him. His car was blown up—he wasn't in it, alas. One of his lawyers went to meet Jesus, so we all put it in the win column. Couple of snipers took shots at him, and for a fun five minutes we thought Bishop was down, but the wily bastard actually had doubles. Not clones or anything that cool. Just actors hired to impersonate him and, as it turned out, die for him. Someone torched his house, and someone else mailed him a birthday card filled with anthrax.

None of it got anywhere near Bishop.

His empire was crumbling, but he still had enough money to hire actual loyalty from some of his super soldiers.

Which brings us to why I'm not drinking cold beer and watching the Orioles spank the Phillies.

When Mr. Church called me he said, "Myron Bishop wants to come in."

"'Come in' as in…?"

"He wants us to protect him."

If I'd been drinking coffee I'd have snorted it out of my nose. "I saw a t-shirt with a bull's-eye on it. Can we just mail that to him with a nice card saying 'have a nice and very short life'?"

"Tempting as that is, Captain," said Church, "the State Department would like some quality time with Bishop."

"Wait, he wants to confess?"

"In a very limited way. He claims that he has become aware of some improprieties in his foreign holdings, has become alarmed by them, and wishes to bring them to the attention of the appropriate authorities and cooperate in every way possible."

"It must hurt your mouth to repeat that."

"I'll take an aspirin later."

"What's the play?"

"Unclear. Bishop is difficult to trust under any circumstances. However, even someone like him must feel the pressure of being under constant threat of assassination. He can't go out, he can't date, his social life has become nonexistent."

"And I feel so bad for him, too. I may cry."

"Try to rein in your emotions long enough to pick him up."

"How far 'in' does he want to come? Are we putting him in WITSEC?"

"No. He doesn't trust the Marshal's service to protect him."

"Fair enough. Most of them would want to shoot him."

"He requested you."

"Me as is in the DMS or me as in—?"

"You personally."

"Not sure I like the sound of that. When we met at that café, I pretty much told him I thought he was dog shit on my shoe. Words to that effect."

"Ah."

"I also threatened to tie him to a chair and wire a car battery to his nutsack."

"Well...I don't think he's entranced by your charm," said Church.

"Then—?"

"He considers you a professional."

"I am."

"You didn't try to arrest him. You didn't actually use violence on him."

"I insulted him."

"Irrelevant. He's in biotech, so he's used to that. He said that you didn't try to provoke him into any action that would have allowed you to use force on him."

"Wasn't that kind of moment." Which was true in its way. I'd heard he had a bad temper, so I was deliberately rude in hopes he'd swing on me. He didn't, so the whole thing stayed in low gear.

"You could have turned it into one," said Church. "It was probably the only time when someone could have. You chose not to. He said it was very professional. It engendered a degree of trust. Now he wants to come in and talk to us and there aren't many people left whom he trusts."

"So I lose a day at Camden Yards for a dickhead everyone wants to see in a body bag. How did I get so lucky?"

"Perhaps you were too charming for your own good."

"Cute. So what do I do with him once I have him? We putting him in a hotel under guard or do you want me to take him to the safe house in Elkton?"

"Did you ever finish the repairs on the holding cell at the Warehouse? The one where the toilet backed up?"

"No. The plumber comes in next Monday and...."

"Put him there," he said.

He disconnected without further comment.

Chap. 5

I considered the way Frick and Frack flanked me on the elevator. I was in the center of the car, they were fanned to either side, quarter-turned toward me. Both had their jackets unbuttoned, which meant they were carrying. If they were both right handed, the guy to my right—Frack—was going to have to reach into his jacket toward me, which meant I could jam him back against the wall and keep the piece in its holster. Frick would have to reach across his chest away from me, because his piece would be hanging under his left armpit, the barrel facing away. If it came to a watershed moment, I'd bodyblock Frick and kick Frack's kneecap off.

I generally don't rehearse this sort of thing, preferring the fluidity of spontaneous reaction. But these guys were not top tier. I doubted they were graduates of a super-soldier program. More like meat in off-the-rack suits.

They didn't make a play, so we didn't need to explore the extent of their health plan.

Fair enough.

Maybe this would go by the numbers.

The car stopped and the doors opened and my assessment of the day changed.

Myron Bishop was right there, waiting directly outside. He was well dressed in a five-thousand-dollar suit and a million-dollar smile. There were four very, very large men behind him. They were smiling too.

Myron Bishop said, "Fuck you."

And he jabbed me in the throat with a stun gun.

Chap. 6

So, there I was.

Buck naked.

Duct-taped to a chair.

I was never completely unconscious, though Bishop and—I think—both Frick and Frack kept juicing me with the stun guns.

Stun guns fucking hurt.

I twitched and jerked and pissed myself and screamed.

They laughed their asses off.

Despite the constant shocks, I didn't make it easy for them. I strained my muscles, fought them, made them earn it.

One of the big goons with Bishop took my rapid-release knife and cut my clothes off. Except for my Orioles shirt. He pulled that off and set it carefully aside. Everything else was slashed to ribbons. He even looped my socks over the knife and cut them in half. While I can appreciate attention to detail, that seemed somewhere between petty and psychotic.

I hadn't been wearing my earbud because this didn't seem like that kind of situation. The bad call was entirely my own. No radio, no backup.

Had one of my guys done something as rookie as this, I'd have fried him.

There's a lesson about hubris in all this. Balls.

The big goon with my knife was one of the ugliest men I've ever seen. His face was lumpy and distorted, his nose flat and crooked, his eyes buried in little pits of gristle. And damn if he didn't stink. Worst body odor I've ever smelled, and I've been to the great apes exhibit at the zoo. When he turned away to unload my weapon and place it on the table, I saw that his thighs and buttocks were unnaturally lumpy and huge. Not sure whether this was a bad side effect of the super-soldier formula or the wrong kind of manic weight training. Or whether he was simply a freak.

The other two goons were merely big. Six-five, six-six. Muscles upon muscles. No mercy at all in their eyes.

While all this was happening, Myron Bishop sat on the edge of a desk, swinging one foot and listening to a smooth jazz station. Kenny G or some shit.

He finally waved the goon squad back. He sent Frick and Frack down in the elevator.

"Nobody comes up until I say so," he told them. "That means no calls, no nothing."

They grunted like obedient dogs and disappeared.

Bishop pushed off from the desk and strolled toward me. "You know, I've seen every James Bond movie. I have them all on DVD. Great stuff."

"Yeah? Who's your favorite Bond?"

"Not my point," he said. "In the movies there's always this scene where the bad guy captures Bond, ties him to some kind of device...."

"Like the laser table in *Goldfinger*," I said, trying to stretch this out.

He snapped his fingers. "Exactly. Or the villain invites him to dinner. Either way, the bad guy does this info dump where he brags about his evil master plan and basically tells Bond all the information he'd need to fuck him up if Bond ever got free. And Bond *always* gets free and then fucks him up."

I said nothing.

"Which is crazy, 'cause why the hell would anyone do that? I mean, how stupid is that?"

"It doesn't adequately reflect the real world."

He grinned and nodded. "It's a plot device. You read the books?"

"Sure. When I was a kid."

"Same problem in the books," said Bishop, nodding and grinning. Couple of guys bullshitting about movies. Like any other day. "But in the real world the hero would almost never meet the villain. Bond might tear down Blofeld's plan or infiltrate Dr. No's hollowed-out volcano with a bunch of ninjas, but if the super villain was there he'd be killed in any resulting firefight, am I right?"

"Ideally."

"Unless—?" he prompted.

"Unless," I said, "the op was to apprehend the bad guy and turn him over to an interrogation team."

"Bingo. The hero and villain aren't really going to meet and have a heart-to-heart. That doesn't happen."

"It doesn't *always* happen."

"What, you mean it does sometimes?"

"Life's weird like that."

He thought about it. "Fuck. I didn't know that. You've done it? You've had that James Bond info-dump moment?"

"Not over dinner," I said. "And never with a laser cannon."

"But you've had it."

"I guess."

He looked excited. "I'd love to hear about it. Could you...you know...*tell* me about it? Just one or two."

I smiled at him. "You are, of course, shitting me here."

"No, I'm dead serious."

"I'm tied to a chair with my junk hanging out."

The goons laughed at that. The ugly one, Stanky McButtchunks, laughed hardest.

Bishop chuckled.

I did, too. It was a funny moment. Mind you, you'd have to be a few steps along the path to psychosis to find it funny, but I think we all qualified.

Bishop said, "I really would like to hear about it. Seriously."

"Sorry," I said. "It's classified."

"Unclassify it. I won't tell anyone."

"Ummm….no. I don't see it happening."

He leaned casually on the wheeled cart on which the generator sat. "Try."

"Can't and won't."

"I'm pretty sure you're wrong about that."

It wasn't something I wanted him to rush to prove.

So, I said, "What's this all about, Myron? I thought you were going to go all Bond-villain on me and tell me about your master plan. Wasn't that what you were leading up to?"

"No. I wanted to point out how stupid those movies are. Villains don't have confessional moments with spies or assassins."

"I'm not technically a spy."

"You're an assassin, though."

"Labels are ugly things, Myron."

He grinned, showing me expensive dental work. "Christ, I really like you, Joe. I even liked you that day when you were fucking up my life. You have balls—"

"As we can all clearly see."

"—And you got a weird way of looking at the world. Skewed is the word, I think."

"I prefer 'unique perspective.'"

"Whatever. Point is, I got no evil master plan to reveal. I'm fucked. And I mean bent over a barrel with everyone from the SEC to NATO waiting in line to pull a train. I'm in total crash-and-burn mode here. My former customers and most of my business associates would like to see my head on a stick, and except for a few guys in my inner circle, I've got no one at my back." When he mentioned his inner circle he gestured to Stanky and the other two.

I didn't comment.

"So I am well and truly screwed here, Joe. A baby-raper in prison has a better chance than I do."

"Nice comparison. You sure you want to run with that?"

"You're missing the point."

"No, I get you. Your empire has crumbled. Cut me loose, and we can go cry about it over some beers. Bring the goon squad if you want."

"I think that ship has sailed."

"Actually, it hasn't."

"You're a federal agent. I'm pretty sure we committed about nine felonies in the last few minutes."

"Which I'm willing to forgive and forget. No, don't smile, I'm serious. So far all that's happened is a little fun and games. I'm a big boy, I can let it slide. We'd rather have you come in where we can protect you—"

"—And interrogate me."

"Let's call it an extended interview. If you came in it would be with the understanding that you're willing to cooperate, name names in exchange for immunity."

"No one's going to give me immunity."

"No? Look in the front right pocket of my jeans."

He did. The paper was in three pieces, thanks to Stanky and the knife, but Bishop smoothed them out on a desk and puzzled the pieces together. He grunted.

"That is an Executive Order from the President of the United States. It offers full immunity from prosecution in exchange for complete and unreserved cooperation. That means we protect you, we give you a completely new identity in a place no one will ever look, and we go out and arrest anyone who would ever want to do you harm. It also gives the State Department some iron boots with which to kick the ass of a few countries on our current shit list. The bottom line is that you get to have a good life and get to *live* that life. That was the offer I came to deliver today. That offer still stands. I can get a new copy of the Order. We can all step back off this diving board and end the day with everyone smiling."

"I'm supposed to believe this after we kicked your ass?"

I laughed. "Dude, having my ass kicked is pretty much on my day-planner on any day that ends in a 'y.' I don't burn up a lot of calories holding grudges. For me it's all big picture, and my job gets easier if you're in a nice split-level somewhere with no one shooting at you and the two of us swapping YouTube videos of kittens, you dig?"

"You really buying this shit?" asked Stanky. Even his voice was ugly.

For a moment it looked like Bishop was, in fact, buying it. Lots of different expressions crossed his face. Doubt, interest, some fear. The guy was an emotional train wreck, and I could see what months of stress were doing to him. Under his fake tan, his skin color was bad. There was a little tremolo in his voice, and his hands shook. I'd bet my pension that he was drinking too much and not getting any sleep unless he rode a sleeping pill down into troubled dreams.

In a weird, detached way I almost felt sorry for him. We'd done an even better job of ruining his life than I'd thought.

Now, understand me, when I say I felt sorry for him, it was only a fleeting thing. Like gas pains after a plate of nachos. He was a scum-sucking bottom feeder whose business deals had probably cost thousands of people pain and maybe put a few hundred in the dirt.

So, yeah, I'd actually kill him without blinking, but in that moment I felt bad. He looked like a hurt, scared, little kid.

Bishop turned away and paced the office for a few minutes. We all waited him out. Now was not the time to push. After a dozen turns back and forth, he stopped by a tall metal cabinet, opened it to reveal shelves filled with office products and cleaning supplies. He took down a box of Hefty trash bags, tugged one out, and turned to one of the other goons.

"Red," he said, "put his stuff in here. Dump it somewhere no one will find it."

He handed the box of bags to the other goon. "Billy, there should be enough here to wrap up the parts."

I said, "Ah, fuck, Myron."

Bishop looked at me for a few silent seconds. "Sorry, Joe. The truth is that you fucked me over pretty good. You know how many days I've had diarrhea? My blood pressure could blow bolts out of plate steel. You ruined more than my business. You ruined me."

"So let me make it right," I said. "We're not the Marshals. They'd hide you away in some Podunk town and make you live small. The DMS can give you a better life than clerking at a shoe store in East Galoshes, Iowa. I'm serious. We have some places on some islands. Palm trees, ocean views, the works. Like a resort."

"I *had* that."

"Have it again. Have it forever."

"Even paradise would get boring if I could never leave."

"Well, shit, man, what's your plan now? Go on the run for the rest of your life? Defect to North Korea and live in some underground bunker until you stop being useful?"

He shook his head. "No," he said, "I have other plans."

"*What* other plans? What other options do you have left? I'm offering you the best deal."

"Sorry, Joe, I'll pass."

"Tell me why."

He smiled. A thin, small, slightly weary smile. "This isn't a James Bond movie, Joe. Guys like me don't have confessional moments. You don't get to know our plans. All you get to do is know that you fucked up and failed. Maybe that'll give you a little taste of what I've been going through."

He came over and stood right in front of me. If I hadn't been taped to the chair I could have reached out and strangled him.

Without breaking eye contact with me, he spoke to his goons. "Make it last," he said. "Ruin this motherfucker the way he ruined me."

Bishop bent forward and patted my cheek.

"No offense, Joe."

Chap. 7

Here's the thing about duct tape.

It's tough, we all know that.

Breaking it through sheer muscle power is pretty much not going to happen. Especially if it gets folded over while you're struggling. That increases the breaking strength.

Here's the other thing about duct tape.

People trust it way too much.

They tape you up and they think you're good, they think you're there to stay.

Try that shit on someone like, say, Houdini. Or a Vegas stage magician worth half a shit. Try it on some of the really smart street thugs. They'll all slip out of it.

Like I slipped out of it.

The trick is to have them tape you while you're struggling, and to make sure your wrists are flexed out and all your muscles are bulged. These assholes helped with that with their damn stun guns. They thought they were wrapping my wrists and binding me to the chair. Actually they were wrapping my muscles and bones while they were expanded. And, yes, you can expand the width of your wrist by splaying your fingers and tensing the muscles. It separates the radius and ulna. Look it up, this isn't a science lesson.

Point is, I was not nearly as tightly bound as they thought I was.

All the time Bishop was talking shit to me, I was relaxing my muscles and easing my right out of the loop of tape. Same way magicians slip out of handcuffs.

When Bishop leaned close to pat me on the face, I whipped my hand out of the last strand of tape and punched him in the throat.

Not my best punch.

Probably the hardest punch he ever took, though. He wasn't the physical type.

He made a horrible gagging-choking sound, and I stood up, spun him, and wrapped my left arm around him, my forearm pressed to his right carotid and laying on the windpipe, my bicep pressing the left carotid shut.

The goons, Red, Billy and Stanky—I never found out his real name—surged forward and I lifted Bishop onto tippy-toes and clamped my right hand behind his head to increase pressure and secure the lock.

"Stop right there," I growled. "Anyone moves and he dies."

They hesitated.

"Tell them to back off," I ordered.

Bishop, whose face was turning a nice shade of puce, could only gurgle. I shook him a little bit and added another couple ounces of pressure.

"Tell them to stand down," I ordered. My feet were still taped to the chair, so I wasn't in any shape to fight these guys. Besides, they had guns and I had duct tape and my birthday suit. Not a good mix. "Tell them or I will kill you."

He couldn't exactly tell them, but he gesticulated with great enthusiasm.

The three goons towered over us. They looked so big and scary and mean that I was scared out of my goddamn mind. Talking trash does not actually make you brave. It doesn't win you a fight. They knew it and I knew it.

My only weapon was Bishop.

I gave him another squeeze, careful not to bring him to the point where he choked out. If he suddenly went limp, they'd think he was dead, and then they'd tear me apart.

Bishop waved wildly, making shoving motions to order them back.

They took a step back.

"All the way to the wall," I said. The office was about forty by twenty. They retreated about half that distance but no amount of threats, commands or wild gestures would get them to go all the way.

Shit.

I began shuffling backward. There was about two inches of play in the tape around my ankles, so I had to move in little retreating baby steps. I dragged Bishop with me all the way to the elevators.

That was a tricky moment. I had to release the restraining clamp on the back of his head in order to flap backward and unearth the button. Bishop gurgled out a plea. The goons surged forward. I punched the button and then clamped my fingers over his eyes.

"I'll tear your eyes out and make you eat them before they can take me down. Do you believe me?"

"Yes! Oh, Christ…yes."

"Tell them to back the fuck off."

He did.

They only backed about half a fuck off, though. Not even as far as before.

Behind me the elevator went *bing!*

I shuffled us back. Naked guy ankle-tied to an office chair with a chunky business guy in a choke hold. Not a pretty picture.

The doors began to shut.

The goons started rushing forward before the doors closed completely.

Bishop screamed at them.

The doors closed.

Chap. 8

I used my right hand to slap the buttons for the twentieth floor.

I needed time to get my shit together, get armed, call for help. If I showed up in the lobby, Frick and Frack would gun me down. If I got off on a floor too close to the top, the goon squad would simply run down a few flights of stairs. To confuse things I hit all the buttons from twenty down to the lobby. Let them guess.

Then I choked Bishop unconscious. When you do it right, compressing both carotids, it takes eight seconds. Compress one and you double the time.

He went out right away, probably because his throat was already a mess.

I coveted his trousers. Big and baggy.

But as he sagged in my grip I smelled a bad smell.

I said, "Ahhh…shit."

Which was accurate, because Bishop's bowels failed him as he went out.

So much for a clean pair of pants.

Or, let's face it, any pants.

Damn it.

I threw him into a corner of the elevator and went to work freeing my ankles.

We hit the twentieth floor before I was out, so we stayed on.

I got my right foot out on seventeen and the left out just as the doors were opening on sixteen. I kicked the chair out, grabbed Bishop by his hair and tried to drag him out.

Turns out he wears a toupee.

I tossed the rug away, grabbed the shoulders of his suit coat and hauled his limp, smelly, flabby ass off the lift.

The doors closed.

We were on a floor with several suites of offices. All closed.

A kinder God would have given me a men's clothing designer, a knife shop, and an armorer. Instead I got a CPA, an investment broker, and a real-estate attorney.

You take what you're given.

I let Bishop lay there. He was dead weight for me now. He wasn't my problem. Instead I picked up the chair and swung it as hard as I could at the big picture window of the attorney's office. I cowered back as it shattered.

Bishop didn't need his jacket, so I pulled it off. I considered taking his shoes, but he had small feet—maybe eight or nines. I have thirteen wides. No joy there, but I took one to smash out the last of the glass in the window frame. I did a quick reappraisal, then stripped off his dress shirt and spread that over the glass on this side of the frame; and bent over the frame and laid the jacket on the other side. Then I vaulted the frame, which was waist-high, crunched over the padded glass, and entered the offices.

First thing I looked for was a phone. Found the secretary's desk, figured out that I had to dial nine for an outside line, and called the duty sergeant at the Warehouse. I gave him the address, a quick rundown on the situation, and my location inside the building. I told him to scramble everyone who could pull a trigger.

As an afterthought I told him to bring me a pair of pants.

Then I told him to patch me through to Bug, our computer guy.

"This is an open line," I said as soon as Bug answered.

"Copy that, Cowboy. What's going on?"

I gave him an even briefer version of the story.

"I don't have my com with me," I said, "and I'm probably going to have to keep moving. Kind of a *Die Hard* situation."

"How can I help?"

"Be creative. I need the power out and I need some distractions. See what you can do."

"No problem."

"And call Church. He knows I'm here, but he doesn't know this. I need him to control local law and the press. I do not want to be on the front page of the paper with my dick hanging out."

"You talking literally or figuratively?"

"Literally. I'd give a month's pay for a thong and ballet slippers."

"Jeez."

"Get moving, Bug."

"Already working on it."

I hung up.

The cavalry was coming, and that was good news.

I heard a sound—Bishop groaning. Soon he was going to start yelling.

Shit.

I ran back, vaulted the frame again and spent some quality time kicking him unconscious. Brutal? Yeah. Uncivilized? Sure.

Satisfying?

You betcha.

If he survived today he was going to need a damn good dentist. I did give him the courtesy of angling him so that he didn't choke to death on his bridgework.

Then I ran back into the lawyer's office to look for a weapon.

I found exactly nothing. No guns, no knives, nothing.

"Okay," I told myself, "plan B."

In jujutsu, which is the hand-to-hand combat system developed by the Samurai, there's a nasty little subscience called hadaka-korosu. Loose translation is the art of the naked kill. No, it isn't the art of fighting in the buff. Naked kill refers to self-defense and combative offense using commonplace objects as weapons, meaning those things that aren't designed for that purpose. It's basic tool use. Any object has some combative potential so long as it can be seen, heard or felt. You couldn't use, for example, a single tear or a soft contact lens because they can't be perceived in any useful tactical way.

Everything else falls into a basic weapon category. There are blunt objects, things you can throw, items that will cut, flexible things useful in binding, objects that will distract, and so on. It's like MacGyver if he wanted to go medieval on people. Or, as one of my instructors said, "Imagine fifty people trapped in a building during the zombie apocalypse. One of them is a handyman, the kind of guy who can fix anything, make stuff, and use tools. Which of those fifty people is going to survive? Which one is going to become the most valuable person in the building? In a real-world crisis, when everything is falling apart, the handyman always gets out."

I've taken that sort of advice to heart. I once strangled someone with a bikini top. Long story. Done a bunch of other bad things to bad people using whatever was to hand.

The irony of actually being *naked* was not lost on me; but I wasn't amused. Ha-fucking-ha.

There was another sound from outside.

A voice. Not Bishop's though.

I snatched a few things off the secretary's desk and ran back to the hall where I caught a snatch of what the voice was saying.

"Nothing on seventeen. Heading down one."

There was a squawk of feedback from a walkie-talkie. Nothing I could understand.

"Roger that."

The voice was close. Right outside of the fire tower door.

The lights went out.

Bam, just like that.

It plunged the whole building into utter darkness.

Thank you, Bug.

A yard away a line of pale yellow appeared in the wall of featureless shadows. The door opening. Lights from the fire tower emergency lights spilled out, pale and weak.

The door began swinging inward, and I rose up and rammed it with every ounce of body mass, fear, and rage. Steel hit flesh. There was a single bang, and something hot burned past my ear, but I didn't care. I had Bic pens in each hand and began chopping at a shadowy figure. I hit him in the chest, the throat, the mouth, the sinuses, the left eye. I buried one pen so deep into his eye socket that as he screamed and reeled back the pen was torn from my hand. His hands went up to try to fend off the assault, but he bungled it. His gun went flying. I tried to grab it, but it spun over the rail and dropped into the stairwell. It fell so far I never heard it land.

It was the goon called Red, and he was screaming too loud.

I grabbed his tie, jerked it out and then slammed my forearm down on it. The leverage, plus my two hundred and ten pounds of mass snapped him down to his knees. His screams stopped, and as an after-echo I heard the bones in his neck break apart.

He didn't die right away. Broken necks aren't always an off switch, but I let Red lay there and die. Fuck it.

I crouched and did a fast pat-down.

He had one extra magazine. No backup piece, though. And no knife.

Damn it.

I started to pull off his clothes, but the stairwell was suddenly filled with shouts and the sound of pounding feet. Ten floors down and coming fast. Those big sons of bitches.

I ran back to the lawyer's office for more goodies.

I was very fast about it.

By the time I got back to the fire tower, the spry sons of bitches were only three flights below me.

I decided against the stuff I'd just grabbed. Not enough time. So, I squatted and hoisted Red onto the rail.

"Yo!" I said in a bad imitation of the dying man. "Fucker went up."

I saw a head and shoulders lean out from one floor down. Billy.

I dropped Red on his face.

Big, wet crunch that could not have boded well for either of them.

Then there were bullets from the level below them filling the fire tower and whanging off of everything.

I got out of there fast.

The emergency lights were on in the office now. Not good.

Using Bishop as a shield was not going to work. Not this time. He was covered with blood and looked dead.

I returned to the offices and looked for something that would give me some kind of chance. I was pretty sure it was my friend Stanky coming up the stairs. He was huge, and if he was truly a super-soldier, he could tear me apart with his bare hands. Plus he had a gun.

My odds sucked.

Time to change the math.

I grabbed a heavy stapler and ran from one emergency light to the next, smashing the bulbs and bringing back the darkness.

Darkness was my weapon to use. Not his.

I heard the fire tower door open.

I heard his growl of anger when he found Bishop. I'd left the security light by the elevator intact for that reason. I wanted Stanky to see what was out there.

I prayed that he'd grab his boss, cut his losses, and bug out.

Nope.

He was a big shape in the gloom.

I crouched down in a cleft between a desk, a wheeled chair, and a file cabinet. He came creeping, letting his pistol lead the way.

"I know you're in here, dickhead," he said.

I said nothing.

"When I find you I'm going to rip your balls off. That's not a joke. I've done it before."

I believed him.

"Make you eat 'em before I—"

I gripped the chair and rammed it at him. There was a lot of desperate energy behind that shove, and I hit him as hard as I've ever hit anyone in my life.

He crashed down. The gun went flying into the shadows.

I piled on top of him, needing to end this fast because surprise was the only advantage I had on this brute. I still had the stapler and I smashed it down on his face.

Except he got his forearm up instead and took the hit. He cried in pain, but it wasn't the kind of cry that said "I'm done."

Which he proved in the next second by twisting his hips and shoulders into a wild hook punch that caught me over the ear and rang every bell in the world. I went flopping sideways into a metal trash can, sure that my skull was fractured.

With a display of rubbery agility you wouldn't expect to find in a man of his size, he popped to his feet and came for me. In the dismal light I saw him swing again, so I whipped the trash can at him. His punch collapsed it like it was foil, but the impact deflected his aim. The punch flattened the can against the plastic chair pad under the desk.

I tried for a kick to his nuts, caught him on the thigh, and knocked him back four feet.

That gave me a half a second, so I scrambled up and snatched the first thing I could find on the desk. It was a thick three-ring binder. He swung again. There was no finesse in his punches, just a lot of speed and power.

I shoved the flat of the binder toward him and his knuckles slammed into it. The shock knocked me back against the desk, but he had to have felt it. You can't punch through a loose-leaf binder filled with a hundred pages of paper. That is, for all intents and purposes, a block of wood. He jerked his hand back, hissing in pain. So I followed the fist back to its source and slapped him forward and back with the binder, rocking his head side to side. He stumbled back two steps, and I reversed the binder so that the covers opened to form a Vee. I rammed that into his throat.

It would have stopped him had it connected.

He got a muscular shoulder up and took the shot, then backhanded me, catching the binder and sending it flying across the room. I narrowly avoided his return shot by back-rolling over the desk. As I landed on the far side I shoved the desk at him, hit him in the thighs, and, as he abruptly bent forward, grabbed the back of his head and slammed him facedown onto the desk. He rebounded from that, and I saw a black line following him. A trail of blood that looked like ink in this light.

With a roar like the gorilla he resembled, he grabbed the edge of the desk and hurled the heavy mahogany aside like it was cheap particleboard from Ikea.

I backpedaled until I hit the desk behind it, hooked the chair with my foot and kicked it at him as he rushed me. It caught him at knee level and he almost fell. I swept the contents of the second desk toward him, hitting him with a bunch of debris that did him no harm at all.

However it gave me a chance to dive for a coatrack closer to the door. He staggered to his feet and swung another punch at me, really putting some hate into it. I swung the wooden coatrack into the arc of the punch and that's what he hit.

That time I heard his hand bones break.

Nice.

I kicked the base of the coatrack into his groin. It doubled him, but he hugged the rack to his body as he hunched forward, tearing it from my hand. I whirled, fumbling at the desk for something useful. Found a vase and broke that over his left ear. Picked up a couple of paperbacks and slapped them together with his head in the middle, right over his ears.

His scream was ultrasonic. Pretty sure I burst one of his eardrums.

But the son of a bitch kept coming.

He staggered toward me, reaching with long punches, both of us knowing that with his level of strength he only had to hit me once to win this fight.

I pivoted, grabbed a fistful of pencils from a cup and as he came up off the floor at me I slammed my fist down, hoping to get an eye or his face.

I missed both.

Instead I hit right above his collarbone. Right below the sweeping curve of his trapezius muscle. There's a sweet spot there. The subclavian artery.

On any other person I'd have opened the faucets and he'd have sprayed his life all over the walls.

But Bishop's science had given him tougher skin and thicker muscle tissue. The pencils stood up like porcupine quills, but not one of them went deep enough.

With a howl of inhuman rage and pain, he tore them out of his shoulder and threw them away. He swung punches left, right, left, right, and I fell back. He was so goddamn strong that even if I blocked him I'd break an arm. I could feel the wind of each punch and the way my heart was beating way too fast.

I dove sideways, rolled, came up onto my toes, and ran for it. He bellowed and ran after. I threw chairs in his path. I ran onto and over desks. I made it all the way to the back office and slammed the door in his face. He burst through it. I don't mean he rushed through the doorway. He actually exploded the door itself as he slammed into it. Splinters of wood and glass filled the darkened room. I couldn't see most of them but I could feel them cut me.

I stumbled backward, out of time, out of places to run.

Out of luck.

He backed me all the way into the corner. My shoulders thumped against something I couldn't see. Draped cloth of some kind. And a shaft of wood.

A flagpole?

In a flash of panic I grabbed the cloth and tore at it, hoping to get the pole. Maybe I could beat him with it. Instead the cloth tore free and the pole fell out of reach.

The office was nearly pitch-black, which gave me a second as he tried to sort out which piece of shadow was my face so he could punch it to goo. I had the cloth.

It was all I had.

I looped it over his head and jerked downward. He bowed forward, and I kneed him in the face. Missed the nose. Got the cheekbone, which hurt like hell. My leg felt cracked and numb. Couldn't care about that. In the split second while he was still bent over I jumped onto him, shoulder rolling over his back like an acrobat and dropping to my feet so that for a moment we were back to back. The cloth was still around his beck, so I looped one end over my opposite forearm and twisted to create a tourniquet, then I jammed my knee up between his shoulder blades and threw myself backward.

It was a hard damn fall, and he had to weigh two ninety or three hundred. The impact nearly dislocated my hip. I brought my other knee up so I was on the bottom, and he was splayed backward on my shins with the flag cinched tight around his throat. The impact constricted it even tighter and I twisted with every last bit of desperate energy I had.

He had the mass and the muscle. He was genetically engineered to be a superior soldier. Faster and stronger. More durable.

Cutting-edge genetic science made him a monster.

I used one of the oldest bits of practical physics. A turnbuckle. It's torsion and leverage. Only simpler machine is the wheel.

I turned the cloth loop until he gagged.

Until he choked.

Until there was not enough room inside that loop for a human throat to exist in any useful structure.

And then I tightened it some more.

If the bones and cartilage made any sounds as they collapsed, I couldn't hear it over the sound of my own screams.

Chap. 9

When I let him go, empty meat fell sideways.

I lay there. Gasping. Hurt. Flooded with adrenaline. Seeing exploding stars in the darkness.

I lay there for maybe a full minute, unable to move.

When I finally peeled myself slowly—so damn slowly—from the floor, all the lights in the building switched back on.

And Echo Team—my own goddamn team—came pouring out of the stairwell, guns up and out, shouting, yelling, staring.

I was covered in blood, naked as an egg, and I still held the coiled flag in my hands.

I looked down at it.

It would have been extremely cool if it was an American flag. Very poetic.

It was from the Rotary Club.

Less poetry. Still effective as a son of a bitch.

Chap. 10

The postscript is brief.

Bishop's great escape plan was South America, a face job, a false identity, and a villa in Argentina. Bug picked that apart in seconds.

They carted Bishop off to the hospital, and then he headed off to Gitmo for a long, long time of soul-searching and water sports.

He should have taken the deal.

Really should have.

~The End~

Borrowed Power

NOTE: Parts of this story are set between the novels *Assassin's Code* and *Extinction Machine*. If you haven't yet read *Assassin's Code*, there are some spoilers in this story.

Prologue

They say that gods cease to exist when people stop believing in them.

Others say that the gods of Olympus and Valhalla and all of the other pantheons are merely sleeping, waiting for that one person in whose breast a spark of belief is rekindled.

Secrets are like that. Particularly the kinds of secrets governments hide and people like me kill to either defend or destroy.

A secret doesn't stop being important because it's forgotten. Or buried.

These secrets wait like dreaming gods until one person reaches into the darkness to stir them to wakefulness.

Part One
1983

Chap. 1

Les Égouts de Paris
(The Sewers of Paris)
March, 1983

The killer descended from the glimmering lights of Paris into a black underworld of rushing water, stagnant pollution, raw sewage, savage rats, and forgotten bones.

He carried no map, but the route was imprinted onto the front of his mind. He went deeper and deeper into the underworld, carrying with him the tools of his trade. A gun, a knife, a silver garrote, and a mind far colder than the waters that rushed through the bowels of the earth.

It had been the work of four weeks to obtain legitimate permits and credentials from the correct departments within the streets management offices, then copy those documents, and return the originals. If anyone ever checked, everything would be in its proper place. The level of proficiency at which the killer worked was both a source of amusement among his peers and the reason this man had never failed in a field mission. The jokes at his expense—"My grandmother's slower, but she's old"—were swapped out of his earshot. Or, at least, so the jokers thought. The killer usually heard what was being said, though through means that were only ever supposed to be used on the Russians or Chinese or North Koreans. Never on the home team.

The killer did not recognize most of his peers as being on the same team as himself. He had a separate and entirely personal agenda that he chose not to share.

Even the members of his own team—none of whom were on this particular mission—knew only what he wanted them to know. Just as his superiors knew only what he wanted them to know, and that included many of the details in his personal file. Most of it was a fabrication that had taken years, much thought, and a great deal of money to construct. Everything there—photos of his childhood, his school records, his medical history, even the samples of blood and hair on file for DNA testing—belonged to other men. Dead men whose lives he had borrowed, combined, and then otherwise erased.

The killer was as certain as he could be that his real name existed in no database in any computer on earth.

Except Pangaea.

His computer.

A computer the killer had obtained in the way he'd obtained many useful tools in his personal arsenal. He'd killed the man who built it and the men who guarded it.

And then he completely rebuilt the computer to suit his own needs.

Now Pangaea was a killer, too. Like him in many ways. It intruded where it did not belong and destroyed things that were too valuable to let stand. For Pangaea the path of destruction was through the memory banks of other computers. It sought certain information and retrieved it, often deleting the information on the target mainframes, then it deleted all traces of its own presence.

The killer spent a great deal of time erasing all records that a computer system called Pangaea ever existed.

One of Pangaea's secret weapons was a new feature that the killer had developed and added to its operational system. A subroutine called "Kreskin," designed to search for patterns and collate any relevant information into a set of projections as close to human intuition and guesswork as a binary computer mind could achieve. At least with the current technology.

That pattern search had located a target the killer had sought for a long time.

It was why he was down here in the sewer.

It was why he was hunting in the darkness like the predator he was.

He moved as quietly as possible, running lightly along the narrow ledges to avoid splashing through the sluggish runoff from last night's rain. The storm drains were vast, stretching for twenty-one thousand kilometers beneath the sprawl of the city above. These tunnels held the drinking and non-drinking water mains, telecommunication cables, pneumatic cables, and traffic light management cables. Following the tunnels took planning. Getting lost was simple. Dying down here was common.

He took care. He planned every step.

If his information was correct, he was near the target.

The killer slowed to a walk and then stopped at the entrance to a chamber that was part of the channeling system that took water from dozens of culverts and combined it in a larger chute that flowed to the Seine. He crouched in the shadows, silent and unmoving, allowing his senses to fill him with every bit of detail about where he was and what was here. He was not a man to make assumptions, even about an empty tunnel.

There was a rusted service door in the far wall. A weak bulb in a grilled cage mounted above the door threw dirty yellow light over the churning water. A child's ragdoll bobbed in the current, and the killer paused for a moment to look at it. The doll was dressed in the checkerboard clothes of a harlequin jester, with bells on its hat and a broad smile of stitched red silk.

It was an expensive doll and it looked well-worn, and not just from the passage through the drain. This was a doll a child had held close for many nights. Something loved, something treasured. And now it was lost here in the darkness, on its way to oblivion in the ocean. Perhaps if the child knew where it was then he, or more likely *she*, might imagine her tattered friend to be off on some grand adventure. Otherwise…it was a friend who was lost and would never be found.

That thought came close to breaking the killer's heart.

So many of his friends were lost to him.

So many.

He almost reached for the doll, almost pulled it from the water as the thing bobbed past, but he did not. He remained as still as the shadows and the grime-slick walls and the bones of dead rats. Instead, he watched the harlequin doll drown in the froth of converging sewer water and rush away into the great nothingness.

After a moment, he turned his attention to that rusted door. According to the records Pangaea had filched for him, that door led to a disused valve station whose purpose had been superseded by a more modern system controlled in an office on street level.

At a glance the door appeared to be forgotten, with years of rust crusted to the hinges and knob. The low-wattage service light was there to aid with routine inspection of this rechanneling chamber.

That was how things looked according to all official records and even on the service logs of the men who worked these tunnels. They knew the door was there, but they ignored it as they ignored hundreds of similarly disused doors, tunnels, chambers, holding tanks, ladders, and other detritus of an older age of public sewage. Like the subway systems in New York and London, here there were layers of new built on forgotten bones of the old.

However the killer had a separate source of intelligence that insisted that this door was not at all what it seemed. And that there were more than rust-frozen valves on the other side.

The killer was about to rise from his crouch when he heard something.

Very faint, very soft.

A footfall. A scuff.

Not an animal sound.

Human, though he could not tell more than that.

He did not move, aware that he was so deep inside a bank of shadows that he was invisible. His clothes were as black as his balaclava, and he had black greasepaint around his eyes. Only the whites of his eyes were visible in the light, and no light touched him where he crouched. The gear he carried—grenades, knives, and more—was arranged on his belt with cushions so they didn't clink or rattle.

The sound came from a side tunnel to his left. From the memory of the tunnel schematics in his mind, he knew that the closest street access to that tunnel was at least a mile away. A long way to go in the dark. He raised the black cover of his watch and touched the face, reading the position of the arms. Three minutes past four in the morning. Far too late for the evening maintenance crew, two hours early for the day shift.

He waited.

There wasn't another scuff. Whoever it was knew how to move quietly. The scuff had probably been a rare accident. An unseen patch of slime.

The killer drew his pistol. A .22 with a sound suppressor. It was poor at long range, but this man never killed from a great distance.

He was selective and careful. It was not because killing up close provided some men with a physical thrill. That was not a factor in the function of either his heart or mind. It was a matter of not liking to make errors. Distance, especially in the dark, increased the risk of errors.

Errors were the result of sloppiness, nerves, or poor process.

He crouched, the pistol held in both hands, barrel pointed down, his forearms resting against his bent knees to keep the muscles from fatiguing.

Forty feet down the tunnel the shadows changed. A slender fragment of the darkness detached itself and crept forward with catlike grace.

In the bad light it was difficult to tell much about the figure.

Small, slight of build, moving with the ease of a dancer or a martial artist. Someone who knew how to move. No visible weapons in the hands; however, the black handles of knives stood up from sheathes on each thigh.

The killer pursed his lips in appreciation.

He watched as the figure approached the downspill of yellow light and paused, becoming as motionless as the killer himself.

Suddenly a sound broke into the moment as the rusted metal door opened. Despite its decrepit appearance, the door opened with a soft *click* and swung outward on nearly silent hinges. Three men stepped out. Two of them wore boots, jeans, and t-shirts; both wore identical shoulder holsters with .45 pistols snugged into them. The third man wore a hazmat suit with the hood off. The men in jeans drew their pistols and walked to the edges of the runoff trough, looking up and down into the shadows. The killer knew that they saw nothing, that they *could* see nothing; neither had allowed his eyes to adjust to the darkness before trying to look through it. They didn't see the killer, and they didn't see the other figure crouched barely six feet from them.

The two thugs nodded to the man in the hazmat suit who reached through the doorway and lifted out a Styrofoam cooler of the type used to transport medical or biological materials. A red biohazard symbol was stamped onto the white plastic side. He walked to the edge of the trough and stood for a moment looking down into the eddying water. Then he set the cooler down.

The killer raised his pistol.

His intel had brought him here to this place, this time. His mission projections had him back at street level within eight minutes from first trigger pull.

Then everything changed.

The figure crouched in the dark moved.

There was a rasping sound, steel clearing leather, but no flash of metal. Like British commando knives, the blade was blackened. The figure rose from a crouch and swarmed among the men. The blade swept right and then left, and suddenly arterial blood geysered, spraying all the way to the curved top of the brick tunnel. One of the thugs reeled back, fingers scrabbling to stem a flow that could never be stopped. The second man staggered away and turned in an almost graceful pirouette, hands reaching out to break a fall that turned clumsy and artless. They collapsed like discarded puppets onto the stone walkway so quickly that the man in the hazmat suit was unaware of their deaths until bone and slack flesh struck the stones behind him.

He twitched and spun and was on the verge of crying out in shock and alarm, but the figure moved past him, sweeping an arm across his throat with such speed that arm and blade vanished into a dark blur. The man in the hazmat suit dropped to his knees and then fell forward, his slumping corpse humped over the Styrofoam chest.

It was the fastest thing the killer had ever seen.

How quick? Three seconds? Two?

The thugs and the other man lay dead. Blood ran in slow lines down the walls.

The shadowy figure stood facing the open doorway, knife gripped in one hand. The cuts had been so fast, the edge so sharp, that no blood clung to the weapon except a single pendulous drop that hung for a moment from the tip and then fell with the softest *splash*.

The killer watched all of this down the barrel of the .22 he held in hands that neither trembled nor swayed. He was thirty feet away, and if he'd to paint a fourth corpse onto this tableau he could have done it with impunity. Fast or not, the kill shot was his to take.

But the figure turned.

Slowly, with grace and without haste.

Toward him.

A gloved hand reached up and hooked fingers under the edge of a mask. Lifted, pulled it away.

In the weak lamplight the hair which spilled out from under the mask looked yellow, but the killer knew that it was not. He knew that it was as white as snow. Thick and lustrous, but paler than death. The face it framed was nearly as pale, except for a red mouth and eyes so dark they looked black. It was a beautiful face. Regal and cold and cruel. A face unused to smiles. A face like a death mask of some ancient queen, or a temple carving of a goddess of war.

The killer knew that face.

He held his pistol on her for five long seconds.

As always there was a fierce internal debate. His finger lay along the outside of the trigger guard. It would be so easy to slip it inside and take the shot.

The air between them seemed flammable, as if a word or even a thought could ignite it.

She lifted that proud head and looked down her patrician nose at him.

"Saint Germaine," she said quietly. There was equal parts contempt and admiration in her voice. "Or do you prefer 'Deacon'? I've heard that people are calling you that now."

He kept the gun on her. "It doesn't matter."

It didn't. Neither was his name, and he was sure that, as smart and as connected as this woman was, she would never know his real name. No one would.

"Deacon, then," she said. "It's less pretentious."

He lowered his pistol and pulled off his balaclava. "And we wouldn't want to be pretentious," he said. "Would we, Lilith?"

Chap. 2

Deacon rose to his feet, his pistol still in his hand but the barrel pointed down. It made the statement he intended.

Lilith flicked her wrist the way a samurai would when shaking blood from a *katana,* and then slid the black-bladed knife back into its sheath. Without taking her eyes from Deacon, she knotted her fingers in the back of the dead man's hazmat suit and with no apparent effort lifted his body off of the Styrofoam cooler and casually swung it up into the rushing water. It was an act that demonstrated a level of physical strength far in excess of what should have been possible for a woman of her size. A very strong man might have had difficulty lifting so limp and heavy a burden and tossing it aside so casually.

That, too, made a statement, and it was in no way lost on the Deacon.

He moved closer and stood a few feet from her and the cooler.

"Are you here for that?" he asked, then ticked his head toward the open door. "Or what's in there?"

Lilith took some time answering that. Her expression gave little away, even to someone as practiced at reading expressions as Deacon. She nudged the cooler with the toe of her boot.

"Do you know what's in here?"

"I might," Deacon said. "Do you?"

Another pause. "No."

"Ah."

They both looked at the open door.

"That's going to set off an alarm," he said.

"I know."

"If they think they're being raided they'll dump their hard drives and—"

"It's an old burglar's trick," she said. "Set a smoky fire and watch through a window to see what people rush to save. A good man will save his family bible. A blackmailer will save his cache of evidence. And a scientist—"

"—Will save his research. Yes, I've read Sherlock Holmes."

Lilith gave him the tiniest sliver of a cold smile. Not at all friendly, but not as hostile as the flat, reptilian glare.

"Why were you waiting over there? You could have picked the door lock."

"I wasn't trying to get in. I wanted this." He squatted down and removed the cooler's lid. Inside were three aluminum cylinders packed into carved slots. Each cylinder was pressure locked with a tight metal cap.

"What is it?" asked Lilith. "A bioweapon? Some kind of germ warfare thing?"

"A performance enhancing synthetic steroid," said Deacon.

She actually smiled. "'Performance'? What kind of performance?"

"Not the kind you're thinking," he said, returning her smile. "It's the first generation of a formula that combines the select lean-mass-building steroids with a synthetic *nootropic* compound that significantly increases and regulates the hypothalamic histamine levels. In normal pharmacology these drugs are wakefulness promoting agents often prescribed to prevent shift-work sleepiness. This version is designed to build stamina and wakefulness to a point where the treated person won't tire and won't lose mental sharpness."

"To what end? Super soldiers?"

"Hardly. Indefatigable factory workers."

Lilith blinked. "Factory...?"

"These drugs are intended for use in third-world countries to increase the efficiency and output of unregulated factory workers. Shift workers who can work twenty-four or even forty-eight hours at maximum efficient output." He sighed. "It's a new tweak on legal slave labor because it's for use in countries where there is no enforceable human rights presence and where governments are easily bought. Earlier versions of these drugs are already being used in Southeast Asia and some places in Africa."

A sneer twisted her mouth. "The new face of slave labor."

"Yes," he agreed.

"You're American," she said. "Most of the companies that would use this sort of thing are American."

"Many are, yes."

She cocked an eyebrow. "Are you here with official sanction?"

He shrugged.

Lilith shifted to get a better look into his eyes. "Why do *you* care?"

She leaned on the word *you*.

Deacon didn't answer. Instead he closed the cooler and replaced the lid. Then he took the container and placed it in the shadowy spot where he'd been crouching. It vanished from sight as if it ceased to exist.

"I didn't see you in the dark over there," said Lilith after a few moments. "Not until you pointed your gun at me."

"Your back was turned when I raised my weapon. You could not have seen the movement."

She shrugged.

"One of these days," said Deacon, "I would like to obtain a drop of your blood."

"To test?"

"Of course."

"You wouldn't understand the results," she said.

"I might."

"No."

"Why are you so sure?"

Her tone was flat. "Because I'm not like you. Not like anyone you know. You'd see the numbers and the chemistry, and maybe if you had the funding you would run some tests on my DNA, and all it would do is confuse you. Maybe scare you."

"Fear is seldom a deterrent," he said.

"Wouldn't that depend on what there is to be afraid of?"

"Generally not."

She made a moue of irritation. A very French thing, although Deacon knew that she was not French. He did not know everything about Lilith's heritage—and some of what he'd been able to piece together was apocryphal or at least doubtful—but he knew that her mother had been a Warsaw Jew who had died badly at Sobibor. Deacon had no information beyond wild rumors as to who her father was. The only other family member Deacon could reliably identify was a daughter whose real name, like Lilith's own, was buried beneath layers of secrecy and obfuscation. Although he would never say so, to her or anyone, it was the fact of having one genealogical foot planted in horror and the other planted in obscurity that engendered within him small feelings of kinship for her.

And, like his own history, there were questions about her past that most people would find difficult to answer and, if answered, challenging. Life, however, is far stranger than the greater population of this troubled old world would readily and comfortably accept.

While Lilith watched, Deacon dragged the two dead thugs, one at a time, to the stream and rolled them in. It was clear to them both that it required more effort on his part than she'd used to dispose of the man in the hazmat suit. Neither felt the need to comment on it.

When the last man vanished into the swirling waters, Deacon consulted his watch, glanced upstream and then over at the still-open door, and pushed his sleeve down to cover the watch.

Lilith said, "Those men were out here to hand that cooler off to someone."

"Yes. A four-man team. Two Americans, a Brit, and their local contact."

"When are they due?"

"Five minutes ago," said Deacon.

She opened her mouth to ask for clarification, then thought better of it. She glanced at the rushing water as if expecting to see four bodies float by.

"Ah," she said.

He nodded.

"So, your part in this is over?"

"I did what I came to do," he answered. "Now tell me...what's your interest here? Arklight has never expressed an interest in this area of *human* rights."

Deacon, for his part, leaned on the word *human*. Making the point and leaving much understood but unspoken.

It seemed to both amuse and annoy Lilith, since various partially formed expressions came and went on her face in rapid succession.

He noted that Lilith did not flinch or rage at his mention of "Arklight." Once before she had tried to kill him for speaking that name, for even knowing it. The fact that she had been unsuccessful formed one of the somewhat shaky pillars of the truce between them. The truce, he knew, was as substantial as vapor and existed only because they had yet to have directly conflicting agendas. Her tolerance of his use of the name of the highly secret and extremely dangerous group, of which Lilith was nominal head and chief operative, was as close to an olive branch as he ever expected to receive from her.

Finally she gestured to the open doorway. "The lab in there is partially funded by *Ordo Ruber*."

Deacon said, "Ah."

The Red Order was something that he had on his to-do list but which he currently lacked the funding and manpower to tackle. If his intelligence could be trusted, it was an ancient order along the lines of the Templars. Secretive and dangerous, with tendrils tangled into the underpinnings of several world governments, the OPEC nations, and the Catholic Church. He had not yet had the time to verify much of what he had heard and therefore had no framework for a cohesive case he could make to the President and Congress.

Lilith said, "There are rumors that the Order has been hiring scientists of all stripes—molecular biologists, geneticists, and others—to try to rebuild the genetic lines of the Red Knights. You know who they are?"

The Red Order was rumored to employ a group of special operatives known as the Red Knights. Like the ninja of ancient Japan, however, there was layer upon layer of misinformation and deliberate disinformation about who and, more importantly, *what* the Red Knights were. Some of the stories were preposterous. Others merely frightening.

"Rumors only," admitted Deacon. "Feel free to share."

She ignored that. "They want the Knights to become a more powerful and effective organization than ever." Something, some strange fire, ignited in Lilith's eyes. "I can't allow that."

"Then this is a straight hit?"

"No. This isn't the central lab. We don't know where that is. This is more of a processing and distribution center for research materials to be sent to researchers in the Order's pocket."

Deacon nodded. "And you mean to do what? Get hold of their bulk research materials and notes and use them to find leads to the scientists working for the Order."

"You were always cleverer than the other little spies, Deacon. Yes, that's exactly it."

"Do you have a team coming to help you?"

"It's only a small lab," she said. "Staff of ten or twelve." A pause. "These are scientists, lab techs, and a few foot soldiers. Three are already down."

"What about the Red Knights?"

Lilith shook her head. "They don't do guard duty. They won't be here."

Deacon looked at the gun he still held. He was about to say something when a buzzer suddenly sounded from inside the open doorway. Loud and insistent.

"Finally," she said, resting her hands on her knives. They could hear shouts and running feet. "This part is mine."

Deacon smiled and shook his head. "To be fair," he said mildly, "you helped me when you eliminated the three men who came out here. I feel as if I should return the favor."

But Lilith shook her head.

"I don't want your help," she said. "Be a nice little spy and go play James Bond somewhere else."

The shouts grew louder.

Deacon took a breath and let it out slowly. Then he holstered his pistol and turned away. He picked up the cooler and faded into the shadows, watching over his shoulder as Lilith drew her weapons and moved like a blur of shadows and steel through the open doors. The tunnel immediately echoed with the rattle of automatic gunfire and the screams of men in terrible pain.

With the cooler under his arm, Deacon began walking back the way he'd come, a frown etched on his face.

He got almost a hundred yards before another scream split the air.

It wasn't the dying scream of a man.

It was the shriek of a woman in terrible pain.

And in terrible fear.

Deacon dropped the cooler, tore the pistol from its holster, whirled and ran back along the edge of the black water as fast as he could.

Chap. 3

As he ran toward the door a man staggered out, blood streaming from deep crisscrossed cuts that gouged him from shoulders to hips. His belt was severed and with each step his trousers slipped further down his bloody legs. But he still held an AK-47 in his hands, finger jerking spasmodically on the trigger, bullets punching into the chamber beyond.

Deacon put a single .22 round into the back of the man's head and shoved him out of the way.

He jumped through the doorway, pivoted as he dropped into a crouch, gun up and ready in both hands, eyes taking in the scene. He was at the end of a short tunnel that doglegged to the left and opened onto a large stone room that had been converted into a rough field lab. There were long work tables, banks of computers, and various kinds of processing machinery. Blowers pushed cool, clean air into the room and pulled dust out. Two men lay in a red tangle at the mouth of the tunnel. Automatic rifles lay inches from their dead hands. Three other men, a guard with a handgun and two men in white lab coats, were down inside the room, their faces and throats slashed to ribbons.

Inside the chamber there were seven uninjured men. All of them had weapons—guns, a fire axe, and a burly man with a black t-shirt held one of Lilith's daggers. They were strung out in a wide half-circle around three figures who fought and tore at each other in the center of the room.

Lilith and two tall, pale-faced men dressed in dark clothes.

All of them were bleeding.

But Lilith was limping as she backpedaled from them. Her left arm curled gingerly around her middle. At first Deacon thought that the arm was broken, but then he saw the lines of bright red running down her loins and thighs.

She had her arm clamped over a stomach wound.

The men surrounding her were yelling and pointing weapons.

Lilith coughed, and there was blood on her lips.

The two men in dark clothes laughed.

Lilith's invasion had gone horribly wrong.

Deacon took all of this in within the space of a heartbeat.

He did not pause, did not waste time processing or strategizing. He tore a grenade from his belt, pulled the pin, hurled it.

It was a flash-bang, a stun grenade developed by the British SAS. Deacon dropped into a crouch and covered his head with his arms. Even so the bang was almost unbearably loud. The burst of light stabbed him through his shut eyelids.

The men in the room screamed.

Deacon immediately opened his eyes, took his guns in both hands again and began firing as he rose. He was peripherally aware that the two men with Lilith were beyond the effective range of the flash-bang and yet they had their hands to their ears, hissing in pain.

He noted it, but it was far from a matter of first importance as he felt his gun buck in his hands.

His first shot took a scientist in the side of the face. It was not intended as a kill shot, though the bullet punched a wet hole through cheekbone and out through the opposite cheek. The intention had been to drive that man into the men beside him. The collision took three of Deacon's opponents out in one second. He swung his pistol and fired four shots, two each to guards, hitting them as they turned toward him, the first shot to each hitting bodies to jolt them to a stop and the second hitting them in the head. Small caliber rounds lack the power to exit the far side of a skull, so instead they bounce around inside and destroy the brain. It was why the caliber was the preferred weapon of assassins.

That left two men immediately able to respond.

One man had the fire axe.

The other had a pistol.

Deacon shot the second man in the face and then put the axeman down with a head shot.

He calculated his ammunition. Eight shots fired. Four dead, one wounded, two recovering from the collision with the scientist. That was a full magazine and the one he'd chambered. He dropped the magazine and reached for a second, but one of the two survivors rushed him so fast he had no time to finish the reload.

Deacon stepped into the attack, pivoting his body as he tilted his weight onto his front leg. Both hands moved out as he simultaneously blocked with his left forearm and rammed the unloaded pistol into the attacker's face hard enough to jolt the man to a stop. Deacon recoiled his gun-hand and chopped the man in the Adam's apple with the gun.

The man dropped at once.

But now the second man was up and in motion, bringing his rifle to bear. If he'd dropped the gun and used his hands, or if he'd swung the rifle stock at Deacon, he might have had a chance. Instead he tried to aim the weapon.

Deacon stepped into him, dropping his own pistol as he intercepted the swing of the barrel and grabbed the long-gun with both hands. He turned his second step into a flat-footed kick that shattered the man's knee so badly the leg buckled and bent the other way. Deacon tore the gun from his hand, reversed it and pulled the trigger.

The gun bucked as two rounds hit the man in the chest, but then the slide locked back.

Empty.

Deacon tossed the gun aside.

Twenty feet away the two men in black and Lilith had all turned toward him.

Her eyes were filled with pain and hate.

Their eyes were filled with a pernicious delight that was appalling to behold. And those eyes were all wrong. The irises were not brown or blue or green. They were red. As red as the blood that painted this room. Instead of round pupils, theirs were slits. Like the eyes of reptiles.

The two men smiled at him.

Deacon felt the blood in his veins turn to ice.

The intelligence reports, the rumors about the killers called the Red Knights...so much had been beyond belief. Horror stories. Crazy lies.

Except....

Except now the truth was like a punch over the heart. It stopped the world for a terrible moment. It tore the mind open and jammed in like daggers.

As their lips curled back, Deacon saw their teeth.

So white.

So long and sharp.

They had teeth like dogs.

Like wolves.

Like monsters.

"They're Red Knights," screamed Lilith. "Deacon, they'll tear you apart. For God's sake...*run!*"

Chap. 4

He could have run. He was closer to the door than the Red Knights. He could be outside, reloading as he ran, safe in darkness.

He should have run. This was Lilith's fight. His government— even the small, clandestine groups that endorsed Deacon's personal agendas—had in no way sanctioned any contact with Arklight. The few people in the U.S. government who even knew of Arklight considered it a borderline terrorist organization. So this was not his fight, and Lilith was not his ally.

He would have run. But that would have meant that he was a different person than he was.

Instead, Deacon let the empty assault rifle clatter to the floor.

"No," he said.

The Red Knights—whatever they were—smiled with their wicked teeth. Their red eyes flared with the joy of a coming slaughter.

One of them stepped closer to Lilith. He had black fingernails, and blood dripped from them. Was that the weapon that had torn the screams from Lilith? Deacon was sure it was.

"I'll finish the whore," said that one, speaking in thickly accented French. He pointed at Deacon. "His blood is yours, my brother."

The second Knight laughed, every bit as coldly and cruelly as a villain from an old-time movie. A stage laugh, and it should have been comical, should have inspired laughter or groans from the audience. And, in any other place, under any other circumstances, it might have. But this was a monster laughing at the thought of red slaughter. An actual monster.

A fanged killer.

A drinker of blood.

A thing that should not exist outside of fiction or nightmares or the tortured dreams of lunacy.

One vampire said something to his companion, rattling off a few terse sentences in a strange language that sounded vaguely like Latin but wasn't. It gave no clue to the nationality or ethnicity of these Red Knights.

These *things*.

Deacon neither needed nor wanted a translation. Death was coming for him. That was the gist; he didn't require details.

The Red Knight began moving toward him. Not fast, not using its speed. It *stalked* him, anticipation twisting the smile on its face. This was what it enjoyed. The hunt. Maybe more than the kill.

The Knight held out his hands and flexed his fingers, displaying thick fingernails as sharp as bear claws. Claws for tearing the humanity from a person, claws for rending to the bone.

Deacon began backing away.

This made the Knight laugh. A low chuckle, echoed by his companion. Lilith sagged to her knees, blood streaming from between the fingers of the hands she pressed to her stomach.

"Run," she said weakly. "Run...."

Deacon turned and ran.

The Knight howled with delight and ran after him.

It took only six steps for the monster to catch the man.

Suddenly Deacon dropped to the ground, arms wrapped around his head, knees drawn up into a fetal ball.

The Knight paused, confused.

Not at that, but at the thing that floated toward him. Something his prey had thrown as he twisted and fell.

There was only a fragment of a moment to react.

The Knight said the same thing Deacon himself had said a few moments ago.

"No."

It meant something entirely different.

The object exploded.

With a flash.

With a bang.

Six inches from the vampire's face.

The Red Knight screamed. Caught point-blank inside the blast zone, the Knight was slammed backward, blood bursting from his nose and ears. Red tears fell from its traumatized eyes. It staggered sideways, clawing at its face, shrieking in its strange, alien language.

The second Knight was thirty feet away, outside of the blast zone, but even so, he staggered, too. Extraordinary hearing and eyesight were powerful tools in the quiet and in the dark. Less so in the presence of a light-amplified concussion grenade.

Deacon rolled out of his fetal ball and snapped a kick at the closest Red Knight's knee.

The scream of pain from the flash-bang and the scream of pain from the shattered knee hit different notes. The second was sharper, higher, and as filled with fear and surprise as it was with agony.

Deacon came up off the floor and attacked the Knight. He did not enjoy fighting. There was no sense of style to what he did, he made no comments, he wasted no time.

As he rose, he hooked an uppercut into the monster's groin. That folded the Knight forward, and Deacon met the sudden bend by grabbing the thing's head and yanking him face-forward onto a rising knee. As the Knight rebounded from that impact, Deacon punched him three times in the throat with the extended knuckles of both fists, left, right, left. Cartilage collapsed. Deacon did not know how strong this thing was; he didn't know what kind of damage he could sustain or how fast he could recover. Centuries of lies and half-truths and myths masked the truth. All he knew, all that he had to work with, was that the Red Knight could be hurt and could bleed and needed to breathe.

That was enough.

He attacked the Knight, giving him no chance, no advantage, no mercy. He blinded him and broke his arms, he stamped again on the shattered knee, destroying the leg completely, then he used a kick-sweep to cut both legs out from under his screaming enemy. As the Knight fell, Deacon twisted and followed it to the floor so that his punch to the solar plexus landed at the same instant the man's weight hit hard ground. The effect was to drive whatever air was trapped in the Knight's throat upward against the wreckage of his throat. The extra force tore apart whatever was left of the structure of the throat—using the fragments of the hyoid bone as razors. Blood immediately began filling the Red Knight's lungs; he began thrashing and flopping around with hysterical force.

Deacon hurled himself backward and spun away from a dying enemy to face the other vampire.

He froze at the spectacle before him, and he knew immediately that it would live forever in the darkest parts of his mind.

The second Red Knight was down.

Lilith sat astride him.

She had not been at the point of death from the wound in her stomach. It was immediately clear that she'd been faking, exaggerating the severity in order to find a moment to make her move.

In the confusion, while Deacon killed the first Knight, Lilith had attacked the other.

Not with her hands.

Not with her knives.

She crouched over him, her mouth buried in the side of the vampire's throat. For the oddest little fracture moment, Deacon thought she was kissing the Knight.

But, of course, that was wrong.

Everything in this moment was wrong.

There was a feral snarling, tearing, ripping sound. The Red Knight thrashed beneath her, tearing at her clothing and flesh with his nails. Weakly, though.

And weaker still with each pulsing moment.

Blood pooled beneath the Knight's head.

Then, with a terrible spasm, the creature shivered and flopped and lay utterly still. Lilith still bent over him, her face buried beside the Knight's neck, half-hidden by the corpse's profile.

"Lilith…," murmured Deacon.

Nothing.

Only the sound of a wild animal. Wet and awful.

"Lilith," he said again.

Nothing.

He bent and picked up his fallen pistol and the second magazine he hadn't been able to use. He slapped it into place. The sound was loud, harsh.

Lilith froze.

The sounds stopped.

"Lilith," Deacon said once more as he raised the pistol and racked the slide.

Only then did she lift her head. Her face was completely covered with dark red blood.

And her eyes.

Her eyes.

They were entirely black. Without pupil or iris or sclera.

Black within black within black.

Deacon pointed the pistol at her.

"Come back," he said.

His voice was gentle. The barrel of the gun was a promise.

Blood dripped from Lilith's chin and lips.

"Come back."

She blinked at him.

Once.

Twice.

And then her eyes were human again.

No, thought Deacon, that was an imprecise way of understanding what had happened. She was not human again, not even *more* human.

In that moment, as Lilith stepped back from the edge of the abyss, it was simply that for now she was less of a monster.

They stayed like that for a long moment. She, kneeling astride a savaged corpse, he standing with a gun in bloody hands. The world ground on its gears around them.

Lilith spoke a single word, and it came out thick, and wet and harsh.

"Deacon."

His heart beat many times before he lowered his gun.

Part Two

Now

Les Égouts de Paris

Chap. 5

I was ankle-deep in water that smelled like shit and garlic.

Charming.

It had been dry in Paris, and the only thing sloshing around in the sewers came from toilets and bidets. Which made me weigh my pay scale and benefits against the benefits of saving the world. I'm pretty sure I was being shortchanged.

And I was pretty sure I was lost.

The Paris sewer system was a bitch. It would have given Daedalus a boner.

I tapped my earbud. "Bug, where in the wide blue fuck am I?"

Bug said, "Two turns to go, Cowboy."

Although this was in no way a high-profile mission we were using combat call signs. Well…I was, at least. Bug was Bug at all times.

"You said that before the last turn."

"No, that was a bend, not an actual turn."

"Yeah? When I get back I am going to bend your head and shove it up your actual ass."

Bug chuckled. He's the computer guru for the Department of Military Sciences. And a world-class geek.

And a friend, so the threat was only half serious.

If I couldn't find my target soon, it was going to get a lot more serious. I'd been down here in the smelly darkness for too long, and I was beginning to suspect that this whole thing was a wild goose chase.

The mission briefing went like this....

My boss, Mr. Church, received intel about a new player in the international black market for stolen technologies. The guy's actual identity was unknown, but the rumor mill said that he was paying top dollar for certain kinds of software, bulk research, or hardware. Interpol had formed a task force to hunt the guy, but so far he'd been as elusive as Professor Moriarty. A few associates had been bagged, but the big man himself always seemed to vanish like smoke. Barrier, the British equivalent of the DMS, reached out for our help—mostly to have our super-duper computer system, MindReader, interface with their computers and collate data from a dozen enforcement agencies in Europe, looking for useful patterns. MindReader got a whole bunch of hits, and since then every police department and intelligence service on three continents had been running down leads.

I got into this because I was on vacation at Argentière in the French Alps and was therefore officially "not doing anything." Vacationing shooters get no respect. No respect at all.

Thirty-one hours ago I was swooshing down a ski slope.

Now I was sloshing through French poop.

Happy? No, I wasn't.

Mr. Church had called me to ask if I could check a place under Paris that had once been used as a processing facility for bioweapons and similar threats. The place had been emptied of anything dangerous and sealed off and, apparently, forgotten and left to rot way back in 1983. I was learning how to play with Legos in 1983 and never thought that I'd grow up to be a spotless hero for truth, justice, and the American way. I kicked a dead rat out of my way and plodded on, wishing all kinds of horrible deaths on Mr. Church.

"Fifty feet and left," said Bug.

"Yeah, yeah."

I'd asked Church why I had to go and not the French *Brigade des Forces Spéciales Terre*. This was, as I remembered it, their fucking city. Church took a moment before answering, and when he did that I knew that he was sorting through all the things he knows about something to decide what little sliver of the truth to tell me. Especially about things that happened—or that he might have been involved in—prior to his forming the DMS. I don't know a lot about his past other than that he was some kind of spook and almost certainly either Special Ops or the equivalent for some deep-cover black ops group. You know the expression "he knows where the bodies are buried"? I made that joke to him once, and he gave me a sad, old smile and told me that, indeed, he should know where they're buried...he'd buried a lot of them. Anyone else makes a comment like that, you think they're talking trash.

You never—*ever*—think Church is talking trash.

I don't know that he's ever outright lied to me, but if I had to live on the tiny scraps of information he fed me...I'd starve to death.

What he actually said was, "Captain Ledger, there may be nothing left of value to anyone. However in the remote chance that there *is* something to find at that lab, we need to put eyes on it first and then either retrieve it or destroy it. This needs to be handled with secrecy, immediacy, and finesse."

I have seldom been accused of possessing finesse, but I understood his point. This was never going to make it into an official report—even for the eyes-only crowd; and I suspect that his initial involvement back in the eighties likewise was never filed.

I came to the end of one branch of the sewer system. There was a big tank-like chamber from which six side tunnels branched off.

"Bug," I said, "talk to me."

"Take the second tunnel on your left," he said. "Follow that for a hundred and twenty meters, make another left and you'll be there."

"You're sure?" I put just a little edge in my voice. Bug was like a little brother to me, but if I got lost one more fucking time I was going to feed him to the tigers at the zoo.

"The intel's rock solid," said Bug.

I followed the second tunnel, took that second left, and found myself in another chamber, this one a reverse of the one I'd just left. Dozens of smaller tunnels seemed to converge here into a larger waterway. If there had been even a light rain, this would probably be a fairly brisk stream. As it was the filthy water merely rose above my ankles to midcalf. Thank Christ, Church gave me enough of a heads up so that I wore a waterproof Saratoga Hammer suit. It was a biohazard rig designed for combat troops. I wasn't wearing the hood, though, because I needed to see where the hell I was going. As a result I had the full snootful of the aroma of human waste smacking me in the face with every step.

I know, my life…just like James Bond. Beautiful women, clever gadgets, dinner jackets, and martinis.

I climbed onto a narrow stone ledge that ran along the edge of the water. It was wider here than in the tunnel, allowing me to be on moderately dry land. Less noisy, at least. I knelt at the shadowy edge of a spill of yellow light thrown by a bulb in a rusted cage. There was a niche in the wall with a door set into a frame of bricks. Black mold and lichen coated the bricks, and the door was completely covered in dark red rust. The door was at the far end of a small concrete pad just big enough for half a dozen people to stand on, though right now I was the only person down here who wasn't a rodent or cockroach.

"Cowboy to Bug," I said. "Target acquired."

"Proceed with caution," said a voice in my ear. Not Bug this time. Church.

"Roger that, Deacon," I said, using his combat call sign.

"Good hunting, Cowboy," he replied.

Yeah, I thought, *hunting for what? E. coli?*

I squatted, studied the ground in front of the door, and felt the first tickling of alarm.

A fine sheen of moist grime covered the light gray concrete, and as I bent close I could see the impressions of shoes. Several pairs of shoes, the prints overlapping and partially obscuring each other. Impossible to tell how many.

"Rut-roh," I said in my best Scooby-Doo voice.

Then I heard voices.

Men's voices. And, I think, a woman.

Muffled, distant. Impossible to understand.

Any sewer is an echo chamber, and the sewers of Paris are virtually endless stone tunnels in which sounds are distorted, carried for miles, buried, or combined into an auditory mélange that can drive you nuts. I cocked my head to listen, trying to determine from which side corridor or tunnel the voices were coming from.

Then I realized that they were not coming from the tunnels.

The voices were coming from the other side of the rusted door.

I crept toward it, and as I did so it was clear that the door, though closed, was not shut tight. It was slightly ajar, not even enough to slip a business card through but enough for voices to slip out. As I drew closer I could tell why.

The voices were shouting.

Yelling.

And, then one of them started screaming.

The woman.

Before I knew it, my knife was in my hand. There was too much raw methane in the foul air to risk sparks from a pistol.

I pushed the door open and moved inside, fast and quiet, keeping low, taking in everything I could. Church had given me the basic layout of the lab: a short tunnel and then a larger chamber, with many small cubby holes used for storage, bathrooms and utility.

All of the action was happening in the main room.

And I walked into a weird tableau.

Truly weird.

There were ten people in that room. All dressed in black. All men.

Well, all of the people left *alive* were men. There were three dead people on the ground in space around which ten men knelt. One of the corpses was a woman. From her clothes—satin shorts and a tiny halter—it was pretty evident she was a prostitute. The woman lay in a pool of blood. Her throat had been cut from ear to ear.

On either side of her lay skeletons dressed in the rags of old black clothing. Even from where I crouched I could see that one of the skeletons was busted up—clear breaks in one leg and both arms. The other had a broken neck. From the condition of the bones and the scraps of old clothing, it was evident they'd been here for a lot of years. The vermin in the dark had been busy with them. Now they lay on either side of the murdered woman so that the pool of blood under her touched both sets of bones.

The men wore nondescript clothes—black shoes, pants, and sweatshirts, but they also wore turbans with scarves covering the lower halves of their faces. The turbans were loose and wrapped in the same fashion. I've been in the Middle East enough to know that there are a lot of methods of wrapping a turban and that each method usually denoted a different ethnic or religious group. A Sikh's turban and one worn by an Afghani village headman are entirely different. These guys, though, didn't fit any group catalogued in my head.

This whole thing appeared to be a weird kind of religious ritual and that matched no part of my mission objectives. The gathered men stared at the blood and bones with absolute intensity, wide-eyed, as if they expected something miraculous to happen.

They watched.

I watched.

Not a goddamn thing happened.

So far no one spotted me, and since the odds were ten to one I was thinking about the many benefits of running away. The woman was beyond help, and none of this made a lick of sense, so I backed out of the entrance corridor and crept a dozen yards down the walkway to call Mr. Church.

Chap. 6

I described everything I'd seen.

"Cowboy," he replied, "verify that there are two skeletons. Describe their clothing."

I did. I expected him to tell me to bag it and call this in to the locals.

"Captain," said Church very tersely, "listen to me very closely. The two skeletons are the remains of Red Knights. Confirm understanding."

I think I actually staggered. I remember the wall slapping me in the back.

Red Knights.

Jesus, Mary, and Joseph.

I'd encountered Red Knights before. Fought them. Killed some of them. Watched them slaughter some of my team.

They almost killed me.

It came close.

So close.

The Red Knights were genetic aberrations. Monsters. Not entirely human. They are the descendants of a freakish schism in the evolution of our species. Like *Homo sapiens idaltu* and *Homo floresiensis*, these were members of a race of cousins to *Homo sapiens*.

They're proper scientific designation appears in no medical or scientific textbook. It exists, as far as I know, in only three places—the archives of the Department of Military Sciences, in the secret traditions of the Red Order, and in the bloody history of the covert group called Arklight.

That scientific name?

Homo vampiri upierczi.

Vampires.

No, these weren't pasty-faced noblemen in opera cloaks. They couldn't turn into bats and they weren't in any way supernatural. These bastards—the *Upierczi*, as they called themselves—were all too real. Relatives of humanity but set apart. First as slaves of the Church and assassins for the Red Order, later as their own self-governing shadow kingdom.

The world doesn't know about them. The truth of what they are, the fact of their existence, is buried beneath layers of false histories, folklore, myths, lies, and legends.

Last year the DMS teamed up with Arklight to bring them down. It was not a war of our choosing. They started the game and were playing by some nasty rules. If they'd won...?

Well, if they'd won, I wouldn't be here up to my ankles in shit beneath Paris because there wouldn't be a Paris. There wouldn't be much of anything left except a wasteland suffering through an unending nuclear winter.

The fact that the two Red Knights down here with me were dead—and had been dead for a long time—was no fucking comfort at all.

When I could speak I said, "Any idea who the guys with the turbans are?"

But even as I asked it, I think I knew. Church confirmed it, though.

"*Hashashin.*"

Yeah. Fuck me.

The Red Knights were killers for the Red Order, an illegal and unsanctioned group operating on behalf of Christianity. They were formed during the Crusades. Their enemies—and in many sick and twisted ways their co-conspirators—were the *Hashashin*, a sect of superb killers formed in 1080, before the First Crusade. The Anglicized version of their name is *assassin*.

You can see why I was sweating bullets.

One of me, ten world-class assassins. The bones of two vampires.

"What the hell have I stepped into here?" I demanded.

"Something that should have been entirely past tense," said Church, and there was definitely sadness in his voice. "It was a mistake not to have cleaned up the leavings."

I don't know that I've ever heard Church admit to a mistake before. Rather than humanizing him, it gave me the chills.

"I'm wide open to suggestions," I said. "As long as they don't involve me going back in there. I'd like to see the cavalry come riding in pretty damn soon."

"Is now fast enough?"

It was not Church speaking in my ear. Or Bug.

The voice came from behind me.

There are very, very few people who can sneak up on me.

But she....

Yeah, she manages to do it all the time.

And despite everything, I was smiling as I turned around.

She stood there. Lean, fox-faced, with erect posture and the slightly splay-footed stance you see in ballet dancers. Thick auburn hair pulled back into a pony tail. Black form-fitting fatigues. Lots of weapons.

I said, "Hello, Violin."

She said, "Hello, Joseph."

Chap. 7

Violin beckoned for me to follow her down the tunnel, away from the rusted door and the room filled with killers and death. I was happy to follow.

In the shadows, as we stood precariously on a one-brick-wide ledge, she grabbed the front of my shirt and pulled me into a ferocious kiss. It was immediate and scalding, and it filled all the dark spaces—inside my head and here in the tunnels—with fireworks.

Then she pushed me back. I wobbled unsteadily and her strong grip kept me on the ledge.

I said, "Wow."

She said, "What are you doing here?"

"What are *you* doing here?"

Violin shrugged. "My mother sent me."

I told her about the routine scut work for Interpol.

She looked past me to where the dirty light splashed down over the metal door. "Do you know what's in there?"

"Some," I said and told her what I saw. "What do you know about it?"

Violin's eyes are difficult to read at the best of times. I saw shadows flit and dance. Eventually she said, "A long time ago, when I was a little girl, my mother came down here."

"Your mother? Lilith? Why?"

It was a dumb question to which I already knew the answer.

But Violin answered anyway. "Hunting monsters."

She didn't have to explain. The women of Arklight were survivors of the hell that was life in the Shadow Kingdom of the *Upierczi*. The vampires were all male. In order to breed, they stole women. The tales I heard about the immense suffering of women trapped in the underground breeding pens still gives me nightmares. Lilith had been a prisoner for twenty years. She had ultimately led a rebellion and took more than thirty women with her to freedom. Some of the women left their babies behind, unable to bring themselves to suckle the children of rape. Others brought their children out.

Violin had been born in captivity. Now she, like her mother, was a practiced hunter and killer. Part of Arklight.

I've had a long, bad life, and I've suffered some terrible tragedies. But when I think about what Lilith and the other women endured, I am humbled. And I'm also filled with a dark red, murderous rage. Together, Violin and I had vented some of that rage when we stopped the rise of the Red Knights. But, like most wars fought against a concept rather than a nationality, the struggle continues.

"Those are *hashashin* in there," I said. "What are they doing with the bones of Red Knights?"

Violin made a face. "They're superstitious," she said. "The Shadow War created by the Red Order and their counterparts in Islam is out of balance. The Red Order is in ruins, the Knights are scattered, the goals of the Shadow War are threatened."

"So?"

"So, they think they can resurrect the Red Knights with a blood sacrifice."

"Tell me you're joking."

"You saw it, Joseph."

"No, tell me that it can't work."

She punched me in the chest. Hard. "Don't be an idiot. Of course it can't work."

I was relieved. Kind of.

"But," she added, "I sincerely doubt that blood ritual is part of their mission objectives. That's something the assassins might think up, something fed by their own mystical beliefs, but if they're here, then they must have been sent by their masters who in turn must have intelligence from Red Order operatives."

"Again…so?"

"So, they want the bones of the Red Knights."

"Why?"

"DNA. The Red Order has no intention of letting their pet monsters become extinct. Not if they can find a way through some avenue of science to strengthen the Knights they have left or somehow create new ones. My mother thinks they are planning on using gene therapy to transform human operatives into Red Knights. A new and improved model, so to speak. They want to borrow the best genetic qualities of the Knights and graft it to humans who can otherwise be trusted. After all…the Knights did ultimately betray the Order."

Five years ago I would have laughed at her. Gene therapy to build super soldiers was science fiction, right?

Over the last few years I've encountered that kind of madness in several forms. Science was growing faster than sanity or common sense.

I looked past her.

"I don't suppose you have an Arklight strike team back there waiting for a go-order?"

She grinned. "I don't suppose you have Echo Team locked and loaded."

We both smiled as if this was all funny. Like it was a sunny day and we were looking at kids playing on the beach. Like the world made sense and we were ordinary people.

Except that neither of us would ever be ordinary.

And the world was totally mad.

I kissed her again.

Who knows if I'd ever get the chance again?

We crept back along the edge and moved to flank the rusted door. Quietly I asked, "Do you have a plan? 'Cause as tough as we are, darlin', there are ten of them and two of us. I am not hugely sold on those odds, and last time I checked I did not have a big red S on my chest."

"It's not about being tougher than your enemies, Joseph," she said. "After all, the Red Knights are bigger, stronger and much faster than anyone. Certainly much more powerful than my mother, and she's personally killed thirty-one of them."

"Christ." I glanced at the closed door. "That still leaves ten of them, two of us, and an explosive environment, honey."

"The reason my mother has survived this long is that in combat she was always smarter than whoever she fought. Always." Violin placed her palm on my chest, right between the two flash-bang grenades clipped to my Hammer suit. "One of these days, ask Mr. Church how he killed his first Red Knight."

"Huh?"

"He and my mother would have made a very good pair."

She removed one of the flash-bangs.

"Whoa, now. Wait, we can't," I said. "Too much methane."

Violin ignored me. She pulled the pin on the grenade but left the spoon in place. Then she carefully fitted the flash-bang into the space between the doorknob and the frame.

It was so simple an idea that I felt like kicking myself.

Violin stood on her toes to kiss my cheek. "Time to go."

We stepped slowly, softly and quietly away. We didn't start to run until we were fifty yards down the tunnel. And then we ran like hell.

It was just beginning to rain as we emerged from the darkness via a duct near the Seine. The water was stingingly cold, but it washed the filth from us.

We knew exactly when the assassins left the chamber with their stolen bones. We could tell down to the second. The blast blew manhole covers into the air for twenty blocks. Towers of flame shot a hundred feet into the air, transforming the City of Lights into a city of fiery red and gold and yellow. The earth shook beneath us. Windows exploded outward all along the avenues. People screamed and panicked and ran as if the world itself was exploding.

Violin and I sat on either side of the open duct as a fireball belched out between us. We were laughing like fools.

Like lunatics.

Like children.

I tapped my earbud and called it in. Church only said, "Good work." Nothing else. Some instinct told me that he wanted to say more, but I knew he wouldn't.

Bug said that he would make sure that no trace of DMS involvement hit anyone's radar. As for the lab down in the sewers? Tomorrow someone would go in.

The fire brigades, the police.

Maybe the *Brigade des Forces Spéciales Terre.*

Who knows, maybe even Interpol.

They'd go in looking for the source of the explosion. If the right people went in, there was a marginal chance they'd find the bones. Many bones now. Charred beyond recognition. The DNA in the marrow utterly destroyed, and all the potential for corrupt science to borrow the unnatural power there gone.

There would be nothing worth salvaging. And nothing worth learning. No secrets, no horrors, no nightmares.

And for once I'd come out of it whole.

It was a strange fact of my life that when I went to work I seldom came away with a whole skin. This time...I hadn't so much as skinned my knee.

It felt weird.

When the flames died down, I crossed the open duct and sat down next to Violin. The night was alive with sirens and car alarms and shouts. None of that mattered. The danger was over for now, even if we were the only two people in Paris who knew it.

"Look," she said, pointing.

Far above us a falling star carved a white line across the sky.

It was so corny that we both laughed. So poignant that I sought out her hand and when I took it she gave me a squeeze.

"Make a wish," I said.

I expected her to laugh at that, too. But instead she turned away, and in the light of stars and moon and Paris I caught the tracery of silver tears on her cheeks. I wrapped my arm around her and pulled her against me.

"The war never ends," she whispered. Softly, more to herself than to me.

For that I had no answer.

What response is really adequate when we both knew that, for us and those like us, the war could never really end? Ever. I thought about Lilith, the hell she lived in and the war she fought. I thought about Church, whose war was ongoing, fueled by some personal reasons I doubted I would ever fully comprehend.

Violin was a child of conflict and atrocity, bred as a slave, forged into a weapon.

I had been reshaped by horror and loss into a killer.

People like us were meant for war, and that is a tragedy I can't look too closely at or I start to really lose it. Four people who craved peace—and who understood both its cost and its vulnerability—but who would never be allowed to share in it. Even if we somehow managed to win this unwinnable war.

Violin leaned into my arms, and I bent and kissed the silver tears on her face.

We sat there on the edge of the river and above us the wheel of night turned from this day toward the next.

~The End~

Inside The DMS

THE GOOD GUYS

JOE LEDGER

Combat Call Sign: Cowboy

Rank: Captain

Brief Bio: Joe Ledger is a former Baltimore cop recruited by the Department of Military Sciences to head a team of special operators against terrorists with cutting-edge bioweapons. Joe is a dangerous man but a badly fractured one. The victim of terrible childhood trauma, Joe has three separate and distinct personalities inside his head: The Civilized Man—that idealistic and moral part of himself; the Cop—the investigator who is all about control; and the Warrior, also known as the Killer—who is savage and unforgiving. Thanks to years of therapy with his doctor and friend, Rudy Sanchez, Joe is able to use all three of those aspects and keep them under control. Joe Ledger is tough, resourceful, and a professional smartass. Ask anyone.

First Appearance: *Patient Zero*

MR. CHURCH

Combat Call Sign: Deacon
Real Name: Classified
Rank: Director
Brief Bio: The enigmatic man known variously as Church, the Deacon, the Sextant, Colonel Eldridge, Dr. Pope, St. Germaine, and a dozen other names, is the founder and director of the Department of Military Sciences. Brilliant, cold and dangerous, Church brings enormous financial and technological resources to bear in his crusade against terrorism. He is apolitical, ruthless, and well-connected. The running bet is that he's a former Cold War era special ops shooter. But that might be simply another layer of cover.
First Appearance: *Patient Zero*

DR. RUDY SANCHEZ

Combat Call Sign: Aztec (honorary)
Rank: Chief Medical Officer
Brief Bio: Mexican-born Rudy is now an American citizen and the Chief Medical Officer for the DMS. A psychiatrist specializing in post-violence trauma, Rudy was one of the doctors who helped Ground Zero workers cope with their experiences after 9-11. Since coming to work for the DMS, his job is to help the field teams cope with the horrors they encounter and the violence they're forced to commit.
First Appearance: *Patient Zero*

AUNT SALLIE

Combat Call Sign: Auntie
Real Name: Classified
Rank: Director of Field Operations
Brief Bio: Only Mr. Church knows who Aunt Sallie really is. And, though she could pass for Whoopie Goldberg's twin sister, she has none of the actress' charm and compassion. A former field agent and assassin, Aunt Sallie is the only person who knows Mr. Church's secrets. She runs the Hangar, the DMS headquarters located at Floyd Bennett Field in Brooklyn.
First Appearance: *The King of Plagues*

DOCTOR WILLIAM HU

Combat Call Sign: Dalek

Rank: Science Director

Brief Bio: Dr. Hu is one of the most brilliant scientists in the world—proof that Mr. Church never hires second best. He runs the advanced sciences division of the DMS and oversees research and development. He and Joe Ledger have failed to bond on a spectacular level.

First Appearance: *Patient Zero*

DR. CIRCE O'TREE

Combat Call Sign: Greek Fire (honorary)

Rank: Director of Strategic Intelligence

Brief Bio: A bestselling author whose books explore the ways in which religion and political ideologies are used as the basis for war and terrorism, Dr. O'Tree joined the DMS to help stop the terrorist organization known as the Seven Kings. She has since become a valuable member of the team and, most recently, the wife of Rudy Sanchez. Only a handful of people know that she is the only known surviving member of Mr. Church's family.

First Appearance: *The King of Plagues*

LEROY WILLIAMS

Combat Call Sign: Bug

Rank: Director of Computer Sciences, Deputy Director of Field Support

Brief Bio: Bug is the heart and soul of the DMS. His genius with computers brought him to the attention of Mr. Church, who hired him to manage the supercomputer MindReader. Bug and his team also provide real-time intelligence support for DMS field teams. He's one of Joe's most trusted allies and closest friends.

First Appearance: *Patient Zero*

GRACE COURTLAND

Combat Call Sign: Amazing

Rank: Major, Special Air Service, UK (deceased)

Brief Bio: Grace Courtland was the first woman to make it through the experimental program for women soldiers in the SAS. After distinguishing herself in that notorious boys' club, she helped Mr. Church form Barrier and later its American counterpart, the DMS. She and Joe Ledger became lovers for a brief time before Grace died a hero's death saving billions from ethnic genocide.

First Appearance: *Patient Zero*

VIOLIN

Combat Call Sign: Violin

Real Name: Classified

Rank: Arklight Senior Team Leader

Brief Bio: Violin was born into horror, as the child of one of the breeding slaves kept by the horrific Red Knights. When her mother, Lilith, escaped the Knights and formed the covert counterterrorism hit-squad Arklight, Violin quickly rose to prominence as their top field agent. Beautiful, deadly, and not entirely human. She is Joe Ledger's former lover and sometimes ally.

First Appearance: *Assassin's Code*

JUNIE FLYNN

Combat Call Sign: Bookworm (honorary)

Rank: n/a

Brief Bio: Junie has a complex past as the subject of a breeding program initiated by the Majestic Project in the years following the Roswell Crash. She is the former host of a conspiracy theory podcast and an author, and currently heads up a foundation dedicated to repurposing technologies illegally developed by the Majestic Three. She and Joe Ledger became romantically involved during the Majestic Black Book affair.

First Appearance: *Extinction Machine*

GHOST

Combat Call Sign: Ghost

Rank: Sergeant

Brief Bio: A big, strong, occasionally goofy and entirely dangerous white shepherd who is partnered with Joe Ledger. He has been awarded official rank as a sergeant in the DMS.

First Appearance: *Dog Days*

BRADLEY SIMS

Combat Call Sign: Top

Rank: First Sergeant, Army Rangers

Brief Bio: Top Sims is Joe Ledger's strong right hand and the most trusted field agent in the DMS. A former Ranger who came out of retirement after his son was killed and his daughter wounded in the early days of the Iraq War, Top now runs Echo Team.

First Appearance: *Patient Zero*

HARVEY RABBIT

Combat Call Sign: Bunny

Rank: Staff Sergeant, USMC

Brief Bio: Bunny is a big, blond, former competitive volleyball player who joined the Marines and went from Force Recon to the DMS. He and Top are best friends, and they joined Echo Team at the same time as Joe Ledger.

First Appearance: *Patient Zero*

LYDIA RUIZ

Combat Call Sign: Warbride

Rank: Chief Petty Officer, USN

Brief Bio: Apart from Top and Bunny, Lydia is the most experienced DMS field agent. Quick and ruthless in a fight, she's been on some of the most terrifying missions with Echo Team.

First Appearance: *Assassin's Code*

SAM IMURA

Combat Call Sign: Ronin

Rank: Lieutenant, US Army

Brief Bio: Sam is one of the best snipers in the U.S. military. Cool and patient, he provides Echo Team with long-range punch.

First Appearance: *Extinction Machine*

MONTANA PARKER

Combat Call Sign: Stretch

Rank: FBI Special Agent (retired)

Brief Bio: Montana is a former FBI agent and the newest member of Echo Team. Tough, outspoken and reliable, she fits in well with the other top professionals on Joe Ledger's top squad.

First Appearance: *Code Zero*

SGT. GUS DIETRICH

Combat Call Sign: Bulldog

Rank: Command Sergeant Major, retired; US Army (deceased)

Brief Bio: Retired Command Sergeant Major Dietrich was Mr. Church's personal assistant, aide and bodyguard. Bulldog tough and fiercely loyal, Dietrich was one of the few people Church trusted completely.

First Appearance: *Patient Zero*

BRICKLIN ANDERSON

Combat Call Sign: Stonewall

Rank: Gunnery Sergeant, U.S. Army

Brief Bio: Brick Anderson is a former DMS field agent who lost a leg in combat. He originally ran the Field Support team for the Hub, the Denver Field Office, then worked out of the Warehouse before becoming Mr. Church's personal assistant and bodyguard.

First Appearance: *The Dragon Factory*

BRIAN BIRD

Combat Call Sign: Birddog

Rank: Logistics Specialist

Brief Bio: Birddog works closely with Brick, making sure that the field teams get all of the hardware they need to get the job done.

First Appearance: *Extinction Machine*

HELMUT DEACON

Combat Call Sign: The Kid (honorary)

Rank: Junior Executive for FreeTech

Brief Bio: Helmut is a teenager whose parentage is both complicated and horrific. In a move to separate himself from his father, and prove to the world that beyond nature and nurture there's a third option: choice, Helmut has used his genius and specialized knowledge to help humanity. He is currently on the science team for Junie Flynn's FreeTech.

First Appearance: *The Dragon Factory*

THE BAD GUYS

THE SEVEN KINGS

A secret society made up of some of the most powerful and dangerous men in the world. To build their mystique, the Kings hijacked much of the conspiracy theories built around other groups—such as the Illuminati. Though defeated by the DMS, the Kings are far from destroyed, and it's likely they'll be back in force before too long.

First Appearance: *The King of Plagues*

HUGO VOX

The cold-hearted genius who built the Seven Kings was also one of the leading experts in anti-and counter-terrorism. He used his high security clearance to obtain insider knowledge that allowed the Kings to do untold harm.

First Appearance: *The King of Plagues*

THE RED KNIGHTS

The *Upierczi* are a genetic offshoot of humanity that live in the shadows and hunger for human blood. Although they're not supernatural—just products of genetic aberration—they are the basis for the myths of vampires. The Red Knights are incredibly strong and fast and utterly ruthless.

First Appearance: *Assassin's Code*

BERSERKERS

These super soldiers are the result of transgenics and gene therapy undertaken by the Jakoby Twins. Given DNA from silverback gorillas, the Berserkers are enormously powerful and highly dangerous.

First Appearance: *The Dragon Factory*

SEBASTIAN GAULT

The former pharmaceutical developer has used both his genius and his vast fortune to fund terrorist groups and to provide them with dangerous bioweapons including the fearsome *Seif al Din* pathogen. Gault was recruited into the Seven Kings of Hugo Vox.

First Appearance: *Patient Zero*

ALLIES

BARRIER

Barrier was the first of the modern wave of counterterrorism organizations designed to respond to enemies with the highest level of technology. Based in London, Barrier's teams are made up largely of the best-of-the-best agents from the SAS, MI5 and MI6. The senior consultant on the design and protocols for Barrier was Mr. Church.

First Appearance: *Patient Zero*

ARKLIGHT

The covert and militant arm of a secret organization of female assassins, Arklight operates according to its own agenda. They are the principle enemies of the Red Knights and the Red Order. Arklight is run by Lilith, a former breeding slave of the Knights; her daughter, Violin, is their senior field agent. It's rumored that Mr. Church and Lilith have some significant history, and they've shared a number of adventures in the years prior to the establishment of the DMS.

First Appearance: *Assassin's Code*

TOYS

Alexander Chismer is a former criminal who worked with Sebastian Gault and Hugo Vox. When he helped bring down the Seven Kings, Mr. Church offered him a chance at redemption by entrusting him with billions of the Kings' ill-gotten gains and challenging him to do as much good for humanity as possible with it. He is the private financier behind Junie Flynn's FreeTech. Whether Toys will earn redemption or slip back into his corrupt ways remains to be seen.

First Appearance: *Patient Zero*

FREETECH

An organization formed to repurpose technologies originally created by terrorist organizations such as Majestic Three, the Seven Kings, the Jakoby Family, the Red Order and others. Funded by Alexander Chismer and run by Junie Flynn, FreeTech brings these technologies to the people who need them.

First Appearance: *Code Zero*

THE DEPARTMENT OF MILITARY SCIENCES

THE ORGANIZATION

The Department of Military Sciences was created by Mr. Church and is chartered by Executive Order. It is tasked with searching out and responding to terrorist threats involving cutting-edge science.

The DMS operates out of regional field offices. Currently there are seventeen field offices that run thirty-six active teams. Joe Ledger's Echo Team was originally based at the Warehouse in Baltimore, but was later relocated when Ledger opened the Pier in San Diego.

The DMS's primary weapon is the supercomputer system called MindReader. This system has two primary and overlapping functions. Using an elegant pattern-recognition software package, MindReader collates information culled from all domestic law enforcement and intelligences services as well as those from trusted international allies. MindReader sifts through the data on an endless hunt for terrorist activity. Its second function is as an intrusion weapon. MindReader can hack its way into virtually any known computer system and then rewrite the target computer's memory to erase any trace of its presence.

Unlike other covert agencies, the DMS is not buried under mountains of red tape. Field team commanders are given superior mission support and encouraged to act autonomously. Naturally this requires a certain kind of leadership personality, and screening new DMS agents is done with utmost care. Everything about the DMS is built around the accuracy of its intelligence and the speed of its response.
First Appearance: *Patient Zero*

ECHO TEAM
Joe Ledger's group of first-chair shooters. This SpecOps team has logged more field time than any other DMS unit; and they've tackled some of the most dangerous threats to humanity imaginable.
First Appearance: *Patient Zero*

THE WAREHOUSE
The Baltimore Field Office and home to Joe Ledger and Echo Team from *Patient Zero* through *Code Zero*. The original Warehouse was destroyed by the terrorist Erasmus Tull, taking with it the lives of nearly two hundred agents. It was rebuilt by Ledger in the days following that tragedy.
First Appearance: *Patient Zero*

THE HANGAR
The main headquarters of the DMS, housed in an old hangar on Floyd Bennett Field in Brooklyn. The decrepit exterior hides the world's most sophisticated counterterrorism organization on earth.
First Appearance: *Patient Zero*

THE PIER
The DMS's latest field office. Built on an actual pier in San Diego by Joe Ledger, this office is dedicated to Special Operations and runs four teams—Echo, Slingshot, Deep Six and Kraken.

The Joe Ledger Series
Novels and Short Stories in Chronological Order

COUNTDOWN
(A teaser prequel to *PATIENT ZERO*)
"I didn't plan to kill anyone. I wasn't totally against the idea, either. Sometimes things just fall that way, and either you roll with it or it rolls over you. Letting the bad guys win isn't how I roll." Meet Joe Ledger, Baltimore PD, attached to a Homeland task force...who's about to get a serious promotion.

PATIENT ZERO
NOVEL #1/Published in 2009 by St. Martin's Griffin
When you have to kill the same terrorist twice in one week there's either something wrong with your world or something wrong with your skills... and there's nothing wrong with Joe Ledger's skills. And that's both a good, and a bad thing. It's good because he's a Baltimore detective that has just been secretly recruited by the government to lead a new taskforce created to deal with the problems that Homeland Security can't handle. This rapid response group is called the Department of Military Sciences or the DMS. It's bad because his first mission is to help stop a group of terrorists from releasing a dreadful bio-weapon that can turn ordinary people into zombies. The fate of the world hangs in the balance.

ZERO TOLERANCE
Short Story
This sequel to *PATIENT ZERO* brings Joe Ledger back into action, hunting for zombies in the deadly mountains of Afghanistan.

DEEP, DARK
Short Story
In an underground bioweapons lab a team of scientists working to develop super soldiers instead create something that is far deadlier and infinitely stranger. Joe Ledger and Echo Team must hunt—and be hunted—deep down in the dark.

MATERIAL WITNESS
Short Story
A stand-alone short story that takes place in the early days of Joe Ledger's service in the Department of Military Sciences, a top secret division of Homeland Security. Joe Ledger and the DMS must protect a Pine Deep spook and author who is in over his head with the wrong people and may know more than he is letting on.

THE DRAGON FACTORY
NOVEL #2/Published in 2010 by St. Martin's Griffin
Joe and the DMS go up against two competing groups of geneticists. One side is creating exotic transgenic monsters and genetically enhanced mercenary armies; the other is using 21st century technology to continue the Nazi Master Race program begun by Josef Mengele. Both sides want to see the DMS destroyed, and they've drawn first blood. Neither side is prepared for Joe Ledger as he leads Echo Team to war under a black flag.

DOG DAYS
Short Story
Joe Ledger returns in this tale that follows the tragic conclusion of *THE DRAGON FACTORY*. In the wake of a devastating personal loss, Joe Ledger and his new canine partner, Ghost, go hunting for the world's deadliest assassin.
***An audio exclusive story available from Blackstone, read by Ray Porter.

CHANGELING
Short Story
Joe Ledger teams with a mysterious British agent named Felicity to investigate a dangerous bioweapons factory.
Originally published in *Midnight Echo Magazine* (Australia), June 2013.

THE KING OF PLAGUES
NOVEL #3/Published in 2011 by St. Martin's Griffin
Saturday 09:11 Hours: A blast rocks a London hospital and thousands are dead or injured.... 10:09 Hours: Joe Ledger arrives on scene to investigate. The horror is unlike anything he has ever seen. Compelled by grief and rage, Joe rejoins the DMS and within hours is attacked by a hit-team of assassins and sent on a suicide mission into a viral hot zone during an Ebola outbreak. Soon Joe Ledger and the Department of Military Sciences begin tearing down the veils of deception to uncover a vast and powerful secret society using weaponized versions of the Ten Plagues of Egypt to destabilize world economies and profit from the resulting chaos. Millions will die unless Joe Ledger meets this powerful new enemy on their own terms as he fights terror with terror.

ASSASSIN'S CODE
NOVEL #4/Published in 2012 by St. Martin's Griffin
When Joe Ledger and Echo Team rescue a group of American college kids held hostage in Iran, the Iranian government then asks them to help find six nuclear bombs planted in the Mideast oil fields. These stolen WMDs will lead Joe and Echo Team into hidden vaults of forbidden knowledge, mass murder, betrayal, and a brotherhood of genetically engineered killers with a thirst for blood. Accompanied by the beautiful assassin called Violin, Joe follows a series of clues to find the Book of Shadows, which contains a horrifying truth that threatens to shatter his entire world view. They say the truth will set you free.... Not this time. The secrets of the *Assassin's Code* will set the world ablaze.

A FOOTNOTE IN THE BLACK BUDGET
Short Story
Joe Ledger, Top and Bunny go to the bottom of the world all the way to the Mountains of Madness in this crossover with H. P. Lovecraft's Cthulhu Mythos.
***This story is not yet released. It will be included in the anthology *The Madness of Cthulhu*, edited by S.T. Joshi.

MAD SCIENCE
Short Story
Joe Ledger and Violin go after a kill-squad of Red Knights in this sequel to *ASSASSIN'S CODE*.

BORROWED POWER
Short Story
Joe Ledger teams with a mysterious British agent named Felicity to investigate a dangerous bioweapons factory. A story told in two parts: A young Mr. Church teams with Lilith to hunt monsters in the sewers beneath Paris; and when that ancient evil rises again, Joe Ledger and Violin close in for the kill.

EXTINCTION MACHINE
NOVEL #5/Published in March 2013 by St. Martin's Griffin
The President of the United States vanishes from the White House for five hours. Next morning he is found, apparently safe and sound. Except that he claims that during the night he was abducted by aliens. A top-secret prototype stealth fighter is destroyed during a test flight. Witnesses on the ground say that it was shot down by a craft that immediately vanished at impossible speeds. North Korea's ultra top-secret weapons research lab is destroyed by a volcano—in an area where there has not been an eruption for forty millions years. All over the world reports of UFOs are increasing at an alarming rate. Key military personnel, politicians and scientists begin disappearing. And in a remote fossil dig in China, dinosaur hunters have found something that is definitely not of this earth. Joe Ledger and the Department of Military Sciences rush headlong into the heat of the world's strangest and deadliest arms race, because the global race to recover and retro-engineer alien technologies has just hit a snag. Someone—or something—wants that technology back.

ARTIFACT
Short Story
Joe Ledger goes after an enigmatic device that could hold the key to permanent sustainable energy—or could become the most dangerous weapon on earth.

THE HANDYMAN GETS OUT
Short Story
Joe Ledger is naked and unarmed and has to escape a high-security facility armed with whatever he can find. Expect Joe to get cranky.

CODE ZERO
NOVEL #6/Published in March 2014 by St. Martin's Griffin
A direct sequel to *PATIENT ZERO*. A rogue scientist within the DMS takes the *Seif al Din* pathogen (and dozens of other deadly and exotic weapons) and begins selling them to the highest bidders. Bizarre science-based terrorist attacks tear the nation apart—and at the heart of it are new outbreaks of the zombie plague that first brought Joe Ledger into the DMS. Joe and his crew team up with Arklight (from *Assassin's Code*) in a running battle that leaves a trail of bodies from Los Angeles to the steps of the White House.

THREE GUYS WALK INTO A BAR
Short Story
Joe Ledger teams with Malcolm Crow (from the *Pine Deep Trilogy*) and Sam Hunter (from *Strip Search*) to tackle a team experimenting with genetically engineered werewolves.
***This story will be included in the anthology, *Limbus II*, available in 2014 from JournalStone Publishing.

PREDATOR ONE
NOVEL #7/To be published in March 2014 by St. Martin's Griffin.
Someone is turning airliners and fighter jets into murderous drones. Joe Ledger needs to discover if the enemy is a supercomputer hacker or an advanced Artificial Intelligence program gone rogue.

Also....JOE LEDGER makes cameo appearances in…

FLESH & BONE
Book #3 of the *ROT & RUIN* series from Simon & Schuster.

TOOTH & NAIL
Ebook tied to the *ROT & RUIN* series.

FIRE & ASH
Book #4 of the *ROT & RUIN* series from Simon & Schuster.

ROT & RUIN: THE COMIC
Coming in Fall 2014 from IDW Publishing.

A Conversation between Jonathan Maberry and Ray Porter

NOTE: Actor Ray Porter has become the official 'voice' of Joe Ledger since his first performance on the audiobook of *Patient Zero*. Since then Ray has read all of the novels and a slew of novellas and short stories. Author Jonathan Maberry discusses with Ray the process of bringing Joe Ledger to life in the audio performances.

JONATHAN MABERRY: What's your process for preparing to read an audiobook?

RAY PORTER: I like to familiarize myself with the characters. Often I can gain insight into how the character sounds from a gentle pre-read of the text. I say "gentle" because I don't want to get too heavily into the read until I am recording. "Save it for the stage." Most important for me is to get an idea of the author's "voice." Nine times out of ten, the author will help me find the voice of the book just by the way they have chosen to tell the story. As much research as necessary before recording is a good idea. Thankfully, Blackstone Audio has great proofers but I always feel a little embarrassed when I have pronounced something so hideously wrong that I feel like taking an English class.

JONATHAN: Walk us through the steps of recording a book?

RAY: Well, as I said before, a gentle pre-read helps me a great deal. Since I record at home, I am the narrator and engineer. I read the book from my iPad, which is mounted to a music stand next to my microphone. There is a monitor above me and a mouse and keyboard handy so that on the very rare and vastly infrequent times that I make a mistake (between 1 and 1000 times per page), I can simply punch-in in ProTools and continue recording. I also have to stop for helicopters flying overhead. No matter how well insulated your recording space, some sounds just get through. Los Angeles is sometimes not the most tranquil place, and I have had to take extended breaks at times to wait for the noise to lessen. We live near Forest Lawn, and on the day of the Michael Jackson funeral there were so many choppers in the air that I just took the whole afternoon off.

JONATHAN: How do you pick the voices for each character in the Joe Ledger books? What goes into that process?

RAY: It's hard to describe how that happens. Sometimes the author will say "He had a high, thin reedy voice and a thick Bulgarian accent that still lingered behind his Texan drawl and cleft palate" (don't get any ideas, Jonathan!) and so you just do that. Other times, it just kind of happens. I don't know how to describe it better. When I first came across Mr. Church, I saw him in my head. I had a clear picture of his face. His voice just sort of fell out of my mouth. I tend to get a clear visual of faces and then their voices arrive from that. There are also clues from the author. The description of the way a person looks can tell me what they may sound like. You gave me such a gift in your initial description of Rudy that I only needed to follow suit. Others can be tougher to find, but it is so important that the person listening knows who is talking and when. In a scene between two women I really need to be as specific as I can so you don't get lost.

JONATHAN: What's the role of the director in the performance process?

RAY: I usually work alone but when I have worked with directors it is always a great experience. I am fortunate to work with Grover Gardner at Blackstone and I can get his input whenever I need it. Imagine getting help with your science homework from Stephen Hawking and it is kind of like that.

JONATHAN: You read books all day long. Do you still have the energy to read for pleasure?

RAY: I do. I have always been a voracious reader and I really love books. I even collect antiquarian books. I was initially worried when I first started narrating that it would be the ultimate busmen's holiday to read a book for pleasure, but quite the opposite is true. I find I am reading more now that I narrate books than I did before. I read to my three-year-old son every night at bedtime, so you could say I also narrate for pleasure.

JONATHAN: Readers have told me how much they enjoyed your reading of *Patient Zero*. Do you have a favorite character from the book?

RAY: Everyone has been so kind in their reviews of that book. I had an utter blast reading it. I feel a great affinity for Joe Ledger as we are very similar in a lot of ways. Except for the killing zombies thing, that is. I like Gault and Toys a lot, Mr. Church is endlessly interesting, Rudy is great, Grace….

At the risk of sounding lame, I kind of love all of the characters in that book. I can't decide a favorite.

JONATHAN: Do you feel like the character as you portray him, and how much of yourself do you bring to the role?

RAY: I think I have to have a personal investment in a character to make the character work. But I really try to let the characters speak for themselves. You didn't buy "Ray Porter reads *Patient Zero*," you bought *"Patient Zero."* I have to stay the hell out of the line of communication between you and Jonathan so that his work will affect you. If I do my job right I am just narrating the book, you are *reading* it.

JONATHAN: Do you have a favorite character from *Patient Zero*? Or from any of the other Ledger novels or stories?

RAY: Well, as I said before, choosing one character over another feels a little like "Which cute puppy do you want to keep?" It is just too hard for me to choose. As for *Dragon Factory*? Oh my, there are some fun people in that one!

JONATHAN: Do audio performers get any kind of recognition—like an Oscar or Emmy?

RAY: There is actually a spoken word Grammy, believe it or not. Jim Dale won for his narration of the Harry Potter books. There are also the Audie awards from the Audio Publishers of America. I am up for one this year (nonfiction) and my fingers are crossed. *Audiofile* magazine has monthly Earphones awards that they give each month from reviews in that magazine. I have won a couple and felt very proud indeed.

JONATHAN: Do people ever recognize you by your voice because they've heard you read an audio book?

RAY: This question made me smile. I think it would be very cool, but it hasn't happened yet. I actually would prefer it not to happen. I feel it is very important to stay out of the way of the text in my narration. I know I made some strong choices in the first Joe Ledger book (and the second!) but they were justified by what Jonathan wrote. He created a book that was so much fun to read, but I really was never conscious of "performing" the book. Jonathan wrote it, not me. I am so happy and grateful beyond words that people like my narration of his work but the most important thing for me is that you get to experience Jonathan Maberry's story, not mine. That being said, I still think it would be the coolest thing ever to be on the phone with AT&T or something and have the person on the other end say "wait a minute, you sound like the guy from *Patient Zero*." That would be excellent. Although with my luck I'd get "I know you. You narrated

The Complete Idiot's Guide to String Theory. You broke my brain! Damn you!" I actually did narrate the aforementioned book. I really liked it. But truth be told, zombies and evil geniuses hell-bent on world destruction are more fun than a barrel of transgenic simian commandos. Keep 'em coming, Jonathan!

JONATHAN: When you get the next book in an ongoing series, what's your process for getting back into the groove with those character voices/personalities?

RAY: A lot of getting back in the groove with recurring characters depends on the author. In your case, every character has such a well-defined personality that, if I really "listen" to what you are saying, the voice just naturally comes back. A perfect example of this is when I was reading a phone conversation made by an obviously distraught person who was unidentified. I got three lines in and realized "it's Toys!" You write such full characters that I hear their voices just by reading the text. Which brings me neatly to the next question.

JONATHAN: Nowadays when I write a new Ledger story I hear your voice interpretations in my head. How weird is that?

RAY: It is weird and wonderful that you hear my interpretations as you write. I cannot think of higher praise. Your writing is such a great pleasure to read. I'm one of the few, if not the only, ones who gets to read it out loud (there may be a Joe Ledger fan out there annoying his flat mates with his interpretations). I once said that Mr. Church's voice literally fell out of my head, and many of your characters are like that for me. Joe and I just talk alike, always have. I am amazed that I get to read these stories, and I miss them between books. You'd better not let Joe retire! People have spoken about how well these books work as audiobooks, and I am grateful indeed that I was assigned *Patient Zero* way back when.

Jonathan Maberry is a *New York Times* bestselling author, multiple Bram Stoker Award winner, and freelancer for Marvel Comics. His novels include *Assassin's Code, Flesh & Bone, Ghost Road Blues, Dust & Decay, Patient Zero, The Wolfman,* and many others. Nonfiction books include *Ultimate Jujutsu, The Cryptopedia, Zombie CSU, Wanted Undead or Alive,* and others. Jonathan's award-winning teen novel, *Rot & Ruin,* is now in development for film. He's the editor/co-author of *V-Wars,* a vampire-themed anthology; and was a featured expert on The History Channel special *Zombies: A Living History.* Since 1978 he's sold more than 1200 magazine feature articles, 3000 columns, two plays, greeting cards, song lyrics, and poetry. His comics include *Captain America: Hail Hydra, Doomwar, Marvel Zombies Return* and *Marvel Universe vs The Avengers.* He teaches the Experimental Writing for Teens class, is the founder of the Writers Coffeehouse, and co-founder of The Liars Club. www.jonathanmaberry.com/.

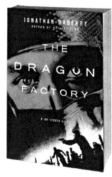

JONATHAN MABERRY, JOSEPH NASSISE,
BENJAMIN KANE ETHRIDGE,
BRETT J. TALLEY, and ANNE C. PETTY

LIMBUS
INC.

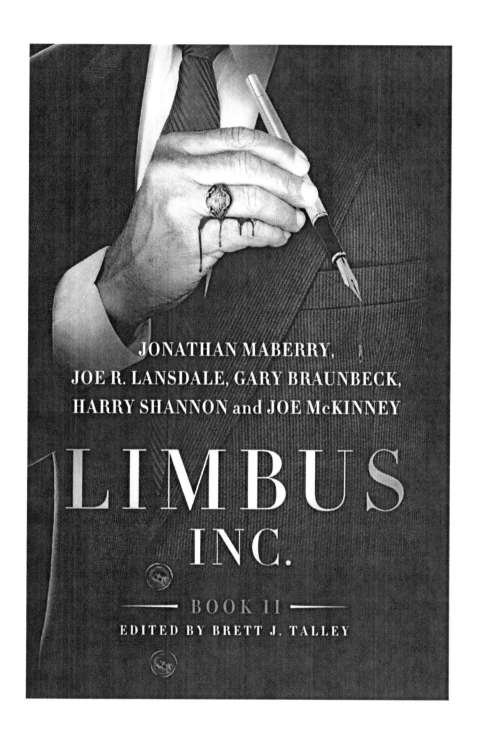

JONATHAN MABERRY,
JOE R. LANSDALE, GARY BRAUNBECK,
HARRY SHANNON and JOE McKINNEY

LIMBUS
INC.

—— BOOK II ——

EDITED BY BRETT J. TALLEY

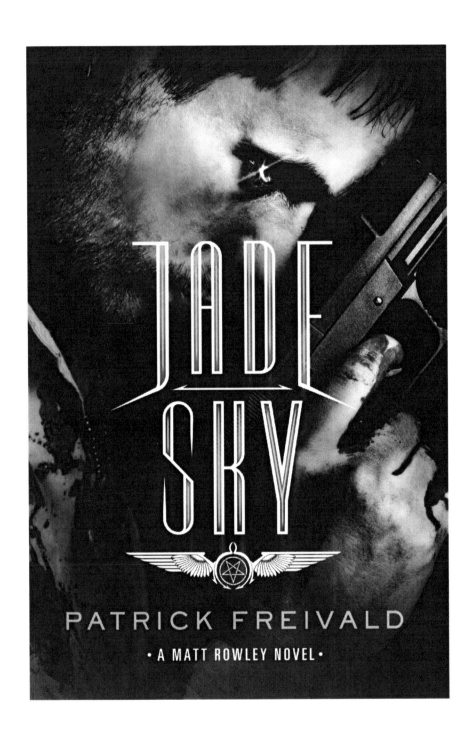

JADE SKY

PATRICK FREIVALD

· A MATT ROWLEY NOVEL ·